Having It and Eating It

Having It and

Riverhead Books
a member of
Penguin Putnam Inc.
375 Hudson Street
New York, NY 10014

Library of Congress Cataloging-in-Publication Data

Durrant, Sabine.
    Having it and eating it / Sabine Durrant.
        p.   cm.
    ISBN 1-57322-215-1
    1. Unmarried couples—Fiction.   2. Mother and child—
Fiction.   3. Motherhood—Fiction.
    I. Title.
    PS3604.U77 H38   2002   2001048777
    813'.6—dc21

Printed in the United States of America
10 9 8 7 6 5 4 3 2 1

This book is printed on acid-free paper.   ∞

Book design by Lovedog Studio

Eating It

Sabine Durrant

Riverhead Books

A MEMBER OF PENGUIN PUTNAM INC.

NEW YORK ✦ 2002

Having It and Eating It

June: Ants

Chapter 1

It is not often you really want someone else's life. You might say you do: wouldn't mind being her or him with her or his looks, or wealth, or fame. But you don't really mean it. It would involve far too much upheaval for one thing.

But Claire Masterson. I'd have given anything to be her. I'd have sacrificed friends and relations, not to mention my guinea pigs and my Donny Osmond posters, for one week in her shoes—the patent leather pumps with shiny buckles, for example, or the pink ballet slippers with real blocks in the toes or those big red clogs she wore when clogs were it.

There were lots of Clares in my class, a whole register full of them, but only one of them had an i. Claire Masterson had other extras too. She had long, tawny legs under her gymslip and marble blue eyes, flecked with green, and hair the same color and texture as the straw in our regulation summer boaters. And her parents were actors: God, that was exciting. Her mother spent long nights in the West End, whole days in bed. Her father, handsome, famous from some ad—Schweppes was it?—pulled our cheeks and pretended to pull our mothers at the school gates and gave us all rides in his car with the roof down. Her parents were untidier than you generally found along the green streets of our London suburb, where even the trees were pollarded as if to avoid any verdant vulgarity, but they were trendier too: they didn't wear A-line skirts or Prince of Wales check, but kaftans and cheesecloth. And their house was messier, but bigger, grander. There were piles of dirty dishes in the sink and food left out and furniture that didn't *match* like ours. "Family money," said my mother coolly, dropping me at the mossy stone lions at their gates.

And Claire was amazing. Claire lunched with "Olivier" and holidayed in New York ("NY" she called it). On Wear-Your-Own-Clothes-Day she wore glamorous scarves and real faded jeans, and later just black. Black with a tan. She brought Pepsi to school when the rest of us brought clanking Thermoses of tomato soup. She was the first at everything too: the first to know the facts of life, the first to hitch the waist of her gray serge skirt up under her money belt, the first to Sun-In her hair, the first, easily the first, to go all the way. She was certainly the first, and probably the last, to go all the way behind Pizza Hut in Morton High Street.

And then she left. She was the first to do that too. At sixteen, sweet 'n' sour sixteen, she went. For another thirty-five years, or so it felt, we padded about our all-girls sixth-form common room, thwumping down into beanbags with our mugs of Nescafé from the calcified kettle in the corner. We dreamed of the life she was leading, off, away, in her progressive mixed boarding school, experimenting with hard liquor and soft drugs and English teachers, small acts of rebellion adding up to some blissful alternative program, far from our secure, stultifying teenage existence. She said she'd write, but she never did. Instead, you'd hear the odd piece of news over the breaktime snack, picked up from someone who'd met her mother's secretary in a line at the bank: the parties, the dorm fire, the time she "got caught." Later, there was other news too: the *Vogue* talent competition, the shiny, glossy job at the shiny, glossy magazine, the newspaper column ("Girl, Uninterrupted: the nights of a party animal"), the journalistic assignments abroad. She was everything we, I, wanted to be. And wasn't. She was our Sylvia Pankhurst, our Isadora Duncan. She was our free one, our wild one. The one that got away.

So it was quite a surprise to bump into her in Morton High Street that day. I'd got the double stroller caught on a slightly raised curb—you have to angle it right, get your foot on the back supports and really yank it up; mistime it, as I had, and you're lost—so, what with reassembling Fergus's electric Thomas the Tank Engine, which had lost a battery in the maneuver, and repositioning Dan's Winnie the Pooh pacifier, which had fallen out, I didn't see her until she was standing right in front of me.

"Maggie?" she said. "Maggie Owen?"

The moment I heard her voice, creamy with catches in it, like chocolate chip ice cream, I knew it was her. She looked the same too. She hardly seemed to have aged at all. It's funny how close friends can suddenly put on ten years in a week, how the whole texture of their face can shift in an evening, so that you can hardly bear to look in their eyes for pity and fear of what you might see back, and yet people you haven't seen for eons quite often confound you by looking just how you remember them always looking. Teachers who looked fifty then still look fifty years later. And Claire Masterson, sixteen plus twenty, was a sophisticated version of her younger self, not a line out of place.

"Maggie?" she said again. She was smiling at me, slightly quizzically. Her hair was longer than when I'd seen her last and the once thick black eyeliner around those bright Aegean eyes had gone the way of all black liner (though perhaps, on reflection, not the way of mine, stubbed and cracked, to the bottom of Fergus's crayon box). She was thinner than she had been too, her body brown and lean in a dazzlingly orange cotton dress with velvet straps and purple ribbon around the neckline. On her feet were a pair of embroidered slingbacks with kitten heels and in her hand a hard candy-pink handbag, clashing with everything else in a manner that only models in a magazine, or Barbie, or Claire, could carry off with style. I felt suddenly sick. I wished I hadn't seen her. More to the point, I wished she hadn't seen me. My unwashed hair. My sleep-deprived makeup-free face. The oatmeal on the sleeves of my left-over-from-pregnancy white/beige/whatever T-shirt. The mud Fergus's shoes had left on the thighs of my jeans the last time he'd demanded to be carried halfway through a stomp in the park. I thought fuck, fuck, fuck. And then I pulled myself together. Never mind, I thought, never mind: quick, a wave, a smile, a waft of contented motherhood and into Woolworth's. Come on, get wafting.

"Juice. I WANT MY JUICE!" Claire was still smiling at me, peering now. Fergus wasn't. Fergus was scowling. He'd twisted his lean, wiry body around in his seat and was pushing against the foot rests to stand up, straining against the straps. His arms were flailing in the direction of Dan's dark head. He was beginning to tip the stroller backwards. Dan, struck, spat out Winnie the Pooh and started screeching. A motorbike screamed past. I lunged. The stroller tipped. The Safeway's bag dangling on the back of the stroller split. There were jars of Organix baby food in the gutter, fish fingers underfoot. And Winnie the Pooh was in a puddle, eviscerated, tire marks across his silicone neck. Claire was still standing there, patience on a monument, smiling at my grief. I burst into tears.

There was a hand on my shoulder. "How about a coffee?" Claire said.

"So was she nice?" Jake asked over supper that evening.

"Yes," I said. "No. Yes. I don't know."

We'd made our way, me wiping my eyes, saying sorry I'm stupid, blaming the humidity, to Pollyanna's, Morton High Street's contribution to the coffee revolution. My arms were full of broken plastic bag, so Claire took control of the stroller, pushing it gingerly at arm's length so that she looked like someone walking barefoot on pebbles, pausing only to produce half a Snickers from her matchbox bag to appease Fergus (bit close to lunch but never mind; and *how does she stay so thin?*) and to coo charmingly to Dan until, astounded by the attention, he stopped crying. When we got there, we ordered two cappuccinos; I was busy sorting the children at the table while she was getting them from the counter so I didn't hear what she said, but it was enough to make "Polly-anna," a burly, grumpy Spaniard whose mouth had been set at four-forty for the last five years, his brows forever furrowed with cross thoughts of tax returns and sugar wastage on table ten, look across and laugh and squirt an extra dose of St. Ivel's spray cream onto our hot brown drinks.

Claire turned and came toward me, bearing two cups. But just before she reached me, she turned sideways to negotiate the stroller which was blocking the way and as she did so, she became somehow entangled with someone else who had just gotten up from his seat, someone in a polyester beige rain-coat, shoulders heaving with annoyance, elbows jerking at cross angles at the inconvenience. Someone whose tutting followed me like the ticking clock in Captain Hook's crocodile. It was, I realized before she even turned, my neighbor Mrs. Allardyce, who had, I had long learned, very little time for "ridiculous modern contraptions" or "today's mothers."

"Mrs. Allardyce," I said, jumping to my feet. "Sorry . . . Won't be a . . . Just let me . . ."

Mrs. Allardyce glared at me, her lips pursed, her chin folded down onto her neck like a cross toad. "Sorry," I said, holding Dan up so I could yank my ridiculous modern contraption out of her way with my knees. She shook her head and said, "Tt'ahhh," which I didn't take as a form of thanks. "Sorry," I said again weakly to her departing back.

"Who was that?" said Claire after she'd gone.

"Mrs. Allardyce," I said. "She's a neighbor. She hates me."

"Ooh, that's grown up."

"What, being hated?"

"No, having neighbors. Having neighbors that have an opinion about you at least."

"It goes with the territory," I said, gesturing at Fergus and Dan. "People do have opinions about you when you have children. You become sort of public property somehow."

"I wouldn't know," she said, putting the cups down on the table.

The vinyl tablecloth was damp from a recent mopping, and she sat at an angle to it so as not to get her knees wet. This wasn't an option for me: Dan was making powerful splashing movements on my lap, and Fergus was trying to get the salt and pepper, squirming in his chair, every inch of him twitching with the shock of constraint like a salmon on the end of a line. "Ants in your pants?" said Claire, which made him laugh.

"Pants!" he giggled. "Pants!"

She reached across to take Dan on her knee. "Can I?" she said.

I had forgotten how charming she was. In fact, for the first five minutes, as we conducted that "catch-up dance," in which you move from subject to subject, leaping great chasms of time, plunging into giant life-altering moments, while so rigid with the social trauma of unexpected encounter that you don't actually listen or follow up a word the other person says, she did such a good job of blowing raspberries for Fergus and kisses for Dan, I tried not to mind when she pulled an ashtray over from the next table and started to blow cigarette smoke over them.

"So, hey," she said, exhaling. "So, hey, God. Who do you still see from the old days? Do you ever see Serena? Serena La-Di-Da Mills?"

I told her I thought Serena Mills was in hairdressing, which made Claire hoot. "Natch," she said, grinning. "Patricia Wells?"

"Someone told me she was an airline pilot."

She laughed even more. She said, "That figures." And I laughed too. That was the thing about Claire. She made you feel in collusion with her against the rest of the world, blissfully superior until in a quiet moment you would wonder what she might say about you.

"And what about the boys' school? Do you ever see any of the old gang from there?"

"Well actually," I began.

"You know, what about whatsisname? That hunk with the floppy dark hair we all pretended to be in love with. God, what was his name? Jock. . . ?"

"Oh—well . . ."

She was laughing. "What did we see in him? He was in that crap band wasn't he? What were they called? The Nasal

Passage, was it? I almost got off with him once, glad I didn't. Handsome, but dull." She opened her eyes wide to make a face for Dan and then said with exaggerated mouth movements, as if to entertain him more than me. "Dullsville."

"No. Yes," I said. "I do. See him I mean. Actually, um." I tried to laugh. I took a mouthful of muffin to pretend to be relaxed. "Actually, I *did* get off with him. These I'm afraid"—I shrugged hopelessly through the crumbs to show no hard feelings—"are his kids. Er, and . . . The Snot Goblins. The band was called The Snot Goblins."

"Oh shit. I'm sorry." Claire flushed. She put her hand out to touch mine. There was a moment of silence. Then she gave a loud exaggerated gulp, which sounded like a coin landing in the bottom of an empty charity tin, and raised her eyes to the ceiling. She could always self-dramatize herself out of trouble, could Claire. "My big mouth," she said, opening her eyes wide and clasping her hand to her forehead over Fergus. "It has a life of its own. I don't know why I said it. I never really even knew him. And twenty years is a long time. He's probably changed. I mean, not that there was anything wrong with him before. Oh God, I'm digging myself deeper into a hole, aren't I?"

I laughed. Claire's eyes were darting over the café for assistance. She made a goofy face at Pollyanna who appeared to blush. I said, "It's all right. Dull's good. Dull's fine." I watched Dan, who was trying to wriggle out of her arms, grab the sugar bowl and begin to chew on the end of a pink saccharine sachet. "Anyway, what about you? Last I heard you were with *Vanity Fair* in New York." I pulled the sugar bowl back to the other side of the table. "NY," I added.

"Yes I was," she said. "But I was running away . . . you can be away too long, do you know what I mean?" I didn't, but I nodded. Her voice had shifted gears now that America had been mentioned, her sentences beginning to go up at the end as if turning into questions despite themselves, statements of fact in search of approval. "It was fine when I was working for the *Sunday Times*. You know, they pay for your flat and your expenses and . . . you know me, Maggie, I was never very diligent, not like you, and all I had to do was write a weekly diary column, make a few jokes about Woody Allen or satirize Starbucks' bid for global domination, and then interview the odd film star for the mag. And it was great. It suited me fine. But then *Vanity Fair* offered me a contract and I was flattered so I took it."

"That's good though, isn't it?" I said. "I mean, they must have been really impressed by your Woody Allen jokes . . ."

"No, it was awful. They never ran any of my pieces and I was having to travel all over the US all the time, doing proper stories, investigations, and it was all crap. I was crap. And I was in this relationship with this English bloke. And he was over here and I was over there, and I was beginning to think it was make or break time . . . and then luckily my grandmother died, no I don't mean luckily of course, I mean unluckily, but *coincidentally*—she was old anyway—and the *Times* were on the phone and . . . I thought I've got to get out. And Granny's flat was just sitting there. And I'd come into a bit of money from . . . oh, just from this little screenplay I'd sold . . ."

"Screenplay?" I had to try very hard not to yell it.

"It was nothing much. I was just lucky. I wrote this little thing about an English woman in New York and . . . I suppose I just tapped into something a bit zeitgeisty? Anyway, Disney wanted it and . . ."

"DISNEY?" I cleared my throat and repeated the word more quietly. "Disney?"

"Well, one of their offshoots. Anyway, look Maggie. None of that matters. It was just time to come home. I had a lot of issues. I saw a therapist for a bit out there—God, can of worms or what?" She raised her eyes to the ceiling. "Anyway, what with one thing and another . . . I thought it was time to stop running away? And maybe it was time to start healing things with my parents?"

I was giving a little nod to coincide with each verbal rise, but at this I felt a little shake was required so I gave a little shake, opening my eyes wider a notch in an interested manner. "Your parents?" I said.

She had lit another cigarette and had began puffing on it furiously as if pursuing a private line of inquiry. "Well, Rowena's always had everything." Rowena was her younger sister, who was, I'd noticed, the new face of *Animal SOS,* the latest early evening animal rescue program on ITV. "She was the actress. She was the one whose talent they respected. Forget the fact that I was the youngest person ever on the *Sunday Times*'s Style File. That at one point I was writing for *Real Life* and had a weekly column in *Life* . . ." Fergus had got down from her lap and was pretending to be a lion under the table. A lion with his mouth full of sugar. "Mind your head," I said.

"Anyway," Claire was saying, "it's time to shift priorities. It's time to reassess what I want from the people around me . . ." Dan was stuffing her necklace into his mouth. She pulled it out of his grasp and tucked it into the top of her dress. He tried to grab it again. She jerked her chin away from him. "I've been running away from decisions, you know? And letting time run away from me. And as for men . . ." She stopped and passed Dan across to me. He was making irritated thrusting gestures with his legs and waving his arms about, which meant he was bored or hungry or needed changing, or all of those things. For a moment I was

distracted, thinking how I didn't have any wipes and that perhaps we ought to go before Fergus the Lion reared up and
knocked my coffee over, so I missed what she said next.
Something in a quiet voice about clocks ticking and a birthday coming up.

Fergus the Lion reared up and knocked my coffee over.
Only some of it splattered on Claire's dress. "Don't worry,"
she said with a fixed smile, "it will dry clean." By the time I'd
mopped the greasy brown liquid off the table and the floor
and the sides of my chair, apologized to the man at the next
table whose paper was ruined, and paid, she'd changed the
subject.

"Anyway," she said brightly as I kicked the stroller into life
and strapped the children in. "I'm having a party on Saturday
and I'd love it if you came. Catch up properly. And bring
Jock. I'd love to see him too. Honestly." She made a silly-me
eyes-to-the-ceiling face and, producing a pen from her
clutch purse, scrawled her address on the back of a napkin.
"Bring the kids!"

"That would not be a good idea," I began to tell her, boring even myself with my sensible tone. "They'd be a nightmare . . ." I studied the napkin. I knew the road—elegant
Georgian houses overlooking the common. "But I'm sure
we'd love to come. I'll ask Jake. See if we can get a baby-
sitter. It's quite short notice, but . . . And I don't know
whether Jake has anything planned. But . . . yes."

Claire had started smiling politely then, and I could see she
wanted to get going. "See you then, then," I said. She kissed
me on both cheeks. "Great to see you, Maggie. You look . . .
fulfilled. Really you do." And she walked off down the road,
young and tall and free and lovely. I watched her go.

"Carry," whined Fergus.

"No. You've got to stay in the stroller," I said.

"CARRY!" he shouted. "I NEED A CARRY!!"

I picked him up and sat him on my hip. It was only as I turned to go home, trying to steer the recalcitrant stroller with one hand and secure my eldest child with the other, that I realized cold coffee had seeped all the way down the inside of my thigh.

· · ·

"So what's she doing now?" asked Jake that evening.

"What isn't she doing?" I said. "Film scripts, columns here, assignments there . . ."

"And is she back in Morton for good?"

"I don't know."

"Is she married? Does she have children?"

"I don't know. I don't think so. No, I think she would have said."

"You didn't get much out of her then."

He put his tray down and went through to the kitchen. I heard the fridge door open, the clatter of unidentified objects falling onto the floor, and a muttered "oh fuck."

"Well, you know what it's like. I had both children with me," I called. "Fergus spilled some coffee . . ."

Jake came back into the room holding two yogurts. He chucked one of them and a spoon onto the sofa next to me.

"Is she still as selfish as ever?" he said.

"She's not selfish," I said.

"Oh go on, of course she is. I know she was good fun, but always on the lookout for herself, wasn't she, Claire Masterson? Claire with an i. Don't forget the i."

I felt a sudden dark twist of pleasure—fault found with perfection—which was immediately overwhelmed by irritation. It was unlike Jake to be like this. What right did he have to criticize my friend, my past? He always seemed to like her enough when we were teenagers. He had tried to get off with her, she'd said. "Well, she always thought you were . . ." I stopped.

"Thought I was what?" he said.

I tore the strip of lid off my yogurt and licked it. It was gooseberry and stung my tongue. Could I tell him he was dull?

"Handsome," I said, deflating. "She thought you were handsome."

. . .

During the period that these events took place, Jake and I and our two children were living in a terraced house in a nice street near a common on the outskirts of London. Morton, or Morton Park as our particular patch was called, was ideal for children—green spaces, fresh air, Pizza Express—and only ten minutes by train, if you wanted it, from the center of town. Not that I ever went there. I'd found family life to be a gradual process of zoning down, like old age: any trip involving more than a packet of breadsticks or one flight of steps or too many restroom unknowns was out of the question. So we tended to stick within a crutch's length of home, plumb in the middle of what the property supplements called "Cape Cot": it was said to have the highest concentration of under-fives in Europe. As Jake used to say, most of them seemed to live in our house. As the money had begun to float across the river, real estate agents had started referring to "Morton Village," though there was no village hall, no village school, no village festival, no village pub (well there was, but it had been bought up by some huge chain) and the streets seeped very quickly into the bog-standard Edwardian sprawl of the sub-urb in which we'd both grown up.

Jake and I had met at school. We'd do our homework together sometimes and on the nights when a gang of us would trawl south London in search of a party, it had always been Jake who'd lend me his jacket and find us a night bus home. But I had never thought I was his type back then. I was too mousy. Jake, stocky and dark like a walk-on in *The Godfather,* was famous for his gap-toothed blondes. They'd drape themselves over his shoulder in the pub on Fridays and stand shivering on the side of the field during his Saturday morning soccer commitment. ("Nothing," he used to say, "comes between me and my soccer. Nothing.") He went off to Oxford and had a wild old time, juggling work and women and his Saturday morning soccer commitment. "Wotcha Mags," he'd say when we'd bump into each other during the holidays. "Wotcha Jake," I'd say, mocking him back.

I was far more sober. I didn't juggle anything. I balanced. Through school and at Bristol, where I wandered aimlessly through college, and in my early working life, I was always "married" to someone. My friend Mel, who's generally single or up to her neck in some disastrous romantic intrigue, used to say I was the queen of the long-term monogamous relationship. Two years here, four years there, five . . . Though I always got out before they did. I wasn't going to follow the example of my mother: abandoned by my father when I was a baby and in personal turmoil ever since. Oh no. Not me. I always had an eye out for the signs.

I was going out with David the summer Jake and I got together again; in fact we'd just got back from staying with his parents in France, fresh from celebrating his new job as a lawyer. We were at a wedding, a posh do with a tent on the lawn and strawberries bobbing in the Spumante, when Jake came up behind me in the line for coffee. " 'Ello, 'ello," he said in the mock Cockney he used to bring out when he was nervous. "Fancy a turn?"

"A turn at what?" I said crisply.

"A turn round the dance floor, you pillock," he answered.

David was talking to a woman farther up the line about the benefits of joining a central London dining club. He'd just got his coffee—I saw the glint of his Palm Pilot as he whipped it out of his top pocket. "So," David was saying, "I don't know if you've ever eaten in a panelled room before . . ."

Jake was giving me a wolfish grin. "Okay," I said.

We danced and at midnight—by which time there were rings of wet on his white dress shirt and his bow tie was hanging loose around his neck and the dark hairs of his chest were just visible through the damp fabric, and my dress was torn at the hem and my face flushed, and after I'd given up searching for David who appeared to have left with his Palm Pilot in a huff—he walked me to the taxi stand outside Marks & Spencer, his jacket slung over one shoulder, and kissed me.

That time, it felt grown up, as if now I was playing it for real, no more rehearsals or trial runs. David said I was a heartless hussy, or similarly unoriginal words to that effect—but I was too much in love to care. Jake, this newly discovered adult Jake, interested me. It wasn't just sex, though there was a lot of that. It was more that he touched me in other places too. He was sexy and funny and kind, but he also had a different take on life than the men or boys I'd known before. Beneath the jokes and the fooling about were unmined seams of seriousness, self-confidence, and strength. He didn't, when it came down to it, care very much what other people thought. Oh, I know he wasn't perfect: he could be moody and distracted, and sometimes, when overpowered by the strength of somebody else's self-obsession, he could be quite tactless, but he also had an ability to rise above the pettier aspects of life. He didn't get cross, or insanely irritated, like most of the other men I'd known, with silly things, like parking tickets, or mistimed video recorders, or the time I spilled a ten-liter can of paint (eggshell) on the back seat of his car (new). He made me look at the world differently, from a higher perch, and when my mother was telling one of her long, condescending anecdotes involving the doubtful manners of a member of the working classes, I'd see his mouth twitch and I'd want to laugh not cry. Most of all, he made me feel really cared for. Not just in a mimsy, doing-the-bills, filling-out-the-census-form kind of way. But because I knew he wanted me. Though, I'd have to add for the sake of balance, he was good at the census forms too.

So, we moved in together, and we moved back to Morton Park because it seemed like the natural thing to do. A homing instinct. And there we were, eight years and two children down the line: Mr. and Mrs. Convention. Minus the Mr. and Mrs., though. This, as they say in advertising circles, was the Nitty Gritty of the situation: Jake did not want to get married. He must be the only offspring known to man to have been put off not by his parents' divorce but by the occasion of their silver wedding anniversary. This took place in the banquet suite of the Horse and Groom pub in Norwich, where they now live. Jake's mother, Angela, wore her wedding dress. "Can you believe, it still bloody well fitted?" Jake said when he told me. "And all the bridesmaids were there. Twenty-five years in lace." (Jake has a complicated relationship with his mother. She still keeps for him the picture cards you occasionally get in boxes of PG Tips Tea. It was only after we got together that he stopped putting them in a scrapbook.) That was his excuse. But of course it was more than that, and a lot less at the same time, more bound up with a resistance to doing what was expected, or an aversion to form, or, at the very least, just laziness. "Who needs a piece of paper?" he'd say, as people always do, but it wasn't the piece of paper I cared about, it was the ringless left hand and the awkwardness I'd feel fifty-eight times a week, or maybe it wasn't fifty-eight times, maybe it was five but even still, when I'd refer, pregnant, or small child in hand, to "my boyfriend." Sometimes, I'd lie and say "my husband" and that would feel worse. Anyway, the long and the short of it (probably short: I always imagined I'd wear kneelength—a tight pearled bodice with a fifties puffball skirt, sort of classic with a sense of humor) was: no wedding. At first I had minded a lot—I liked things to be clear; I liked things to be black and white—but I had got used to it. Sometimes I even forgot I was still waiting for something to happen.

Jake worked then for TMT&T (Titcher, Maloney, Titcher, and Titcher), a medium-sized advertising agency in the center of London. He was a planner, a board planning director to use his correct title, which was as far removed as you can get from your average red-glasses, sling-it-up-the-flagpole-see-if-anyone-salutes kind of advertising person. Planners are quieter, more cerebral, "the brains" of an agency, who think about strategies and consumer profiles and brand definition, and well, that sort of stuff. Whatever he did, it took up a lot of his time. He often worked late, usually missed bathtime. And if he wasn't working, he was socializing. There was a lot of socializing in his line of work. He'd sigh and say he hated all that, the client lunches at Le Caprice, the agency bashes. He'd much rather, he'd say, be at home with us, kicking a ball about with Fergus in the garden, as he would on the summer evenings when he did get back before dark, elbows neatly at his side, head wobbling, just a subtle gentleness in the lower half of his body to indicate his opponent was only two, or in winter, sitting back on the sofa, his tie undone, a small child tucked under each arm, three heads in three shades of brown watching *Scooby Doo* with expressions of pure concentration on their faces.

But that didn't happen often. And his long day was one reason why I gave up my job. I had always wanted children, always wanted to create the perfect family life I had never quite had myself. And it was all right when we just had one child, but once we had two, both of us working didn't seem fair anymore. And of course it was me who gave up. That's the way things were in our circle. People talk about "having it all," but you can't. You can have some of one thing and some of the other, but you can't have all of everything. You might be able to have the company car and the nativity play; you might be lucky and even get home in time, in your company car, to see your baby's first step. But what you wouldn't see is the six attempts that went before your baby's first step, the six brave wobbling strikes at independence, and the six aston-ished expressions when their little legs give way. To some women that might not matter. But I minded enough, when the day-care worker told me about the face Fergus had made at his first sip of water (horrified, all screwed up as if she'd plied him with gin—apparently) or, I don't know, about this or that daily nothing and everything, that I decided, after Dan was born, that I was going to be around.

Actually, I wasn't very good at my job anyway. I was never going to have a company car. I was several escalators down from the glass ceiling. I wouldn't have recognized one if it had shattered about my ears. I, like Claire, was a journalist, but I'd never made it like her. I just burbled around on the sidelines. I'd worked in newspapers for a bit and then in pub-lishing, and before I gave up I was working for a literary jour-nal, owned and edited from the basement of his flat in

Bloomsbury by an eccentric elderly Czech called Gregor. I'd harry his contributors—mainly academics who took five months to get back to me—and sort through the piles of correspondence that provided the most comfortable of sleeping quarters for his copious cats and proofread, and get articles off to the typesetters (we weren't exactly cutting edge on the technology front), and, sometimes long into the evening, listen to Gregor's reminiscences of his life in Paris in the fifties, of drinking with Beckett and lunch with Cocteau. It was nothing. Dispensable, poorly paid, easily surrendered.

I missed it like hell.

But I had the children. And really I couldn't complain. Oh I know there were days when I was subsumed by the *task* of it, by the things none of the manuals tell you: the mess and the noise and the chaos and the clobber and the palaver, and the squeezing of the person you used to be into this dull, one-tracked, *loaded-down* creature with opinions on the introduction of solids and an encyclopedic knowledge of diaper absorbency; the sense, in those early years at any rate, of being swallowed whole. But things would change. The children would get bigger. They'd go to school. I'd read a grown-up book again. And it seemed important not to become entirely a member of The Bleat Generation. Because there were moments even then, "trapped at home with the children," when I would feel my soul soar with the freedom of it all. And it might just be hearing the theme tune to the two o'clock broadcast of *The Archers* that would do it. Or it might be the sense, waiting at the station on platform 2 for a train to take me to the seaside or the swimming pool or a distant park, when everyone else was on platform 1, briefcases at their ankles, irritated fingers tapping watches, pinched, impatient faces scanning the empty tracks behind, that I was going against the tide, that I was my own boss, the big cheese in a corporation of one—and two halves. Or it may simply have been that I felt in touch with my own life, with the diurnal nothings of it, aware of every change in the weather, each kaleidoscope shift in the day's light. You may have no time to yourself when you have small children, but you also have all the time in the world.

I know, of course, that if I had bundled on to their train, the train for busy, serious commuters, with my slow, wobbling toddler and my knee-bumping hideous stroller and my wailing baby dripping a bottle from his pudgy fingers into the ridged floor, I would have seen pity or contempt in their faces. But I didn't care. Or I tried not to. Because I thought what I was doing was what really counted. I thought I was doing the really big stuff. Even putting aside the genuine satisfactions of it, the physicality of children, the toughness of their hair, the softness of their skin, the bones in their back, the dough of flesh on their *knees,* there were things to take value from—just keeping them alive, keeping them off the road, out of reach of the kettle, getting nourishment into them, keeping illness out. So you could keep your spread sheets and your projected figures for 2005. I made life-and-death decisions every day.

Not that Jake's sister Fran believed it. She called us "Them Indoors" because we were so boring, still to be living round the corner from where we grew up, squatting like over-fed Toms on the same patch of territory. But I found familiarity comforting. I liked the sense that I was continuing a life that had been lived before. I loved our garden for this reason too. The woman before us, who'd lived there for years until she was moved into a retirement home by her relatives, left us a forty-foot Eden, of hip-height lavender and mature viburnum, twisted honeysuckle and crooked apple. I used to spend every weekend out there, tending and cultivating (though with Fergus's arrival this had dwindled down to the odd snatched moment, and then, after Dan, to almost no time at all).

And I liked hanging out, woozy with boredom, with my take-out polystyrene coffee in the same playgrounds (safer now of course with their flexi-firm floor coverings) that I used out to hang out in, woozy with boredom, as a child. I liked knowing that The Drunken Stoat, the winebar on the corner, was once a hardware store, that Blockbuster's used to be a shop called Cuff's selling school labels, that the man I lived with, Mr. Advertising Exec with a bag of clubs in his trunk, used to bleach his hair and play drums for a band called The Snot Goblins. I was a creature of habit, I suppose. And I could have sworn, until the day I met Claire again, that Jake was the same.

. . .

"Did she really say I was handsome?" said Jake that evening.

"*Were* handsome," I said, chucking a cushion at him. "She said you were handsome when you were sixteen. She hasn't seen you now you're old and gray and love-handled." I grabbed him around the waist. "Get off, woman!" he yelled. "I'll report you!"

"Come here," I said. I pulled me to him and stroked the stubble on his face with my thumb. "Come here," I said again, more softly. But Jake turned away, almost imperceptibly, bringing his own hand up to his chin as if we were both simply checking if he needed a shave. He hunched his arm across my shoulder.

"Hey," he said, reaching for the remote control, "we don't want to miss *The Sopranos.*"

Chapter 2

The next day was Thursday, the day when Fergus went to playgroup—Little Badgers (or Little Buggers, as Jake called it)—so I took the baby around to see my mother.

"Darling, how nice. Have a sherry," she said.

"Mum, it's eleven in the morning."

"Is it? Just a little one then. Oh Daniel . . . why's he crying? Does he want a little something?" For a moment I thought she was going to pour him a sherry. "How about a cookie? Oh Daniel, don't you want to come to your grandmother? What's this on his head?"

"Cradlecap," I said. "And his name is Dan. Just Dan."

"I just can't understand it. I suppose I'll get used to it. But all these short names. I'm sure he won't like it when he grows up. Moira at Nadfest thinks it's most odd. Are you sure there isn't something you should be putting on it?"

She was very well meaning, my mother, and devoted to her grandchildren. She'd do anything for them, except on a Wednesday when she had tennis, or a Friday when there was art class, or Monday or Tuesday or Saturday or Sunday, when there were music groups and upholstery sessions and Nadfest, whatever that was, and trips to the National Theater, and she and her new husband had just a few friends around—the Thomases or the Bloxons, the Flotsams or the Jetsams—for a bite to eat. My mother, who was taller than me and hadn't lost the figure I never had, was what she would call "with it." On the day in question, she was wearing a canary yellow jogging suit which might have meant she was fresh from some sporting activity but was, more likely, a fashion statement.

I put Dan down on the floor, and he crawled gratefully out of the room.

"I met Claire Masterson yesterday," I told her. "You know, from school."

"Which one was she?" she said absentmindedly, riffling through her bag and pulling out a packet of photos. "Have I shown you our trip to Bruges? The one whose father was big at IBM?"

"Yes, you have," I said, looking at them again anyway. "This one's nice of you. I'm not sure if I like the hot pants though. No, Claire Masterson. You remember. Parents were actors. Henna'ed my hair that time. Ran away on the French exchange."

"Oh, Claire Masterson," said my mother, "Clive Masterson's daughter." She paused to remember something, while a small smile played about her lips, then she added sharply, "Claire with the painted finger nails. The girl you all wanted to be."

There was a silence while I registered this uncharacteristic moment of insight. I picked up a carriage clock on the side table next to me and fiddled with its brass handle. "Yeah, I suppose so."

"Still looking out for herself is she?" she said.

"Not you too," I said, turning it upside down to see what happened.

"What do you mean, 'not you too'?"

"Oh nothing," I said. I put it back down with a clatter. There was a silence. "What do you mean?"

"I don't know, dear. I know you all thought she was terrific fun, but I just remember that party she took you to and she got offered a lift home and you rang from Virginia Water on your own in tears."

"That was a long time ago, Mum. Anyway, I just . . . you know . . . seeing her, it's just made me feel a bit funny somehow. I love my life, of course I do, and I was feeling perfectly happy, I think, until I bumped into her and now I just keep thinking of all the things she's done and all the things I haven't."

"She was certainly always very independent," said my mother.

"Yes, that's right—she's been places, she's done stuff. I mean, she never *settled*. In any meaning of the word. You know, she's been living abroad. New York. She's written a screenplay . . ."

My mother took a sip of her sherry. "But she's back now, then?"

"Well . . ."

"Married?"

"Well . . ."

"Children?"

I didn't say anything.

"Well there you are, dear." Problem solved. Anguish over. "I had the most terrible night," she said, moving on to more important matters. "I didn't sleep a wink. Frank"—that was her latest husband—"had to go and sleep in the other room. I had to take two of my pills in the end." My mother was of a generation for whom ongoing supplies of prescription-only pills and lunchtime sherry were as normal as vitamin C supplements and bottled water to mine. She reached into her bag and bought out a matted sliver of tissue. For a moment I thought she was going to use it to clean my mouth—you never know with mothers—but she pulled it into a usable shape and blew her nose as if stifling some enormous grief. "I don't know if you've been away," she said when she'd finished, "or perhaps you don't listen to your messages these days, but I did call on Tuesday to let you know about Ann and Rupert."

There was a clatter and a clank from the kitchen as Dan began an onslaught on the cupboards. It sounded like saucepans. Then there was a wail—he'd probably reached the Le Creusets. I fetched him back into the sitting room. "What about Ann and Rupert?" I said, sitting back down again with Dan on my knee, fondling his toes through his socks with my fingers.

"Well, didn't you know? Their daughter's got cancer."

"Oh, how awful," I said. "I am sorry."

"Breast," she hissed.

I held Dan tightly against my chest. Digging his feet into my thighs, he put his fingers in my mouth and tried to pry it open like an oyster. He was a sturdy little chap at that age, all pudge and muscle and thick dark hair, not a delicate rabbit like his brother. He started bouncing up and down, using my legs like a trampoline, chanting "ehda, ehda." My mother was slipping her photos back into her bag.

"Well, they're being most odd about it," she said, reemerging. "We were so good to them when they found out. You know, she said to me, she said, 'Sue, you really have said the right things.' Because you do have to be careful, you know.

People can be so terribly sensitive. Anyway, I rang last week and left a message asking them if they wanted to come to supper—just potluck in the kitchen—and they didn't ring and they didn't ring: more people who don't seem to listen to their answering machines"—this pointed at me—"so on Monday I rang again and this time I got Rupert and you think they'd leap at the chance to get out, you can't just sit in and mope, and he said, 'Can we ring you back, we'll see how the chemotherapy goes.' Well, I mean don't you think it's odd? And it just puts me in an awkward position? Do I shop or not?"

"It depends how lucky your pot's going to be, I suppose," I said.

She looked momentarily floored. Then she said, "And yesterday, on top of everything, Margot rang. In floods. I thought, this is just what I need. Her Burmese had run out into the road and a horrible, horrible van driver ran over him and didn't stop—I mean, people are awful—and poor Petrushka . . . Well, she rushed her round to the vet and that lovely Mr. Pelt did what he could. Cost her £240—well, I told her she should have had PetPlan but too late now, of course."

She had begun to gulp with tragedy recollected in tranquillity. My mother's response to misfortune never failed to astound me: she skirted over the horrors of life, but was thrown by small things. Take the time she was burglarized. The thieves threw her underwear all over the bedroom, smashed the glass in the family photographs she laid out like chess-pieces on the mantelpiece, and defecated in the bath. I found my mother with a bottle of spot remover on the stairs. "You'd think they could have wiped their feet," she said. She also never talked about my father, the Gentleman Bolter, though she had plenty to say about the unscheduled departure of her last cleaner: "And did she bring the key back? No she didn't. And it wasn't for want of asking."

I propped Dan into a nest of cushions on the sofa, where he sat fiddling with his fingers, bringing them up to his eyes and examining them as if he'd only just discovered them, and went through to the kitchen to put the kettle on. My mother still lived in the house I grew up in, and it never changed, just accrued. She only ever seemed to add things: utensils, ornaments, husbands. Frank, number four, was always tinkering about with his toolbox trying to make shelf space.

I filled the kettle, pulling a couple of thick Italian mugs (lugged back from their last holiday in Puglia) down from their place next to the decorated pasta bowls (free with 180 gasoline tokens from the local garage). The kettle, I noticed, was new, rounded white plastic: an ocean liner compared to the old aluminum tanker (still visible on a shelf above the fridge).

"New kettle?" I said when I went back into the sitting room with two cups of coffee.

"Ah, yes. I didn't tell you, did I?" she said, fully recovered now. "I bought it in the store the other day when we went to buy the new dishwasher. Now, that was an adventure. In the end . . ." Her voice slowed down and hushed in preparation for some momentous news. She stretched out the fingers of both hands in a "wait for it" sort of way. "We went German. There was this lovely girl assistant. Black, but she couldn't have been nicer. Lovely hair. And she just persuaded us it was worth the difference. And it really is a super machine. I couldn't be more pleased with it. Very quiet."

"That's good," I said, and I drank my coffee.

"Well, lovely to see you, darling," she said into Dan's face as I carried him to the door. "Give my love to 'Jake.'" She always said his name in inverted commas, as if I'd made him up. "Is he still working so terribly hard? Is it so necessary? I only ask . . . How's Angela?" This sudden casual reference to Jake's mother may have seemed innocuous on the surface, but then so does sinking sand. A lot was going on here. When had we last seen Angela? How often exactly had we been in contact with her? How did that tally, exactly, in divvied up hours, minutes, with the amount of time we'd spent with her?

"Fine," I said, giving nothing away.

"And do bring both the children round soon. I'd love to have them both for an afternoon. We could go for a lovely walk, couldn't we, Daniel?" Dan didn't respond.

"Well, actually," I said. "You're not free on Saturday are you? You couldn't baby-sit if you are. We've been invited to a party and . . ."

She thought quickly. "Saturday? Saturday? This Saturday? What time? I know I'm free in the afternoon—we've got lunch at the club but nothing after that."

"I meant the evening," I said.

"Oh, what a bore," she said. "It's Morton Park Music Society at the church. They're doing Flanders and Swann. I'd give it a miss but . . . I do love them, don't you? In a wheelchair, poor man, but such a lovely sense of humor. 'I'm a gnu'—do you remember?"

"No, I don't," I said, gnu-like. And left.

•   •   •

I was first in the line of parents at Little Badgers so Fergus was very cheerful when I picked him up. Second's good, third's fine, fourth was a disaster with tears all the way home. Today, though, he was chipper and really quite forthcoming. Apparently, a girl bumped her head on her chair and they put water on it. And the story was about a bear. It usually was. "And do you know?" he said, bounding into the back of the car, his arms full of sheets of paper still wet with paint. "I bumped my head too and I was very brave and I went to the moon in my helicopter."

He was so busy telling me about his adventures in space he didn't notice me take a detour from our usual route and drive slowly down the road where Claire lives. I stopped when we had just passed number thirty-eight. "What are you doing, Mummy?" he said then, jolted from his mental moonscape.

"Just checking something," I said, craning over my shoulder. It had been bothering me, the house. Property envy can be a terrible thing. When anyone I knew bought a new house, I wanted to know three things: one, how much—exactly—did it cost?; two, how big was the garden?; and three, that, however big it was, was there a Tube line at the end? Claire's writing said "38b," b for basement or b for beautiful view? I couldn't see any numbers, but there were steps up and steps down. Four floors of windows. Not a maisonette, surely? Please, I thought, don't tell me *two* whole floors of beautiful view?

The door of the raised ground floor opened then and suddenly there she was on the doorstep. In some sort of robe. One o'clock in the afternoon—in middle of the week—and wrapped in something soft and textured. It was the color of pigeon—the more expensive an item, the more indistinct the color—and she was clasping it around herself in a caress though you could still see a slip of lace underneath. She was holding the door open while talking to someone back in the recesses of the hallway. As she turned to look into the street, a man came up behind her and pulled her around to face him. They kissed. Lingeringly. One of his hands slid down her back and clenched her behind through the fabric of her robe; the other was tangled in her hair. They wouldn't have noticed me staring at them, but through some sort of modesty I turned and watched them in the mirror anyway.

"Baa baa black sheep, have you any tractors?" bellowed Fergus.

"Ssh," I said. "Don't wake Dan." The man was coming down the steps. He turned and said something. Claire laughed and shut the door. Quickly I grabbed a map from the glove compartment and studied it intently until he'd passed by the side of the car. Then I looked up again. He was wearing a suit and carried a pigskin briefcase. He was walking quickly, flicking shoulder-length hair away from his face. Just after he passed me, he paused for a moment, retrieved something from his pocket, brought it to his nose, and sniffed deeply. In the time it took him to walk to the end of the street, he did that twice more. He turned the corner.

"Twinkle, twinkle, little tractor. I want my lunch," shouted Fergus.

"OK, OK," I said, turning the key in the ignition and pulling out. There was a screech of brakes, the scrunch of metal, and a jolt. "Oh fuck," I said, opening my door and getting out, braced, as you are in London, for aggression. The other car was a red transit van, with writing on the side, and was now at a funny angle to the road. There were hunks of colored plastic on the tarmac. I could see that the rear passenger side of my car was bashed in. The front of the red van was a bit of a mess.

A man in combat trousers was coming round towards me. "I'm sorry. I'm really sorry," I said. "Are you all right? I'll give you my details. It was all my fault. I wasn't looking. I'm sorry. The children . . ." I gestured to the inside of the car. Dan was still asleep. Fergus was pushing his bottom out of his seat in excitement, gesticulating wildly. "Crash," he said, laughing. "Crash, crash, crash."

"Calm down," said the man, smiling. I realised he was Australian when he opened his mouth—"Ca'm deyeown" he'd said—but you could have guessed from his stance, legs apart, arms out at an angle, a body not closed like English bodies against the elements, but open to the warmth. He had blond curly hair with darker roots, scrunched up as if he'd been through a hedge backwards, and coppery freckles on his forehead. His hands were broad, the fingernails ingrained with dirt. He said, lazily, "Look, I was probably as much to blame myself. I wasn't looking where I was going. Are the kids alright?" He opened the back door. "Fuck, fuck, fuck," continued Fergus. "Oh shit," I said, and shut it again.

The man laughed. He was younger than me, nice looking. "Hey, let's look at the damage." He went to the back of my car and poked about. "It's not too bad. New bumper probably, new headlight. I expect they can beat the panel out. And as for mine . . . Well, it was about time"—abo' tiym—"I had a new one anyway."

He gave a half smile, half grimace. His eyes were ginger. There was a fan of white lines on the outside corner of each as if he'd been squinting into the sun. "You're being so nice," I said. "People are usually so horrible about these sorts of things. What shall we do? Shall we swap details anyway?"

His T-shirt was creased oddly. He tweaked it at the shoulders. "Yeah, perhaps that wouldn't be a bad idea."

I found an old parking receipt on the dashboard and wrote my name and number on it. He handed me a card. *"Peat and Dug"* it said beneath a pen-drawn spade. *"Garden services. No job too small."* Then there was a name, Pete Russ, and two phone numbers. So he *had* been through a hedge backward. "Oh, you're a gardener," I said. "No wonder you're nice."

He smiled, looked at the used ticket, and then, I could have sworn, at my ringless left hand. "And you're a meter maid."

I felt myself go pink. "Not really a maid," I said. He looked at me for a bit but didn't say anything.

After a moment or two, I said, "So is there a Doug?"

"Come again?"

"Peat and Dug. Is there a Doug?"

"Oh no. No, there's no Doug. There's a Lloyd. Will you be all right?"

"Yup, yup, of course," I said, getting into the car.

Fergus said, "Are you going to call the police?" The baby was stirring, screwing up his face in his sleep in preparation for Armageddon.

"Thanks," I said through the window. He was bending down and trying to wedge something back onto his car. "And sorry again."

"No worries," he said, not looking up.

And I drove, or rather clanked, off down the road—back to microwave baked beans and do some laundry and feed the baby, screaming at full throttle now, and persuade Fergus to have a rest and do the ironing and then get out the crayons or make some fairy cakes and remember to call the garage and if I was lucky later and the sun was out maybe collect some stale bread and go and feed the ducks. It was my life. I loved it. It's just . . .

What was Claire doing, all this time? Had she watched me from the window? Had she seen me, a boring thirty-something mother, flirting stupidly with a kind, indifferent man? Or had she, after kissing her lover, returned, sleepy-headed, to her warm, crumpled sheets? Percolated herself a tiny cup of strong, dark espresso and curled up in an armchair with the papers or the latest copy of *Vogue?* Slipped into a long, deep bath fragrant with amber or mimosa or fleurs d'oranger? I wondered about that intently all the way home.

．．．

That night, Jake called to say he'd be late. He had an important "strategic development meeting" to prepare for. All his
meetings were called things like that. Sometimes he had
brand definition meetings; other times he had campaign definition meetings or status meetings. But it all came down to
bread in the end. Bread (Wheato), spot cream (Zap-it), pot
noodles (Ecram Foods), and cars (Kyushi, the Japanese multi-
national). Those were his accounts, his bits of business, the
things he filled his head with. Today it was the zit cream. He
had the results of some focus group to go through. To spot
check.

"Ha, ha. Go on," he said at this. "Squeeze it for all it's
worth."

"I'm squeezing," I said, "I just wish it would pop."

Then I told him about the car and he said as long as we
were all okay, and I said we were, and he said, "Okay then,
sweetie. Laters."

"Laters," I said.

After I'd put the phone down, I sat, quite still, for a
few seconds and then I got on with putting the children to
bed on my own. Later, when they were asleep, I called some
baby-sitters to try to find someone—unsuccessfully—for Saturday night, spoke briefly to Jake's mother, who wanted to
know how his nasty cold was (I didn't have the heart to tell
her I didn't know he had one), and then, after I'd tidied the
sitting room and swept the kitchen floor, I settled on the sofa
and called Mel.

I'd known Mel since my second year at college. Our paths
shouldn't have crossed—she was a medic and I did lan-
guages—but Adam, the boy she went out with in her second

year, was a friend of Tom's, the boy I was going out with (and whom I once thought I'd marry, but that's a different story), and we were hurtled together in a series of double dates in the days when double dates were easier than having to talk to each other on your own. Our romances both fizzled out before the end of the summer but our friendship didn't, and it was Mel and I who ended up moving in together at the beginning of the third year. She was different from me. She was a scientist; I was an arty-farty nothing. She came from a big family in the center of Manchester, not an inconsequential one on the outskirts of London, and she had a resilience and a toughness on her delicate shoulders that I envied and admired. She also made me laugh. Nowadays, she lived, with her three-year-old daughter in a two-up, two-down terrace near our local hospital where she used to work. She was going to be a surgeon but, as for so many women, ambition became impractical once she'd had Milly. She was a GP now. A doctor, and a single mother: every inch of her life was a reproach to mine. As she rarely let me forget. She was my dearest soul mate and my harshest critic.

I said, "I have sooooo much to tell you."

She said, "Well, be quick. I'm on another call."

I said, "I met your future husband today."

She said, "I'll phone you straight back."

Mel's daughter was the result of a brief relationship with a consultant in Obstetrics and Gynecology who left her, when she was pregnant, for a drugs rep. Mel said he'd obviously had enough of the National Health and wanted an easier life. Mel was slim and dark and compact. Milly had unruly blond hair and blue eyes the size of petunias and big fat three-year-old thighs. Mel used to say Milly needed a proper father, that she herself needed a proper man in her life, not just a signature on the end of a monthly check, but I was never so sure she meant it. For the moment she was seeing a very nice anesthetist called Piers, who would have done anything for her. But Mel asked for nothing. Secretly, I suspected she liked her life just the way it was. Which is not to say I didn't still try.

The phone rang. "God," she said, as soon as I picked it up. "Middle-class mothers! Nonworking middle-class mothers, no offense—they are the worst. I've just had one on the phone. Whine, whine, whine. Why won't I give her daughter antibiotics? She's sure it's not viral. Blah, blah, blah. She came into the surgery earlier today and her kids were running riot and trying to dismantle the weighing machine and I told her then that she didn't need them, but she thinks she knows best and that, just because I know her a bit from Milly's nursery, I'm going to give in. Well, I'm not. Honestly, there was a bloke in the surgery today who cut up nasty because I said I didn't have the authority to renew his Methadone prescription—he's got to see Andrew, the head of practice, for that—but I can tell you, this woman was scarier."

"Are you going to let this nonworking middle-class mother cheer you up, then?" I said.

She sighed. "Yes. Go on. Who's this bloke?"

So I told her about bumping into Claire and the party invitation and the pigeon robe, then I told her about bumping into the red van. "And this man comes out," I said, "and starts walking toward me and he's smiling. You know, he's being nice. And he was sweet with the children, and he didn't get nasty or start talking about insurance details. He was Australian—does that matter? Do we like Australians?—and . . ."

"Handsome?" she interrupted.

"Yes," I said. "He was. Very handsome. I mean leagues above anyone we normally meet. I suppose that's because he's

Australian. Very blondish and . . . an amazing body. Great muscles. You could see them, under his T-shirt, they sort of rippled sweatily."

"Go on," said Mel. "What does he do?"

"Oh. He's a gardener." I started laughing.

Mel did too. "A gardener?" she said.

"Yes. Isn't that great? We never meet gardeners, do we? It's always solicitors or managing directors or advertising executives, men who spend their whole time indoors, worrying about money and accounts and business portfolios, not out in the open air, in touch with the elements, up to their arms in soil. I mean, how sexy is that? Anyway . . . well, I just got the impression he was available. Don't ask me why. I might be wrong, but it's worth a punt. Honestly Mel, he was really fit . . . To be frank, if Jake doesn't begin to show a bit more interest, I wouldn't mind . . . Well, anyway, the best thing is I've got his number."

"He'll do," she said, after I'd rabbited on for a bit longer, "though I don't know how you're going to get us together."

"Leave it to me," I said.

. . .

I was reading in bed when Jake finally got home that night. I'd had my nightly flick through my stash of pornography. Mini Boden, with its privileged sun-kissed six-year-olds in their stonewashed boxy sweatshirts, dipping for crabs on a Cornish beach; Toast—that new one—full of willowy women with enough time on their hands to lie languidly in the shade in their Cambodian hand-woven ikat-dyed shot silk sarongs and duck-egg blue thong sandals. I knew I had to kick my mail-order catalog habit because I always felt cheap and guilty afterward. Wistful too. In my most down-trodden moments, I used to think it was a pity that they were offering only the clothes and you couldn't send off for the life. Mind you, you probably wouldn't want to hang around for too long in those thong sandals: they looked like they'd be murder between the toes.

I was deep into a Georgette Heyer—comfort reading, the literary equivalent of a rice pudding—when the front door slammed. "Hello," Jake said, poking his head round the bedroom door. He came in with a sheepish air about him, kissed me, and sat on the edge of the bed to take off his shoes. There were dark shadows across his cheeks and his green eyes looked bright—with tiredness perhaps. He smelled of cigarettes and taxis and something else almost floral—the summer night air or the scent of another woman.

"What's that smell?" I said, pulling a corner of polo shirt toward my nose.

"What smell?" he said, bending his face too. "Oh that. I popped my head round the door of Charlotte's going away party on the way home. I wasn't going to but Ed persuaded me. He said we needed cheering up. It was at La Renne and they spray you in the gents there. Like aftershave. Or air freshener. You know what they're like in these posh restaurants."

"Actually, I don't," I said. I tried to keep the *tone* out of my voice. Because there certainly was a tone to be ushered in if I'd let it. There seemed recently to be a going away party every week at his office. It had a faster turnover than the McDonald's in Morton High Street. And as for Jake's colleague Ed: he always seemed to be leading Jake astray, or turning him back from the Tube at the last minute, anyway.

Jake had gotten up and was rattling about in the bathroom. When he came back, he said, "Sorry. I tried to ring but you were engaged."

"It doesn't matter," I said.

Jake threw his clothes—his polo shirt, his chinos—on the back of the chair and clambered into bed, pulling the duvet off my legs as he did so. "Oi," I said playfully, yanking it back. Jake wasn't in a playful mood. He switched on his light, and reaching down for *Campaign* on the floor, said, "It's getting worse and worse. I had to see the managing director today. More bad news. Those bastards Kyushi want a European realignment. I've got a nightmare month ahead of me. We're going to have to get a pitch together to blow all the other European agencies away. One thing is I think that means we won't be able to go on holiday this year. Not until it's sorted at least. We're going to have to do it well. We can't afford to lose them."

"Oh," I said. "Oh well."

He looked at me. "Sorry."

"It's okay."

He turned back to his magazine. After a bit, I turned on my side and pressed against him. I rested my cheek on his shoulder. "But this weekend: will you have to work then? Or can we go to this party?"

"What party?"

"You know, Claire's."

"Oh, Maggie." He still had his eyes on his page. "Do we have to? I really, really don't want to. Anything but that. Claire Masterson's? Do we need that? I wouldn't feel comfortable."

"Why not?"

"I don't know. Who would we know? It'll just be her Disney crowd."

"I'd like to," I said. "It'll be fun, won't it?"

"Okay, then." His expression was blank. "If you want to."

"I do," I said. I was moving my chin farther up his shoulder, in little jerky movements, trying to get him to look at me. He didn't. After a bit, I lifted my chin away, shifted back over to my side of the bed, and went back to my book. "Who shall we get to baby-sit?" I said.

"I don't know," he answered shortly, turning a page. I felt a flare of unexpected anger. Of course he didn't know. He didn't know any of our sitters' names, let alone their numbers. It was something since I'd give up work that I always dealt with, just as I always got the dry cleaning. And cleaned the kitchen floor. And cleaned it again. And did all the mundane things that kept our life together. I didn't mind the chores, but I did mind any inkling of his contempt for them.

I put my book down and closed my eyes. Other things had changed between us recently too. Jake used to go to the gym, played tennis on Saturdays. But over the last year, it was as if he'd partially retreated from the toughness of having two children, as if the very thought of it made him feel weary. And around him instead there seemed to be a gradual accretion of middle-aged things: predictable clothes, corporate entertaining, golf. It was all very well growing old together, but did it really have to happen this quickly? "Night," I said, thinking all this, thinking of Claire. Claire and her screenplay. Disney. Had I told Jake about that then? I must have done, or how else would he know?

"Night," he said, not looking up.

I turned onto my stomach and thought about cotillions and Corinthians for a while, Hessian boots and neckcloths tied Trone d'Amour. And then I thought about Claire's gorgeous robe—maybe that was from Toast?—and her man in his suit and the gardener, and the gardener with Mel . . . They could meet at my house. I could babysit Milly. We could rendezvous for drinks, in an outdoor pub, by the river, there would be birdsong, and the two of them would laugh and kiss and thank me. There was a crackle of pages next to me. I opened my eyes and half-turned. Up close, Jake smelled of wine and smoke and a day in the office. The duvet smelled stale too—the old sheet smell of marriage. It had been a month or so, now that I came to think of it, since we'd last had sex. That was another thing that had seized up. It was fine when it was still the topic of jokes between us, but less fine now that it had passed into silence. I wondered if I should make another approach, not so obvious as to make rejection, if it came, feel too awkward, but obvious *enough*. I stroked my hand low across Jake's stomach. His skin felt soft and fuzzy. He didn't even run these days. He said, not moving except to turn another page, "So, as a result, I'm going to have to go to the agency office in Amsterdam next week."

I said, "Oh right, fine," and took my hand back.

"Night," I said, curling away from him into my corner of the bed. Claire had said I looked fulfilled. Was I fulfilled? She'd said Jake was dull. Was he?

"Night," he said.

Chapter 3

"I'm going to start with Jamie Oliver's slow-cooked and stuffed baby bell chilli peppers. Followed by the River Cafe's pan-roasted pigeon stuffed with cotechino with wood-roasted whole organic carrots. And then for dessert—well, I'm not quite sure. Have you ever done Nigella's almond and orange blossom cake?"

It was Friday afternoon and, after taking the car to the garage across the common, I was sitting on a warm, damp bench in the playground talking, or rather listening, to Rachel, another playground mother. There had been a quick burst of rain, but the sun had come out again. Dan was in the sandbox, seeing how much of it he could fit into his mouth, and Fergus and Rachel's son Harry were trying to climb up the slide. A smaller child in a white sundress and pink Tele-tubby boots, which she was banging crossly on the metal at the top, was waiting to slide down. One of us needed to intervene—playground etiquette is very strict on the subject of equipment violation—but I couldn't be bothered.

"Nigella?" I said. I wasn't really listening. Rachel was a good cook—it's where she put the energy she used to expend as a conference organizer—and always assumed I was too. She didn't hear me. "It does seem to take an awful lot of eggs," she was saying. "Do you think it might be a bit rich after the cotechino?"

"Maybe," I said.

"Really? Even with the loganberry and mascarpone coulis?"

"Maybe not then," I said. She darted me a look but then luckily noticed the situation building on the slide.

"Fergus!" she yelled. "Harry! Get off the little girl! We go *down* slides, not up them." She pursed the corners of her mouth and held her hands out apologetically in the direction of the pink girl's mother who inclined her head stiffly. "Now go and play on the monkey bars you two. And Fergus, stop pushing Harry please." Rachel, who approached mother-hood like a military exercise, was convinced that my son was out to get hers. It was a sort of persecution complex by proxy. Child-on-child violence: a greater source of tension among adults than the threat of nuclear action. Personally, I thought Harry should learn to fight back. Little whiner.

Rachel came and sat down next to me again. She had fresh, young skin, Rachel, but there were firm lines edging their way down from her mouth and across her forehead. Her hair was always pulled back tightly as if defiant of the new threads of iron in her temples. She was one of my new friends, one of the "playground mums" as Jake called them. The personal criteria for friendship changes when you have kids. You don't need to get along too well or to have that much in common—in some respects, that can get in the way. Better to withstand the constant interruptions that children bring to a conversation about recipes than one that really interests you about, oh I don't know, what did interest me those days? Playground friends take the same role as work friends: someone to gossip with at the photocopier, when half your mind's on something else (only, of course, it's not a photocopier any more, it's a slide in the shape of a moose). Someone, anyway, to gang up with against the strain.

I said, "Oh look, it's Maria."

Rachel said, "Oh yes, so it is."

That's the kind of conversation our sleep-deprived brains stretched to. It wouldn't, now I come to think of it, have lasted two minutes at the photocopier.

"Maria!" I called her over.

"Oh, hiya!" she said. Maria, slim and toned and usually in Lycra from hours in the gym, was several years younger than us and married to a banker. She had two small children, a house the size of a hotel, and an irritating habit of always pretending to be more humble than she was, a pretense which only served to draw attention to her position of wealth and privilege. "Ohmigod," she said, wiping the seat with a muslin that had been hanging off the back of her three-wheel all terrain mountain stroller and sitting herself down next to us. "Another riotous night at Casa Jennings. I'm so hung over. I couldn't tell you how much I drank. God knows what the neighbors think of us. It was supposed to be just a quiet kitchen supper—we had Flossie's godfather and his new girl-friend over. But it ended up with Patrick out in the middle of the road at midnight on Flossie's Microscooter. It was hilari-ous. I was laughing so much I'm sure I woke the whole street. Down our way, they're not used to that sort of behavior."

"Thursday night," remarked Rachel. "I don't know how you do it."

We both knew how she did it. I said, "You don't think Merika might be free on Saturday night do you?" Merika was her au pair, a devastatingly attractive and capable twenty-five-year-old, whom Maria called "My Slovakian." Merika was a pediatrician before she came to England, one of many Slovaks putting their qualifications at the mercy of the British middle class. Having made the grade as brain surgeons in their own land, they then submitted themselves to the ultimate challenge of nannying in south London.

"Oh," said Maria, sounding dubious. "The thing is, I've got people coming over, just a small party, and I was rather hoping that once the children were in bed she might help out. I thought she might enjoy that—she could throw on a black frock and pass around the nibbles."

"What sort of nibbles?" asked Rachel, with genuine interest.

"Oh, I haven't asked . . . we've got this sweet girl coming in to cook—she's just a friend of a friend; I'm just having Merika to help her out really . . ."

Rachel turned to me. "I served this delicious hors d'oeuvre last week," she said. "Crostini di fegatini di pollo e acciughe. River Café 2—I do think it's better than River Café 1, don't you?"

"Artemis! Octavia! Heel." A loud voice pealed across the green swade. "Shit," I said, under my breath. Rachel elbowed me in the ribs. It was Lucinda, an investment banker who, on the rare occasion that she was spotted in the week, did her utmost to undermine the rest of us. More polished, more efficient, more organized than us, morally, intellectually, and financially superior in every way (or so she believed), she was Public Enemy No. 1 in the battle between mothers-who-work and mothers-who-don't. She towered over us physically too: with the body of a tennis player and the thick, long, springy hair of Medusa. Only, Lucinda's hair was never wild—she was not a woman you ever imagined letting her hair down—so if Medusa she was, she was Medusa after a visit to Vidal Sassoon.

"Hiya," we chorused as she tied her leash of Highland terriers to the railings and bustled her brood through the child-friendly, finger-grabbing swing-back gate. Lucinda's children were called Cecily, Gwendolen, Ned, and Sid in accordance with a peculiar Morton Park fashion for naming girls after Noel Coward characters and boys after New York pickle salesmen. All four (she bettered us in child-bearing too) were delivered by elective Caesarean because she was, as they say, too posh to push. "Off you go, children—swings. WHAT A DAY!" she said, marching over to the bench. She adjusted the grip of her padded hairband, which, on "family days," replaced the tight chignon she wore to work. "The Audi wouldn't start. And Cecily was late for ballet and Miss Trisha gets so cross if they're not there for their barre exercises. And Ned and Sid had Toddler Massage on the other side of Morton and I've been lugging Gwendolen around with me when really she should be at home practicing for her violin grade five. Her teacher suggested she skip two to four as she is really very advanced," she added as an aside. "*And* I should be at work. This is a very important week for me. But Hilda, our nanny bless her, is in the hospital. Can't be helped I know, but it is typical. Honestly, you lot don't know how lucky you are. It's not the work that's so backbreaking, or the child care, but the *juggling*."

"Nothing serious I hope," I said.

"What?"

"Hilda."

"Only a perforated appendix, but the fuss she's making . . . Two months off? Quite absurd. And guess who's paying?

Well anyway, enough of that. I expect she needs the rest. Who doesn't?" She fixed Maria in her sights. "I haven't got nearly enough help. Your Croatian is super, isn't she?"

Maria began to look helpful and then frowned.

"No poaching," said Rachel.

"Slovakian," I added.

"And the house is still a state after the builders," said Lucinda, bending down and rubbing a chink of mud from the buckle of one of her little velvet shoes. "I don't know what Matty, my cleaner, does all day. Well, that's an out-of-work actress for you. Maybe I should go back to the agency and get someone a bit more committed."

"To a long-term future in lavatory bowls," I said.

A mobile phone started ringing. An eerie silence fell as mothers and nannies throughout the playground stopped dead for a moment, listened, and then scattered from the play area and charged back to their stroller baskets or handbags to rummage for hand-held salvation, leaving children hanging from the top of monkey bars, dangling from swings, thumping to the ground on suddenly vacated seesaws. Only Lucinda emerged triumphant. Apparently, her country needed her, or the city did at least.

"Oh no," she screamed into her Nokia, red blotches of anger beneath her foundation. "Gregory, I told you . . . All right, I'll deal with it. Okay, okay. Yes, I know. Okay, okay." Pause. "Okay, okay. See you later. Okay." She slipped the phone back into her stiff olive-green Mulberry shoulder bag. "Ach," she said. "I said to Gregory it's all very well this new house with all its acres of space and huge garden, but I can't be the one who has to take responsibility for it on top of everything else. This sort of thing never happened when we were in Fulham."

"What *has* happened?" asked Rachel.

Lucinda closed her eyes, as if the light was hurting, but kept on talking. "Flower Power were due to come today," she explained with exaggerated calm, "to prune the cherry and mow the lawn and plant out a few pots for the terrace so that it looks halfway decent for Sunday when Gregory's boss is coming for lunch. And the main woman has rung Gregory to say she can't come today, will Monday do? Well, no, it won't do." She stopped as if even she was pulled short by her own bossiness.

"What's her excuse?" asked Rachel. "Stung by a nettle?"

Lucinda ignored her.

"I know a gardener." Everyone looked taken aback including me.

Lucinda looked at me directly for the first time.

I pulled out of my wallet the card that the man from the crash had given me. "Here," I said. She looked at it.

"Peat and Dug," she read. "Any good?"

"Someone I bumped into. Seemed very nice. Ask for Pete."

"Should I mention you?"

"You could. But he probably wouldn't remember."

Lucinda jotted down the number, and I went off to find Fergus.

It took me a while. He'd broken out of the playground through a vandalized gap in the fence and was poking about in the roots of a tree with a long stick. There was earth in his pale brown hair, and his face, flushed with exertion, was screwed up into an expression of intense concentration, his tongue resting on his lower lip.

"Bang," he said when he saw me. "You're dead."

"I know," I said. "But it's also time to go home."

"NO," he shouted. "I DON'T WANT TO GO HOME." He went rigid and dug his heels in.

"Yes," I said patiently, trying to undig them with my fingers. Rachel, Maria, and Lucinda were looking over at me with pained sympathy. "Pleeze," I whispered. He slackened. Sometimes even under-threes respond to desperation. We set off for home and, in gratitude, I let him walk all the way.

•   •   •

When we finally got there, Fran, Jake's sister, was sitting on the doorstep.

"Oh God, I'm so sorry," I said. "I had to take the car to be repaired and then we walked back by the playground and I completely forgot you were coming."

She heaved herself up. She was twenty-two weeks pregnant and already into the self-righteous, martyred stage.

"It's all right," she said in the tone of one for whom it wasn't. "You're here now." She fondled her tiny bump, which was on proud display between a crop top purple vest and a pair of shocking pink draw-string trousers. "As soon as I've had a drink, I'll feel better." She sighed and rubbed both hands up and down her lower back.

Fran, who was an interactive artist, had never been one for strict time-keeping, for such conventions as appointments and routines—unless you were the one keeping her waiting, in which case punctuality suddenly seemed to rise on her list of priorities. She was twenty-nine, seven years younger than Jake, a much longed for second child, a girl at that, and had the kind of looks—a large, vulnerable mouth, deer-like brown eyes, tumbling curls, and pale white skin that bruised easily—that made you want to look after her. I loved her and was infuriated by her in equal measure. Her parents just gazed at her most of the time with open mouths. There was Italian blood somewhere in their veins, but it was as if Fran had gathered up every unconventional gene the Pritons had ever had, and run off with them, carefree in the knowledge that she could do her own thing and no one could stop her. Her own thing had included psychotherapy, aromatherapy, that spiritual movement when you only eat air—one of her more short-lived fads—and finally moving in with a fellow artist called Rain. He may not always have been called Rain—his parents lived in the very conventional suburb of Croydon— but Fran accused us of being bourgeois when we asked. They lived in West Kensington—"in town" she called it—in the mansion flat the Pritons once bought for her and Jake to share, but which appeared since to have become wholly hers. She made virtual art on the Internet. Rain . . . well I'm not quite sure what Rain did. Something to do with Thames debris. Rain, who was so handsome you wanted to weep, didn't say much.

"How are you feeling, sweetie?" I said. "And how's Rain?"

"Rain, rain, go away," said Fergus.

Fran ignored him. "Just so, so well," she said, slipping out of her Birkenstocks at the door. "I feel as if the world has just begun to make sense you know? As if it's been black and white, and now it's in color."

"Jolly good," I said, steering her through the house and into the garden. "I like your toe nails. What color do you call that?"

"Daylily." She plonked herself down into a deck chair. Fergus ran off to find his fire engine. I put Dan on a blanket on the grass. He immediately made for the borders. I had a few minutes before he found a snail and started eating it.

"Tea or coffee?" I said. "Or fizzy water?"

"Have you any raspberry leaf?" she asked.

"No."

"Dandelion?"

"Nope."

"Ginger? Blackcurrant? Red Zinger?"

"No, no, and no."

"What about chamomile? Surely you've got chamomile."

"I think we're out."

"Sod it, I'll have coffee," she said and lit a cigarette. "Low tar," she said defensively. "Nothing in them. Anyway, they're organic." She took a few deep drags and then twisted it out on the grass and chucked the dead end into the impatiens.

"Fran!" I said.

"Sorry," she said and rubbed her eyes.

I grabbed Dan by the legs and pulled him away from a daffodil bulb that he was on the verge of sinking his two rabbity teeth into. I could tell Fergus was all right because I could hear him shout "Emergency, emergency, fire on the sofa, fire on the sofa" in the sitting room. I put my arm around her shoulder. "Are you okay Fran? You seem a bit down."

"Sorry," she said a bit tearfully. "I've just convinced myself I've had a missed abortion. You wouldn't know, would you? It's been a while since I felt the baby move. And I was reading last night about detached placentas. And I'm sure I felt a sharp pain when I was waiting on your step. So it could be that. I just don't feel that things are right."

I laughed. That may sound like an unsympathetic response, but one of Fran's more touching characteristics was incorrigible hypochondria. I had had four months of this, of early pre-eclampsia, of threatened toxoplasmosis, of blighted ovums. She looked at me through watery eyes. "Why are you laughing?" she said in a little voice.

"Fran, there's nothing wrong with you. Or the baby. You've had your scan. When did you last feel a movement?"

"At breakfast?"

"Well then, the little mite's obviously having a nap. I'll get you some orange juice, and we'll wake him or her up. How about that?"

I put my finger under her chin, but her eyes had filled again. "Fran?"

"Oh God, I know you don't get any sleep either, but I'm just so tired you know? And I've got these funny little veins on my legs. I'm sure they're new. And . . . and . . ."

"What?" I said.

"I've got piles," she whispered.

"Poor you," I said with genuine sympathy. "I know. It's all awful. It's an awful business. But it's worth it in the end."

"Is it?" She looked at me keenly. "Oh God, I don't know. I suddenly feel really scared. I feel like I've been invaded. And I feel so fat. And I'm desperate to smoke all the time. Typical, the one time when you really need a cigarette it's the worst thing for you. And I don't know if I'm going to be able to cope. And . . . I mean Maggie, do you ever look around yourself and think how have I gotten here? How has all this accumulated? Where has my life gone?"

"Oh God," I said, straightening up. "Don't go down there."

Luckily Fergus came into the garden then, clutching a packet of frozen dinosaurs nuggets. I could hear the deep-freeze alarm beeping. Fergus said, "There's a fire in the freezer, but I got the animals out."

"Well done, you," I said, taking them back off him. Dan had crawled off to the steps and was about to plunge down headfirst. "Actually," I said, going after him and then returning the ice-age pterodactyls to the kitchen, "it's not the big things I miss so much, the freedom and the independence, as being able to finish a sentence without interruption, have a proper conversation now and again."

"Sorry?" said Fran, trying to wrest her packet of cigarettes from Fergus.

"Doesn't matter," I said. "Now, guess who I saw yesterday? Claire Masterson. Do you remember, my year at school?"

"God, yes," she said. "Wasn't she always going off with everyone's boyfriends?"

"Ye-es," I said doubtfully. "Anyway, she's invited us to a party. Tomorrow night . . ." I paused.

"And?" she said.

"And I don't suppose you could baby-sit? All my regulars have gone AWOL. Good practice . . ."

She cast her eyes at Fergus and Dan. Fergus was on top of Dan, trying to chew his ear off. "All right," she said.

I almost fainted. "Are you sure?"

"Yes," she said doubtfully.

"Good," I said. "Good, good, good, good, good. As Dr. Seuss would say."

"Who?"

"Dr. Seuss. *The Cat in the Hat.* A lot of repetition."

"Oh, right."

"But anyway. Good," I said again, before she could change her mind. "Thanks."

Before she went, Fran came upstairs with me to find me something to wear. I left Fergus in front of *Thomas the Tank Engine,* lined up for his favorite crashes, with a big pile of floppy Marmite sandwiches and strict orders not to wipe his fingers on the sofa. Fran held Dan while I flicked self-consciously along the hangers in my rickety pine wardrobe. She said: "You can't wear that!" and "What the hell is that?" and "Doubt you'll get into that" and "Hm. Thought not."

"It's all too black and middle-aged in here," she said. "You need something with color. Haven't you got an old nighty and a little cardy?"

"I've got an old nighty," I said, producing it.

"Not that old," she said, grimacing.

"This is hopeless." She put Dan onto the floor and picked up my dog-eared Fcuk Buy Mail catalogue. "Oh, what about this?" She held up the page with the white sprinkle sequin dress. I loved that dress. It had tiny straps beneath the model's tumbling auburn locks and was about four inches long. It probably would have fitted me—three years earlier. I wrinkled up my nose. "Dry clean only," I said.

Fran looked bored. "Oh right."

I turned back to my closet. Dan had started pulling out the shoes from the shoe rack: one of Jake's old loafers, now dusty and slope-heeled; some Docksides, cracked and sand-encrusted; several pairs of gray-white sneakers, a red suede stiletto!

"What about this?" I said, holding it aloft like Cinderella's prince, spinning it round on the top of my finger. "Would this jazz something up?"

Fran laughed. " 'Jazz'?" she said. "Oh, Maggie, you are funny. You sound like my mother." She started to talk as if she had a plum in her mouth. "How about a nice silk scarf with horse stirrups on it. That can *jazz up* any outfit. Oh God, Maggie. This is what I'm worried about. Am I going to start talking about 'jazzing things up'? Am I going to have a closet full of yesterday's clothes? It's fine for you, you're Maggie. But does motherhood automatically mean letting yourself go?"

I was smiling at her, but I could feel the blood draining from my face and then flooding back into all the wrong places. It was throbbing under my eyes. My throat suddenly felt tight. I had to keep smiling or I would cry.

"I don't know," I said, still smiling. "I suppose it, well I mean it . . . It depends on . . ." I couldn't seem to get the words out.

"Oh, God. Have I upset you?" She got up and put her hands on my shoulders. "Oh sorry. I didn't mean to. Was that very tactless? I didn't think you minded about things like that. Not like old frivolous me. I'm such a body fascist. It's the inside that counts. And you're so relaxed with things and people love you for it. Jake I know, I'm sure, loves you for it."

I turned away and picked up Dan who had emptied the shoe rack now and had started on Jake's ties. When I stood up, I was standing by the mirror and I turned to give myself a long look. It was like catching my face in a Tube window. I knew I was going through a dowdy phase—it's a *time* thing as much as anything—but I saw my face properly for the first time in ages. There it was: distorted and flattened, with hard angles for cheeks and dark rings where the eyes should be, as if all the old bad points were accentuated, all the good ones dissolved. This wasn't a phase. This was how I was. I looked hollowed out. I looked middle-aged. I said, quietly, "Yes, well, I wouldn't know, because he's hardly ever here . . ."

Fran had diverted her attention back to the clothes on the bed. She was holding a pair of black leggings against her bump. She said, "Oh, that reminds me. Tell him I saw him last night. I yelled at him from the car window, but he didn't see me. He was too busy yakking. Can I borrow these? They look blissfully comfy."

I turned. "Who was he yakking with?"

"Oh just some girl." She chucked the leggings back on the bed, stretched, and whirled her hands around above her head—a pregnant ballerina. "So can I have them?" She looked at her watch. "Oh shit. Better go. I've got prenatal yoga. Bugger, I meant to buy some almond oil to massage my perineum."

"The little touch that means so much," I said.

"What?"

"Nothing," I said. "Of course you can borrow them. They're probably too tight for me anyway."

At the door, she said, "Sorry if . . ."

And I said, "Doesn't matter. Thanks for baby-sitting tomorrow."

And she said, "Give my love to Jake."

And I said, "I will if I see him." And we both laughed. So everything was all right then.

I was bathing the children when Jake got home. He came straight upstairs hollering, "Where's my family!" like a hungry monster and made Fergus laugh so much he went under the water. While I was fishing him out, Jake came up behind me and kissed me on the head. "You're early," I said, putting my arms back to keep him there.

"I bunked off," he said. For a moment, he buried his nose in my hair, but then he was tickling Fergus and hauling him out of the bath, and chasing him, squawking and shrieking and wet, up the stairs and around our bedroom and over our bed and got him so overexcited I couldn't get him to sleep for hours.

Chapter 4

Saturday started early. It was 5:30 a.m. when Fergus began hollering for his breakfast in the other room and then, a few minutes later, in my ear.

"Whose turn is it?" Jake muttered.

"Yours," I said, but he didn't move. I got up with big exaggerated getting-up noises and, on the way out, left the door open which was code for "I'm happy for you to carry on sleeping if you can bear to do so through the guilt." Nobody ever warns you about the guilt quota in family relationships. "Shut the door!" yelled Jake after me, which was code for "shut the door."

I took Fergus down to the kitchen where he played on the floor, driving his Matchbox cars along the ridges between the tiles while I emptied the dishwasher. I loved my house in the early morning. It felt cool and clean and monastic without the toys out and papers everywhere. The kitchen was small—I'd never wanted to waste garden space by expanding out like all the other newcomers on our street—so it had windows on two sides and on June mornings like this the sun slipped in, past the pots on the sill, still sleepy, not bright enough yet to glare accusingly at the egg stains on the table or the crayon on the woodwork, but strong enough to throw the creamy whiteness of the walls into relief and send geranium shadows dancing up the cabinets. The cabinets were painted an off-white called "Casablanca." "White with a hint of Bogey," said Jake.

It was almost nine when he stumbled down the stairs with Dan in his arms. Fergus and I were watching Saturday morning television by then, curled up around each other on the sofa, and while half my mind had been actively following Buzz Lightyear's conflict with Evil Zurg, the other half had been mulling over "things," worrying at them like a tongue at a sore tooth. The previous evening Jake and I had had what we used to call, in the days when nights could be anything but, a QNI (a Quiet Night In), but this one had been even quieter than usual. Jake had been preoccupied once the children were asleep, and we had eaten and cleared in silence. He'd gone to bed early, leaving me in front of *Frasier*, so I hadn't told him about Fran seeing him with "a girl." I hadn't asked him who she was. I hadn't made a joke of it, got to the bottom of it, as I would have done a few months before. A few months before, I would never have believed it for an instant. But now? I didn't know what I thought. I just felt uneasy and distant. I hadn't, now that I came to think of it, even told him that Fran had agreed to baby-sit tonight, though if I had he would probably just have groaned and moaned about going. I was thinking about this when he came in. I said, idly, "Oh, hello. By the way, I meant to say, the good news is Fran says she'll baby-sit tonight."

He looked bemused. He frowned. He handed me Dan who snuggled into my neck. "Why?" he said, waving his hands in front of Fergus's eyes to distract him from the television.

"So we can go to Claire's party."

He groaned. Here we go. "Oh, God," he moaned. "We're not really going, are we?"

"We have to," I said firmly. Then more weakly, "I said we would."

Jake was walking around the room with Fergus standing on his feet, using them like human stilts. He sighed heavily and put Fergus back on the sofa. "I'd better go and have a shower now then."

It was only an excuse of course. Like "Just popping out to get the paper" or "I've just got to get this off in the post," "having to have" a shower is one of the few times you ever get to have any time to yourself when you have small children.

So Jake had his shower—a long shower, you could have cleaned the Statue of Liberty with a toothbrush in the time it took him to wash—and Fergus and Dan and I sat on the kitchen floor and studied the ants. Children are the gods of small things. When I was little, I was always finding dying fledglings in the garden. I'd make a bed for them in an old plastic breadbin and bring them milk and worms. And then I'd rush home from school and up the stairs and into my bedroom to see them . . . and, well, usually my mother had discreetly cleared them away by then. Or I'd find money on the pavement and stag beetles in the gutter or powder blue blackbirds' eggs cracked open on the grass: objects you never find when you're grown up. You have to be a mother for your nose to be brought back to the ground, for little things to matter more than the large.

The ants in our kitchen knew they were on to a winner. No pesticides in this house. Far too toxic. Over the previous days, Fergus and I had studied their advance on the kitchen cupboard, one, two, three, up the cabinet, into the jam. At the moment, they were marching in a line from the back door across the tiles to a hole in the baseboard.

"Is that their house?" Fergus asked.

"Maybe," I said. "Or maybe they live in the garden and they just come here to shop."

"They're busy," said Fergus. "Aren't they?"

"Busy doing nothing," I said. "They are amazing things, ants. The industry, the organization. They live in finely developed communities. Did you know that when . . ."

"OH MUMMY!" Fergus cried. "Dan's eating them!"

The phone rang just then—in time to divert a crisis. It was Angela, Jake's mother. I told her Jake was in the shower, but she was quite happy to talk to me—as long as the subject was Jake. Like many women I knew, I had taken on the role of mediator between my cohabitee and his parents, a domestic hostage negotiator. I was the one who remembered birthdays and anniversaries, who made interested inquiries about the garden and the Nile cruise. I was the one who cooked Sunday lunch and made sure we had the right sherry and kept them up to date with their son's career advancements. Angela always complained that Jake never told her anything, whereas I'd say, "Oh yes, I know, he's *dreadful* about keys" or "Yes, I've told him he should get that mole seen to." She babied her only son, and we all colluded in it. Only sometimes did I let it irritate me. After I'd put the phone down, promising he'd ring her when he was dry (and resisting the temptation to add "between the toes and behind the ears"), I rang Mel. I said, "What are you doing? Why don't you bring Milly round to play?"

She said, "I would, but I've got a half leg, an underarm, and a bikini at 11."

"Well, come after. Isn't the bikini agony?"

"Absolute agony but not as agony as the underarm, which is major agony. I'll ask Milly. MILLY! Do you want to go and play with Fergus?"

Fergus was jumping up and down next to me trying to grab the receiver. "What do you want?" I said. He muttered something. "What?" He pulled my head down so that my mouth was on a level with his ear. He hadn't really gotten the hang of whispering.

"Can she bring her guns?" he begged.

Mel came back on the line. She said they'd come for lunch. I told her to come armed.

Jake clumped down the stairs then, looking spruce. "Hello, gorgeous," he said, happy about something, and unstringing the belt of my robe.

"Hey," I said. We kissed—a brief moment of happy family: parents united, baby frolicking on the carpet, toddler busy with a box of matches—before Fergus jumped on Dan and the usual mayhem broke out, everybody shouting and yelling and trying to kill each other. Jake didn't look so happy again after that. I was still feeling disgruntled.

"Ring your mother," I said. "You never ring your mother."

.   .   .

Mel and Milly arrived at midday. Milly and Fergus threw themselves into each other's arms and ran upstairs giggling. Mel said, patting Jake's stomach through his shirt, "What's this?"

"Oh no," he said, anguished.

"It's all right," she teased. "It's nice. Makes you look cuddly."

"I don't want to look cuddly," he said.

"All right then: commanding."

"That's better," he said. "How's Piers?"

"Don't."

"Poor Piers," I called from the kitchen where I was making coffee.

"Poor Piers nothing," called out Jake. "He can always get out if he wants to. He doesn't have to stay with her."

"I know," I said, coming back in with the coffee pot and a packet of chocolate chip cookies. "It's just . . ."

"Excuse me," said Mel from the sofa where she had put her legs up. "It's my love life you're discussing if you don't mind. I am in the room."

"Well?" said Jake. "How is it?"

Mel sighed. "Uninspiring. He's sweet, but . . . there's no spark."

I handed her her coffee. "Sex?"

"Yes please, but no sugar."

"Ha. Ha."

She lay back down. "Darling," she camped. "He's an anesthetist. It passes in a blur. I count to ten, and when I wake up, it's all over. Completely painless."

Jake said, anguished, "Oh no, I can't bear it. The thought of anyone talking about me like this . . ." He got up from his chair. "I've got to go and do some work anyway." He mussed Mel's hair. "Staying for lunch?" She nodded. "Good. See you in a bit."

After he'd gone, Mel and I went into the kitchen. She took Dan on her knee while I defrosted a quiche and told me about this man in his fifties who'd come into the clinic the day before, particularly requesting her, and how he'd stood shyly in the doorway, slightly stuttery, hands in his pockets, a bit greasy looking but otherwise harmless, and told her how he had a problem "down there." "So I said, all serious, not wanting to jump to conclusions: 'down where?' and he kept saying 'down there,' so finally I said I'd do an examination and a funny look came over his face and he dropped his trousers and shrieked, 'it goes all hard, it goes all hard' and started cackling with laughter. I had to push him out of my room. Apparently, he's done it to all the women doctors, just no one had warned me!" I laughed with her at this, but maybe I stopped too soon, because she said, "Are you all right?"

I said, turning away from her and looking out of the window, "What would you say if someone told you they'd seen Jake with a girl?"

Mel said "What?"

I turned back. "A girl."

"When?"

"Late at night."

"Doing what?"

"I don't know. Yakking."

"Who told you this?" She was looking at me as if I was mad.

"Fran. She said she saw him. He told me he was with Ed."

"Well, I'd say you, or Fran, need your head examined. Why would Jake see a girl? He's got you. Or if he did, it was probably someone from work. Why don't you ask him?"

"I can't bear to." I sat down next to her. "In case it's true."

"Oh Maggie. How could it be? He loves you. You're the best couple I know." She looked into my face. "He adores you. You've got no reason to . . ."

"I don't know, Mel." I cleared the papers on the table into a pile, sorted Jake's mail from mine.

"Things aren't great at the moment. He's distant, disengaged. I thought relationships were supposed to get easier. But they don't. Everything speeds up and intensifies. Things that used to take weeks to happen take place in a day. One minute we love each other and the next, we seem to hate each other. Honestly, I really do. I hate him sometimes. It's frightening. And then I love him again and it happens so fast. It's so changeable." I stood up. "Like the English weather."

Mel said, "Well, in my experience, these sorts of feelings are easily solved."

"How?" I'd opened the fridge and began spooning puréed carrots into a bowl of left-over rice for Dan.

"A good shag's what you need. Clears the air like a thunderstorm."

I gave her a rueful look over my shoulder.

"What?"

"Yes well, easier said than done."

"Oh dear." She grimaced.

I took Dan off her knee and, plonking him in his high chair, began coaxing purée into his mouth. I looked at the door and back again and mouthed, "And it's not like him."

"Oh dear."

"So something's up," I whispered.

She ran through a few suggestions. She advised adding a new spark to the relationship. She mentioned that *Cosmo* staple of coming to the door in a negligee. I told her that, as in most grown-up relationships, my cohabitee had his own key. She brought up candlelit dinners.

I said, "Puleese."

She said, "Well, why not do something different for once. Experiment."

"You mean anal sex?" I said and winced.

Then she said, "Oh fuck, I don't know. Maybe it's just a phase?"

"Yes, or maybe it's me," I said. I gave up on Dan, who didn't seem hungry or certainly not hungry for puréed carrots and chucked his bowl behind me into the sink. "Maybe he just doesn't fancy me any more." I wiped Dan's mouth and hands with his bib. "Or maybe it's inevitable. Maybe this is always what happens after a bit. Maybe it takes two years or five or ten, but finally you can't summon it up anymore. I mean"—I got up to find Dan a hunk of bread—"do you think you can ever go back to the days when every pore seems to tingle and you can't wait to tear off his clothes? When sex really is preferable to a good book? Do you think it's a choice between that and settling down? Can you ever have both?"

"I haven't got either," said Mel, laughing.

"I know but . . ."

"Maggie. It'll be fine. You're just stuck in a rut. My sister Siobhan felt just the same when her children were this little. You just need something to get you out of it. What about this party tonight? Why don't you dress up? Make yourself feel like a proper woman again."

"I do feel like a proper woman."

"Exactly," she said darkly. "Too proper."

I got up to set the table. I wanted to ask her more, seek more reassurance, but I felt I'd probably had my quota so instead I handed her the cutlery. "I wonder what you'd think of Claire," I said.

"Would I like her?" she asked, as she mimed cutting a piece of meat before placing the knives and forks around the table.

I reached up to get the plates from the cupboard. "I don't know." I put them down and then leaned for a moment against a chair. "She's quite high maintenance and she doesn't let you get a word in edgeways. But she's . . . remarkable really. She has this glamorous life and she's funny and successful and she's got nice clothes."

"Oh well, if she's got nice clothes."

"She's definitely got nice clothes."

"Are you a teensy bit jealous?"

The microwave beeped. "LUNCH!" I yelled up the stairs. "Of course not," I said. "With a life as glamorous as mine? Of course not."

·   ·   ·

After we'd eaten, Mel and I and the children went over to the common to laugh at the weekend dads. It was one of our regular pleasures. There was a whole different scene in the park at weekends. There were two types of weekend dad. Type one: the lawyers and city men, shiny black shoes poking under their razor-sharp jeans, crisp work collars folded like envelope flaps over "fun" weekend jackets, white-lipped and dazed by the limitless potential for wildness and disagreeableness of children they had only seen flush-cheeked against their pillows all week. There was one there then, desperately trying to get his daughter off the monkey bars. Mel ducked because she thought she recognized him from the clinic ("Athlete's foot," she mouthed, "or was it warts? Can't remember now"). He wouldn't have spotted her anyway. He was half in, half out the bars himself. "Cressida, out of the jungle web now, time to go. I mean it, Cressy. I'm counting to three, Cressida. One. Two. Three. Where are you going now, Cressida?"

And then there was type two. Maybe they worked in the music business or film; either way, they were at home in their weekend Timberlands (laces undone), their plaid shirts and Ralph Laurens. They were *so* busy showing you how they could squeeze a week's worth of "quality time" into forty-eight hours, chasing their children around the playground—crazy people, crazy guys—they almost forgot to keep an eye on their microscooters or their expensively kiddy-seated mountain bikes. There were a couple at it today, playing crocodile tag for, oh, at least five minutes before two of their children clonked their heads and another crashed into a brown Labrador and everybody left in tears. "It's enough to put you off family life for good," said Mel, as we sat together on the metal fence around the swings, legs dangling, knees warmed by the bars, rough girls against the world.

I didn't answer. I was too busy watching two people farther away under the trees. They were lying on their stomachs on a blanket, with the papers spread out around them and a bottle of wine beside them on the grass. Their ankles were entwined.

"All right?" said Mel.

"Yup, fine," I said, "Let's go."

When we got home we had tea and cake. *Homemade* cake. Banana and walnut to be accurate. I could hardly be trusted with a stew, but I was fine with a sponge. You have to be if you don't work, otherwise people don't understand what you do all day. When working mothers talk about their guilt, it's always bringing store-bought treats to school events they mention first. The humiliation of that or the misery of being up at midnight creaming eggs. As if it really mattered. It must be a conspiracy between the PTA and husbands whose mothers were always baking. You could write a thesis on the subject. Cake: Its Role in Family Politics.

"Hm," said Mel. "Very moist."

"I want a chocolate cake," said Fergus. "One of those shiny purple ones." You see, children prefer Cadbury's minirolls anyway.

I had just cut a slice for myself when Jake came in, yawning, leaned over me and picked it up clumsily for himself. Half of it fell on the floor before he got it to his mouth.

"Jake," I admonished. "That was mine. Anyway, what happened to the packet of chocolate chip cookies? They've all gone."

"Funny you should say that," said Jake, putting his hand to his forehead and waving his head around woozily. "I was just making myself a cup of coffee earlier and suddenly—brwwwwww—I woke up and I was on the floor and there were crumbs all over my face."

Mel laughed. She hadn't heard it as many times as I had. She picked the slice off the floor, put it on a plate, and handed it to him. "Bit of dust won't hurt anyone," she said.

Chapter 5

Jake became quiet after Mel and Milly left. It was as if they had taken all his energy with them, as if they'd switched the light off when they went. He had to answer some phone calls and then he got cross with Fergus for trying to disturb him, and Fergus, who was tired, continued banging on the door of the room Jake was in until he came out and said, "Maggie?" in a pointed voice. By the children's supper time, something with edges was flying around in the air, catching in our hair and jangling our nerves. "Do we have to go?" said Jake behind me, as I pushed eggs around in the frying pan. "We won't know anyone. And anyway, what about our curry?" Saturday was, traditionally, take-out night in our house.

"Okay." I turned abruptly, fish slice dripping fat onto the floor tiles. "Let's stay in like we always do and wallow in biryani instead."

Jake held out his hands and turned. "Fine, fine, fine. We're going. Forget I said anything."

Which is how it was left until there we were at 9:15 p.m., scrubbed and stilettoed (well, I was stilettoed, having found the second one at the back of my closet), on the steps of Claire's house. "Let's not go," I said suddenly. "Let's go and have a meal instead."

"WHAT?" mouthed Jake in a silent-shout.

"I'm nervous," I said. "We won't know anyone."

"Oh behave," he said. "We're here now and we're going in."

The buzzer rang, Jake pushed the door open, and we went through to another open door. And there was Claire. She was dressed in a curve-clinging aquamarine frock, with a thick band of darker green velvet around the hem and tiny sequinned straps over her shoulders. "Beautiful dress, Claire," I gasped. She wrinkled up her nose. "I bought it in America," she said. On her feet were deep-water blue silk Aladdin slippers, and her blonde hair was piled up high, tendrils tumbling around her ears. She was either wearing a very clever bra or her breasts had magical floating properties. Most of them were bobbing above her dress. They looked new to me. I wondered if she'd bought them in America too.

"Gosh hello," mumbled Jake. "Long time no see."

"Jake!" she said. "How lovely that you've come. Maggie too. And how nice that some of my married friends have made it. All the others have cancelled."

"Children?" I said.

"No, wives," she said, winking at me over her shoulder as she threaded her arm through Jake's. "Now, come in you handsome man and meet some people."

She took us, or him, me tripping along behind, feeling clumsy in my heels, into a wide drawing room where a waiter handed me a glass of champagne. You could see the sun floating low over the common through the floor-to-ceiling windows (definitely b for beautiful view), throwing pinkish gold light across the bare floor and up faded green walls. There was no furniture. It appeared to have been moved out of the way to make room for the candles. There were candles every-where: thick ivory church candles flickering in gilt-framed mirrors; small round candles bobbing like lost ships in silver bowls of water. It certainly didn't seem to have been moved out of the way to make room for the people. There weren't any.

"Everyone's in the garden," said Claire, and led us through some French doors to the top of a wrought-iron spiral stair-case below which, in a dusky grotto of urns and figurines and sculpted box trees, a small throng milled and swayed, cigarette ends glowing. "I hope you're not going to find it all horribly media," she said, waving to a chap with a bald head behind a bay. "Political editor of the *Independent*," she said, "married to Sue Batsby on the *Mail*. Darling." She broke off to kiss a young man with sideburns the shape and size of New Zealand. "How's life on *Culture*? Oh I know, they're all absolute Philistines. Except for Gav who's a poppet, and of course he's gone to *Harper's* . . ." She was still gripping Jake tightly by the arm. He was smiling inanely. She said, "Remind me what you do again, Jake."

"I'm in advertising," he said patiently.

"Ah, well you must meet Omar," she said. "Or have you already met? He writes 'Back in five' in the *Guardian*."

She pulled Jake away behind a mossy angel but, before I'd quite finished sinking to the ground in horror, was back. "Now, Maggers," she said. "Who shall I get for you? Now . . . there's Pool-ey who edits my copy at the *Times* but looks a bit tied up at the moment talking to Caggers from the *Speccy* . . . Ah—" She put out her hand and grabbed a woman with plas-tic pansies in her hair. "Katya, Katters, quick, meet my oldest, oldest friend in the world. Katya does 'Talk of the Town' for *The New Yorker,* and writes a column in the *Sunday Telegraph* on American politics. She's also studying at Columbia for her doctorate in comparative literature. And Maggie . . ." She broke off and then resumed an octave higher, "isamum!"

Katya, who seemed about twenty-five, looked at me wonderingly, and then reproachfully at the departing back of Claire. "Hi," she said kindly.

"Hello," I said. And then, "Sorry, you don't have to talk to me if you don't want to," which was the worst thing I could have said because of course it meant after that she did. She was very nice. She made a good show of it. She asked me lots of questions about my children's ages (one probably would have sufficed) and was sweetly generous in the information she was happy to impart about life in the Big Apple (I must remember to try Cello at 53 East Seventy-seventh Street next time I'm there). But I knew she was desperate to escape. Not because she looked over my shoulder the whole time—only the socially gauche do that—but by the way her eyes bored into mine, unflinching in their determination to do so, her whole body rigid with the effort of staying upright. After a while, once she'd explained, nodding earnestly, why she didn't think she could ever give up work herself ("I value my own identity too much and I think, if I ever have children, they'd respect that"), I said, "Oh your glass is empty," and she caved in with relief and disappeared.

After she'd gone, I scanned the crowd for Jake and could just about make out his top half through a crush of bodies. He appeared to have taken off his jacket. He was bending down to hear someone over the hubbub and was laughing. I was just about to go over to him when someone next to me said, "Any chance of another drink?"

"Sorry?"

"A DRINK," the man said, as if I was deaf or mad. "Are you serving or not?"

"Not," I said.

"Oo, I'm sorry." He turned and giggled to the woman next to him. "Oops," he said to her.

I sat down on the step. My toes had begun to hurt. I was wearing a short-sleeved white linen shirt that looked like the kind of jacket worn by milkmen and that I only ever wore because it had been expensive, a short black chiffon skirt that I'd thought made me look sexy but that I now realized was an inch too short, and black tights because I hadn't had a chance in the end to shave. None of the other women here had sullied their brown legs with anything as tacky as nylon. Or as dull as black. Nobody else had dressed like a waitress. Not even the waitresses.

"Maggie. What are you doing? Not on your own already!" Claire was back again.

I said, "I'm dressed all wrong. All your friends look like they've stepped out of *Vogue*. I look like I've stepped out of *Bon Appétit*."

She said, "Maggie, you look great. You always do. You just have a problem with your self-image." She broke off. "I know. Aha. I've just got the person for you to meet. Wait here." She scurried off into the party to return a few minutes later, dragging an attractive red-headed woman in bright orange trousers and striking turquoise shoes with blunt toes like a dolphin's nose. "Meet Yonka," said Claire. "She's a personal shopper. Oops, better go, the band's here," and she disappeared again.

Yonka smiled. "Hi."

"Nice to meet someone else who's not in the media," I said. "How do you know Claire?"

"She's doing a piece on me for *Harper's Bazaar*," she said.

"Oh," I said. "I like your shoes."

"Mew, mew," she said.

I said, "I'm not being sarcastic, I mean it. They're nice."

"It's the designer," she said. "Mew mew. M.I.U. M.I.U."

"Oh right."

Silence. Someone had to fill it. "So what exactly does a personal shopper do?" I said.

Yonka raised an elegantly plucked eyebrow. "I'm involved in realigning the individual look. I'll create an image for someone, or I'll work with the client to discover what they themselves would like their personal presentation to say about them."

"What, clothes-wise, you mean?"

"Clothes-wise and, um . . . yup basically clothes-wise. A lot of it is about undoing the damage created by years of laziness or bad habits."

"Oh. I could do with a bit of that." I looked down at my legs. "I bet black tights are pretty damaging."

She smiled politely.

"No, I mean it. Are they pretty damaging?"

She made an amused hm!, half-laugh, change-the-subject sort of noise.

"No, are they?" I almost shouted.

She stopped smiling. "Yes," she said. "In June certainly. Have you considered a St. Tropez Tan?"

"It would be lovely, but we're not planning on a holiday this year."

"No, from a bottle. You need to have it applied at a beauty salon. And you have to be careful which one. Some of them smear."

"Oh."

"And I'd definitely lose the stilettos," she added.

"I thought heels were in."

"Yes, but *tubular*."

I groaned. "I wish I'd never come."

Yonka leaned forward and pressed her card in my hand. Before she turned away, an expression flitted over her face, not unlike that of a priest about to administer Communion.

"Call me," she said.

Alone again, I returned to my perch on the steps. I didn't have a pocket so I screwed Yonka's card into a twist and poked it into a hole in the wrought-iron banister. Jake was no-where to be seen. Nor was Claire. I looked idly for Rowena, her actress sister, but I didn't see her either. I felt beached. It had been so long I'd forgotten how parties could make you feel like that—sometimes they pick you up and roar and crash about your ears and carry you along with them, but most often they just leave you stranded.

"Angel on horseback?" said a voice above me. It was a waitress, a waitress in hot-pink chiffon, bearing a tray.

"No thanks."

"What about a devil then?"

"Do you have something in between?" I said, but she didn't smile.

I stood up. I wanted to find Jake to check that he wasn't having too awful a time. I should never have made him come. He recoiled like an anemone from this sort of thing. It was wrong of me to have insisted. We should leave, find some quiet restaurant, our local Indian maybe, in which to sit and be ourselves, to sort things out between us. I manipulated my way through the crowd, thicker now, louder now since the band—a salsa band—had struck up in the sitting room, until I reached the place where I thought I'd spotted him before. He wasn't there. I grabbed a glass of Perrier from a passing tray and navigated a path through some more jostling bodies ("Soho House," they were all saying. "Oh yes, The Ivy,

Babington") until I got to the bottom of the garden. He wasn't there either. I sat on a wall, took off my shoes, and fiddled with the feet of my tights, unpicking the net at the toes. After a while, I thought I might as well go to the bathroom, the last resort of the socially desperate.

I had made my way halfway back when I realized there were a few people in the drawing room now. It was dark and the room stood out like a magic lantern. Two or three couples were dancing to the music, holding hands and coming together and apart again, rubbing hips and rocking shoulders. Up close they probably looked self-conscious, but from a distance, up there in the candlelight in that big empty room, they looked enchanted, like inhabitants of some suburban Grand Meaulnes. I was almost at the steps before I realized that one of the men, the one holding his partner's hand above his head and spinning her round in an enclosed circle of his own making, his mouth open, laughing, was Jake. And then I realized that the girl was Claire.

My first thought was surprised pleasure. Jake danced so rarely in those days, so rarely let himself go. And he looked young and free and handsome, twirling Claire and her green dress around. He was bending over to reach her, his shoulders rounded, his hair pushed back from his face, at ease with himself, not cuddly, but, yes, *commanding*. For a moment I reflected on how cool, how together he looked. He had always been a good dancer. And then I felt dizzy with something less charitable, with the sense that I was lost and alone, and socially inept, and he was up there, part of it all, part of the party. And even though I recognized it as self-pity it didn't make it any easier when I thought: when was the last time he danced with me?

I had stopped on the spiral staircase, one foot on the first step. In the next moment I would, I think, have continued up—gone to join him, make a joke to Claire, and cut in—but in that moment a small middle-aged man with straggly gray hair and a pregnant-paunch under his camel V-neck started coming down, feet tumbling after each other in an erratic manner, so I had to jump quickly, back down into the garden, to get out of his way. I backed into a tub of marguerites to let him pass. But he didn't. He lurched toward me, using his girth to block my escape. I said brightly, "I'm just on my way up."

He swayed precariously, spilling red wine from his glass onto the York stone, and grabbed my arm to steady himself. "D'I know you?"

"No," I said, maneuvering halfway around him. "You don't."

"S' what's a pretty girl like you doing on your own?"

"I'm not on my own," I said, trying to sound upbeat and relaxed with his drunkeness, and trying not to sound stiff and sober and slightly censorious, which was how I was really feeling. "I'm on my way up to see my husband."

"Waste of time: marriage," he said, suddenly vicious, kicking a private wound. He let go of my arm then and the loss of security sent him reeling. He grabbed the wrought-iron banister. More wine slurped; this time onto my stilettos. That would jazz them up. He said, comically, "Ooopss."

I said, caught now, "Have we perhaps had a drop too many?"

"You mean, am I drunk? Yes I am. I'm a cunt."

He bent his head toward me. His face was all twisted. I could see the hairs lurking in his nostrils, the broken white ridges on the back of his purple tongue. I thought, for a moment, that he was going to kiss me, so I put my hands out and was about to push him off when a man came up behind me, put his arm on the drunk's shoulder, and propelled him gently down the stairs. The newcomer said, "Language. There're ladies present."

The drunk said, "Fuck off."

"Hey," the newcomer said. "No need to be like that. Maybe you should be going? Shall I get you a cab?"

"I'sfine. Got the car."

"Okey-dokey. I'll just go and find our hostess, shall I?" The man straightened up and for the first time he looked at me. With a shock of recognition I saw who it was. It was the gardener from the crash. My gardener. *Mel's* gardener. "Hello," he said, squinting as if he couldn't quite place me.

"Maggie," I said. He looked blank. "The meter maid. From the crash," I added.

His face relaxed. "Oh yeah." He put out his hand—"Pete. Pete Russ."

He had had a haircut since I'd last seen him and his head now looked like a recently sheared sheep, the curls surprised into tufts before they'd even begun to unfold, and he was smartly dressed in an ash gray linen suit, but he still looked out of place in this company, a footballer in his interview-best, a cat among the pigeons, a fox among the hens.

"I remember," I said, taking it. "But what are you doing here?"

"I live here," he said flatly.

"Oh, with Claire," I said, suddenly understanding. Bad luck for Mel: he was taken.

"Claire, Claire, the moment I met you I swear," droned my friend on the steps, his chin now sagging onto his chest.

"No, downstairs. The basement." He gestured to a dingy barred window abutting the ground (b for basement). "With my partner. Look, I'd just better go and call matey here a cab. I'll be back in a sec."

He jumped over the man, leaped up the steps two at a

time, and disappeared into Claire's drawing room. I waited, crocheting my fingers in and out of the cast-iron railings, not sure whether to leave, wondering if I was supposed to be standing guard over the now almost comatose drunk at my feet. A minute or two later, though, Pete was back, this time with Claire. She said, "Ooh dear. What have we here? Oh shit, Cyril. Why do you always do this?" She turned to me and added, "I knew I shouldn't have invited him. But he's the chief sub on Features, and I dreaded to think what he'd do to my copy if I didn't." I made a face. "I'm joking," she added. "I feel really sorry for him, actually. He's always pissed."

"Has he got far to get home?" I said.

"No, since his divorce the poor sod lives in Tooting."

"A fate indeed," I said.

She and Pete heaved him to the top of the steps, where they stood in conference for a while, and then Claire took Cyril, leaning against her, off into the house.

Pete came back down the steps. "Your partner?" I said, when he got to the bottom.

"My partner?" Pete had bent to inspect the pot of marguerites next to him. Some of the flowers had bent under Cyril's weight and Pete snapped off the damaged stems with his fingers.

"You said you lived with your partner?"

"Oh yeah, I do." He patted down the compost at the base of the plants, then stood up and brushed his hands on his trousers. "Lloyd."

"Oh, as in Doug?" Maybe there was still hope.

"As in Doug?" Pete was frowning.

"Pete and Doug, I mean."

"Yeah. That's right. Yes. My business partner." He was scanning the crowd. "I'm parched. Do you want to find a drink?"

I looked around me. I looked up into the sitting room. There was no sign of Claire or Jake now. I hesitated, then I said, "Yes, all right."

We worked our way back through the throng. Pete walked ahead of me. There were wrinkles in the linen at the back of his knees. He moved with his arms at an angle to his body, hands out, as if his muscles got in the way of smart clothes. He stopped at a table with an abandoned tray of drinks on it at the far end of the garden. "There you go," he said, handing me a glass. It was half full of red wine, but had a smudge of lipstick on the rim. "Get that inside you. You look as if you need it."

"Do I?"

"You look a bit . . . tense."

"Well, someone just thought I was a waitress and then I thought that poor man was going to be sick on me, but apart from that . . ."

"A waitress?" He laughed. There was a scar under one of his eyes and little dimples above each side of his mouth, as if someone had prodded him with a pen. "You mean you're the hired help?"

"Like you," I said. "Do you do Claire's garden? It's very nice."

"I looked after it for her grandmother, yeah. Not recently. She was a nice lady. That was very sad." He glanced down at the back of his hands.

"Her dying, you mean?"

"Yeah."

"Yes, it was," I said. There was a silence as we both contemplated the passing of Claire's elderly relative. "Though, um . . ." I felt an inappropriate giggle rise in my throat. "Actually, I never met her."

"Oh?" He started laughing. He nudged me with his elbow, and then nudged me again more roughly on purpose so that I spilled a tiny bit of my drink.

"Hey!" I said.

"Sorry." He was grinning.

Then I remembered Lucinda and I told him about giving his number out to her and he said he'd already been in touch and it seemed like she had a lot of work for him. "Which," he said, suddenly earnest, "I really appreciate. Thanks." I told him I thought that it was the least I could do after our little prang and he laughed. And then he stared at me, and said, "And what would be the most?"

"What would be the most what?" I said.

The corners of his mouth were twitching. "What would be the most you could do?"

Was he flirting? Or was he one of those men who was so aware of the effect of his looks that he always behaved like this? Either way, my cheeks tingled. Afterward, I imagined myself saying coquettishly, "Well, what would you like me to do?" or enigmatically, "Less is more." But, of course, at the time I said neither of those things. I said dumbly, "I don't know."

I felt suddenly awkward. A man pushed past me. I raised my glass out of the way, but he jogged my arm and sploshed the wine onto my shirt. He apologized and I said it didn't matter and after he'd gone I was able to turn to Pete again and say brightly, starting the conversation afresh, "So, no garden of your own, then?"

"No garden," he said.

"But at least you have a nice view."

"I have a nice view," he said, looking deeply into my face.

It had been a long time since anyone had talked like that to me. Or had looked at me in that way. It was not how things

were supposed to be conducted, but I felt a flicker of something inside.

Pete seemed to have stopped looking for conversation
now that he had found a seam of his own to mine. I said,
scrabbling about for safer ground, "Look, seriously, is your
van all right?"

"It's fine," he said in mock-exasperation. "Let it rest,
okay?" He put his hand out to stop me from jabbering on. It
was covered in scratches, and there was dirt around the top of
his fingers that looked as if it was ground in. Then he said,
"Do you wanna dance?"

I thought about it for a moment and then I thought about
Jake so I shook my head. "Actually I'd better go," I said. I put
my glass down and nodded my head a few times. "Got to find
someone." I rubbed my hands together and then did a sort of
half clap. "So, um, bye then. Maybe we'll bump into each
other again."

"Not if I see you indicating," he said very cheerily.

I turned my back on him and went up the spiral staircase
and into the drawing room. I stood there for a bit, getting my
breath back, stopping my head from spinning. That's red
wine on an empty stomach for you. I should find an angel or
a devil—one or the other.

There were lots of people dancing now. Jake wasn't one of
them. He was leaning against a wall with a group of people
having a whale of a time. Spouting with laughter.

"Sorry to interrupt," I said. "But I think we ought to be
leaving. Baby-sitter . . ." I added. The people he was with
smiled at me politely. Blankly. "Righty-ho," he said, though,
as I stood there like a teacher waiting for homework, it took a
good ten minutes for him to extricate himself from what had
clearly been a fascinating and side-splittingly amusing conversation about market positioning and it was a further twenty

before, once he'd said good-bye to all the people who suddenly needed saying good-bye to, we were out on the street.

"That wasn't so bad after all," he said, balancing, one foot in front of the other, on the edge of the curb, arms bent from the elbow on each side, surfing an imaginary wave. He toppled and jumped across the pavement, twirling an arm across my shoulders. "I actually quite enjoyed myself."

"So I can see," I said, turning for a moment to look back at the house.

July: Wasps

Chapter 6

There was an old man who lived near us somewhere. I didn't know where exactly but I would see him wobbling down the street in his paper bag–thin raincoat, one arm plastered to his chest in a dirty-edged bandage. He used to be out with an elderly woman, a worn face and a crooked body gaily clad in a Sunday best of years back, jaunty hat perched on her ashen hair. She had trouble walking and she'd lean on him, arms held stiffly at armchair angle, an old, old rose kept just about upright by a tired and ancient post. But you'd see her less and less and then not at all, and he began to look very alone as if walking the streets by memory rather than design.

You see a lot of people you recognize on the street when you walk about, pushing small children in a stroller. For a while, if you've just left a job, you keep seeing people you think you know from the office—oh there's Pauline from Personnel, oh no it isn't; hi, Larry, Larry from Design! oops sorry—as if so engraved are they on your internal landscape it takes a while for the blueprint to fade, for the visual nerves to stop twitching. But the real people, the people who are really there, when do you start smiling? When do you stop and say hello, or wave, somehow recognize the fact that their faces and gait are becoming as familiar as the cracks in the pavement?

I never did. I stared through most of them as if I'd never seen them before, or as if they'd never seen me. So there were faces that I knew and said hello to, but there were others that for some unfathomable reason I blanked. I'd done it at school too. There was my clan, the Claire Masterson clan, and we'd fall on each other in the morning as if we hadn't been on the phone until 9:00 p.m. the night before, but there were other girls who wouldn't even merit a smile. Perhaps it's a tribal thing, a class thing, or a city thing, certainly none of those people ever smiled back, or perhaps, and this is something I thought about late at night, it was particular to me. My life was just fine thanks. I had just what I needed. And I didn't need anything, or anybody, to muck it up.

But that all changed after Claire's party. It rained all day Sunday and Monday—heavy gray skies above the common—and it was so cold in the house I almost put the heat on. But on Tuesday the sun came out. It felt hot on my face when I opened the back door, and before long the shine had been taken off the roofs across the street and the puddles on the pavement began to slip away.

"Right, we're going out," I told my offspring, gathering them up before they had time to protest. We set off down the street, the stroller back-heavy with its usual package of diapers, wipes, juice, emergency cookies, jackets. But there was a new lightness to my step. There were people out there you could meet. There were other lives to cross.

The private schools had broken up. In a couple of weeks the skateboarders would be ruling the streets; there would be teenage girls loitering at the corner. But for now the private school children had the place to themselves. Two little girls in pink fairy tiaras were trotting along ahead of me behind their mother, who had a Little Red Riding Hood wicker basket in one hand and a rolled-up rug in the other. I turned and smiled gaily as I passed. Outside the café, a man and a woman I've often stood behind in the post office sat making conversation with a son who looked as if he'd just been picked up from boarding school. He was wearing a gray uniform and looked hot. "Much homework?" said his father as I passed by.

"Vacation already!" I called. The parents tittered. The son scowled.

At the pharmacist, Mrs. Allardyce, my nemesis in a beige raincoat, was sitting on a chair waiting for her tablets. I braced myself in preparation for the tutting. She had once told me at the bus stop that I didn't know my own luck. Like many older people who, in their own time, managed without disposable diapers or washing machines, she did not suffer The Bleat Generation gladly. I suppose there was less pressure on women of her age to be anything else. Or perhaps if you've lived through a war or directly in the aftermath of one, you have a different perspective. I mentioned this theory to Rachel once and Rachel said, "Well, yes, I suppose if you'd been through a worldwide conflagration, you'd have a rough idea what to expect with children," and I laughed a lot. But then I realized she was serious.

Still, I usually tried to steer clear of Mrs. Allardyce. Not that day, though. That day I went up and said, "Hello, Mrs. Allardyce" and before long found myself offering to drive her to the hospital for her lung X ray.

"You're a good girl," she said, as I left. "But you still can't control your kids."

When we got home later, I felt quite pleased with myself as if I had begun a program to open up my own life. And then I decided to open up Mel's for her by phoning the gardener. I put Dan to bed and Fergus in front of the television and then I dialed the number.

"Hello," I said. "Is that Peat and Dug? Is that . . . Pete?"

The line was crackly, as if the person on the other end was entangled in the branches of a tree.

"Sorry?" shouted a voice at the other end. "Can't hear you. Hold on." There was more crackling, crashing. And then, "Sorry, I was entangled in the branches of a tree. What can I do for you?"

I said, "Oh sorry, sorry to have got you down. Er . . . it's Maggie. Maggie Owen. You know, the . . . um."

"Yes, I know," he said. "Of course I know. How are you?"

"Fine, thanks."

"Good. Did you enjoy the party the other night?"

"Yes," I lied. "Very much."

There was a pause. I realized I was gripping the bridge of my nose between my thumb and forefinger. My toes were curled. My eyes were closed. My mouth was twisted in something between a rictus and a grin.

"And?" he said. "What can I do for you?" I could hear voices in the background. A loud noise started up, sending zigzags down the line. "HOLD IT A MINUTE," he yelled. The noise stopped.

I bit my lip. "Just wondered." I said. "I mean I don't know how busy you are, or whether you've got time or whether this isn't the sort of thing you do, but um . . ."

"Yeah?"

"Well I just wondered whether you'd come and look at my garden." I'd taken the phone to the back door and was looking out at my little loved patchwork of cherished plants and rampant weeds. The vinca major had really taken over this year. Next door's cat had been sleeping in the choisya. Fergus had driven his trike into my lace-cap hydrangea and left it there. "It needs a bit of work and although I love doing it and I'm not the sort of person who . . . I just don't have time at the moment what with one thing and um. . . ."

"Another?" he said.

"Exactly," I said gratefully.

He sounded businesslike. "Fine," he said. "Let me think. It's a very busy time of year, but . . . Where do you live? Right . . . Um, tell you what. I'll pop round on my way to a job tomorrow afternoon. Between two and three: is that okay with you?"

There, I thought, when I put the phone down, feeling all trembly and taking big restorative gulps from a glass of water: don't say I'm not a good friend, Mel. See what lengths I'm prepared to go to for you. Then I rang Mel to tell her as much, and she agreed to slip round between appointments. "I think I'll have a sicky tomorrow anyway," she added. "I haven't had one for a bit." Mel was always having sickies, and she didn't seem to suffer from the paroxysms of guilt that the rest of us feel. I think meeting so many sick, or malingering, people on a daily basis must distort your impression of how much time off the average person takes. "Oh, all doctors have sickies," she said when I raised this. "It's because we work so hard we need them. Plus, it's kind of our medium."

I was halfway to the front door to put the garbage out after this, when the phone rang. I ran back in, snagging the trash bag on the children's pegs in the hall, dripping burst teabag and eggshell on the carpet, assuming it was Mel to say she couldn't make it after all. It wasn't.

"Maggie!" gushed the voice on the other end. "I'm so glad I've caught you. I was sure you'd be out somehow. I just wanted to say how glad I was that you both managed to come on Saturday. But I've been feeling dreadful that I didn't get a chance to talk to you. Did you have an awful time? Was it the worst, worst party you've ever been to?"

"Hello, Claire," I said, taken aback. "Not at all. It was very nice. I should have rung you to thank you. I had a great time. And Jake did too. In fact, I haven't seen him enjoy himself so much in . . . well, for years." I was clearing up the eggshell and thinking, why is she ringing me? It was so out of character. The old Claire never rung me. I was always the one who rang her. And then when I went around, I'd often find someone else already there, and they'd have already played with her makeup, and be in the middle of trying on her mum's old clothes, and I'd feel plain and wan standing in the doorway. Now she wanted me. The thought pleased me, flattered me.

"God, you are an angel to say so," she was saying. "Listen, when are we going to meet? I'm longing to see you properly and really, really catch up. It was fantastically frustrating not to talk to you properly at the bash. I wanted to just wrench everybody else aside to find you, but you know what it's like . . ."

"Of course," I said.

"And . . ." Her voice shifted a gear. "I wanted to ask if you were all right. You were looking quite tired and . . ."

"Children," I said.

". . . and run down."

Oh great. "Probably goes with the territory," I said.

". . . and . . ."

"What?"

". . . and what's happened to your hair? Didn't it use to be curly?" Her voice was over-burdened with sympathy.

"Yes," I said. "No, it has changed. I think that's pregnancy. Tragedy really." I meant it facetiously. I didn't really care if my hair was straight or wavy. Those days all that mattered was that it was out of my eyes.

"Oh Maggie," she said. "We do need to sort you out, don't we?"

"Yes," I laughed jollily, hollowly.

"So listen, get your date book, girl. Right now."

I went and got my date book. I used to be rather fussy about date books. I'd had a Filofax stage, in both big and small format. I'd had a classy buttoned-up Coach stage and, when I was at the journal, a big cloth-bound desk-job stage which had also kept me abreast of the birthdays of various dead literary figures. But, since the children, and since giving up work, there wasn't much call for any form of date book, really. I could keep most of my appointments (a dental appointment here, a swimming pool meet there) in my head. At that stage in my life, I was scrawling the odd thing in a freebie off the front of *Cosmo* the woman at the newsagent had given Fergus (she was always saving things from magazines to give Fergus—sometimes he hit pay dirt with a Sesame Street fridge magnet from *Tots TV;* other times he'd leave the shop with a baffled expression and a plastic artists modelling scalpel from the front of *Craft-Works*).

Open in front of me then was my *Cosmo Girl* freebie. Blank.

"You must be busy, busy, busy," said Claire. "What with the children and everything. And I'm quite tight this week. Tomorrow, let's think. . . . I've got a meeting with my agent in the morning. I'm seeing a publisher to discuss turning my *Times* column into a book in the afternoon . . . And then on Thursday . . ."

"Busy, busy, busy," I interrupted.

"No, actually, Thursday is quite clear. I've got to write my col some time, but . . . I don't know. Thursday morning? Coffee?"

I was staring at my blank date book. I panicked. I grabbed the nearest other thing to hand. The *Yellow Pages* (South London) was underneath a pile of unpaid bills on the kitchen counter. I opened it at random.

"No good, er, electrolysis," I said.

She didn't miss a beat. "Lunchtime?"

"Engine tuning."

"What?"

"The engine, the car engine, got to take it to be tuned."

"Thursday evening?"

Escort agencies. No. Frantically I turned the page. "Exercise equipment. I mean exercise class."

"Okay then. Friday morning?"

I'd reached explosive engineers. "That's great," I said, closing the book. "I can make that. Here?"

"Fantastic. Can't wait."

I was about to put the phone down when she added, "Oh and just one other thing. Jake said . . . he was being very interested about 'pester power' the other night, about how advertisers target purchasers through their children, and it struck me it would make a very good piece and I just wondered . . . Could you ask him to give me a ring some time?"

"He's working very hard at the moment," I said. "You might be better off trying him at the office."

"Actually, I have. I just thought if I left a message here too . . ."

"Of course," I said. "Right. Bye then. See you."

And then Claire said, "Ciao."

When I put the phone down I said "ciao" crisply to myself in the mirror. And then I said it again, with a provocative curl to my lip, "ciao." And then I twisted my body away, so I was looking at myself over my shoulder, and I pushed my nose up with my finger and, with my top teeth digging into my tongue, I said, with comic exaggeration, "Ci-ao. Ci-ao. Ci-ao." And then I felt much better.

. . .

Jake hadn't gotten back before midnight all week, creeping into bed long after I'd gone to sleep, but that night he'd promised to be home in time to see Fran and Rain, who were coming around for supper.

Fran had left her birth plan behind on Saturday. In the meantime Jake had defaced it. He'd replaced "Mozart, Elderflower, Birthing Pool" with "Pethidine, Epidural, Emergency Caesarean."

"You. Are. Such. A. Child," she said, chasing him around the kitchen with the birth plan curled up in her hand like a rolling pin.

"Help me. Help me," he squawked, trying to hide behind me while I was cooking. "Mad pregnant hippy on the loose."

Later, when they were setting the table, he pretended to be intensely interested in something above her waistband. "What? What?" she said, craning her neck and panicking.

He peered closer and closer. "Fran," he whispered. "Maggie, Rain, quickly come and see. It's . . . a . . . yes . . . it's . . . a . . . STRETCHMARK!!!!!"

She screamed and hit him on the head with the paper.

I said, "Fran. Ignore him. He wouldn't know a stretchmark if it bounced off and twanged him in the eye."

I suppose I was asking for it because Jake just laughed and said, "Oh yeah?"

"Oh yeah?" I repeated.

"Well . . ."

"Charming." I said it jokingly, and normally it wouldn't have bothered me, but a bit later, after we'd eaten our cannelloni with spinach and ricotta (Fran was a vegetarian) and when the others were settled in the sitting room listening to Rain's CD of whale sounds set to a garage band back track, I went upstairs to the bathroom. I undid the top button of my jeans and pushed them down over my hips so I could inspect the marks left behind by my pregnancies: white ridges across the outer reaches of my stomach like bad embroidery. Then, just for good measure, I yanked my T-shirt up and round to look at my breasts. There were thin white traces here too. I pulled my T-shirt back and rummaged around in the bathroom cabinet until I found the "maternity lotion" that I'd once bought and never used and went back downstairs.

"Here," I said to Fran, handing her the lotion. "This might have worked if I'd bothered to use it."

"Maggie, you're an angel," she said. She closed her eyes and rolled her shoulders around. "Did you manage to buy some peppermint tea yet?"

After they'd gone, I said to Jake, "You have to be nicer to Fran. It's very difficult being pregnant, you know. You can be very sensitive about your body."

He was standing up but still flicking through the channels. He wasn't looking at me. He said, "Don't be silly. She can take it. Tough as old boots, my sister. One thing you don't have to be is touchy on her behalf." He stopped flicking, seemed suddenly engrossed in a man swinging a club on a piece of green sward somewhere where the sun was out. "She can look after herself," he added.

I said, "Well, maybe I'm being touchy on my behalf."

But he wasn't listening. He said, "Oh yesss." And I don't think it was directed at me.

I was halfway out of the room when I remembered the message. I said, "Oh, can you ring Claire? She rang for you earlier. About some conversation you'd had . . ."

That certainly got his attention. "She rang here?" he said.

"Yup. The number's in the kitchen."

He looked uneasy. "I'll ring her tomorrow," he said. "I'm sure it's not urgent."

When I went to bed I thought about the old man in the raincoat and his absent companion in her Sunday best. And I wondered how long they'd been together and whether they'd had children and whether she had had stretch marks to bear witness. And I wondered how much he missed her.

Chapter 7

The next day, Jake got up early, packed a suitcase, and left. Bound for Amsterdam. A taxi arrived, containing Ed Brady: colleague, best friend, and chief leader-astrayer. Ed Brady was an account director at TMT&T. His job involved dealing with the clients and, as far as I could gather, a lot of slipping things up the flagpole. He was charming and smooth and whenever I overheard him talking about work to Jake, he'd be saying things like, "We had a very, very positive meeting with the client yesterday; they thought the presentation from the creatives was fantastic . . . Absolutely terrific. They just have a teensy-weensy concern with the central concept . . . If they could just have a couple more options, to put it in context."

Jake: "So you mean they think it's shit?"

Ed: "Er . . . yeah, well . . . maybe . . . yes."

That day, I heard the taxi purr throatily outside the window first and then I heard the door knocker clatter and then I heard Ed calling, "Get your sorry arse out here, my son" through the letter box.

"Bye, sweetie," Jake said, bending down with his elbows buried in the pillow on either side of my head. He kissed me. "Will you miss me?"

"You'll only be gone one night," I said.

"It might be two—or three."

"Oh?"

"I'll ring." He kissed me again. There was more banging from downstairs. "I'm coming. I'm coming." He jumped up, grabbed his bag, and charged from the room. I never quite knew what to think about work trips. Jake said he hated them, but it was hard not to detect, when he was poised for departure, a lightness in his step. The father of young children leaving on a business trip: the definition of the Great Escape. He slammed the front door behind him. The baby upstairs started crying.

But it was another beautiful morning, and I couldn't feel put out for long. There was a hazy softness in the air, light slanting already through the apple tree at the bottom of the garden. Fat gray wood pigeons were waddling across the lawn like elderly women whose thighs were rubbing. There were motes dancing in the bathroom. I changed Dan's diaper and took him downstairs to give him his bottle. It was peaceful with just the one child for a bit. There were moments when I thought we made a mistake having two. When we had Fergus, we still felt like a couple who just happened to have a child. Now we were a family, and you can get lost in families. Or if you don't get lost, you get sat on. Or bitten. Or shouted at and sent up to your room. And that's just the parents.

The phone kept going that morning. Fergus had come down eventually in just his pajama top. "Where are the bottoms?" I said.

"Oh!" He looked down at his willy, surprised, as if he'd just noticed. "I don't know!"

Then the phone rang. It was Rachel. She wanted to know if I'd have Harry while she "whizzed round" Safeway. "Of course," I said, "Fergus would love it. He gets bored playing with himself." Fergus was sitting dreamily on the stairs proving me wrong. "The more the merrier," I added.

I still hadn't got dressed when Lucinda, in super-efficient, hair-in-chignon mode, rang from her city office—a sleek modern high-rise, I imagined, with windows on two sides and a view of St. Paul's and the Thames—to inform me that, due to complications arising from nanny Hilda's appendicitis (peritonitis), who was supposed to have masterminded the operation (so to speak) from her hospital bed, invitations to Cecily's third birthday party had been late getting in the mail. She told me the party was "Bring a Barbie." I told her, in rather dubious tones, that we didn't have one, and she said, "Well improvise," which panicked me a bit. How could one improvise a Barbie? Do something imaginative with an egg box and a teddy? I rang Mel at her clinic to ask her. She had a line of patients, but took my call anyway.

She said crisply, "Oh God, just buy one. They're quite cheap."

"I know," I said, "but I hate them."

She asked me how one could feel anything such as strong as "hate" for a Barbie, and I told her it was something to do with the bosoms and the hair. "So it's competition?" she said. "Get a life."

I know some people—people like Lucinda, say—think nonworking mothers spend the whole day sitting around chatting on the phone with their friends, drinking coffee while the children pleasantly amuse themselves, but it really isn't true. Not the whole day, anyway. I was trying to fill the washing machine while holding a struggling Dan with one arm and preventing Fergus from opening all the remaining detergent packets with all the patience I could muster when there was a banging on the door. She was earlier than she said, but it had to be Rachel.

"Coming," I called. "Now Fergus, put that one in the drawstring bag. Ye-es. And the other. No. No. That's enough. Fergus put that one down. Coming."

She had started banging again, more insistently. "COM-ING," I shouted. I thrust the machine shut with my knee, yanked Fergus's fingers away from the controls, and made for the front door.

"All right," I said opening it. "I'm here. I'm here. You don't have to break the door down."

I looked out. It wasn't Rachel. It was Pete. What the hell was he doing here? He was due that afternoon. To coincide with Mel. This was a disaster. My beautiful plan. "What are you doing?" I said. "You're early. I wasn't expecting you until this afternoon."

"I can see that," he said. He was wearing big dusty boots and a faded T-shirt with a button missing on the shoulder, and he had a wide grin on his face, that tightened his dimples. He made a big play of looking me up and down. "Just got up, have you?" There was a slit in his combats at the knee.

I was still in my robe.

"I've been up since six," I said. "I haven't had a minute to get dressed yet."

It was not a glamorous robe—not like Claire's. I think it might once have belonged to Jake's father. It was tartan and too big and rather holey. I pulled it round myself.

Pete said: "It's just that one of my jobs was canceled. So I thought I'd see if I could come now instead of later? I can come back if . . ."

For a moment, I wavered. "Well, actually . . ." I began. I was staring at his knee. There were light golden hairs on it.

I gave up. "Now's fine," I said. I steered Fergus, who had come to stand meekly beside me, back against the hall wall. "Come in. The garden's this way. Out the back."

"It usually is," he said.

We went through to the kitchen. I was still holding Dan and I had to reach up to turn the keys at the top of the back door. Pete was right behind me. I could feel his breath on my neck. "You have to give it a shove," I said.

He put his arm past me and shoved. "There you go," he said. I moved to one side so he could get by, but the cupboard was in the way and there was a moment of awkwardness as he squeezed past me. "You're going to have to lose some weight there," he said grinning once he'd gotten through. I laughed and pulled the belt of my robe tighter around my waist. Fergus, awed by his presence, had followed him out. The two of them, the big man and the small boy, wandered around the garden for a bit, in and out of the sunshine like pieces on a chessboard. Occasionally Pete would bend down to study a plant, explaining something to Fergus as he pushed the fronds aside authoritatively. At one point, he bent to coax something onto the palm of his hand with his finger to show Fergus, and the two of them studied it for a while before Pete gently placed whatever it was back on a leaf. Finally Pete came back to the house, followed by Fergus. "It's a nice little garden," he said. "You've done well. Was there anything major you had in mind?"

Fergus said, "Mummy. Come and look. We found a caterpillar."

"Um . . . I'm not sure." Fergus was pulling me out to the garden. "Maybe. Not really. Just a few things here and there really." I pointed to a gnarled stump by the side wall. "It would be great, for example, if you had something which could get that out." Pete pried at it with his fingers. "I could probably get it out with my hands," he said. "What else?"

"Maybe some new trellis?"

"But you've got perfectly decent trellis."

"But at the back?"

"What? Over there?" He walked to the scrubby end of the garden and stood under an apple tree by the shed. He stood still for a minute, sizing something up, while Fergus and I tried to find the caterpillar, and then he came back.

"Not much point," he said. "What were you thinking of growing up it?"

"Wisteria?"

"Too dark," he countered. "You'd do better growing that up the back wall of the house. You could train it in with the ivy."

"Well what about that then?" I said.

He laughed. He said, "You don't really know what you want, do you?"

I said, "No."

He said, "I tell you what I think. I think it's just general maintenance you need. The basics are all here, but it could do with a bit of love and attention, couldn't it?" He put his hand out and cradled the head of a hydrangea. It was blue. I thought it might change to pink any minute.

"I think general maintenance might be a good idea," I said.

I looked at him straight on for the first time. I had tidied up his face in my mind, ironed out its irregularities. His eyes were closer together than I'd remembered, and his mouth was almost the same freckly color as his face so that it seemed to disappear into it. But he was still more handsome than anyone else who'd ever been in my garden. I could still imagine how you might want to put your hands in his tufty wavy hair, run your fingers along the knotty veins in his forearms.

I cleared my throat. "I'd better get dressed," I said.

"You don't have to on my account." He smiled. He was tapping his hands on his trousers, his fingers wide apart from each other.

"Do you want coffee?" I said.

He looked undecided. "Ooooh," he said in a "go on then" tone of voice. And then the door went again. "Actually no," he said. "Don't worry. You're busy. I'd better be off."

"No, stay," I said.

I went to the door. Pete came with me and sidled out as I opened it. "Hello," he said to Rachel and Harry, who were standing there. "I'm off. Cheers," he said to me.

"Are you sure about the coffee?" I said.

"Nah. Give me a buzz if you think you need me." And then he was gone.

Rachel raised an eyebrow and said, "Not dressed?"

·   ·   ·

That day, it got hotter and hotter. For the rest of the morning, Harry and Fergus splashed about in the wading pool, raiding the kitchen cupboards for utensils with which to empty the water on to the flowerbeds and then demanding the hose for refills. Harry was fine until Rachel came to pick him up, when he developed a sudden passion for Fergus's spatula and threw himself onto the grass in despair when the passion turned out, at Fergus's insistence, to be unrequited.

"Oh *honestly.*" Rachel sighed heavily. "I just don't know why these children don't get on. Fergus, please share."

It was quite an innocuous comment, but it was just weighted enough in her own son's favor to ignite something in me, to set me stamping off across the unexploded minefield that is competitive motherhood. I said, sympathetically, "Oh dear, is Harry a bit tired? Is he still waking up every night?"

She said, "Yes, but you can't have everything. At least he's a good eater" (a veiled reference to Fergus, who, as Jake said, lived on snot and air). I surrendered then, arms up.

This is how we measure out our children's days.

She had a quick cup of coffee before going. She told me she'd seen Lucinda out for a jog with the dogs across the common; that even in the throes of physical exertion, she still looked immaculate. "Hair band?" I said.

"Absolutely," she answered. "I think she sleeps in it. Probably more comfortable than all those pins you need for a bun."

I told her Jake was away again. Rachel's husband, Guy, who was a physicist, didn't get out much, let alone abroad. There was still some tension zinging in the air so there was a little too much sympathy in her response. She said, "Oh, poor you. It's a bit much again, isn't it? Does he have to go away so much or does he choose to?"

I mumbled something or other. And then she said, "Do you think it would be different if you were married?"

Smiling broadly, I said, "Not a jot!"

She stirred her coffee absentmindedly—dipped her little finger in sideways to remove a tiny floating object. "Why *aren't* you married?" she said. I'm sure she'd asked before. Most people asked at least twice.

"I don't know," I said. "It just always seemed too late."

"It would be nice, though, wouldn't it?" she said. "For the children."

After she left, I felt miserable, but it wasn't long before Mel got there. She had Milly with her so she must have left work in the end. I greeted Milly at the door with a big hug and, arms outstretched in an attitude of despair, greeted Mel with the news that the Pete plan was in tatters, that he'd come that morning and left. She didn't seem too concerned. "Oh well," she said. "Nice idea. Never mind. Got anything to eat? I'm starving."

Later I told her what Rachel had said about Jake and me not being married. Mel laughed and said I was being stupid and that it didn't make any difference and that a blind man could see Jake loved me. "How is he, by the way?" she said.

"Away," I said.

She laughed "Oh, well he clearly doesn't love you that much then."

"Still no sex," I said.

"Give him a chance, Maggie, he's *away*. Wait till he gets back . . ."

We were lying on a blanket on the grass, cups of tea making scalded patches on either side of us. The children were filling the wading pool with earth from the flower beds. "Shall I . . . ?" said Mel.

"Don't bother," I said. "Leave them."

It was too hot to move. The air was heavy, like a rich pudding, silent except for the distant roar of traffic. I was about to ask whether she really did think he still loved me, when she plucked a blade of grass and, putting it in her mouth to chew, said, "Actually, I went on a blind date last night. And it was such a disaster, I didn't really feel up to meeting someone new today anyway." She spat the grass out, tucked the bottom of her shirt into her bra to sun her midriff, and lay back down again. I sat up.

"A blind date?" I felt suddenly outraged as if my gardener wasn't good enough for her.

"Tara, our receptionist's brother. Called Leo. Works for some bank. In the City. Divorced."

"And? Kids?"

She turned over. "Two. Nine and seven. It was fine. He was perfectly nice. Talked a *tiny* bit too much about his ex-wife. And didn't quite pick up the signals that I wasn't *that* interested in paint balling."

"What sort of signals?"

"Oh, you know, the usual. Putting my finger down my throat and pretending to be sick. That sort of thing. Funny, really, because Tara's such fun. Anyway never again."

"Did he try and kiss you?"

"Did he try and kiss me? They always try and kiss you, Maggie. You've been out of the game too long. But I turned just in time and he got my ear. Milly! Not in his mouth. He's only a baby."

"Gave you an earful then?" I got up to comfort Dan, who had a mouth full of flowerbed. From behind me, Mel said, "What I don't understand is, why you didn't nip to a phone and ring me? About the gardener being here, I mean. I could have been here in five minutes."

She said it wonderingly, but not so inquiringly that I felt I had to answer. I was busying myself with Dan, finding an animal cracker to cheer him up. But then she said, all singsong, her voice a stick to poke me with: "I know. You fancy him yourself, don't you? Maggie? Am I right? Are you blushing?" I was about to turn round, about to say something, when there was a yowl from Fergus.

"Nyowooooooooo," he cried, clutching the side of his neck. "Mummmmmmmyyyyy. NYoowooowowwo."

"What darling? What?"

He was sobbing. There was a bright spot on his neck, with a surrounding welt getting wider by the minute.

"Oh dear. Has he been stung?" said Mel coming to look.

"Poor Fergus," I soothed. "It must have been a wasp. Is it better now?"

"Nerrrrrrrrrrrr. Nerrrrrr," he said, which I took to mean no.

You always think you've got Bactine, you can visualize it at the back of the bathroom cabinet, underneath old tubes of whitening toothpaste and, in my case, all the free samples of Zap-it Jake brought home from work, but when you go to find it when you really need it, it turns out to be hemorrhoid cream or insect repellant. I couldn't remember either if it was bicarbonate of soda or vinegar you're supposed to apply, but Mel, the doctor, said, "Oh don't bother. All that matters is that he hasn't gone into anaphylactic shock," while Milly went to get her Teletubby doll to cheer him up.

"You can borrow it if you like," she said. After about ten minutes Fergus stopped gulping, reached out for the Teletubby, and put his head on my shoulder.

"Poor Fergus," Mel cooed. "Wasp stings really hurt, don't they?"

He lifted his head. "Where's the wasp now?" he said.

"In the garden," I said.

Mel and Milly left soon after that. They wanted to get to the shoe store before it closed. If they'd stayed a little longer, I'd have answered her question. It wasn't like I had anything to hide.

Chapter 8

Jake didn't ring on Wednesday evening—which was unusual. Normally he tried to talk to Fergus before bedtime. He spoke, Fergus nodded, or said, regardless of what he'd been asked on the other end, "Yup, yup, yup. Byeeee." And he didn't ring on Thursday morning either, which was doubly odd. No playgroup for the summer break, so we met my mother for an early lunch—"a quick bite to eat"—at the café attached to the local garden center.

"Does 'Jake' have to work so terribly hard?" she said among the hardy perennials. My mother didn't really approve of advertising. Or of Jake, to be honest. I don't think she ever entirely forgave him for not marrying her daughter. Or, for that matter, for The Snot Goblins. Then she said, "Still, is it rather nice to have the bed to yourself for a bit? I had another *terrible* night last night. Tossing and turning like a ship at sea. And I've run out of my pills. I must get a new prescription."

I was in listening mode so we got on fine, the two of us (and she had a point about having the bed to myself) until we were in the snack bar and were halfway through lunch. The children had gotten down from the table, unimpressed by their broccoli tart, and were mucking about in the flower bed just outside the door, so we were alone at the table. And when a silence unexpectedly gaped in the middle of my mother's latest anecdote—"My Traumatic Trip to Waitrose"—I said, "It's funny how relationships can change, isn't it? I mean, it's good that Frank's so supportive, not every man would ask to see the manager on your behalf, not just over an out-of-date pack of sausage meat. I mean Jake . . . well . . . At the moment I think he'd definitely leave customer complaints to me . . ."

"Hmmm," said my mother, thoughtfully exploring the zucchini quota in her vegetable stirfry.

I carried on: "We're not really communicating at the moment. Well I hope that's all it is. Actually I'm beginning to feel a bit worried . . ." I looked up to see her expression, but her face was turned away. Her attention seemed to have been caught by a woman at the next table, bleached hair, forty-odd, who was feeding a sweetly compliant baby in a high chair. I moved my own head forward, and I could tell then that my mother was about to strike up conversation because she had a bright smile on her face.

She said, in a high, approachable, interested voice: "How old is your little . . . oh grandson! Oh . . . Eight months!" This, wonderingly. Then, "Oh, the same age as Daniel." She gave a nod to the open door. Then she said, with an undercurrent of sharpness, "Is he crawling yet?" She made a moue of concern. "Oh dear. Gracious. Oh well." A beat and then, vaguely, "Of course, Daniel's been crawling for a couple of months now!"

"Mum," I hissed. "You don't say things like that."

"I don't know what you're talking about," she said firmly. "You'd think you'd be glad that I take an interest. Very common," she mouthed when they'd gone to the cashier to pay.

We didn't stay long after that. Fergus, who had been standing on one of those industrial-sized plant trolleys shouting "I'm a dirty rascal," fell backward into a display of heartsease. "They're going to seed anyway," said my mother, bending to help me repot.

"Aren't we all," I said.

. . .

When we got home, Jake had called and left a message. I couldn't make out most of what he said because of the background noise—hollering and laughing as if he was in a bar or at a dog track. He broke off halfway through the message to say something to somebody else—"Mine's a Pilsner," I think. I tried to call him on his mobile, but it was switched off. "What's your father doing in a bar on a lovely day like this?" I said to Fergus.

"Hunting," he replied sagely.

"He'd better not be," I said. I opened the back door.

"WASPS!" shrieked Fergus, fleeing back into the bowels of the house.

"It's all right—they're not here now. There's nothing to hurt you in the garden. I promise."

He went out reluctantly and hovered on the steps. I took Dan, who'd fallen asleep in his car seat, up to his crib, lowered him gently in, and then tiptoed gingerly across to the door. The last board creaked. It always does. I stood in the doorway listening to him stir and then whimper, and then open his lungs and cry. He was standing up and shaking his bars when I went back in, so I picked him up and took him downstairs again. "My life," I muttered to myself. "Where has it gone?"

The phone was sitting by the back door. I picked it up and dialed. Just like that. He picked it up straight away. His voice sounded drowsy.

"Were you asleep?" I asked.

"No, no," he said sleepily, rubbing the dust from his voice. Or rather, "Neouw, neouw." No one, child or adult, ever likes to admit to having been dozing.

I said, "Do all Australians either use loads of vowels or miss them out all together?"

"Come again?"

"You see, you just said, 'Cm 'gaeyn.'"

"Who's speaking please?"

"It's Maggie. From Chestnut Drive."

"Hello, Maggie from Chestnut Drive."

"Hello. Sorry. I just . . ."

"Mumeeeeee." Fergus was calling from the garden. He sounded desperate. Maybe it was another wasp.

I sped up. "Look, just to say, I'd be really keen if you could fit me, fit my garden, into your busy schedule . . . I really do think it needs it. So whenever suits you really."

"Mumeeeeeeeeee."

"Hang on, let me just look in the date book." There was a rustle. I wondered what his date book looked like. A big brown folder with bits of paper falling to the ground like leaves, loose-sheafed and chaotic, notes and numbers scrawled, a manly, outdoor kind of date book.

"Okay," he said, "Palm Pilot at the ready. Just wait for it to boot up. A-ha. I've had a cancellation tomorrow afternoon. Would that do you?"

"Mumeeeeeeeeeeeeeeeeeeeeee."

"Tomorrow afternoon would do me fine," I said.

When I got out to Fergus, he was sitting on a deck chair. "There you are!" he said with that disconcerting shift of tone that children have, like the sun poking its head from behind a cloud. "I needed you, but now I don't."

• • •

I was half expecting Jake home that night, but only half, so it wasn't that much of a surprise when he rang instead.

"Hi, hon," he said, all soft and conciliatory. "How are things?"

"Fine. Where are you?"

"In my hotel room," he said, as if it was obvious.

"It's just that you . . ."

"What?"

"Nothing." I thought he'd be on his way back by now.

"When are you coming home?"

"Tomorrow," he said, as if it had always been the case.

"Oh right. You've missed Fergus. He's in bed. He was whacked."

"Oh well. Kiss him for me. Has it been all right?"

"Yes, it's been fine. I told you. How's it going there?"

"Tortuous. Crap hotel in the middle of nowhere. Horrible sandwiches for lunch. And we've just been stuck in this room, going round and round in circles. We're just fighting our corner really."

"What corner is that?" I said.

"You know, the new Kyushi Pondura. Hatchback. Second car. Kyushi wants to target women twenty-five to forty. They want the same advertising campaign throughout Europe, and we want it to be ours. So I've got to get them to accept my brief."

"You'll be fine, won't you?" I said reassuringly.

Jake snapped, "I don't know."

"All right, you don't have to snap."

"I'm not snapping. I'm just saying I don't know. I hope so." He took an intake of breath, a suspiciously sharp intake.

I said, "Are you smoking?"

"No," he said, breathing out loudly. "No. Hang on, got to go, that's Ed at the door. We're meeting the others down in the bar at nine."

"Okay then, bye," I said. "Love you," I added. But he'd already hung up.

It is an unpleasant but unavoidable truth that women who don't work soon become resentful of the fact that their husbands do. The office can very quickly become The Other Woman. Jake's Other Woman was young and glamorous and hung out in bars and spoke with a sexy cigarette-laced foreign accent. She drove a Kyushi hatchback. And she ate sliced bread. And her skin had blemishes. I began to feel better.

I was standing in the kitchen, looking out of the window at the darkening garden. A month ago, in June, it had looked fresh, budded, full of expectation; it was beginning now to look overblown, straggly in places. But never mind that, I thought, tomorrow Pete will be here and he'll make it look beautiful again. I went upstairs to the bedroom and tried on lots of summer clothes. And then, with the windows open and a light breeze ruffling the curtains, I danced around the room in my underwear. And then, when it was quite dark outside, I curled up on the sofa in my pajamas and watched a movie on Channel 5 about twin sisters, one of whom has an affair with the other's husband before being murdered—or you think she's the twin that's been murdered, but in fact it's the other one; it turns out the husband did it to be with her sister. A true story, it said. Honestly, other people's lives.

Chapter 9

I'd forgotten Claire was coming. I was cooking when she came to the door on Friday morning—"Smiley Carrot and Lamb Faces" from *Bigger Helpings!*—Anjelica Knurgle's latest guide to feeding children. Knurgle, the tormentor of all microwaving mothers, was worshiped among many women in Morton Park for having introduced marinades to the nursery. I was not one of those women, but Rachel was. She'd lent me the book a few weeks previously after witnessing me remove a packet of sausages from the freezer. "Have you seen what's in these?" she'd said, appalled.

"Lips and arseholes?" I'd countered.

"No, much worse," and she'd reeled off a list of additives.

"What about fish fingers?" I said.

"Well, okay," she said. "But take the breadcrumbs off Harry's. The sulphur dioxide in them turns him into a raving lunatic."

So there I was, resentfully poking shepherd's pie by any other name into the compartments of an ice cube tray, when there was Claire, immaculate in velvet-trimmed denim pedal-pushers and a T-shirt the whiteness of which hadn't been seen in our house since Fergus discovered you could pick up the coals in the real-effect coal gas heater.

She said, standing on the doorstep, head tilted to look up at the roof, "What an angelic house. *Sweet.*"

I said, "Come in. It's a bit messy I'm afraid."

She squeezed past the stroller into the hall, "*Adorable.*"

We went into the kitchen and she sidled into a chair at the table. The back doors were open and a fresh breeze was toying with the corners of the tablecloth. Fergus had retreated, dog-like, to the garden. Dan was asleep, cat-like, in the hall. A couple of flies were bumping their heads against the skylight in the ceiling. Claire seemed on edge. "God, I'm gasping for a coffee," she said.

I should have gone to the store. "Is instant all right?" I said.

She made a polite wincing face. "Do you have any real?"

I checked in the tin, though I knew what I would, or rather wouldn't, find. "Sorry."

"I'll have tea," she said bravely.

I'd meant to buy flowers, spray a bit of perfume on the lightbulbs, tidy up the Duplo, to show her how fragrant my life was, how together. But I hadn't. There were no clean mugs either so I fished a couple out of the dishwasher to run under the tap. It burped a waft of dried ketchup and stale garlic. I closed it quickly.

She said, "How are things?"

I said, "Fine. Great. Terrific. You?"

She said, "Don't ask."

She took a packet of Silk Cut out of her basket and lit up. Her hands shook a bit. There was a clot of lipstick on one of her teeth.

I said, "I love your bag."

She said again, closing her eyes this time, "Just don't ask."

I started to say something else. "How's your . . ." I began.

"I mean. Christ," she said. "Just. Do. Not. Ask."

I smiled. "What?"

She looked around for an ashtray and then, as if forgetting what she was looking for, dropped her cigarette to the floor and rubbed it absentmindedly into the tiles with the toe of her sneaker. "Do you really want to know?"

"Of course. Tell me."

"It's a long story."

People don't normally mean long when they say this, they mean emotionally intense. But with Claire? Well, let's just say her love life had always been complicated. I said, "Go on."

"It's so nice to see you, Maggie. I'm in such a mess. My love life is just . . . I mean, how do you keep things together? How have you got this far? I'm all over the sodding place."

"No, you're not," I said. "You're amazing. You've got everything—job, success, Disney contracts! Looks . . ."

"Yeah, but no kids. No husband. Look at me, Maggie. I'm thirty-six." She rocked her head from side to side, making a rhythmic clicking sound with her tongue. "Clock ticking—all that."

"Thirty-six's nothing," I said. "Especially these days."

"Is it? I don't know. I just would so love to have a baby. You know, I see you and other friends and it's like being locked out of a club, and if I knew that one day I would have a child I would feel all right about it, but it's the fear that I might never and I couldn't bear it . . ."

"Oh Claire." I felt sorry for her suddenly. I put my arm around her shoulders. "There's bags of time."

"Yes. But without even a man on the scene?"

"Claire. I don't believe there isn't a man on the scene."

"Well . . ."

"Go on," I said slowly. I turned and busied myself with the kettle and the teabags.

"I'm seeing someone at the moment but . . ." She broke off, paused as if to consider something, and then began again. "There was this other bloke, the bloke I left England to get away from really. We were mad about each other and I really thought he was the one, but . . ."

"But what?" I said, squeezing out the teabag.

"Unavailable. Temporarily off the shelf. Out of stock." She started talking faster. "It's no secret as far as I'm concerned. I wasn't the one creeping around deceiving people. I mean, we had this fantastic time together, great sex and fantastic weekends away—we managed to get to Venice once. It was just heaven—and he gave me lovely presents . . ." She waved her wrist in my direction and I had time to make a quick appreciative "nice watch" face, before she was off again. "He was the love of my life, but it was all just a waste of time. He didn't have the guts . . ." She was staring into my face beadily as if looking for something there.

"What stopped him?" I said. An image flashed into my mind of Claire Masterson at school, on the tennis court with her long legs flashing, in the dinner line passing out snippets of her glamorous weekends, in the school disco with the boys from the boys' school spinning round her in Spirograph circles. And here in the kitchen, with her caramel hair and her velvet trim. Why would anyone not leave his wife for her?

"He said he'd miss his child," she said.

I had been looking back at her in sympathy. But at this I looked out into the garden. Fergus had managed to get into the shed where there was a hose-winding contraption that fascinated him. There was also a lawnmower with open blades and recently sharpened shears and damp boxes of weed killer trailing their sweet-smelling lethal powders onto the floor.

"Honestly," she was saying. "It just wasn't fair on me." She pulled her hair together and tied it in a casual knot. "It completely battered my self-esteem and I had to get out, which is why I moved to New York . . ."

I got up and went into the garden to extricate Fergus from the den of knife and poison. He didn't want to come so I brought him out under my arm like a piece of rolled-up carpet. His back half flapped uselessly. His front half hollered. If he hollers, let him go. Do fish holler, I thought? When I had calmed him down with the help of a trowel and an empty polystyrene plant tray, I went back into the kitchen.

She carried on talking as if nothing had happened. "And it was in New York," she said, "that I met Marcus. He's based in London—I mean he's English—but he was there on business and I was in The Plaza to interview Lou Reed and he was there with clients and we started talking in the lobby. And one thing led to another and . . . business trip led to business trip. He's also married—did I mention that? But he stopped sleeping with his wife months ago. Anyway, I thought he was really keen and that it was only the distance which was keeping us apart, but now that I'm back, he's behaving all oddly and I don't know what to think, or where I stand. And being back's confused me too, I keep thinking about the other guy but he won't answer my calls and . . . I'm just fed up with it all. Anyway, I've given Marcus an ultimatum. He's got until next week to make up his mind: the wife or the mistress. His choice. And this time I'm not going to be fobbed off. I'm worth more than that."

I put her mug of tea down on the table. "How do you know they've stopped sleeping together?" I said.

. . .

After that I thought she'd never go. She wanted to talk about it. She really, really wanted to talk about it. She wanted my angle (the wife's angle), which would have been flattering if it hadn't made me feel so uneasy. It was hard to keep track too. I kept getting the two men confused until finally I had to say, "Look, I think it's number one you need to sort out in your mind, the love of your life. It sounds to me as if Marcus, number two, is a rebound thing."

"Do you think so?" she said. "You're so wise. Yes. I don't know. It's so difficult, so heartbreaking."

What with one thing (Married Man Number One) and another (Married Man Number Two), she was still sitting at the table smoking when Pete arrived. I could see his shape, his height, his shoulders, through the glass in the door. Bugger, I thought. "Oh," I said to Claire, as if it was all totally normal. "It's your downstairs neighbor. He's come to do my garden."

"Really?" she said, intrigued.

"It's a long story."

She followed me to the door. "Pete?" she said, coming up behind me as I got there. "Why hello!" she said over my shoulder, as I opened it. "Sweetie," pushing past me. "Fancy meeting you here!"

"Hi, Claire," he said, surprised. "Hello, Maggie," he said to me. And then Claire had kissed him and thrown an arm around his shoulder and was taking his bag of garden tools off him, making a big lopsided show of how heavy they were and propelling him into the house as if she owned the place. "Goodness," she said, "now I get to see you at work. Muscles and everything. Maggie, are you going to get Pete a cup of tea?"

"Of course," I said. "Milk and sugar?"

"No sugar," he said, winking at Claire. "I'm sweet enough already."

"Don't you think Maggie's house is lovely?" said Claire as I busied myself about the kettle. She'd undone her hair and was twirling it round the ends of her fingers.

"Great," he said. "Probably worth a bit too."

I raised my eyes to the ceiling. "Maybe," I said. "The property prices round here . . ."

Claire was poking him in the side. "Got to get on the property ladder, Pete." She was slipping off her shoes. God it was infuriating: she always became someone else when men were around.

"Oh, I'm not one for owning property," Pete said. "I don't like the responsibility. I prefer not to be pinned down."

Claire gave him a nudge with her bare foot. "Well maybe sometimes," he said. They both laughed.

"Right," I said crisply.

They looked at me.

Claire said, "Good thing I'm here, what with Maggie's husband's being away. Wouldn't trust you on your own with anyone."

"Away is he?" said Pete to me.

"He's always away," I said lightly. How did she know he was away? I must have told her on the phone.

"I hope he knows what he's missing." Pete was giving me a funny look.

"I don't know about that."

"I don't know if I'd always be away if I had this house."

"He'll be back later."

"With a big bunch of flowers and big present from wherever he's been I should think."

"I should think," I said. "Not." He grinned at me.

Claire was stretching her arms above her head so that her breasts were straining against her T-shirt. She'd crossed her legs and was twirling one foot in the air, so that the fabric of her jeans was pulled tight across her thighs.

"Right," she said crisply.

"Right," said Pete standing up. "All play and no work . . ."

"Anyway, we're not married," I added, to no one in particular.

· · ·

It became quite clear, shortly after this, that there was no getting rid of Claire. Now that Pete had turned up, she was in for the duration. That was another thing I'd forgotten about her: her ability to cling to somebody else's interesting situation like a gymnast swinging round the parallel bars. I remember bumping into her in Morton High Street one Saturday when we were young, her on her own, me with a boy called Nigel I was dating. Nigel was pushing his bike, separated from me by the crossbar (the bike was our chaperone: most weeks, it would be 5:00 p.m. before he'd brave my side and we'd kiss). Claire came up and giggled into Nigel's ear and made him give her rides on the bike, and our afternoon fizzled out after she'd gone. I thought she must really fancy him, but on Monday at school she laughed with the others and said, "Zits, zits. My kingdom for such zits!" Poor Nigel. If only I'd had all those free samples of Zap-it then.

"How well do you know Pete?" I asked at one point.

"Oh, we're great friends," she said. "I just love him. Don't you think he's gorgeous? I think he's one of the most fantastically gorgeous people I've ever met. Very uncomplicated," she added.

"Nice body too," I said.

At teatime, I went out and said, "Can I get you anything?"

And he said, "What are you suggesting?"

And I said, "A sandwich or something?"

And he laughed and said, "Never turn down a free feed." And pretty soon after he'd eaten a pile of bread and cheese minus lettuce ("I'm not one for veggies"), he said he'd better be going, and did I want him to come again to tackle the bindweed?

I glanced back at the house, "Yes, yes, I do want you to come again to tackle the bindweed."

"I'll drop by when I'm passing," he said as he went out through the kitchen. To Claire, he said, "Seeya."

And she said, in a singsong, "Darling, I'll be waiting."

And then he left. Halfway out the door, he said, "Don't mind Claire will you? She's quite a one," and then he tousled Fergus's mop of hair and said, "great kid," which made me shiver with delight, and then he was off across the road with a cheery wave. When I went out the back, the garden looked as tidy as if it had had a haircut, though there was a pile of plastic dinosaurs on the steps which he must have found scattered in the beds.

. . .

Jake got back from Amsterdam shortly after 6:00 p.m. He gave me a bear hug at the door and twirled the children around until they almost brought up their carrot and lamb smiley faces. And he said to Fergus, "Guess what I've got you!" and made him rummage around in his leather-sandwich suitbag, until he'd found the miniature KLM 747.

"Anything in there for me?" I said.

"Oh. I was going to get you some perfume in Duty Free but I couldn't remember whether it was Diorella or Diorissima you liked."

"Ma Griffe," I said.

He didn't smile. He was too busy trying to look into the kitchen. "Who's here?" he mouthed.

I said loudly, "Come and see Claire! She's spent the day here. She's waited all this time to say hello."

Claire was standing in the doorway. "Hello," she said.

It was quite rude of Jake not to look up at that point. "Hello," he said, rebuckling his suit bag. He straightened up. "How are you?"

"Fine," she said. "You?"

"Fine."

It was rather awkward for a moment. Maybe Jake was tired because of the journey; maybe finding someone in the house when he got home was the last thing he needed.

I said, "So who wants a drink?"

Jake said, "Sorry I haven't rung you. I've been away."

"Forget it," said Claire, looking around for her bag. "Actually, I'd better be going."

"Don't feel you have to rush off," I said. Jake didn't say anything. She paused for a moment, burrowed about in her bag as if searching for something. I nudged Jake.

"Yes, do stay for a drink," he said, stilted.

"No, no. I must be going. I've been here hours. Maggie must be longing to get rid of me."

I said, lying, "No. Of course not."

Claire wavered. God, either go or stay, I thought. Preferably go.

"Daddy, Daddy, Daddy, Daddy." Fergus was jumping up and down trying to get Jake's attention. He had Milly's Teletubby in his hand, the one she'd lent him after the wasp incident, and was trying to wave it in front of his eyes. He stood on Claire's toe on one of the downbeats.

"No definitely. I'm off," she said, wincing. Suddenly she seemed galvanized. "Fantastic day, Maggie. Just the most gorgeous children. What on earth is that?"

"Tinky-Winky," said Fergus, waving the doll.

She shook her head bewildered. "Anyway, I've had a heavenly time. Good thing I was here to keep Pete away. He's a bit of a devil with the women is Pete."

"Pete?" said Jake.

"I'll explain later," I said quickly.

Claire darted us both a look. She kissed me and then she went to kiss Jake. She went for his cheek at the same time as he made a small movement away from her so that her mouth hit his. She laughed uncomfortably. Jake didn't do anything.

"Daddy, Daddy, Daddy." Fergus was pounding Jake's knees with his fists, desperate to be picked up. I was holding Dan but he was stretching out his arms to clasp Jake too, pushing away from me like someone casting off in a boat.

"Look, you two," Claire said, as something occurred to her, "are you free on Tuesday? Come to supper. I've got some friends coming over. I'd love it if you came."

Jake frowned. "Errr . . ." he said.

I said, "That would be lovely, Claire."

"Fantastic. Right then, I'm off." She was halfway to the door when she turned suddenly and said, "How was Kyushi?"

"Tricky," said Jake.

I was thinking, "Kyushi? Did I tell her that too?"

Later, after supper, Jake said, "Odd to find Claire here when I got back. Why is she inviting us to supper?"

I edged past him to put the plates in the dishwasher. "What do you mean 'odd'?"

"Nothing," he said, picking up the newspaper and studying the headlines as if he hadn't already had a two-hour flight in which to do so. "I just mean I'm surprised you've seen her again. I can't imagine you've got much in common anymore. She doesn't seem like your usual chums."

"My usual chums?" I said.

"The other playground mums you hang out with."

"The other playground mums?" I repeated acidly. "In what way is she not like them? You mean she's more glamorous?" I scraped some mashed potato remains into the sink and clattered the cutlery into the cutlery holder.

"No, not glamorous. You know . . ."

"What?"

He flicked the paper back onto the table. He sifted through his mail, which he'd sifted through half an hour before. "She's just different. You know . . ."

"No, I don't," I said, clicking the dishwasher shut and turning to face him. "You're just saying you fancy her."

"I do not fancy Claire Masterson. She's not my type."

"Why not?"

He sagged his head toward the table as if it had suddenly gotten too heavy. "All I said was I was surprised to see her here."

"It's just that one minute you don't like her and the next she's the most interesting person in the world. What's that about? The fact that she's got great legs and enormous bosoms and lovely hair? And a job?" I went to stuff an empty milk carton into the bin. It was too full; I had to force it down with the flat of my hand.

He put the mail down and looked at me directly for the first time. And then he sighed and said, "It's not what I was going to say at all. But now that you mention it, I suppose it is unusual, not pleasant, just unusual, to meet someone here who hasn't heard of the Teletubbies."

If the children hadn't been upstairs, I would have slammed the door then. As it was I closed it very quietly and went through into the sitting room. I knew I was overreacting but that knowledge never makes you feel better, it makes you feel worse: more impotent somehow. I felt twisted inside as if someone was pulling and tugging me in different directions. I stood in the middle of the floor for a bit. Everything around me was mine. The faded green sofa I'd picked up at a local junk shop, the rugs I'd lugged back from holiday in Morocco, the battered old mirrors I'd restored with chewing gum and gilt paint, the cushions I'd sewn. Then on the table by the television, I spotted the scrapbook Jake kept his PG Tips cards in, still there from a few days before when he'd shown them to Fergus. For a moment I considered taking it outside and stuffing it into the garbage can. Then I relented. Instead, I dropped it behind the toy cupboard. And then I felt a little bit better.

Chapter 10

That weekend, we had a brunch date. Who has brunch in England? Well, Ed Brady, Jake's much maligned (by me) colleague, that's who. The first time he invited us, Jake had called up to double-check what time we were due. "One or one-thirty," Ed had said.

Most people would call this lunchtime. "Yeah, all right," Jake said, when I pointed this out. "Don't blame me."

Of course, I blamed him. The fact is, not only do one's friends' loved ones often leave one cold, so often do one's loved ones' friends. So I did blame Jake. I blamed him for being Ed's friend in the first place.

Ed Brady was everything I dreaded Jake being. He was Jake on a bad day. He was Jake played by Jim Carrey, only he was much thinner under his loose designer suits, etiolated like a daffodil bulb that has been kept too long in the closet under the stairs. He had so much nervous energy you kept expecting him to fizz across the room like a released balloon. He was married to Pea, or Pee, (short for Penelope), who was "in film," which is to say she worked for the BBC. They had one of those baffling marriages in which one side of the equation had so much more power than the other, that you couldn't see how they stayed upright, why they didn't topple over. Jake and I were always convinced Pea was on the verge of leaving Ed. She seemed perpetually irritated by him, wincing when he spoke as if he set her teeth on edge, and so obviously contemptuous of his job (trashy, empty, ephemeral compared to the real nitty-gritty work of addressing the world's injustices on . . . er, television), you wondered what they had ever had in common. Jake thought—he may have had inside information on this—that it boiled down to oral sex. She was constantly down on him. He was constantly going down on her. Whatever, I always felt uncomfortable in their presence, ignoring as far as I could the public front of their relationship while trying desperately hard not to imagine the private.

"Come in, come in, come in," Ed said at the door that brunch time. "Maggie: You. Look. Fantastic. Give us a kiss. And another. And is this the baby? Gosh, isn't she big now."

"He," I said.

"And Fergus, my man!" He gave him a clap on the shoulder that sent him sprawling across the parquet. "Oopla," said Ed, bending to pick him up. (Fergus looked too stunned to complain). "Jaaaaaaake." They shared an ironic high five. This was part of the charade played out by Ed, with Jake's assistance, that they were, contrary to appearances, in fact eighteen. And black. Ed then went straight into some office in-joke. "Kyushi, Kyushi, Kyushi" he chanted, in the tone of one patting a baby. Finally, in his own voice, he said, "What a fucking week, eh?" Jake raised his eyes to the ceiling and pretended to mop his brow.

Ed turned to me again, "Come in, come in, Maggie. Pea is longing to see you. She's just been saying it's been tooo long."

"Hi," said Pea, coming out of the sitting room, switching a smile on and off, and then disappearing upstairs.

Ed cleared his throat and widened his mouth into a mouth-organ grimace. "PMT," he joked to Jake, then tipped his head back. "Dah-ling," he yodeled. "Can I bring you something? Teensy-weensy glass of bubbly?" There was no answer. "Terrible headache," he said to me. "Poor love."

We went through to the sitting room, where their five-year-old daughter, Clarice, was kicking some small carved figures about on the hardwood floor. Clarice had been squeezed into a miniature version of her mother. She took the world very seriously. Or rather, she took her ballet lessons seriously. And her tennis lessons seriously. And her school, where she wore a boater and green and white stripes, very seriously. She took so many things so seriously she seemed to have lost the ability to do what children do better than anyone else, which is play with nothing—or at the very most a piece of electric cord and a bare plug—very happily, and very *un*seriously, for hours on end.

"Clari, Clari darling, mind the coffee table," trilled Ed. "And not against the French doors please. And be careful of the walls." Sometimes, one suspected Clari needed more fresh air. Or her parents did. Ed hurried over and returned the small carved figures to the decorative Chinese checkers board on the coffee table. "Clari, darling, take Fergus upstairs and show him your new lap dancing." Nudge to Jake . . . "I mean Caribbean Holiday Barbie."

Fergus looked as though he was up for it, but Clarice rearranged her hair in its sparkly heart-shaped clips and said in a clear bell-like voice, "No. I don't want to. I don't like Fergus. I want him to go home."

Fergus looked nonplussed. Ed mouthed, "Sorry she's over-tired. Poor love."

"Perhaps she's got a headache," I said. Dan was wriggling to get out of my arms, so I put him down on the floor, as far away as I could from the jagged-edged glass and steel coffee table. Not far enough. He shuffled over to it and, before I got there too, had scattered neatly stacked copies of *Interiors* and *Wallpaper* in all directions. I grabbed him before he reached the Chinese Checkers. Fergus, delighted, scampered over and started yanking at his hair and shouting, "No, Dan. Naughty." Fergus was reprimanded. Dan cried. Jake hid in an armchair. Ed wheeled his arms around suggesting other activities Clarice might enjoy sharing with Fergus. Clarice went to find her mother. Fergus started crying. Welcome to the Brady brunch.

I had just managed to distract Fergus with a page in *Wallpaper* about kitchen appliances—one of those subjects that strangely fascinates small male minds—when another couple arrived, he with pewter hair and thick leather-clad thighs; she with eyebrows plucked to an inch of their life and a pale suede skirt-top combo that merged imperceptibly into the cream sofa on which she perched. He, it was explained to me, was Ed's equivalent at Blue Fish, another agency. She was "in corporate entertaining." Pea must have approved of them because she launched herself down the stairs to greet them, the image of the hostess with the mostest, a blonde pink-lipsticked weathergirl, bubbling over with effusive greetings that reached almost hysteria at the speedy realization that they were all going to be on holiday in Majorca for the same two weeks of August.

"What bit? What bit?" squawked the eyebrowless one.

"The north," squealed Pea. "You?"

"Oh, the same. We always go to the north. The rest is rubbish."

"Absolutely! We must meet up. Jake, Maggie, what about you? What are your holiday plans this year?"

Jake said, "Er. Well actually . . ." His eyes darted across to Ed who was looking nervous. "Well, because of this Kyushi stuff . . . Well, I doubt I'll be able to get away . . ."

Ed's neck was disappearing into his shoulders. He looked as if he was about to sink behind the sofa. Pea said, "But Ed's working on the same account. Surely this . . . Ed?"

Ed said, "Er, yeah." And then he said again, "Er, yeah," and he gave a little laugh and wrinkled up his nose. "Let's . . . er . . . let's talk about it later."

Hefty Thighs said, "Oh yeah, I heard about this Kyushi pitch. What's happening?"

Pea, her blue eyes like drills, ignored him. She said, still looking at Ed, "But . . ."

I said quickly, "So we're just going to enjoy Morton Park this summer."

Ed said soothingly, "It'll all be over by September. And that's a much better time to go away."

Pea said, "But we always go to Pollensa in August."

Ed said, his voice a pointed reminder of social obligation, "Darling . . . shall I go and get the blinis?"

He escaped into the kitchen, leaving the conversation to flounder a bit before Hefty Thighs threw it a lifeline in the form of "house prices." It had moved via "commuting complaints" on to "kitchen extensions" by the time Ed came back in with a plate of smoked salmon morsels. ("Umm," I said. "Ugh," Fergus said, spitting his out on the cream sofa, and from there it was just a hop and a skip to "child care," to the impossibility of finding a good nanny, about the superiority of "Polish girls" to Czechs, of Kiwis to "The French.") In the course of this conversation, I noticed Pea refer to the intervals she herself spent with Clarice as "child care," as in, "I was late getting to the shoot because of child care." Jake had started doing that too recently—"Sorry, can't make it:

child care"—like it was a double math lesson or an evening class.

"What do you mean by 'child care'?" I said. "Didn't that used to be called being a family?" I knew I was being twitchy, but I couldn't let it lie somehow. Pea looked daggers at me and then, while Ed passed round plates of lasagne, gave me a long lecture about the difficulties faced by working mothers in contemporary society, about the lack of adequate provision, about how squeezed you felt, how torn, how you never have any time for *yourself*. She would probably describe me afterward as being part of an army of nonworking mothers determined to undermine her at every turn. I didn't care. I just smiled weakly.

The others meanwhile had moved on and were busy talking about something else. Jake was telling them about a sticky meeting he'd had with the men from Wheato, about how they'd invented a loaf that tasted like toast and how they wanted to target kids and he'd told them that it was pointless, that it was mums who bought bread. And in the course of this anecdote, he mentioned the name of the MD at TMT&T and Hefty Thighs suddenly said, "Oh Philip . . . Oh, we all know about Philip." He opened his eyes wide and pushed his chin into his neck, suggestively.

"What?" asked his wife.

"Yes, what?" said Pea, frowning.

"Philip's women," he said. He was slapping his knees open and closed with excitement.

Ed was looking embarrassed.

Pea said, "What women?"

Hefty Thighs said, "He's a terrible womanizer. He's always got someone on the go."

"Oh he has, has he?" said Pea, glaring at Ed. "He and his wife, Lucy, were here to dinner last week."

Hefty Thighs still hadn't gotten the measure of her frosti-
ness. He said, "Can't keep it zipped up if you know what I
mean."

Pea said, "Yes, I know quite what you mean."

Ed said, "Anyone been watching Wimbledon?"

Hefty Thighs was nudging his wife, chortling to himself.
"At the moment he's seeing a chartered accountant in Barnes.
He even slips out for a shag in the middle of the evening
sometimes. He says he's nipping out to buy some beer. Once
he even said he had to move the car!"

"She must know then," said the cream combo. "She must
have guessed."

"Knows which side her bread is buttered," said HT. "Nice
five-bedroom house in Holland Park, communal gardens,
worth—I'd say at least two mil in the current market. Place in
Wiltshire. Harvey Nichols charge account. Why rock the
boat?"

"Ab-so-bloody-lutely," joshed Ed.

"Excuse me?" said Pea.

There was an awkward silence as Ed registered that he had
said the wrong thing. I concentrated on Delaney, their
Burmese, who had come and sat next to me on the sofa. I
stroked his wet-look papery fur. He yawned, a startled
expression hitting his face. The inside of his mouth looked
like a fillet of Dover sole.

Pea said, "It's not a joke, Ed."

"No, no, no, I know," he said.

"No, I'm serious," she said. "It really isn't funny. I know
you blokes think it's all a laugh and good for Philip and I'm
not interested in that. But it's beyond the pale to think it's
funny that his wife turns a blind eye. Maybe she does. But I
don't think we should find that acceptable. It's a fundamental
betrayal of women's rights. Don't you think? Don't you think

Maggie? Polly?" She was waving her hands around, her face was in mine. I murmured something, desperately tried to drag up an opinion. Where did people find opinions like this? Were they just born with them? "I mean, we each have a responsibility to other women, not to put up with things like that," she continued. "There may be women who are too scared to leave their husbands and . . . well, I just don't think we should laugh, that's all."

Polly was nodding in agreement. Pea went on, "God, advertising! Sometimes it just makes me so . . ."

Ed looked green. "Ab–so–bloody–lutely," he said weakly.

I looked at Jake. He was staring out of the window with an odd expression on his face.

We left shortly after this. Ed said good-bye to us at the door. "Catch ya later," he said, in an irritating fake voice to Jake. I must have given him a look because I heard him say, "Oops, hope you're not in the doghouse too," which irritated me even more, particularly as I knew that Jake would have had a better time if I hadn't been there, radiating ungraciousness.

While we were walking home, I said, "Why on earth do you like Ed? He's so false."

And Jake said, "He's different when he's on his own."

"Aren't we all," I said. I kicked an empty aluminum can out of the front wheels of the stroller only for it to become enmeshed in the wheels at the back.

Chapter 11

On Sunday morning, Jake went to the office, going straight on in the afternoon to the managing director's "country" (if Hemel Hempstead counts as country) club for a round of golf. He didn't get back until late. And on Monday Pete came to the house. I hadn't expected him to come that soon. I thought he'd come on Wednesday. Maybe even Thursday or Friday. I'd have washed my hair if I'd known. I'd certainly have washed my hair if I'd known this time he'd be wearing shorts.

It was just after one when he arrived. Dan was building a tower out of bricks on the kitchen floor. Fergus and I were making chocolate cornflake cakes, as a distractionary measure. "Okay, that's enough stirring," I was shouting. "It's hot, Fergus. HOT."

At the door, Pete said, "Thought I'd crack on with the job now I've started. That bindweed gets into everything. You only need to leave a tiny piece of root in the earth and it spreads."

"Is it the worst thing you can have?" I said, wiping Fergus's chocolatey fingers with the corner of my apron.

"No, Japanese knotweed's worse. Get that in your foundations and you can start getting cracks. Japanese knotweed can bring your house down. Japanese knotweed's a killer."

"I'd better be thankful for small mercies, then." I smiled, trying not to look down at his ginger brown muscular calves. The shorts looked ancient, tatty, army surplus; one of the pockets, combat-style, was half hanging off. There was a scab on one of his knees but an old one, an etching of New South Wales.

"Yes, you had," he said, his eyes crinkling up as he smiled back. "Yes, you had."

He worked in the garden all afternoon, mowing the lawn and digging sharp trenches between the grass and the flower beds, banging in some netting for the vines along the fence, tangling himself up in some of the shrubs with his pruning shears. Fergus was out there most of the time watching him, jumping up and down with excitement every time Pete brought through a new implement from his van. I watched most of the time, too, but from the upstairs window. I watched him bend and hoick and stretch. I watched his T-shirt wrinkle up across his back. I watched the circles of sweat widen under his arms. Occasionally, he'd stand and squint in my direction. But I don't think he could see me through the sun on the glass.

This time, when he'd finished work, he stayed for tea. And a chocolate cornflake cake.

"God, these take me back," he said between mouthfuls. He was sitting opposite me with his feet up on the rungs of the chair next to him and one elbow on the table. There was grass on the soles of his shoes. His forearms were richly sunburned and freckly like the top of crème brûlée, though underneath they were still pale, like the underside of a fish. He stretched suddenly, pushing his arms up in two Vs above his head, and I got a glimpse of the hollow beneath, the whiter skin and the darker damp hairs, like a secret place. "Remind me of my mum," he said.

"Where is your mum?" I said. "Is she still alive?"

"No. She cocked it in ninety-seven."

"Cocked it?" I tried not to laugh.

"Died." He smiled ruefully. "She died."

"I'm sorry. And what about your father?"

"Oh, dad's alive and kicking. He's back in Sydney. He was as weak as a kitten for a bit but he's got used to life on his own now."

"Does he miss you?"

"I guess so. But he's got Mo, my big sister, and her brood to keep him busy."

He did some pretend drumming on his thighs and on the edge of the table. "You got any brothers and sisters?"

"No. I'm an only child."

"Spoiled?" he smiled.

"No, thank you very much," I played mock-hurt. "I don't think I am. I think if anything it's made me more vulnerable, a bit of a loner; it's made it hard for me to read people . . ."

"Uh-huh?"

I laughed. "Oh, all right, spoiled."

He said, "You don't seem spoiled to me." He raised his eyebrows. "I'd say maybe you could do with a bit more spoiling."

I laughed nervously. I said, "And is Sydney where you grew up?"

He leaned back in his chair. "Yeah. Sydney. It's a great place. You should come visit some time."

"I'd love that, but . . ." I shrugged. "In another life."

"You should, you know." He leaned forward. "I think you'd love it. The space and the beaches and . . . You really should come one day. I'll show you round."

I laughed, as if, even in another life, this wasn't worth considering.

Pete said, "And the kids. They'd have a great time. And the food is cheap and the clothes . . ."

"So are you planning on going back soon?" I said.

It seemed important, for whatever reason, to know more about him. It felt nice to have a man in from the garden in the house. Jake never did any gardening. He didn't have the clothes for it, he said.

"I dunno." He shrugged. "Your guess is as good as mine. I like it here. I like London. I like the people . . ."

"So how long have you lived under Claire?"

"If only." Pete raised an eyebrow. I laughed, a haha-not-very-funny laugh. "Not that long," he said. "It's Lloyd's place. I'm subletting my room off someone who's traveling round the world."

"When are they back?"

"You're asking a lot of questions." He looked at me askance, wiggling his eyebrows.

"The Spanish Inquisition," I replied.

"The Spanish what?" he said. He picked up Dan, who was crawling under the table, and dandled him on his knee. His bare brown knee.

I said, "It doesn't matter."

There was a pause. Pete was making Donald Duck noises for Dan out of the corner of his cheek. Dan was chortling. I smiled at them both. "Have you always been a gardener?"

"No," Pete said, still as Donald Duck. "Have you always been a mother?"

"Now you're evading. Do you like it?"

"What evading?"

"No. Being a gardener?"

Dan was wriggling so Pete put him back on the floor. In

his own voice, he said: "In summer I do. I'm outdoors. I like being outdoors. Winters get a bit long. I do decorating and a bit of construction work if I need it. This year I've got some saved up so I might go snowboarding."

"Aren't you a bit old for that?" I said.

"You're as old as the woman you feel."

"And how old is she?" I said lightly.

Pete said, "Now that would be telling."

There was a pause. And then Fergus came in carrying a fork. Pete jumped up and said, "Hey, big fella, want to give that to me before you do some damage?" Fergus handed it over without a whimper and went back into the garden to see what else he could find. Pete said seriously, "You have, you know, you've got great kids."

I had started clearing the table, with Dan clinging to my knees. "They're a handful," I said.

"Spirited. Not a handful: *spirited.*"

"Maybe."

"And good-looking."

I grinned. "I'm biased, but . . ."

"They take after their mum." He was studying me.

I tried not to look flustered, willed the flush back down into my heart. I turned to busy myself, frantically with the washing up. "Flattery will get you everywhere," I said.

"But will it get me another chocolate cornflake thing?"

I wiped my hands on a tea towel. "It will certainly get you one of those."

I passed him the plate, and he spent a long time with his head bent choosing. He held the plate with his hand so I wouldn't move it away. There were some tiny dark green leaves in his hair. Ceanothus probably. Finally, he took one.

"Hey," I said, "That's the biggest."

"I'm terrible that way," he said, still holding his side of the plate. "I always take what I want."

They're tricky, moments like that. You think you know what's going on, but you don't know for sure. You can't say, "Well, here I am, take me," or "Well, you can't have me: I'm not available," because there is always the chance that it's totally innocent banter, no double entendre intended, or at least intended but only to be taken so far.

And let's face it. It had been a long time since I'd embarked upon anything even remotely flirt-related. I had, as Mel had so recently reminded me, been out of the game for eons. Not only did I not know the rules—Jake and I were practically pre-AIDS, certainly pre-AIDS-as-a-serious-consideration; all we had had to worry about was herpes and warts, and who cared about those these days?—but I didn't even know the game any more. At least, I didn't know what I was playing at.

So what did I do? I panicked. I defused. I put the emotional jigsaw back in its box. I tidied up the sexual skittles. I stepped back. I said, "I bet you do. You young things are all the same. Now get those grass-stained boots off my kitchen floor. And how much do I owe you?"

He looked a bit uncomfortable, but his smile didn't shift. He said, without even glancing down, "I'll clear up the mess, no worries. And as for payment, I'll bill you. You don't have to think about that now. Do you want me to come again in a week or two? Just to get you back on track?"

I wavered and told him I'd let him know. I felt breathless and sick somewhere between my stomach and my throat, churned up like the grass in the back garden. I knew what I had to say, though. I had to say it before he left. I took a deep breath, leaned back against the kitchen counter, and said, "This may sound a little odd, but there was something I

wanted to ask you. I'm all embarrassed now, but: are you seeing anyone at the moment?"

He was knocking the grass off his soles on the back doorstep. He turned round, with a lopsided smile. He said, "No.
And?"

I had to say it. It was now or never. I said, through a forced
laugh, "It's just I've got a friend. She's really great and I think
you'd really like her. And I just wondered . . ."

He said, still grinning, "A *'friend'*?"

I said, "No, honestly, I mean it. A friend. My friend Mel.
She's great. She's a GP and she's feisty and funny and . . ."

Pete's smile evened out. He said, not that nicely, "Little
Miss Matchmaker, are you? *Mrs.* Matchmaker I should say."

"Oh well, if you're not," I said quickly.

"I don't think so," he said, coming alongside me to wash
his hands at the kitchen tap. "If that's all right with you."

It was a bit frosty for a moment or two. Then, picking
up his bag, he said, "Do you think I look desperate or
something?"

"I didn't mean that. It was nothing. It's just that you don't
often meet nice single men."

"I see. Well, I'll think about it, okay? Maybe when I come
next time I'll take her number."

"Okay," I said.

After he left, I finished off the chocolate cornflake cakes.
All eight of them.

• • •

I saw Mel that night. I asked Jake to make sure he was home
early, which he did with much puffing and lugging of heavy
papers onto the kitchen table and important phone calls over
bathtime. "They will go to sleep, won't they?" he said, finally

coming up to take over the toweling. "Only I've got to work on this pitch."

"Of course they will," I lied, skipping to the bathroom door. Of course Fergus won't get out of his bed five minutes after you've put him there. Of course he won't want another story. Of course he won't want a drink of water ten minutes later. Of course Dan will let you put his pajamas on without wriggling out of the door. Of course he'll go down without a murmur. Of course Fergus won't wake him up asking for his glass of water. "Of course, they will," I said, halfway down the stairs. I could hear a splash and a crash behind me. That would be Fergus throwing his toothbrush in the toilet, and slamming the lid down after it. I could hear wails. That would be Dan's fingers between the lid and the bowl. "They're angels," I called from the street.

Mel and I met at The Drunken Stoat, the brasserie-cum-Mexican-cum-tapas-bar round the corner. It was all modern steel chairs and lacquered tables and mirrored walls, as if its decor was trying to keep one step ahead of its next change in cuisine. That night it was busy with a post-work crowd. Men in suits with their ties undone. Girls in thigh-skimming skirts and fancy tights. Lots of loud laughter and sitting on knees and piles of nachos with cheese. Sade remastered on the sound system. Could have been us, fifteen years ago, only no one was blowing smoke rings.

"That's because no one smokes anymore," said Mel, as we sat down in the corner. "Haven't you noticed the link between the decline in smoking and the rise of tapas bars, or—" she unslotted the plastic-coated menu from its special metal rest on the table and waved it in the air—"sophisticated bar snacks. Young people have to do something with their hands. People don't smoke any more; they snack.

"Except for doctors," she added, lighting up.

"And advertising execs," I said. I was sure Jake had started again. I could smell something musty on his jacket. And he'd left a box of Chez Gérard matches and a packet of mints on the hall table by his keys.

"Wouldn't he have told you if he was?" Mel said.

"I don't know. I'm not so sure about him these days. He's still behaving a *bit strangely*." I said these last two words in a Vincent Price voice. I might have expanded, but the waiter came along then and perched familiarly on the edge of our table. "Hi guys," he said.

"Hi guy," said Mel.

I ordered the deep-fried Camembert, with gooseberry sauce, starter-size. "I mustn't eat too much," I told Mel. "I've been eating cake all day."

I was about to tell her then about my encounter with Pete. I was longing to have someone to dissect our conversation with, to relive the thrills without the danger, to hear what she thought. But her mind was still on Jake. She said in a sympathetic voice, "In what way is he still behaving strangely?"

I fiddled with the see-through plastic salt and pepper shakers, spilled a little pepper and dipped my finger in it. "I don't know. He's at the office all the time. Still no sex. Something's up with him. It's almost as if he's seeing someone else." I snorted, as if I realized this was ridiculous.

Mel looked serious. She said, "Oh, Maggie. You've always been like this. Whenever someone's really in love with you, you always think they're going to leave you. I mean, remember Robin and Tom . . ." She listed some of my ex-boyfriends.

I cut her off. "Yes, yes," I said. But she had more to say.

"Just because your father left your mother doesn't mean every man leaves every woman. Jake is a good bloke. Talk to him if you're worried about something. Don't be too hard on him. He was looking really tired the other weekend. And actually to be frank you're the one who seemed on the distant side. Is he under strain from work?"

"Er . . ." I said, chastened. "I think so."

She gave me a sharp look.

"Yes, yes, no, he is. He's got a big pitch coming up."

"What pitch?"

"Kyushi wants one agency across Europe or something. TMT&T has got to rebid for the business from scratch, fighting off all the opposition, and then they might lose the account altogether."

"What implications would that have?"

"I don't know."

She frowned. "Why don't you know?"

"I haven't felt like asking."

Mel shook her head. Her brow was still knitted. "Well, maybe you should. You're lucky not having to work, you know. I know you can get fed up at home with the children all day, but it's your choice and Jake has made it possible for you."

"I know," I said.

Mel said, "You don't have to stay at home. You've got a degree. You could go back to magazines or publishing. It's been your decision."

"Yes, I know, but it's not that simple." I was about to talk about the invisible tug between mother and child, the competing forces of selfishness and selflessness, the physical need to be with them, the fear of what they'd be without you . . . my own crapiness in every job I'd ever done.

But then she said softly, glancing away: "Some of us don't have a choice."

"Point taken," I said, putting my hand on her arm.

The food arrived then and, while I picked at crispy Camembert and Mel tucked into a plate of fettucini with salmon, we moved on to Mel's day and the problems she'd been having with one of the other partners, a woman of her age who Mel didn't think was pulling her weight, and we discussed tactics and the redistribution of nights on call. And then she told me about one of her patients, an elderly woman who'd been into surgery a lot over the last couple of years with heart problems and blood pressure issues, and how she'd seen Mel a few weeks back because she'd been coughing for a bit and maybe even seen a bit of blood, and Mel had sent her off for an X ray. "You just knew," Mel said, putting down her fork, "what the results were going to be. She's smoked for years and . . . Anyway, she came in yesterday saying she felt a bit better, and I had to tell her and it's just awful. Awful."

"Oh, God," I said, suddenly stricken, "I have to take my neighbor for a chest X ray soon. Oh, God, I hope that's not cancer. I've only just got to know her."

"Might not be. Anyway, I had to go straight from her to this other woman, a real Heart Sink Patient, who's morbidly overweight . . . really really fat, and she thinks that all her problems will be solved if she could just be slimmer and she keeps coming back, trying to get us to refer her to a specialist to staple her stomach, which is not the answer. So I had a really awful conversation with her, and I could feel myself getting more and more tense, and then Tara the receptionist buzzed me through two 'emergency patients' who, it turned out, were a young couple who'd forgotten to have their jabs. They were going on holiday to Kenya in three days time. Well, I just hit the roof. It was just the end. I mean, there are people who really are emergencies and here they were, anyway, I had a real argument with them but I ended up giving the shots to them, but I was so grumpy."

I laughed in sympathy.

"But." Mel lowered her voice. "After they'd gone, I realized that I'd given the woman the polio and the yellow fever and the Hep A, but I hadn't given her the typhoid . . ."

"Oh my God!"

"I know, isn't it awful. I didn't know what to do. And because we'd had such a barney, I couldn't ring her, so I've just . . ."

"What? What have you done?"

"I've just left it."

"Oh my God!"

"Is that just awful, do you think? It is, isn't it? I think they were just going to a resort on the coast, but even so. It's just that I've had two nights on call and then the cancer woman and . . . Oh," she pushed her plate to the other side of the table and pulled over an ashtray. "I wish I could give it up and do something else. I don't know . . . marry a rich banker or something."

Which took us to Piers, her anesthetist. She raised her eyes to the ceiling when he was mentioned, lit another cigarette, and poured herself another glass of Chardonnay. I told her I didn't understand why she didn't just finish it, that it wasn't fair to him to keep him dangling. "I know," she said guilt-lessly, "I keep trying. I'm so horrible to him. I make thinner and thinner excuses. He must think I have the weirdest menstrual cycle. But he just doesn't get the message. What I need is to fall madly in love with someone else. What happened, by the way, about the gardener chap?"

"Oh," I said. Even to my own ears, I sounded hesitant. "I think maybe we'd better forget it." I took a long glug of wine. "It turns out," I said, "I think he's seeing someone."

Mel looked unconcerned. "Oh drat," she said. "Oh well, I wasn't that sure about the dirty fingernails anyway. Piers's at least are always so clean." She looked around the room. A girl was shrieking with laughter at the next table. Probably because the man next to her—a colleague? her boss?—had his hand up her skirt. "Too clean," she added gloomily.

We left soonish after that. There was a lot of to-ing and fro-ing in the corner and a man in a moustache with a guitar and a mike came and sat, side on, on a stool, so it was clearly time to beat a retreat. Mel said she'd come back to my house for a nightcap. "It would be nice to see Jake," she said. "See how mysterious he is with my own eyes."

When we got in, he was at the kitchen table, surrounded by papers. "Mel's here," I said.

He stood up and stretched and gave her a long hug. "How nice," he said, still with his arms around her.

We sat on the steps up to the garden with a bottle of wine between us. Mel told him about the difficult partner at work and Jake, who as the head of a department knew about these things, told her what to say and how to approach her. ("The thing is to be nice, always nice, but firm. Reasonable, but firm. Explain how things seem to you, and see what she has to say. Then, if there's still a problem, go to the head of the practice. Whatever you do, don't be emotional.")

Mel asked him about Kyushi and, darting me a look, he said it was very boring, very frustrating, very time-consuming. "And how are the pimples?" she said. He proffered his chin for her to inspect. She ran a medical hand over it. "Hmm. Have you tried. . . . ? might I suggest. . . . ?" She pretended to delve into her bag and bring something out, holding it like a dart in front of her eyes, "ZAP-IT!"

"STOP-IT!" he said, pretending to grab it off her.

She stayed only for half an hour, but it was a nice half hour, almost like old times. I felt warm and comfortable with my two favorite people around me. I said, "Let's go away somewhere next Bank Holiday, us and Mel and Milly and maybe even Piers." Mel winced. "All right. Not Piers then.

We could get a cottage, by the sea or something. When is the next one? August. End of August. Let's go then. Can we?"

Mel looked enthusiastic, but Jake gave a weary grimace. "Oh. Maggie. Didn't I say? Or have you forgotten . . . ? you know . . . Ed and Pea?"

I frowned. I didn't remember.

"We said we'd go and stay with them in Suffolk?"

"Did we?"

"To make up for Majorca?"

"Were you going to go to Majorca?" asked Mel.

"No," I said, shortly.

"Never mind," Mel said. "Another time."

When Mel's mini-cab came, I walked her to the curb. "Try and be a bit more understanding with Jake," she said, as we parted. "Otherwise, I'll have him."

When I got back into the house, Jake was back at the kitchen table, head bent over a mess of paper. "Sorry about Suffolk," he said, not looking up. "I think I'm guilty on that one. I was just waiting for an opportunity to slip it in."

"You slipped it," I said.

He still didn't look up.

"Are you all right?" I came up behind him and rested my chin on the top of his head. There were lines of gray in among the dark brown.

"Exhausted actually." He kept his eyes on his paperwork. But he reached behind to put an arm around my legs. "Perhaps you could just go and check on your children. I think I might have just heard Dan."

"They're my children now, are they?" I said. "Only yours when they're quiet?"

"Absolutely," he said, smiling. "Oh, and Fran rang earlier . . ."

"*Your* sister."

"Definitely my sister. She said can you ring her? Something about a tennis machine?"

"A Tens machine," I said. "You know, the thing you strap on your back when you're in labor. Nothing to do with tennis. You idiot."

I was about to give him a playful slap, but he'd already bowed his head again and was back to his figures, so I went upstairs to check on the children instead. Dan's hair was all sweaty on one side from where he must have been lying; Fergus's mouth was squashed open against the pillow and he was breathing through it: thick, wet, rasping snores that pulled at my heart. Still clasped in his hand was the 747 Jake had bought him at the Amsterdam airport. My children. Our children. What had I been thinking of? We were a family. Nothing could come between us. It was just a rough patch, that was all.

I rearranged their blankets and went back downstairs to make Jake some tea.

·   ·   ·

The next morning, I took the children to the urban zoo: held Dan up to stare blankly at the penned-in sheep, let Fergus sit for our entire visit in the rusty old tractor, fighting off the other children with his feet. I dropped in on Rachel on the way home, and we sat in her garden and I chatted happily about Jamie Oliver's pine nut and pancetta penne as if I didn't have a care in the world. She said we should have "a girly night out," which made me smile. "Right," I imagined her saying. "Let's be girly. Come on girls, line up"—but it was a nice thought.

Fergus did some painting while we were there. Mostly he painted on Harry's piece of paper, which made Harry screech and flail his arms in annoyance and spill the pot of

water. I mopped it up with a dishcloth I'd found by the sink.
I should have known Rachel's dishcloths would be color-
coded. "Stop, stop," she shrieked. "Pink's for faces; blue's for
floors." When we left—Rachel soothing, "Please don't worry
about it, he's just tired"—I took Fergus's picture with us,
drove up to the common, and parked at a bus stop. On the
back of the painting (it was just red actually; Fergus often saw
red) I wrote:

Dear Pete,

On further reflection, I think it's best if we do call
it a day on the garden front. I'm thrilled with the
work you've done so far, but on further reflection [I
scratched those last three words out] it's probably
getting a bit too expensive in the long term. Thanks
for untangling the bindweed and [I thought for a
while before adding] your care and attention. It was
much needed! Let me know how much I owe you
for services so far rendered. [I regretted that last bit,
but felt I couldn't cross anything else out without
having to find another piece of paper. I wondered
hard how to finish. In the end I wrote]

Best wishes, Maggie (Owen)

Then I opened the car door, ran down the steps of the
house he shared with Claire, and posted the note through the
basement door. I didn't feel sad as I drove home. I didn't
really feel anything. There was nothing to feel anything
about.

Chapter 12

"I'm going to have to meet you there," said Jake on the phone that afternoon. "I'm sorry. I can't get away early tonight. There's a good-bye party I have to show my face at. And then I need to come back to the office after that. I've got people breathing down my neck left, right, and center. Not just Kyushi, the people at Zap-it say they want a whole new cradle-to-grave strategy by the end of the week."

"Cradle to grave?"

"It's not just teenagers who get spots, they say. They want the new improved cream to be really big."

"You mean, in your face?"

Jake didn't laugh. He sounded impatient. He said, "So, what with everything, Maggie . . ."

I said, "Well, don't stay forever at the party. And then you won't be too late, will you? Don't be rudely late."

"I'll try and be there by 9:30 p.m. . . ."

"Jake!" I said.

"Look, I've got to go. Bye."

I found it much easier finding something to wear than I

had a few weeks before. It might have been because I was browner after a few days on the common. Or it might have been because my self-esteem had been lifted out of my shoes on the fork of a flirtatious gardener. Either way, I happily ironed a spotted tea dress I'd once found at a yard sale. It was rather too wide and rather too long, but I decided, looking at myself sideways in the mirror, that it was just fine. I put on some earrings and some makeup, and felt, in the bathroom light at least, almost glamorous.

Merika, Maria's Slovakian au pair, cycled over from Wandsworth to baby-sit. She was bang on time so I got to Claire's a bit early. I sat in the car for a while, watching the house as I'd watched it before. There was no sign of life in the bottom flat. I wondered what Pete was doing. Who he was with.

At 8:45 p.m. I rang Claire's bell.

"Magsarama," she cried. She was wearing cropped jeans, bare feet, and no make-up. Immediately, I felt overdressed. She steered me in. "Entrez, entrez."

I was not the first. Her sister, Rowena, the television presenter, was reclining on the sofa in the sitting room. She exclaimed, "Maggie Owen, the French-skipping queen of Lower Fourth! Remember me after all these years? Claire's little sister!" I said of course, not adding the fact that I'd caught her elfin figure bottle-feeding a lamb on *Animal SOS* only a few weeks before. Celebrity always made me awkward. She pointed across the room to her boyfriend, Johnny Something, whom I also recognized from the television or the pages of the *Mail* or *Hello*—who was slipping a CD into the machine. He furrowed his handsome forehead into one long eyebrow as he straightened up and, white man's overbite at the ready, pointed his finger at me in a faux familiar "my man" gesture. I pointed my finger back at him and then put it in my pocket.

I said, "What's this?" meaning the music. Johnny said, "M&M."

"Like the sweets?" I said.

He looked pained. "No. E.M.I.N.E.M."

From then on, Johnny Something clearly thought I was an imbecile. Every time anybody said anything about anybody, he turned to me and, sideburns standing to attention, gave me a quick explanation. He'd just said, "That's Guy Ritchie, the film director, they're talking about. He directed *Lock, Stock and Two Smoking Barrels* and *Snatch*. He's married to Madonna. That's Madonna, the pop star," when the buzzer went and almost immediately there were shrieks in the hall. I could hear a high voice and a deeper one. For a gut-wrenching moment I thought this was Pete's—but when the couple entered, the deep voice belonged to a balding, burly-looking bloke who turned out to be a cookery writer on one of the Sunday papers.

"Maggie, er . . . cooks too," said Claire.

"No, I don't," I parried. "I microwave. Though I can make cakes."

The man, who was called Tom, laughed and introduced me to his wife, Lily, a book editor with pouting lips and Louise Brooks hair. They smiled so broadly I liked them both at once.

When Claire was in the kitchen, and Rowena and Johnny were busy flicking through a book of "promos," Tom mouthed conspiratorially, "Any news on Claire's man?" as if we'd known each other all our lives.

I whispered, "Not sure. Do you think he's coming?"

Lily hissed, "I think he's had his chips. I asked Claire on the phone earlier this week and she said, 'Curtains.'"

"Oh really, 'curtains'?" I repeated, interested.

"What do you mean 'curtains'?" said Claire, coming up behind me with a bowl of marinaded olives.

"Nothing," I said, trying to keep a straight face. "Just discussing curtains versus blinds."

"God, you marrieds," she said. "You've got to get out more."

Lily and I exchanged glances.

Soon after that, the buzzer went again, and I thought with relief, that'll be Jake: he's not embarrassingly late after all. But Claire was gone quite some time—you could hear muffled discussions from the hallway. When she came back she looked pink and ruffled around the hair region. There was a triumphant bounce to her gait and in her wake, holding her hand like a reluctant teenager dragged onto the dance floor by a tipsy aunt, was a tall man in his forties with shoulder-length gray-brown hair. Claire said, after a deep breath, "Everybody. Meet Marcus."

Marcus, who was, I was almost sure, the man I'd seen leaving Claire's flat, looked dazed but gave a sheepish smile. He was wearing a pin-stripe suit but the stripes were exaggerated as if to announce his distance from conventionality and proximity to youth. There were deep notches in his cheeks and furrows across his forehead, and a burned-orange hue to his face which didn't look entirely natural. He waved slightly to Rowena to acknowledge having met her before and then rummaged in his jacket pocket to retrieve a nasal spray, which he applied noisily to his nose. Ah, so he *was* the man I'd seen leaving Claire's flat. "Sorry to interrupt," he said, after he'd cleared his throat. Then he looked down blankly at the pigskin briefcase in his hand as if he didn't know what to do with it.

"You're not interrupting," said Claire slowly as if explaining etiquette to a child. "You're invited. Remember."

He made a high-pitched sound, somewhere between a sob and a laugh and took his briefcase through to another room—possibly the bedroom.

"Have a drink," called Claire after him. "He's had a hard day," she said sotto voce to the rest of us. "Sony v. Visconti," she added, wrinkling her nose. She was smiling, but there was something vulnerable in the set of her mouth.

Johnny was whispering to me. "Breach of contract. Visconti, the sixties crooner recently revived through the Ibiza club scene, is . . ."

"Sorry? What?" I said. I was trying to catch Claire's eye. "Yeah, I know," I said, though actually I didn't.

Thinking back to the conversation with Claire in my kitchen, I did some mental calculations. It was, technically, next week. Did this mean Marcus had left his wife? And did this mean Claire had decided to forget the other man, the one she said she *really* loved? Was she happy with this? What was going on? I managed to catch her eye when she was pouring herself a glass of wine, and I opened mine wide inquiringly. She gave me a half-hearted thumbs-up. So he had . . . and apparently she had too.

Marcus sat dazed in an armchair, jacket off, tie undone, nursing his drink, occasionally taking a snort from his spray, while the rest of us chattered around him. Johnny and Rowena had just been on holiday in Madagascar and were full of lemurs ("Nocturnal," Johnny assured me in an aside, "principally found in Madagascar. Similar to monkeys"). Tom and Lily were thinking of downsizing. They'd seen a house in Suffolk. Tom wanted pigs. "For the bacon," said Lily, raising her eyebrows.

Rowena and Claire did a funny double act about their parents, who had moved to an old rectory just north of Oxford. "Handy for Stratford for Mummy," said Rowena.

"And a handy supply of female students for Daddy," said Claire.

And all the while, I surprised myself by my sociability. It was like being single again: I could be who I wanted. So I did impressions of some of the more awful "playground mums" and discussed books with Lily and told tales on Claire that made her squirm with pretend-embarrassment and made the others howl. "And do you remember?" I said, "the day you streaked and Mr. Brown, the geography teacher, escorted you into the staff room? And what about that time we 'slept out' for Wimbledon tickets just so you could snog David Ramsay? Oh God, and all those boyfriends you nicked off the rest of us. Remember Nigel?"

"No," she said, shaking her head, "I don't remember him."

"Nigel? With the bike? My first boyfriend? The man I loved and you took." I camped that bit up. "With the bad skin?"

"No. Blank, I'm afraid."

"Unlike your detention sheet," I said, secretly stung. Everyone laughed (especially, I noticed, Rowena), and I laughed too.

It was almost 10:30 p.m. when Jake finally turned up. The olives had long been eaten and too much wine had been consumed on top of too many empty stomachs. He was definitely rudely late. "Sorry, sorry, sorry, sorry," he was still saying, as Claire brought him into the sitting room. He looked windswept, full of energy. "Hello," he said to the others. "Sorry," he said again to Claire.

"It's all right," Claire said, gaily. "I'm too drunk to care. And it's only risotto. Burned to a cinder. You can have the charred bits from the bottom. Now, Maggie you know. Rowena—you remember. This is Johnny, her boyfriend. Lily and Tom: did you meet them at the party? Oh good. And this—" she put her arm around Marcus as if presenting a soufflé that might collapse at any moment—"is Marcus."

Jake had been smiling and shaking hands, but he turned the charm off for a fleeting moment then. No one but me would have noticed, but it was almost as if he'd met Marcus before, or as if he had something against him. "Hi," he said smoothly, a muscle twitching in his cheek. Then, quickly, he turned to me. "Hello, sweetie." He gave me a single peck. Then mouthed, silently "Sorry, I couldn't get away." I shook my head as if to say, it doesn't matter.

We had finally started eating when the phone rang. We were in the kitchen, which was the most dead-grannyish of the rooms. It had spice racks on the walls, though the jars had gone, and special suction pads on the edge of the melamine counter for tea towels, also empty. The linoleum on the floor had white swirls in it like the trail left at the back of a cross channel ferry. Jake was sitting next to Rowena, who was laughing at whatever he was saying, her head cocked at an angle, so that she could look out at him from behind her hair. Sometimes I forgot how sexy Jake was, what an effect he could have on other women. Rowena was picking leaves of lettuce out of the salad bowl, and then licking the dressing from her fingers, almost, you could say, suggestively. Johnny was looking handsomely pensive at the end of the table, rigid with the effort of not minding about Jake, occasionally frowning winsomely as he caught his own eye in the darkened window. And Lily and I were trying to cheer up Marcus. We were doing party-style good cop, bad cop. I asked the questions, she administered the flattery.

Me: "So what does a showbiz lawyer actually do?"

Marcus: "I'm principally involved with the drawing up of contracts, with protecting my clients' reputation and trademark, and any disputes that might arise as a result of damage to that reputation or trademark."

Lily: "It must be so demanding dealing with all those egos. You must need to be such a patient, strong person."

Marcus, preening: "Well, I don't know about that."

After a while, under the influence of Lily, with a little help from the bottle of Merlot by his side, he stopped looking nervously at his watch every few minutes. He seemed to have forgotten the existence of his nasal spray. He even looked up from his glass to blow a kiss in Claire's direction. "Lovely girl," he said to me, or maybe it was "lucky girl." His voice was a bit too adenoidal to tell.

And that's when the phone rang. It was about 11:00 p.m. Claire had a tray of hot pears in her hand and bent to put them down. Jake and Rowena were still giggling. Johnny was examining the back of a spoon. Tom, who had been helping her whip some cream, was standing by the phone. Claire made a gesture at him to pick it up.

"Hello," he said. "Hello? Hello?"

He put the phone back on the counter. "No one there," he said.

Almost immediately, it rang again. This time, Tom handed it to Claire.

"Hello." Pause. "It's Claire speaking." Longer pause. "Yes, I have . . . Yes, he is. I'm not prepared to discuss that with you." She had gone very red but the blood was now draining away, except for two spots high on her cheeks. Her lips were pale. We'd all stopped talking now. Marcus had stood up. He had his hand out for the phone. Claire said, magisterial, the actors' daughter, "I repeat I am not prepared to discuss that with you. It is my personal business. If you wish to talk to Marcus he is here and you may do so . . . Right. . . . I'm sorry to hear that, but you must understand it is not my concern. Marcus is an adult. I am an adult." Long pause. "I'm sorry, I'm not prepared to listen to this, and I'm going to . . ." She looked as if she was about to hang up, but Marcus grabbed her arm before she could do so, took the phone from her, and left the room.

Claire sat down abruptly in the empty seat next to Jake and burst into tears. She buried her head on Jake's shoulder. He patted her hair.

"Hey, hey," he said softly.

Tom and Lily took over then. "Right," said Tom. "What was all that about?"

"Tell all," said Lily.

Claire took her head out from under Jake's hand and said, through her tears, "She was so horrible. How dare she? She has no right to ring me during a dinner party and say those things. If Marcus wants to leave her for me, it's not my fault, is it? What she's going through shouldn't be any of my business. It's his; not mine."

Her emotion slunk across the room, like dry ice. Most of us shifted in our seats, suddenly awkward and embarrassed, keen to keep our feet out of it. I wanted to hear what Marcus was saying. But he'd closed the door.

Rowena said, "Come off it, Claire. He's a married man. You knew he was a married man. Just like the last one. Married men tend to have wives. And quite a few of them—including this one—have kids. So I have to say it *is* your business."

Claire looked daggers at her sister and said, "But it's not my fault that I fell in love with him. I didn't have a choice."

"I don't think you're in love with him," said Rowena. "Not really. And anyway, there's always a choice. You knew he had a wife and kids when you met him. You could have walked away."

Claire said unconvincingly, "I didn't know actually. He didn't tell me about the meat and two veg until our second date."

"'Meat and two veg'?" echoed Rowena.

Claire looked flustered. "Wife and two kids. You know what I mean . . ." She glanced round the room, and said to the rest of us. "Look, all I'm saying is, we don't choose who we fall in love with and when Cupid steps in and takes over . . ."

"Come off it." Rowena was looking more and more irritated. "Cupid? Which planet are you on? Look, Claire, think about it. Is Marcus the one? Isn't he just the result of panic? What about . . ."

Claire said, "But Ro—" She slumped. She looked suddenly tired.

Tom said quickly, "Those pears look delicious. Let's eat them before they get cold."

Claire picked up the serving dish and was about to dole them out when Marcus came back into the kitchen, looking, despite the orange glow and the exaggerated stripes, like an old man. He said to Claire, his head bent, "I'm sorry. I'm going to have to go."

"You can't," she said wearily. "You've only just come."

"Look, look," he said, trying to draw her into some privacy in the shelter of the fridge. "Look, I've got to go," he whispered intensely. "She's in a state. She's got the letter. She knows. But Alfie has got a high temperature. She's rung the doctor, but they don't know what time they'll be able to come. She doesn't know what to do with herself. I've got to go. I've got to be there." There were a couple of loud sniffs as the inhaler came back into use. "I'll ring you," he said, backing out the door. "Tomorrow. I promise."

"Fucking hell," she said quietly after the front door had closed. "Sorry everyone, but . . . Fuck."

Jake, who had been silent through all this, said, "I didn't much like him anyway."

For a moment, I thought Claire was about to laugh. It could have gone either way. But she didn't laugh. She stood up. She said, enunciating every word very clearly, "Fuck you too," and threw the whole plate of pears on the floor. Luckily they'd cooled down, so no one was hurt.

. . .

"Why did you say that?" I asked Jake in the car. "I can't believe you said it. It was so tactless. Why did you have to inflame the situation? Do you know him or something? You were very odd. And—" I thought I might as well throw it in for good measure, "what was all that flirting with Rowena?"

Jake looked pensive. I was driving. He was slumped against the passenger window. He said, "Calm down. It's just that it all seemed such a charade."

"You didn't help. If you hadn't been so late getting there, we'd have eaten earlier and people wouldn't have got so drunk."

"*I* didn't help?" He was laughing. "What about Claire didn't help? Or Martin or Marcus or whatever he's called, didn't help? Or what about his wife not helping?"

"Marcus. His name is Marcus. And his wife at least had reason."

Jake put his feet up on the dashboard. He seemed oblivious to my mood. He said, chuckling, "Meat and two veg. I haven't heard that one before."

"It's not funny," I said.

• • •

The next night, Claire rang to apologize. Jake was still out. He hadn't rung but I assumed he was at work or at some "do" or another. I had made myself a bowl of pasta with butter and some parsley from the pot on the window ledge and was about to settle down in front of the television, congratulating myself on my ability, "do less" to "make do," when the phone rang. I thought it might be Mel—I hadn't heard from her for a few days—or Fran with some new life-threatening symptom. Neither of them minded me multitasking, in this case chewing while chatting (though Mel got a bit twitchy if she knew I was having a pee while we were on the phone; I had to line the bowl with bathroom tissue to dull the sound). Anyway, it wasn't. It was Claire.

"Hello. How are you?" I said, swallowing and trying to suppress the surprise in my voice, wanting to say, Why do you keep ringing? Don't you have any other friends? What is it with you? Deep down, though, I was flattered, Maggie the schoolgirl sunbathing in Claire's attention.

She said in a small voice, "Are you in?"

"Er. yes."

"It's just that I need someone to talk to. I'm so sorry about last night. I really lost it. I think I'm going mad. I just wondered if I could ask your advice. You were so astute the other day."

"Is this about Marcus?" I said. "I don't know if there's anything more I can say to help."

"Marcus and . . . you know. I'm so confused. Please, Maggie? You've always been there for me. In the past . . ."

"Sure," I said, doubtfully. I tried to remember an occasion when I'd "been there for her" when we were teenagers. I did find her crying once in the bathroom, shortly after the Pizza Hut incident. I think I copied out my wordsheet of Bohemian Rhapsody to cheer her up. I didn't know if I could do anything similar now. "Come round. Jake's out so I'm on my own. Come and have a drink."

She said, "Oh. Where is he . . . Jake?"

I had taken another surreptitious mouthful. I swallowed quickly. "At work."

"Oh." She sounded puzzled. It was past nine, which was nothing these days, but I couldn't lose face.

"Late meeting," I said. "But he'll probably be back quite soon."

"Oh, right," she said.

I plumped up some cushions, assuming she'd be around any minute. I set the video up to tape *ER*. I waited. Forty-five minutes went by before I caught the small thump and clatter that means someone is about to knock at the door. Except there wasn't a knock. There was a louder clatter that means someone is letting themselves in with a key.

"Hi," said Jake, coming into the sitting room.

I was about to warn him about Claire when at that moment there *was* a knock at the door.

"That'll be Claire," I said.

He stood stock still, as if he'd been stung. His nose wrinkled in disbelief.

It was an extreme reaction, but I didn't think too much of it at the time. I went to let her in. She was looking fetchingly tearful, though I noticed her mascara hadn't run. Her hair was damp at the ends as if she'd just washed it. Jake was still standing where I'd left him when we came into the sitting room.

She said, hurling her bag onto the sofa, "Marcus *has* gone back to his wife."

Jake shrugged unfeelingly. "That was obvious."

I said, trying to nudge him out into the kitchen, "Oh Claire, I'm so sorry. What Jake means is that last night . . ."

She said, dramatically, "He rang me this morning. After all that. I really believed him. He said we'd buy a place in Epsom so he could be near the kids. He said we'd get married when the divorce came through. He said we could start a family. I mean, Christ, I'm thirty-six. I thought I'd finally found a man I could trust, someone who was prepared to commit."

Jake snorted. I tried to suppress an image of Claire in Surrey, at Butterfly World or Chessington, with truculent stepkids in tow, a baby wailing in a sling. I said, "I'm so sorry, Claire."

Jake said, "So he wasn't so trustworthy after all."

"Well, at least he almost left his wife," said Claire quickly. "Unlike . . . many men."

"But he didn't, did he?" said Jake coolly.

"Well, he might still."

"What? When his son's temperature goes down? What happens next time the little lad gets a cold?"

"Well . . ."

"How trustworthy, how *committed,* is that?"

"Jake," I said with a laugh, trying to brush over his insensitivity. "You can take your bad day out on me, but not on Claire. She's upset. Leave her alone. Claire, ignore him."

Claire sat down on the sofa; the cushions whooshed as they deflated beneath her. She said quietly, "Oh, it's all a mess. Rowena's right: I don't even know if my heart was in it. But then that makes it all the more awful that he's left me. I can't even keep the second division interested." She looked at the back of her hands and then she looked at Jake. "Of course Maggie said it first: I'm still in love with . . . with someone else."

"Maggie said what?" Jake sounded perturbed.

I explained. "Her ex. Also married." I tried not to sound censorious.

Claire said, still looking at Jake, "I am, you know. I can't get him out of my head. If I'm honest with myself, he was why I came back from New York."

"What about Marcus?" said Jake.

"Even when I was with Marcus, he was the first thing I thought of in the morning, the last thing I thought of at night. I can't forget him."

Jake was staring at her. I said, "I know what we need: tea." And when Jake didn't get the hint, I went into the kitchen and put the kettle on. When I came back into the room, a few minutes later, they were both sitting down on the sofa. Jake had his arm along the back of it. Claire was leaning forward, with her head down, her hair hanging like a veil. They were talking softly. Claire looked up at me when I came into the room. She seemed more cheerful.

When I put the tray down in front of her, she said, "Shall I be mother?"

"You'd better not be," Jake said, which made Claire smile.

Chapter 13

We had a bad night that night. Dan was cutting a molar and started crying shortly after Jake and I went to sleep. He was hot so I loosened his bedclothes and gave him a bottle to soothe him. I was stroking his head through the bars of his crib, on my knees in my pajamas, listening to the rhythmic glugs and snuffles, when Fergus stirred and got out of bed. He was half asleep, still in the middle of a dream, and he went rigid when I tried to pick him up, pulling his head away from me as if I was a night-fright monster, ready to jam his heels into my stomach, on the border of tantrum, and it took a while for me to calm him down. By the time he had woken up enough to snuggle into me, Dan had dropped off and I didn't want to risk waking him again by trying to settle Fergus, so I took Fergus into our room. Jake grunted when he realized what was going on, poured himself out the other side of the bed, and went off to sleep in the spare room.

I lay there, curled around my son, feeling the bones in his back through his pajamas, one arm encircling his head, sensing the warmth of him, filling my nostrils with the smell of crayons and Mr. Bubble, until he pushed me closer and closer to the edge of the bed. And then I lay there, gripping the sheet, uncomfortable, uneasy, as Jake's side grew cold, wondering why I felt so distant from him, and whether we'd ever make love again.

In the morning, after Jake had left, Mrs. Allardyce—minus raincoat in honor of July—came to the door to check if I could still take her to the hospital the following day. She came into the kitchen and had some tea and a comforting moan about the noise and the litter from Pizza Express. When Dan came and clung to her support stockings, she called him "Lamb" and she did "Two Little Dickey Birds" for Fergus, using two bits of tissue on her knobbly fingers. A few minutes after she left, she came back with a packet of custard creams. "There you are, dear," she said, pressing it into my hand. "They can have some of these for their tea."

"You can get people so wrong," I told Jake later when he came in.

"Hm?" he said.

"Mrs. Allardyce. She's really quite nice and . . ."

"Good," he said, looking up absentmindedly from his bank statement. "Good."

I left him to it, found a beer in the fridge, and went into the sitting room to watch my tape of the previous night's *ER*.

I wouldn't have thought anything of the phone call, if he hadn't taken it into the garden. When I heard it ring, I paused the television to hear if it was for me and then when Jake opened the garden doors, I went into the hall to see what he was doing. He had taken the phone over to the bench under the apple tree and was sitting there, legs apart, head bent in concentration. He was too far away to hear from the hall so I slipped into the kitchen and stood to the side of the open window. The light in the garden was only just fading and there were swallows swooping in the navy sky.

Jake didn't say much at first; he just seemed to be listening. Then he said, "Yes," and "I know, I know." And then there was another long silence at the end of which he gave a sequence of sighs and then he sort of groaned and said, "You're very persuasive. Did anyone ever tell you that?" And finally, as if conceding, he said, "Okay. Okay. Lunch tomorrow. Ring me at work in the morning just to check. No, she won't . . . No . . . all right . . . No fine. One-ish. Okay, Claire. Bye."

I hadn't moved. I was standing in the same place. In the same kitchen, gripping the sill as if a wind was ripping through my house. There was a delay between hearing the information and feeling it, as when you stub your toe and there's a moment of nothing when you think you've gotten away with it before the pain hits you. And then it hit me. Claire. Claire Masterson, who always had to have everything I had. *Jake* was the married man she was in love with. The love of her life. At some point, Jake had had an affair with Claire. And now she wanted him back.

Everything suddenly fell into place. The way they had danced at her party, as if they knew each other better than they should have. His attitude at finding her in our house the day he got back from Amsterdam. The fact that *she* knew about Kyushi. That *he* knew about Disney on that first night, before I'd even mentioned it. The smell of smoke on his clothes. His oddly detached attitude at dinner the other night and in our house the evening after. His behavior toward Marcus. *And* his complete lack of interest in sex. With me, at least. This sense I'd had recently that he was slipping away from me, that his life was elsewhere. And her new friendship with me? Ringing me up all the time, coming around whenever she could, inviting us to everything, wheedling herself into my, our, *his,* life. I'd thought, foolish me, she'd wanted to be my friend. But she hadn't, had she? She'd come back from America, determined to get him again, and he must have said no, so at the same time as stringing poor old Marcus along, she'd just used me to get close to him, to thrust herself under his nose, to insinuate herself back into his heart.

I was back on the sofa in front of *ER* when Jake came in from the garden and started clanking about in the kitchen cupboards. After a short while, he came into the sitting room with a pot of coffee on a tray. "Who rang?" I said, without moving my eyes from the screen. I waited what seemed like a million years for him to answer.

"Work," he said. "Just someone from work."

· · ·

That night I lay awake for hours, listening to Jake breathe. I had been on the verge of confronting him all evening. In a minute, I'm going to do it, I kept thinking. Or if not this minute then the next one. I'd open my mouth, and then the words which were jumbled up in my head, the anger, the tears, the how-could-you?s, would disappear, and my tongue would turn to lead, and I'd sit there silent.

In bed, I occupied a ribbon of sheet as far from him as I could. He was hot and restless; once when his legs flailed to kick away the covers, he snagged my shin with a toe nail and I wanted to kick him back; kick him and then push him out of bed, push the duvet down on top of him, and shout and scream and pummel him until he cried for mercy, for forgiveness. But I didn't. I just lay there, everything going on in my head and nothing outside.

I went over and over in my mind when their affair must have started. Before she went to America and she'd been there—what?—two years. So, before we had Fergus? No, it must have been after that because she'd said, that day in my kitchen, that "the love of her life"—of *her* life—couldn't leave his child. Child singular. So after Fergus, but before Dan. It was a horrific thought. I'd believed we were happy then, him and me and our little boy, fussing over the cradle and the stroller and testing the temperature of his room with an over-anxious little thermometer. But all that time . . . As I thought about it, the past moments of contentment went off, like sour milk. Those nights when I'd been working and came back to find Jake at the kitchen table, and he'd made me tea and massaged my shoulders, had she been there with him until minutes before I got home? The weekend he'd spent at St. Andrew's with Ed when I was pregnant, cheering poor Ed up he'd said, one last fling, one last swing, before Dan was born, had that been an alibi? Had Ed been an accomplice? Had he been off on some little holiday with *her,* tucked up with room service in a country house hotel off the M25? And then his behavior over the last year, withdrawn, self-contained, guilty almost, was that bitterness against me, unhappiness at what he'd given up? At Christmas, when we were all bundled together in our bed, sharing smiles of amusement as Fergus hurtled through his stocking, had he, all the time, been thinking of her? I often wondered what my mother had felt like when my father left her. Had she felt like this? As if someone had taken their life together, all the things they'd shared, and thrown a bucket of dirty water over it.

But some things still didn't add up. Why did she refer so dismissively to him the day we bumped into each other? Remember Jock, Jake, whatever he was called, dull Jake.

Dullsville, she'd said. Why would she say that? A smoke screen? To put me off him and prepare the way for herself?

And what was happening now? She wanted him back. That was obvious. Now Marcus had dumped her. But would he go? Whom would he choose? Claire Masterson, the glamorous girl about town, with her Disney contract and her faultless skin and her flat stomach and her keygels all in trim. Or me, plain, mousy Maggie who had none of those things? There was a murmur then from the room next door, a moan with a kick at the end of it, not a cry exactly, not quite a word. Fergus fighting dragons in his sleep. Maybe, I realized, I didn't even come into it. Maybe Jake's choice was between Claire Masterson and his children.

As I lay there, sleeplessness coiled in my stomach like hunger, I realized how impotent I was. Part of me wanted to hurl his clothes out of the window, bundle the children in blankets, and roar off down the street. That's what they did on the television, in the two-part Sunday/Monday ITV dramas Jake and I watched, used to watch, together. But when you have children, life isn't that simple any more. I knew that if I confronted him, I might drive him away. I might force him to make a decision, to do something he might otherwise turn away from.

. . .

I'd intended to take Fergus and Dan with me the following day to the Marsden for Mrs. Allardyce's lung X ray. But at the last minute, I rang Maria to see if I could borrow Merika for the morning. Maria didn't exactly sound thrilled—one of the rules concerning other people's au pairs is that you don't nab them in the day—but I said, darkly, that it was an emergency, and reluctantly she agreed.

It was 11:15 when I knocked at Mrs. Allardyce's door. I felt dazed with exhaustion, but I smiled chirpily when I saw her. She had the traces of talc on her tortoise cheek, pink lipstick across her lips and a turquoise silk scarf, with proper rolled edges, around her neck. She was also, in honor of the radiologist, wearing navy blue heels that squeezed the American Tan flesh on her feet into swollen semicircles.

"Come in, dear," she said. "I won't be a minute. I'm just out back feeding the neighbors' cats."

She left me in her front room, where a gas fire, clagged on to the hearth, was radiating a high heat. There were thick net curtains at the window and a swirly red and black carpet on the floor. On a wheeled table next to the chintz-covered sofa was the *TV Guide,* a magnifying glass, and a tiny plastic beaker, with pills at the bottom of it, and on the mantelpiece and on the sixties sideboard in the alcove, there were jumbled rows of birthday cards—white fluffy cats with cupid mouths, textured red roses with scarlet relief bows, announcing the bestest of wishes for the best gran/mom in the world. There were photographs there, too. I was bending to look at one of the smallest, black and white, of a young man in uniform, when Mrs. Allardyce came in behind me.

She said, "That was Arthur, just after we got married." She paused for a moment before gesturing to another, "And this is us on our silver wedding."

The picture was old, in faded blues and greens. It showed a plump middle-aged couple under a rose swag in a suburban garden. I asked her when it was taken and she said thirty-five years ago, in 1965, and while I was inwardly wondering how anyone's marriage could last that long, she told me that they'd lived in that house since 1950 and seen a lot of changes, but that life hadn't been the same since Arthur had passed on, cancer it was, that not a day went by that she didn't miss him, that he was a good man. I asked how long she'd been a widow and she said twenty-five years, which I said was a long time.

"Yes, dear." She seemed impatient suddenly with my sympathy. She was gripping the side of the wheeled table with one arthritic hand, leaning into it as if it was bearing all her weight. "But I've got my boys." She pointed to another photograph. "That's Philip. He's a teacher, but he's retired now and they live in Newcastle, near her parents. Those are his kids, all grown themselves. I've got four grandchildren, and six great-grandchildren. They're always saying I should come and visit but, well, it's too far for me now. And this is Nicholas. He went to work for Boeing."

I asked her where he lived and she said Seattle and I said that struck me as quite a long way.

She looked at me beadily. "They grow up, dear. You think it's going to go on forever, but it doesn't. They fly off and you hear from them at Christmas, and my boys always remember my birthday. And Flora, my granddaughter, she lives in Streatham and she pops in whenever she's passing . . . But I hope you'll make the most of it while you can, dear. I've seen you around, with your heart in your heels some of the time, and I know it's hard, but . . ."

"But it's not nearly as hard as it was for you," I finished for her.

"Well," she looked oddly satisfied. "Everything's different now."

We had to hurry a bit after that to switch off the fire and lock up the house and get her into the car and to the hospital on time. I parked on a meter and took her arm to guide her in her heels through the long cream-walled corridors and up the cranky lift to the right department. The nurse at the desk said there was a bit of a wait and that Mrs. Allardyce would have to see the doctor after the X ray and then hang around for the results to take back to her GP. It would be a couple of hours, she said. Mrs. Allardyce heaved herself down into a chair with a copy of January's *Good Housekeeping* on her knee and said she didn't mind if I went off for a bit. "You go and do some shopping, dear. I'm fine."

So at 12:30 p.m. I was on the steps outside the hospital. For a moment I wondered whether I *should* do some shopping. We were out of a few things. And there must be somewhere in South Kensington you could buy some soap powder and some ketchup . . . Although, on second thought, maybe there wasn't. But I'd made up my mind earlier. Jake's phone conversation with Claire played in my head. One-ish, he had said. Lunch. I didn't know exactly what, or how much, I expected to see, but if I witnessed them with my own eyes I'd be sure then. I would see where the land lay. I would have proof.

First I asked for change in an expensive jewelry shop to feed the meter, then I half walked, half ran to the Tube, where I waited "4 mins" for a train, though it felt like forty, wandered in a crush of people along endless Stygian corridors to change trains at Victoria, and then, face squashed into the back of someone else's jacket, endured two crowded stops to Oxford Circus. Only one escalator was working, so there was a line to get out. I was hot and sweaty when I finally reached the open air. I came up the steps, turned the corner and then—there was central London.

The sky was deep blue, though the street was in shadow. There were people everywhere, getting off and on the buses that idled at the lights or crossing between cars or selling hot dogs, or weaving purposefully through the crowd, with cups of coffee balanced in each hand or pausing in their lightweight anoraks to consult their maps, or wandering in pairs, amid concertina'ed shopping bags, in and out of shops. There seemed to be a businessman, with his arm out for a taxi, on every corner. No strollers. No three-wheel all-terrain mountain buggies. No babies in slings. No young mums in Boden. No sense of time lingering like you get in the suburbs, but time divided into holiday schedules, dotted with colored stickers, and production schedules, a world of work. Oh, of course I knew central London was *there,* but it still came as a shock.

.   .   .

Jake's office was in a side street between Oxford Street and Soho. It was a big glass-fronted building with rotating doors and leather retro armchairs, in bright colors and bulbous shapes, in reception. Appearances matter in advertising in a way they don't in other businesses. It's how you perceive the product, after all, not the product itself, that counts. Jake's building said, "cutting edge, out there, classic with a twist." There were other buildings adjacent saying other things, but I made for a small old-style café on the opposite side of the road, with sandwich fillings lined up like different types of vomit in the window and hot water gushing into stainless steel teapots from a network of metal pipes.

I sat at the Formica table closest to the door with a can of Coke as cover and waited. Over the next fifteen minutes, a lot of people drifted out of the TMT&T building in dribs and drabs, but there was no sign of Jake. I was beginning to think maybe he wasn't coming, that maybe, perhaps, he'd decided not to meet Claire after all, my stomach tightening in hope, when at ten past one, the doors swung open and there was a stocky dark man in chinos and a white shirt. There he was. There was Jake. He stood for a split second in the street

to shrug on his jacket, slipped on his sunglasses, and then he turned and began to walk briskly down the road toward Soho. I jumped up and was halfway out of the door when someone else came out of the building behind him and called him to stop. It was Ed. He was wearing a lilac shirt with a Nehru collar. I hid in the doorway, suddenly fascinated by the sandwich fillings, as Jake turned and waited for him to catch up. Then they both walked off together.

It isn't difficult following somebody if they're not expecting it. I stayed on that side of the road, twenty yards or so behind them, not even needing to dodge behind a parked car, until they reached a small restaurant on a nondescript street. I knew this restaurant. Jake and I had met there a few times before we had children, before I'd retired to the warm milk world of the suburbs, and I had loved it. It felt dark and Dickensian inside, with its faux cigarette-stained walls and the candles making fairy-tale palaces of wax out of the bottles on the tables. It was full of people you knew, but it still felt like a secret. Jake's and my secret. And now he'd gone there to meet Claire.

The two men were, for the moment, still standing outside. Maybe Jake was trying to get rid of Ed. They seemed to be talking with some heat—Ed was waving his arms about and Jake at one point rubbed his eyes slowly. Finally, hunching his shoulders up to his ears, Ed walked on up the road. Jake stood watching him for a bit and then went inside.

I stood across the street, wondering what to do. There was no café to hide in here. But there was a hat shop that I spent some time in, one eye on the mirror, one on the glass, pretending to be in need of something for a wedding. "Not my own," I jested with the bored young man with snaky hips who worked there. After a while, I ran out of hats and had to leave, promising to return with my Jill Sander suit. I don't own a Jill Sander suit.

I walked up and down the road a couple of times, bought a paper from the newsstand on the corner and hovered as inconspicuously as I could manage. I obviously wasn't that successful because after a bit I noticed the man from the hat shop eying me suspiciously. I gave a half-smile and made a big play of looking at my watch, clicking my fingers impatiently as if I was waiting for something or someone. I even walked directly in front of the restaurant, peering quickly past the menus in the window to see if I could spot them, but it was too dark and too busy. In the end I sat in a patch of sun on some office steps a few doors down and pretended to read the paper. After a while, the sky began to fill up with clouds like steam against a window and the sun went in.

I was about to go—there was only half an hour before I had to pick up Mrs. Allardyce—when the door of the restaurant opened and Jake came out. He was with Claire. She was wearing the same orange shift dress, carrying the same pink bag she'd carried on the day I first bumped into her on Morton High Street. She looked very blond, very fragile, next to Jake. I ducked into the doorway of the hat shop. I watched as he ran his hands through his hair, and then took both her hands in his. He talked earnestly looking into her eyes and then hugged her close.

I turned and ran to the end of the road where a taxi was just pulling away. I threw out my arm, yelled at it to stop, and then hurled myself into the back seat. My limbs felt numb. By the time we reached the Marsden it had begun to rain and the streets had emptied of people.

· · ·

That night, Jake rang to say he would be staying late again at the office and to warn me that he'd have to work all week-end. "Kyushi?" I said. He said yes, in a tired, tense tone. "Or sushi," I said, after I'd put down the phone.

I ranged around the house for a while, feeling lost and impotent. I sorted through the fridge and tossed three tins of half-eaten pickles and unopened jars of Gentleman's Relish, past their sell-by date, into the garbage. In the bedroom, I went through the pockets of Jake's clothes, smelling the col-lars and then chucking restaurant receipts and loose change onto the bed, sorting through them as if they'd bear up a secret. I threw the receipts in the wastepaper basket: there were enough of them to be deeply incriminating. But then Jake was in advertising, so they were nothing of the sort.

And then I did something I'd been putting off all day. I rang Mel.

"Maggie," she said. "I was just about to ring you. I'm off to Shrewsbury tomorrow to meet Piers's parents. I know, I know. Don't say anything. I don't know what I'm doing. You're right . . . blah blah. But I'm doing it. And also I meant to ask you . . . And at some point, I must collect Milly's Tinky-Winky. We had tears about that yesterday. Quite happy without it for days and then suddenly she noticed and it was as if the world had ended. Anyway I told her Fergus was looking after it, but I must get it sometime. And . . . Maggie, are you all right?"

I said, "Yes."

"You're not, are you?"

"No."

"Are you crying?"

It took me a while to say anything. Finally, I managed to say, "Yes."

"Maggie, what's the matter? Do you want me to come round? Milly's asleep but I can get a neighbor to sit."

I blew my nose and wiped my eyes. "No, don't," I said. "I'm fine. It's just . . ." I started crying again but while I was doing so I told her what had happened. She said, "I'm coming round. Give me ten minutes."

When she got there, I'd pulled myself together and we sat in the sitting room and I went through everything again. Mel kept shaking her head and saying she didn't believe it. She said Jake just wouldn't. I was very calm. I said it explained everything, that I knew it was true. She said I should talk to him. I said I thought it was important that I didn't, that all that mattered for now was keeping our marriage—huh, I corrected, with a self-pitying laugh, our *relationship*—going for the sake of the children. "And maybe for the sake of me, too."

She said, "But if it's true, how can you put up with it? And if it isn't, you need to find out."

I was silent for a long time and then I said, "I just don't want to lose him." She put her arms round me and said should she cancel her week away? "No, of course, not," I said. "But you're meeting the parents?" Even under the circumstances, I started laughing at this.

She laughed back. She said, "I know, I know. I'm up to my neck here. It's just he's so . . . nice." She stroked my hair with her voice. "I'm so sorry," she kept saying. "Maggie, I really am. I'm so so sorry."

I was pretending to be asleep when Jake came home, and I was pretending to be asleep when he went off again on Saturday morning. He left me a note. It said, "Maggie. XXX." Either he was kissing me or crossing me out.

Chapter 14

When you're a grown-up, or at least when you're a grown-up who has recently discovered the father of your children in the arms of another woman, there are few things as unimportant as a child's birthday party. When you are two and a half, on the other hand, there are few things that matter more. A week later, after a hot, sticky picnic on the common, I was pushing the stroller past Monkey Business, my mind full of single parenthood, when I remembered. There, on display in the window of the toy shop, was a Barbie hair salon, complete with vanity unit and working hair dryer.

"FUCK," I said.

"What?" said Fergus.

It was a week since I'd found out, a week in which our life had shrunk down to essentials. I had steered past the playground, seen and spoken to no one. I could just about get through pretending everything was unchanged, if I avoided social contact. I had hardly even seen Jake—which made things easier in one way, but also more difficult. He had been at the office (or with her), and when he had touched down at home, I had managed to behave as normally as I could. But I wasn't normal. I was close to losing it.

"We've forgotten Cecily Alberge's birthday party," I said. The invitation was on the mantelpiece. I could just about visualize "3–5 p.m." under a pink cavalcade of dancing dolls. It was just past 3 p.m. now. It was the last thing I felt like doing, face all those smug women. Fergus was looking at me, his features pinched with anxiety and suspended excitement.

"But if we race it," I said.

We raced it. I nipped into the shop. Bought a Barbie hair salon—nothing like emergency for engendering generosity— wheedled a gift wrap, and ran, bent-double with the effort, straight across the common, past the pond, past the tennis courts, past the bowling green, past the flats, over the main road, down some side streets, to the Alberges' double-fronted Victorian residence.

It was twenty past three when we got there.

"Oh, you're early," simpered Lucinda at the door, looking down at me in my dismal T-shirt with its sweat rings under the arms. She was the definition of cool in shades of gray. Her silky trousers skimmed the heels of her camel sling-backs. Her luscious dark hair was tamed back behind her head, only the crinkles at the side to indicate its natural curliness—she was wearing her office chignon, I noticed, a children's party obviously being as close to real work as "home life" gets. My hair was a mess. I wasn't wearing make-up. I was wearing shorts. And flip-flops. My bra itched damply. I'd cried a bit earlier and I was sure there were dirt streaks down my face. "Never mind," she smiled, "everyone else will be here in ten minutes."

Cecily came to the door, in a froufrou party dress with smocking on the front. Her white socks had frills on the top of them like teenage tennis players'. "Is that my present?" she said. "Where's your Barbie?"

Fergus, who had strings of grape juice trailing from his faded blue T-shirt, across his shorts, which were a bit too big about the waist and hung, builder-like, across his hips, to his dusty sneakers, held on to the present tightly and said sweetly, "I hate Barbies. So does Mummy. And no, it's mine. Where's the party?"

"Sweetheart!" said Lucinda. "Come . . . in."

We trooped in. I realized to my horror that Dan's diaper needed changing. Lucinda, whose nostrils, permanently flared, had clearly already noticed the smell and was looking pointedly at Fergus's shoes.

"I'd better just use the bathroom . . ." I said.

I fled upstairs, where I tried to pinion Dan to the fluffy white bath mat while I struggled with his snaps. He was wailing and banging his head against the marble floor. I got the diaper off, but not before I'd got poop on his clothes and poop on the bath mat and poop on his feet and poop on my hands. I'd torn off and wet some toilet paper but it wasn't enough. I tried to grab some more paper with one hand, while keeping him still with the other. He wriggled and twisted, nodules of white tissue clinging to his bottom. I wrested the new diaper on, snapped him up wrongly, and released him while I set about mopping up the floor. All the towels were white. I had to make do with tissue. I dabbed frantically while trying to keep Dan from pulling the Floris soap off the shelf by the bath.

"Maggie? Are you all right?" Lucinda was outside the door. "Fergus wants you. Can you let him in?"

"Yes, yes," I said in a panic, turning the bath mat upside down.

I opened the door and there was Fergus with wet shorts. "Why didn't you tell someone you needed the loo?" I said, despairing.

"I don't know," he said in a small voice.

I gave him a cuddle. It was too late to do anything else, and the three of us trooped back downstairs.

The bad news was now we had pee and poop to add to our sweat and grape juice. The good news was at least the party was in medium swing.

"Hi!" said a friendly voice. It was Rachel with a plate of smoked salmon sandwiches in her hand. "I haven't seen you all week. You look as if you've been in the wars!"

"No wipes!" I hissed.

"I've got a spare packet in the back of the stroller you can have, pink packet for faces, green for bums," she said over her shoulder as she proffered her plate to a passing mother. "Salmon anyone? It's finest Scottish: Loch Fyne."

"Too late," I said.

Fergus ran off to join a group of party-frocked girls, who were playing messily with Lucinda's twins, Ned and Sid, in a plastic sandbox on the patio. Lucinda seemed to be busy altercating with Mr. Twistletoes, a sinister fellow with a beard, about rearranging the furniture in the sitting room. With Dan on one hip, I followed Rachel's raised plate into the kitchen where bottles of champagne and platters of food— sausage rolls and slices of cake and more sandwiches, corporate entertaining on an intimate scale—were laid out on the side (for the adults, it seemed, the children's tea was in individual Barbie boxes on tiny trestle tables outside), and Lucinda's husband, Gregory, was laid out on the sofa. He was wearing a suit, but his eyes were closed.

"Dead?" I asked Rachel.

"Ssssh," she said. "I think the pressure has got to him. Hello, Jill." She kissed an arriving mother. "Pâté? It's wild boar."

Gregory came to as if on cue. "Party. Gosh. Cost a fortune," he said to no one in particular. I was closest so I felt I had to respond.

"I know, awful," I said. "It really adds up."

"Ten pounds a head," he said, searching under the sofa for his champagne flute. "Twenty kids. £200. Plus £180 for the entertainer. Little darling, though, Cecily. Worth it. Wants a pink tent next year. Said we'll have to see. Anyway, better mingle."

He swayed off into the garden. I took Dan into the playroom where Cecily was fighting over the Brio with two small boys. A couple of women were leaning against the video shelf, deep in conversation. They stopped when I entered, paused while they registered the state of my clothes, and continued. I sat on the floor and built Dan a tower of bricks.

"I'm so thrilled he's got into Bolton Prep," the one with gold-strapped loafers was saying. "It's so much nicer than Howarth Hall. Of course I was disappointed that he failed his interview at Howarth—we've been training him to write his name for weeks. Apparently it was just the fridge question that did it. He said, 'for keeping food in,' which is right on the button, but the answer they wanted was 'for keeping food cold.' Well, I mean honestly. He's only three. And a May birthday. He's competing with Octobers and Januarys. It's hardly surprising."

"Hm, hm," said the other woman, tucking a stray bit of hair back into a baseball cap with a Chanel logo on the front.

"And we just really, really liked the atmosphere at Bolton," continued Gold Buckles. "Lovely children. Lovely garden. And I do think it's fairer that they screen the parents and not the children. The headmistress couldn't have been nicer at our interview. And the other parents seem so jolly. My husband John said the meet-and-greet was just like a city cocktail party. And I do like the fact that they curtsy in the morning. Or do the boys bow? I haven't worked that out. But it just gives them a grounding in good manners. Mind you we've still got to worry about what we do when he's seven. Maybe boarding . . . for the sport . . . John hated it himself but thinks it would do Gulliver a world of good . . . And boys do need so much . . . *entertaining*. Anyway, we'll see. What about you? Where's Dylan going?"

"He got in to Howarth Hall actually."

"When's his birthday?" said Gold Buckles quickly.

"March."

"Ah."

I said, to help out as much as anything, "Are all the private schools not much of a muchness?" To which I got a withering look from both mothers. I fiddled with a Playmobil hospital set while the conversation continued above my head. Chanel Baseball Cap had launched into builders.

"They say they'll be out of the house before Christmas," she was saying. "But I don't believe a word they say. I wish we'd got an architect now. But this builder seemed to know what he was talking about. He's done the basements up and down the street."

"Oh," said Gold Buckles, tapping her foot in excited sympathy, "if only you could have had our architects. Everyone who has seen it says our kitchen is quite breathtaking."

Maybe after we separated, I'd move.

Luckily, games were starting up in the garden, so I gathered Dan and, passing Lucinda still in conference with Twistletoes ("I'm sorry. I am not going to move the baby grand"), went to find Fergus.

Blind Man's Bluff had just trailed off when I got there, and a game of Musical Chairs had just begun. Gwendolin, Lucinda's eldest, was operating the tape recorder with an officiousness only a seven-year-old can muster, while a smart elderly couple whom I took—from the height of the man and the thickness of the woman's hair—to be Lucinda's parents, looked on. Harry, the first to lose his seat, refused to leave the game when the music restarted. Cecily, who was sitting under him at this stage, began to kick her legs and scream. Some of the other children, meanwhile, had begun lying on the ground, pretending to be crocodiles. "Come on children, back into a circle. Stop biting, Matilda. Maud, stand up. Charlie, leave her. Stop it. Come on. You—little boy, the little boy in shorts, what are you doing?" Lucinda's mother appeared to be addressing Fergus. I turned away slightly. Perhaps she wouldn't know he was mine.

But then Gwendolin chipped in, giving the game away, "Fergus Priton. We're not being lions now. Leave Matilda alone." I felt a tide of panic in my throat. I could see Maria chatting with Gregory through the kitchen window. I could hear the dogs barking manically, locked up somewhere in the house. Mr. Twistletoes was standing in the doorway, idly folding a long, thin balloon into the shape of a dachshund. Rachel was at my elbow, circling like a bottle top with a tray of food.

Her voice came in and out. "Wild boar, Loch Fyne, more tea." I knew I should move forward to investigate Fergus, but my knees felt weak. The Wheels on the Bus was starting up. Musical Chairs had been abandoned for Simon Says. Lucinda's father was holding Fergus's hand. Children. Husbands. Grandparents. Family life. All this. What was Jake doing now? Was he with her?

"Excuse me," I said, and I turned my back on the party

and made for the bottom of the garden, for the bit around the corner, behind the climbing frame and the shrubbery, where I could have a quick cry in peace.

And there was Pete.

He looked up.

I laughed, partly to disguise my embarrassment, partly to force the tears away. "We must stop meeting like this."

He squinted against the sun. "Hello," he said. "Lucinda said to keep out of the way, but I thought you might be here. I was going to sneak over and have a look."

"My life," I said. "It's just one long party."

We looked at each other. In the silence between us, you could hear Mr. Twistletoes calling the children into the house for the puppet show. When we spoke, we spoke together. I said, "Did you get my note?" and he said, "You've got something in your hair."

I laughed. I said, "I'm a wreck. I thought we were late, which we weren't in the end, so I ran all the way. I probably stink to high heaven."

He straightened up. He said, "I don't think you do. I've got good nostrils and I can't smell anything myself." He leaned forward and pulled a twig from my hair. "But you look better without this."

I half-brushed, half-mussed my hair with my fingers as if to remove the print of his hand. I said, "I'd look better without a lot of things."

He laughed undecidedly, then wrinkled his nose. "I did get your note. Are you sure you don't want me to come anymore? It seems a shame when I've only just got started."

I shifted my weight onto a different foot, which meant I moved away from him a fraction. "Look—"

"If it's a question of money?"

"It's not that." There was a movement, a flash of red, on the other side of the azalea.

Pete said, "Have you met Lloyd? My boss?"

I turned quickly. "No. But it's fine. I'd better get back to my baby."

I started moving off, when Pete put his hand on my arm to stop me. "You okay?" he said.

"Yes. Of course. Just stuff at home."

"There always seems to be stuff at home for you."

I tried to say something, but just a sound came out, like a stifled cry. Pete had his head on one side. "Well, at least let me give you a lift home. If you're under the weather."

For a moment, I thought I was going to cry. I didn't answer. He said, "I can wait for you around the corner if you don't want to be seen hanging out with the staff. It's not a problem."

I said, still with a pain at the back of my throat, "Um . . ."

He winked. "Go on. Live dangerously."

I didn't hesitate then. "All right."

I returned to the party and stood with Dan at the back of Mr. Twistletoes, watching giant magic wands crumble. Then it was time for tea and I helped Fergus to the table to open his Barbie box, and then I helped pass round the Barbie cake and clear all the uneaten sandwiches and uneaten carrot sticks and empty chocolate wrappers and empty juice boxes into the garbage. And then I took my two grubby children to say goodbye nicely and collect their party bags (one model airplane, one bubble mixture, one packet of M&Ms, one pencil sharpener in the shape of a baboon: times twenty, about the value of the gross national product), and we left the house.

Maria was on the doorstep, talking to a woman I didn't recognize. She said, "Oh, Maggie, is everything okay?"

"Yes," I said quickly.

"I mean last week." She gave me a curious look. "The emergency—Merika coming over."

"Oh that," I said, hurrying by. "Yes, thanks. Oh, it's fine. It was nothing in the end."

Pete's van was tucked out of sight around the corner behind Lucinda's Mitsubishi Shogun. He was standing next to it, waiting. The van still had a battered front bumper and missing headlight. "Oops," I said.

"Ye-es," he replied pointedly. He took the stroller from me and put it in the back. I clambered after Fergus, with Dan in my arms, into the front seat.

It didn't take long to round the common to our house. Fergus, strapped in between us, chattered about the gasoline gauge and windshield wipers the whole way. Pete and I didn't say anything much. But when we got there, as I undid Fergus's belt, Pete said, casually, "Maybe I could pop round in the next couple of days?"

"Er," I said. I looked up at him.

"Just to check you're okay."

"Oh."

"I don't like to see a young lady so down."

I smiled. To gain some time, I wiped the dust off the clockface on the dashboard in front of me. "All right then," I said finally.

"Really?"

"Yes." I brushed my finger and thumb together. "That would be nice. Come for a cup of tea or something."

"How's tomorrow?"

"Tomorrow's the weekend."

"Well, Monday then." He grinned. "Before you change your mind."

Maybe it was the cheerfulness of his expression, or the carefree cockiness of his tone, or maybe it was just the inkling of sympathy, of concern, but I couldn't help myself. I leaned across and kissed him quickly on the lips. Then I pulled away. "Okay," I said.

Chapter 15

On Monday, I was up at dawn, to have a shower, shave my legs and armpits, wash and blow-dry my hair before the children woke. "What's up with you?" said Jake when he stumbled down to breakfast. "Nits again?"

"No," I said. "Not nits. Not this time. I just couldn't get back to sleep. Look," I waved something in front of his eyes as a distraction. "I've found your PG Tips scrapbook. It was under the toy cupboard. Fergus must have . . ."

"Thank God," said Jake, putting down his coffee cup. "I'd looked everywhere for it. I was wondering where I might have left it."

"What were the options?" I said. He didn't pick up on it. He was slotting his dirty cereal bowl into the dishwasher. There wasn't much room because it was still full of clean things. He didn't notice. He said, snapping it shut. "I'll be late again tonight. If I even make it home. I'm going to have to go to Amsterdam again this week. We've got to present our pitch to the Central European Office. And on top of that I've got to find time for the Zap-it brief."

"It's amazing what you can find time for when you try," I said. He didn't pick up on that either.

It was now eleven days since I had seen Jake with Claire. Sunday was the first day he was at home for any time during that period. It was surprising how normal things had seemed. There was no confrontation. There was tension but it made itself felt in such small things, such tiny absences—a missing kiss here, a door closed with no good-bye—that an untutored observer would have noticed nothing wrong.

After Jake left for work on Monday, I took Dan and Fergus to my mother's. "Long time no see," she said when I dropped them off. I'd rung her to say I was going to the dentist. "Can you make sure you're back by one? I've got aqua aerobics this afternoon," she said. "And it's absolute murder in the changing rooms if I'm late."

It wasn't that I was excited at the prospect of Pete's social visit. I was too emotionally exhausted for that. It was more that I felt I wanted to meet him looking my best, not tearful and sweaty but together and relaxed. I wanted to look a person who would recognize a Cambodian hand-woven ikat-dyed shot silk sarong, even if she didn't own one. If only for an hour, not to be the woman whose husband was having an affair, but someone a man might flirt with. So when I got back from dropping off the kids, I put on my best accidental-chic linen trousers and a cotton camisole with my bra strap showing. I took a long time over shoes. In the absense of some duck-egg blue thong sandals, I painted my toenails and went barefoot. I sat in the kitchen and waited. I made myself some coffee, got the papers, and spread them around me. I flicked through them and got them tangled. Spilled the coffee. Mopped it up and made some more. Drank it. Remembered I hadn't brushed my teeth, ran upstairs. Dropped some toothpaste on my top. Attempted to lick it off. Finally, took it off and tried to hold just the toothpastey bit under the tap. Stain spread, got the whole lot wet. Panicked again. Up to the bedroom to find another vest, couldn't find one. Tried to dry the first one under the hair dryer. Put it back on damp.

I went back downstairs and opened the garden door. It was a bit chilly, what with me wearing only a vest and everything, so I closed it again. I sat at the kitchen table. It was 9:30 a.m. This was ridiculous. What was wrong with me? I went through to the sitting room and looked out into the street and saw Mrs. Allardyce walking past. I banged on the window to get her attention and went to the door. "So?" I said. "Have you had the results yet?"

"Oh dear . . ." she began. "I haven't. I rang the hospital and they said to ring the GP so I rang him and he said he hadn't heard from them yet and I could ring them if I liked so I tried again, but this time I couldn't get through . . ."

It was then, of course, behind her, coming down the street toward me, that I saw Pete. He was wearing clean jeans and a button-down shirt, and proper lace-up shoes. He stopped when he saw me talking to Mrs. Allardyce, but then carried on coming. "And who's this lovely lady?" he said as he got to us.

"Mrs. Allardyce," I said. "This is Pete Russ. He's a gardener."

Mrs. Allardyce looked flustered and patted her hair. "Marjorie," she said. He took her hand and kissed it. "Delighted to make your acquaintance," he said, like something out of Jane Austen (except with an Australian accent).

When we'd said good-bye to Mrs. Allardyce, gotten into the house and closed the door, I felt suddenly embarrassed and flustered. I said, "You and the ladies, you don't let a chance go by, do you?"

"Aw. She's a sweetie," he said, leaning up against the hall radiator. "She liked it."

I stood there, barring his entrance into the kitchen. "But you are, aren't you? You're a charmer, a womanizer. You're shameless."

"No, I'm not," he said. "I just like women, that's all. I understand them."

"Well, that's good," I said briskly, turning to go into the kitchen. "I'm glad someone does. God forbid." I was talking in short, sergeant-major sentences, trying to make a joke out of it. "Because it would be awful to think we were going un-understood. Or that anyone could mistake you for anything you're not. Of course you're not a womanizer, you're a woman-*liker*. Altogether different."

I had my back to him, filling the kettle with water, but I could tell he had come in and was standing in the doorway. He was silent. Then he said, in a very different sort of voice, "Hey. If you don't want me here, just tell me to go."

I turned round to face him. "I don't want you to go," I said, still holding the kettle. I looked at him hard for a bit, then I smiled.

He smiled too. He put the bag he was carrying down on the floor. He said, "Well at least you got dressed this time, but I can still see your bra."

"That's a style issue," I said, from under my eyelashes. "It's supposed to be part of the effect."

He leaned against the door frame. "Where are the kids?"

"At my mother's."

"Where's your husband?"

"At work. Though, um. . . . we're not actually married."

"Where are your shoes?"

I smiled again. The tension broke a bit. Neither of us had

moved for a while. He said, "How are you feeling? Are things any better with . . . it's Jake, isn't it?"

"Up and down. Mainly down. But . . ." I turned to plug the kettle in, "but that's all boring. My life is boring. I'm sure your life is much more interesting." I took some cups from the shelf. "Is it? I don't know anything about you really."

When I turned back, he was still looking at me with an odd expression. And he said, "What do you need to know?" And he came close to me then and he slipped his hand under my bra strap, which had fallen over my shoulder, and fitted it back under the strap of my camisole. And then, with his other hand, he slowly and deliberately pulled the strap on the other side down. There was a dot of foam in his ears as if he'd just shaved. He smelt of aftershave and breath mints.

I said, drawing a little bit back, "Watch out. I'm a married woman."

"Except," he said, "You keep saying you're not."

And then, his ginger-flecked eyes still looking into mine, very softly, he ran the tip of his finger from my nose, over my mouth and down to the hollow under my neck, circled it there for a moment and then gently trailed it into the crack between my breasts. I was leaning against the kitchen counter and gripping it behind my back with both hands. I wasn't breathing. I didn't move. I was thinking about pulling away, but I couldn't. He left his finger where it was for a moment, coarse against my skin. And then, he coaxed it under the fabric and ran it over my nipple. I leaned toward him finally, lifting my face. And then, with one hand in my bra and the other firm against my lower back, he pulled me to him and brought his mouth down to mine. And then I closed my eyes and kissed him back, and in the course of that kiss he had pushed me up onto the work surface, brushing against the kettle, knocking over a jar of coffee that clattered into the sink, and he had pulled my top over my head and unhooked my bra and then his tongue was on my nipples, and his hands, which were rough and sandpapery, were around my waist and his fingers were down under my linen trousers, pushing against my skin until he'd got the trousers over my hips and down to my ankles, and he moved out of the way for a second, until I had kicked them off and I was naked next to him still in all his clothes. I pulled him back to me, tugging his shirt, but he clamped my hands in his to delay me, holding them back against the kitchen counter as he pressed forward, pushing himself against me, my legs around his waist. I could hear him breathing now, short, deep breaths that were almost gasps, getting louder. There was another sound too: a rising roar that I recognized in the further reaches of my mind was the kettle. Pete's mouth was buried in my neck, and I reached down, forcing his jeans with his boxers over his buttocks. His breaths were coming faster, and deeper, and louder. There was steam rising all around us. He had his hands down below, fumbling. I was seconds from infidelity. "Christ," Pete said under his breath. "Christ. Christ. Shit."

The kettle clicked off. Pete stopped what he was doing. "What?" I said.

"Fuck," he said.

His hands rested slackly on my waist. He sagged his head and moved his body away a fraction. "Shit," he said again. He ran his hands through his hair. He didn't look at me. He pulled up his jeans. "Shit."

I realized that I was completely naked in my kitchen with a fully dressed man who had already come. "Oh dear," I said.

Pete looked sulky, like a spoiled boy unexpectedly told off. He leaned back against the counter next to me. He said, his eyes on the floor, "That wasn't supposed to happen."

I bent my head down to try and meet his eye. "It doesn't matter," I said. "Honestly, it doesn't." The clock above his head said 10:08 a.m.

"Yeah, but . . ."

"Never mind," I said. "It's not the end of the world."

"It's just . . ." he said, his eyes meeting mine for the first time. "Let's have some coffee," I said. "After all, the kettle's boiled . . ."

I disentangled my camisole from the mixer where it had landed earlier, put my underwear back on with as much insouciance as I could muster, and set about scooping the drier grains of coffee out of the sink. Pete sat at the table, kicking a piece of fluff around with his foot, looking embarrassed. I put a cup down in front of him, and then I cut him a slice of the coffee cake I'd made with Fergus the day before and said, "Nothing like manual work for building up an appetite," to let him know he'd done *something*.

He perked up a bit once he'd tasted it. He said, "It's good," then smiling tentatively, holding it up to study it more closely, beginning to feel up to a little ribbing, "but is it supposed to look like this?"

"It sank in the middle," I said. "I opened the oven door too soon. But it's the taste that counts. Do you want some cream with it?"

"Well . . ."

"Go on," I said. "It's not every day you seduce a housewife." I went to the fridge and found a tub of extra-thick and scooped a large dollop into the sunken section of his slice.

"Cream," I said, licking the spoon and sitting down opposite him. "You can't beat it. Or rather you can, although these days it's so thick you don't need to." I reached across the table and helped myself to a bit more from his plate.

"Hey," he said, putting his hand out to stop me. He said, "Give that spoon here," and I told him I wouldn't and he reached across to try and grab it and instead I grasped his wrist and, stretching over him, got some more cream and cake but this time he got my hand with the spoon in it and somehow in the ensuing fracas the cream got splattered and the cake got smeared, and we were fighting and kissing and licking and sliding to the floor and this time his clothes came off too and this time nobody opened the oven door too soon.

Afterward, we lay side by side in silence, getting our breath back. The tiles felt cold behind my back. I could feel the ridges digging into my vertebrae. Pete had his eyes closed. I moved onto my side so I could see the air widening and narrowing his nostrils, the golden stubble across his Adam's apple. There were tight coils of blond hair on his chest, a line of fuzz leading from his tummy button down to his groin. The muscles on his torso were ridged like a piece of armour or the marks the tide leaves on the sand. You saw stomachs like that in advertisements for perfume, and now there was one on my kitchen floor.

"You're so muscley," I said. "I suppose that's working outdoors."

He sighed and opened his eyes, making a "mmm" sort of noise that seemed to express self-satisfaction as much as satisfaction. "Yeah," he said, stretching. "Sorry about earlier."

"It didn't matter in the long run," I said, thinking, What have I done? What am I doing? Not with any crashing sense of shame, but almost wonderingly. There would naturally now be disagreeable things to think about but they were far away, like a phone ringing in the house next door. At this minute, I just felt amazed by what had happened. I began to see how easy adultery could be if you surrendered yourself to the moment. Was that how it was for Jake and Claire? Was that how they managed it? Or had they moved beyond that into something more permanent? Pete put his hand out and, twisting round, tangled his fingers in my hair. Leaning on his elbow, he kissed me on the forehead and the chin and the nose, and then he pulled his head back to study the expression on my face. He said, "You are one very desirable lady."

I emitted a sort of horrified laugh.

"What's the matter?" he said.

"Nothing," I said. "Nothing at all."

After he'd gone, I stood in the bath and ran the shower over myself. Then I put on some old jeans and an old shirt and threw my underwear in the basket. And then I went downstairs again and scrubbed the kitchen floor. Not to wash away all signs of what had happened, but because I'd noticed some dried-on yogurt under the table while I was down there and some desiccated peas. Clean house, as they say, clean mind.

· · ·

Loose woman, light woman, light o' love, wanton, hot stuff, woman of easy virtue, demi-rep, one no better than she should be, flirt, piece, wench, jade, hussy, minx, nymphet, baggage, trollop, trull, drab, slut, mantrap, adventuress, temptress, seductress, scarlet woman, Jezebel, adulteress, nymphomaniac, Messalina.

You can look up the words in the thesaurus, but none of them sounded like me. It was astounding to me how completely the same I felt. This thing that should have been monumental, that should have rocked the foundations of my comfortable Victorian terrace with the force of a buzz bomb, leaving me crouched under the kitchen table, turned out to have no more effect than a standard rocket landing on the roof.

I suppose I felt cheered up—even gently thrilled by the memory of it. Most of all, I felt amused. I wanted to run around the house laughing at what I, Maggie Owen, stretch-marked mother of two, had just done. It was so incongruous, so out of character, so *funny*. And so gloriously clichéd. I'd had sex with the gardener. It wasn't quite a gamekeeper, but still: how Lady Chatterley was that?

I found I could justify it fairly easily too. In light of what Jake had done. In light of what Jake was doing. I was simply redressing the balance. And if it made me feel better about myself, which up to a point I thought it did, then wasn't it time something, or somebody, did that?

These moments of rational clear-sightedness would be offset periodically by waves of withering guilt and dizzying anxiety.

I wasn't late picking up the children from my mother's. I was there at 12:30 p.m. and would have been gone by 12:35 p.m. if there hadn't been a new Kichen Aid to inspect and a long saga to listen to about the new people next door ("they'd invited us for drinks at 7:00 p.m., well that was no good so I said, 'would 7:30 p.m. do?'") which turned out, in the end, not to be about the new people next door at all but about the manners of delivery people ("so by 9:00 when the take-out hadn't come, we began to think about phoning"). But I wasn't listening anyway. I was hugging my secret to me, holding it in my mind, self-contained and separate.

"Anyway," said my mother, "people are rude, aren't they? All we were asking for was a little contrition. An apology never hurt anyone."

That day, I didn't think about the future. I didn't know, or even care, if I would ever see Pete again. Of course it was a one-off. A weird but rather fabulous single occurrence. I was a woman of thirty-five, at her sexual peak. What a shame to let that go to waste—as it had been, night after night, over the last few months. And it didn't mean the end of Jake and me. Just as Claire and Jake didn't mean the end of us either. Don't they say that a little infidelity can jump-start a stale marriage? Aren't there statistics: in forty percent of all marriages someone has slept with someone else? Maybe this would sort things out between us once and for all. Not that Jake and I were even married. Does adultery exist under those conditions? Could he be said to have committed adultery? Could I?

I was a lovely daughter. I raved about the Kitchen Aid. Exulted over the new cushion covers. Drew tears of admiration for the new all-in-one TV remote control. And, for the rest of the afternoon, I was a wonderful mother too. I took Dan and Fergus to the park and played the sort of energetic games with Fergus normally reserved for weekend dads. He laughed and squealed and threw his arms around my knees in delighted exhaustion. Dan crawled around under the trees and I let him play with the Budweiser cans to his heart's content.

When we got home, there was a message from Mel on the answering machine. She was back from Shrewsbury. Was I Okay? Could she come around? I felt the guilt again. How do you tell a friend who, only days before, has been the concerned recipient of your anguish, who has listened to you sob at your partner's betrayal, that actually . . . things have moved on a bit since then? You don't, do you? Not when she sounds so kind and worried about you. So I didn't ring back. Instead, Fergus and I made fairy cakes. With icing. And those little silver balls on top that are supposed to look like metal and taste like sugar—only, of course, they don't: they taste like metal too.

. . .

Smokers who are trying to give up say it is not the first errant cigarette that represents the downhill slope, but the second. It is hard to say, after my one lapse with Pete, whether full-blown infidelity in the form of An Affair was already inevitable, or whether it was the second encounter that led to this. I got through Tuesday and Wednesday, pretending everything was normal. I spent the days looking after my children and my evenings as distant with Jake as two people could be while still sharing a bed and a joint bank account. I even spoke to his mother at length about what I thought he'd like for his birthday (it was getting close; well, there were still three months, but when there's knitting involved . . .). I also rang Mel when I knew she'd still be at the clinic and left a message saying that everything was fine this end, that I'd speak to her soon.

But then it got to Thursday. On Thursday, several events conspired against me, or maybe *for* me, I didn't know. In the morning, Jake left for another "big meeting" in Amsterdam. All his meetings were now big; they were never small or medium-sized these days. This one was so big it was going to last four days. He didn't kiss me as he left. He kissed Fergus and Dan and he said "bye" to us all in a general kind of way, blowing a vague kiss in my direction at the door. Naturally, I found this suspicious: I didn't doubt the existence of this meeting, this big meeting, but I did wonder whether he was flying alone. After he left, I felt empty.

And then in the middle of the morning, Rachel brought Harry around and Maria dropped in with her two on the way to the bank and I served coffee and biscuits and juice and listened to tales of Maria's Club Med holiday in Turkey (drunk every night, etc.) and talked about the rumors that a mobile phone company wanted to erect a cancer-inducing aerial on the church roof and wondered, along with the others, what that would do to the *feel* of the area. And I tried very hard to quell the waves of claustrophobia that had started breaking over me.

And the final straw was the Percy yogurt. It was lunchtime. Dan was smearing mashed up tuna fishcakes ("Have you checked the salt content?" said Rachel in my head) into his highchair. Fergus was fretting over his dessert. I said, "There's *Toy Story* chocolate mousses or yogurts."

"What yogurts?" Fergus said.

I went to the fridge. I said, "Thomas the Tank Engine, though there's only one left of those, Bob the Builder, or Pokémon fromage frais."

He said, "Bob the Builder."

"Please," I said.

"Please," he said.

I brought Bob the Builder to the table, and peeled the lid off.

"Noooooooooo," panicked Fergus. "I want the lid ON."

I tried quickly to stick it back, using the yogurt around the edge as glue. It just about stuck. Fergus took it and eyed it suspiciously. He was momentarily thrown. I thought I'd won. Then inspiration struck: "I said I wanted Thomas. I don't want Bob." He threw his spoon on the floor. His face crumpled.

It's quite clear in the manuals that at moments like this you should not give in. If you give in, a cycle of bad behavior is established. You do not want the lunatics taking over the asylum. You are the boss. It is important to stand firm.

What the manuals never say is, anything for an easy life. I went to the fridge and found one last remaining steam-engine flavored kids dessert. I brought it back to him, my emperor in his booster chair.

"That's not Thomas. That's Gordon," he yelled, his voice rising.

I snapped. "No it's not. It's Percy." And I took it off him and threw it in the sink where its sides dented and splattered against the aluminum.

Fergus started crying, and because he was crying Dan started crying, and I would have cried too if I hadn't been so busy comforting them. And my life suddenly seemed so small and so hopeless and a solution, temporary, but did it matter? seemed so quickly and easily come by, that I couldn't help myself. I rang Pete.

· · ·

He came straight around that afternoon. Fergus and I were playing sea monsters in the garden when he knocked. "As I was passing," he said at the door.

"Well, if you're passing . . ." I laughed back.

I said, "You can come in, but we're playing sea monsters."

He said "Er-aghhhh," which made Fergus, who had wandered up behind me, scream and run back into the garden.

Pete came out with me and I said, "You probably can't stay. It's probably not a good time." But I could feel my mouth stretching into a smile.

He said, "I left my shears. I've only come to pick them up."

"When?" I said.

"Monday," he said. "Must have been Monday."

"And you've done without them ever since?"

"I've got a spare," he said, looking into my face and laughing.

"Er-aghhhh," he said again to Fergus who had come up behind him with a stick. He turned and chased him. Fergus squealed in delight. They fell on the ground and Pete pin-ioned Fergus between his feet and held him high, horizontal, in the air.

"Again, again!" my son shouted.

I felt uncomfortable. It seemed important to keep the chil-dren away from Pete, to keep them pure and untainted even if I wasn't. I said, "Stop now, Fergus, you're overexcited. Come here and find some worms." Pete made a face at him, which made him giggle some more. "Come on," I said. "Calm down." I didn't want him charming my children too. This was nothing to do with them.

"Where do you think you left your shears?" I said to Pete.

He gave me a hot look. "In one of the beds?"

"Well, let's search for them then," I said, looking back. "Fergus, Pete the Gardener has lost his shears in the flower beds. Are you going to help us find them?"

"What's shears?"

"Like big scissors. So get looking."

Dan was having his nap upstairs. Fergus was head down in the bushes. Pete said, "They might be in the shed. Come see." And he pulled me by the arm, with him, to the back of the garden. The door, which was half off its hinges, was kept shut with a big stone. He kicked it out of the way with his foot and pushed me into the shed in front of him. I grabbed him, roughly, after me, and he pushed me back against an old chest of drawers. We kissed hungrily, almost violently. There were old cobwebs in our hair, dead spiders down our neck. I pulled him around so I was pressing into him. We were pulling each other down, dented cans of antifreeze were toppling over on the wobbly shelf above us, there was some clattering as a box of radiator caps tumbled over. A rake slid to one side, scatter-ing rust. Pete was tugging at my clothes. I had my hands in his thick hair, yanking it, my nails in his scalp.

"We've got to stop," I said, not stopping.

"Quickly," he said. "No. Quickly, come on."

It was then I caught a glimpse of Fergus through the dusty window, through the cobwebs, past the tendrils of bindweed that had forced their way under the glass. He was pottering happily across the lawn. He had a stick in one hand and in the other . . . the kitchen scissors. Open. Facing up. I said, "No, no, stop." And I pulled away, disentangled myself and ran out into the light, toward my son.

Pete came out, after a short while, looking amused. He said, "Is that it then?"

I looked at him carefully. "No," I said, sealing my fate. "It's not."

Later that day, Mel dropped around between appointments. "A house call!" I said with unnatural brightness. "How nice!" She frowned. She was worried about me. She wanted to know if I was really all right. I almost told her how things were, but something—guilt? a sense of irresponsibility? fear that she'd stop me doing what I wanted to do?—held me back. Instead, I hugged her and asked if we could leave it for now. I said I didn't feel up to talking about it. And, even though she gave me a funny look, she took me at my word. Big mistake.

August: Dead Flies

Chapter 16

And so it began. In the week in which Jake was away, and when the children were safely asleep, Pete came to the house on three separate occasions. He'd leave the van around the corner. We'd have sex against the radiator in the hall or on the stairs, quick and urgent, half our clothes still on. I wouldn't let him upstairs, in case the children woke up, or in case our reflection was branded forever in the bedroom mirror. And he didn't hang around afterward—just left me with a carpet burn or a radiator ridge and went. Maybe he took a beer from the fridge. Or a slice of cake. And again I would wonder what the hell I was up to.

"What do you see in me?" I asked him once.

"You're wild," he said, through the crumbs. "You seem all English and prissy but inside you're wild."

"Wild?" I said, checking the lights on the baby monitor.

"Okay then," he grinned, "sex."

If he saw sex in me, I don't exactly know what I saw in him. I saw a handsome man, certainly, with the kind of looks

I would once have considered way out of my league; a handsome man who was, of all things, attracted to me. So handsome, and so apparently attracted (or possibly so intrigued), it would have seemed churlish to turn the opportunity down. This sounds flippant, I know, and I have no ready defense for it now. In fact, quite the opposite. My flippancy was a guard, I used it to hide behind, to protect myself from thinking about my actions too deeply, or too carefully. Infidelity brought out the worst in me. I may, in my moments of more pious self-justification, have told myself that I was equalizing things with Jake, that he had started it, that I had been forced into an impossible position by his own digressions, by his absence, by the late nights that continued after his return from Amsterdam . . . But it was much more than that. Something in me, I confess, liked the way Pete was proof that I hadn't completely hunkered down into a cocoon, populated by children and playground mums, that there was a side of me that nobody else had seen—including me up to that point. Some small part of me would have loved Rachel to have caught me in the act, to have seen all her tidy preconceptions about me drain from her shocked and appalled face. And yet, of course, that would have been terrible. The whole situation was ridiculous. Impossible. Miserable. I was full of guilt. But I can't pretend it didn't thrill me.

One day, a couple of weeks in, Pete rang just as I'd got the children into the stroller. He said, "I'm on my way to a garden center down in Surrey: are you free?"

I said, "But we're off to the common."

He made a noise, half whine, half groan, down the phone. And then, wheedling, after a silence, he said, "There's a disused dunny on the path to the fishing lake."

"A *dunny?*"

"You know, a public lavvy. Be there in half an hour."

"Pete, this is impossible."

He had already hung up.

When I got to the playground, Maria's au pair, Merika, was there with Maria's children, Flossie and Patrick. There were a couple of other mothers I recognized from playgroup too—except I only knew them as "Milo's Mummy" and "Jemima's Mummy." I put Dan in the sandbox, let Fergus loose, and then sat, watching them idly. Every now and then I'd nod and smile as a child of one of the other mothers did something nod- or smile-worthy. And I tried to ignore the adrenaline that had started to run inside me along with some feelings of fear and anticipation. After a while I said, somewhat to my own surprise and in a faintly nervous voice, "Shall I go and get us some coffees?"

"Oh, don't worry, I'm fine," Merika said.

"Go on. Cappuccino?" I urged. "Latte? Frappuccino? Mocha frappuccino with whipped cream? Caramel macchiato? You know you want to."

"No really, I'm fine."

"What about a tea then? Iced tea? Mango and papaya juice shake?"

She was shaking her head insistently.

"Cool you down!"

"I'm dieting," she said, tapping a nonexistent belly.

Desperately, I racked my brain for a name for one of the other women. "Laura!" I said suddenly, "Can I get you a coffee? Or an iced tea or a frappuccino?"

"It's Lauren," she said. "Gosh, a coffee. That's a nice idea. I'd love a Caffe Mocha if you're going anyway."

"Absolutely," I said. "I'm on my way. . . . If you could just keep an eye on Fergus and Dan, while I'm gone."

The café was the same side of the common as the boarded-up restrooms. Eventually I puffed up with a corrugated card tray in my hand and hot bubbles of coffee on my shoes. Pete was leaning against the wall, under the trees.

"You're late," he said.

"I'm mad," I replied.

At weekends and in the summer holidays there were strange clusters of teenage boys by the lake. From a distance they looked as if they were dealing drugs or torturing small animals. Or having sex. It was only when you got close that you realized they were sharing a fishing rod, eyes intent on a straggling line that floated motionless on the stagnant water.

I was grateful for their concentration that day. I wondered afterward, as I pulled a leaf from my hair, zipped up my shorts, if they had heard anything, if they saw the undergrowth stir or shake. Maybe they thought someone was dealing drugs or torturing small animals. Or having sex. Uncomfortable sex. Vertical uncomfortable sex. Addictive vertical uncomfortable sex.

When I got back to the playground, Dan was still playing happily in the sandbox, but Fergus was crying. "He wanted his mummy," said Lauren, as I handed her her cup of deflated milk and chocolate powder. "He wondered what had happened to you."

· · ·

Of course I was always meaning to stop it. We had two close shaves. There was one time, when the children were with my mother and Jake was "busy with Kyushi," that Pete and I "went for a drive." That was one of his euphemisms. Pete seemed to prefer making love in his van to anywhere else. The risk, maybe even the grubbiness of it, gave him an extra thrill. We had driven to a road just off the common and parked. On the way back, he needed some gas so he drove into the nearest Shell station. He went into the kiosk to pay and I was just sitting there in the passenger seat, feeling stunned at myself, when I turned and right next to me, so close I could reach down and stroke his hair, was Jake. He was bending over, negotiating the gas cap on our car. He had his back to me, but I dove onto the floor of the car nonetheless.

"What have you dropped?" said Pete when he climbed back in.

"Nothing," I said. "Just drive. Now."

And after that, I did feel awful, though, disconcertingly, the experience seemed to have turned Pete on.

And then there was the day that Pete came round at 7:00 p.m. That summer my children went to bed earlier and earlier. I'd pull their curtains tight shut to block out the sun, which still hit its head on the window like it was midday. Jake had rung to say he had the results of a focus group to go through, and was it all right if he and Ed went for a drink afterward? I said that was fine. It would give me at least two safe hours.

I was wearing my old yard sale tea dress when Pete got there. We took a couple of beers into the garden, which was looking blowsy now that it was August, seedy and unkempt, to drink on the bench under the tree. Pete put his bottle down on the lawn where it wobbled and fell over, glugging into the grass. I bent and made as if to pick it up, but he pulled me onto his lap and, slipping the dress over my head, started kissing me instead.

The bench was concealed from the neighboring gardens by the jasmine on one side and the overgrown honeysuckle on the other, the branches of the tree hiding the upstairs windows. I closed my eyes for a moment as Pete threw off his shirt, breathing in the slightly contradictory scents of midsummer flowers and Australian male. Pete made a humming sound at the back of his throat. He was kissing me and taking off his shorts at the same time. I was drifting. I was almost lost. And then suddenly the atmosphere was split open like a coconut by a voice, not that close yet, not that loud, but inquiring, echoing through an empty house. "Where are you?"

"FUCK!" I yelped. "It's Jake. Quick into the shed!"

I jumped up and, yanking my dress back on, herded Pete, still confused, behind the tree and the beginning-to-run-wild shrubs, into the safety of the shed. I ran back out to the bench, gathered up his clothes, threw them into a bush, called in a high, artificial voice, "I'm here! Coming!" and charged back into the house, where I found Jake bent down, peering into the fridge.

"Oh there you are," he said coolly. "I could have sworn there were a couple of beers left. Ed and I thought we'd head out of the office and go through our stuff here. We both feel like we've been living there recently. Are Fergus and Dan in bed? I thought I'd catch them."

"Oh, I think, we . . . Yes they are . . . I thought you . . ."

"Did we drink them?"

"Yes, we must have."

Ed was in the sitting room, standing with his back to the door, looking out the window. He seemed subdued. "Hi, Maggie," he said. "Sorry to er . . ."

I was curling and uncurling my fists. But my voice managed to be casual. "Hello. I'm surprised you could get away. It's only . . ." I looked at the clock on the video. "Half past seven. Gosh, that is early. You've both been working such long hours." I was studying him carefully.

He said, rather too quickly, "Yes we have, we have."

"No beers." Jake came in behind me. "So how about wine? Or coffee?"

". . . or the pub," I said quickly. "You could go to the pub." I was looking from one to the other. Please say yes. Please say yes. Jake raised his eyebrows. Ed raised his to match. "Go on," I said. "I'm all right here. I've got some things to . . . finish off in the garden."

After they'd gone, I ran back to the shed, my toes fizzy with leftover panic. Pete was sitting on the old chest of drawers, his feet balanced on two of the knobs, looking sullen. "Jesus Christ," he said.

The sight of him, disconsolate and naked, caused me to open my mouth and roar with laughter. "I'm sorry," I kept saying, "I'm sorry," and I'd straighten my face in line with his but then I'd think about it again, and the crosser he looked the funnier it seemed, and I'd start all over again. "Look, look please," I burbled finally, "you'd better go, but don't be angry. I'm sorry. It's just seeing you . . . it's just tension, that's all it is."

"Has he gone then?" he said irritably. "Is the coast clear?"

"Yes, yes," I said, calming. "It is. And you'd better go."

I smoothed him down and got him to the door. He seemed appeased, though he said one more thing before he left. "Don't laugh at me, Maggie," he said. "I don't like being laughed at."

· · ·

And then there were other, more localized, difficulties. Fran and Rain came around one evening in the middle of the month to sort through some baby things and collect the Tens machine. It was a Saturday and I'd slipped off for an hour earlier in the day, under the pretense of buying lightbulbs (as

good an excuse as I could think of: sometimes the more
mundane, the more convincing), and had met Pete in the
parking lot of the hardware store.

We'd had a sticky time. I had been feeling a bit cornered.
I hadn't really wanted to meet—Dan was fretful that day
and Fergus clingy and Pete, for an instant, seemed one more
demand on my time. But he'd rung several times and in
the end I'd gone because it seemed easier to do so than
not. When I'd gotten there, hot and my back sweaty from
the plastic seats of the car, I hadn't even wanted to make
love, though Pete had been insistent. "Be a sport, Mags,"
he'd said. He was fed up—Lloyd was away and he was kicking
his heels, a bored single man stuck on his own on a fuggy
weekend.

"Oh all right," I'd said.

"I'm hoping to do without medical intervention altogether," Fran was saying. She was sitting on the bed in the
spare room. I was standing on a chair, searching the top of the
closet. She took a pillow and squashed it on her lap. "And I'm
not sure if it works in the birthing pool." Jake, who had wandered in with a bottle of beer in his hand, said she'd probably
get electrocuted. I told her I'd found it a waste of time.

"It just set my nerve ends on edge," I said, finally finding
its box tucked behind Jake's Hornby railway set, which he'd
put away until the boys were older (until they'd left home, I
suspected, and he could play with it without them getting in
the way). I reached for it and handed it down to her. "But
take it because it works for some people, and you won't know
until you need it."

Jake said, sitting on the bed, "Actually, it did really help
you. It really helped her, in stage one."

"No it didn't," I said. "I hated it."

"You liked it," he said. "She liked it. She said it helped. It was only after transition that she didn't want it."

"Don't talk about me as if I'm not here. Don't talk about my labor as if you know more about it than me," I said.

"Oooooh. Sorry," he said, getting up and backing away.

"And don't say 'ooooh sorry' like that," I said.

"Oooooh. Sorry."

Fran flicked at him with a muslin, which he grabbed from her and put on his head, folding his hands together and bowing his head like a mullah. Then he went downstairs to the kitchen. I continued folding baby clothes—so tiny, vole-like—thinking with one half of my brain, how quickly my children had grown, and with the other, how quickly my relationship with their father had changed. It was like playing the piano or reciting a poem you know off by heart: everything goes well until you let your concentration lapse, or think too hard about it, and then the words and the notes tumble about your ears unformed and chaotic. When Jake was the unfaithful one, at least I could still take refuge in hating him. Now I just hated myself. I put the baby clothes in a plastic bag and closed the closet door. There were dead flies in the bottom of it—there are dead flies everywhere in August—but I didn't sweep them up. I'd do it later. I'd do everything later.

Fran said, "We've been thinking Lakshmi for a girl. She's the Hindu goddess of wealth. Bede for a boy. What do you think?"

"Heavenly," I said.

Downstairs, Jake and Rain had gotten the menu out and were about to get take-out. Jake ordered chicken biryani.

"Why don't you order something different for once?" I said.

"Like what?" he said, in mock outrage.

I picked up the menu. "What about fish tandoori? Or egg khorma or . . . go on have egg khorma. I've never seen anyone have egg khorma."

Jake looked as if I'd suggested he fry up some diapers. "Give over," he said. "I want chicken biryani. I always have chicken biriyani."

"So you do," I said.

Fran was looking from one of us to the other. She said, "All right, you two?"

I said, "Jake always has the same thing. He's never adventurous. I have something different every time. Jake never takes risks."

"I take risks all the time," he said quietly. "But when it comes to ordering Indian take-out, I like chicken biryani. It is not a crime as far as I know. Unless I'm suddenly living under a new political administration."

"Oh yes, risks. I forgot about the risks," I said.

"Just order!" said Fran.

They went soon after we'd eaten. Fran hugged me. I hugged her back. "Take care," I said. "Ring me if you need anything else."

"I will," she said. "And Maggie? Have you ever thought about Pilates? There's a very good course at the House of Eternal Peace, though it's quite booked up. Or how about You Too Can Heal at the Innerpotential Center. You look as if you need something to take you out of yourself."

"I think, at the moment, I've got enough things with which to take myself out of myself," I said, closing the door.

A few minutes later, I was in the bathroom washing my face when Jake came in. "Are you all right?" he said, reaching past me for the toothpaste.

"Fine," I said as he started brushing. "Absolutely fine."

He spat. I moved my hand. "Are you sure?" He sounded solicitous. He was looking at me carefully in the mirror. He said, "This thing with Kyushi, it's almost over. I know it's been almost three months, but it's not going to go on forever."

I nodded. I turned to go, but he grabbed me by the hand and, still looking at me in the mirror, buried his mouth in my neck. Then he let me go. "How about coming to bed?" he said.

My heart sank. I said, "You go ahead. I'll be a few minutes." And I went downstairs and tidied up the kitchen until I knew he'd be asleep.

Chapter 17

I had managed to avoid Mel since the beginning of my affair
with Pete. She had a course in Bournemouth (Complemen-
tary Medicine in General Practice) which took her away for
one week (including two return trips to Manchester where
her parents looked after Milly). And she left several messages
on the answering machine, which I didn't return. You can
tell you're in trouble if you start steering clear of your closest
friends. I didn't want to see Mel because I knew how shocked
she would be, and, in witnessing her shock, I'd have to confront all the stuff I'd been so busy burying. But I couldn't
hide from her forever.

"So what's going on?" she asked. "I can understand the
eyebrows, but why the bikini wax? I thought you never had
your bikini done?"

It was Saturday afternoon, a week after the hardware store,
and we were lying on our backs, on green cushioned lounger
chairs, naked but for towels discreetly arranged, droplets of
sweat between our breasts, large mango and banana smooth-

ies at our sides, gazing up at a magnolia network of exposed heating pipes.

"This is the life," she said, as a dab of condensation dropped from above onto her forehead. "Ugh," she added, shaking her head like a dog.

It was an annual event. Every year, before our holidays (al though this year, only Mel was going away—two weeks in Tuscany with her brother and his family), we'd get day passes to Paddle, an all-women's health club in the center of London. So far, we'd had a steam and a sauna and a plunge, and we'd frolicked for a while in the pool, where you could dangle above the water on a rope-swing and, with your shoulders against your ears to block out the impossibly thin Sloanes discussing the new Autumn range of Nicole Farhi knits, pretend you were Brooke Shields in *The Blue Lagoon*. And now we were relaxing from the business of relaxing.

"I'm just bucking my self-image," I said. "After all, a bit of pampering never went amiss." And then I turned my face away to take a sip from my fruit shake as I remembered how amiss my pampering was probably going to go.

She said, "Maggie. What is going on? You've been unreachable recently. I know you're avoiding me. I haven't seen you on your own for weeks. I know you don't want to talk, but I think you should. What is happening with Jake?"

I closed my eyes. "Ummmm . . ." I began.

She said, sitting up, "I'm putting my clothes on and walking straight out unless you talk to me. I know something's up. You're not yourself. Please, Maggie. I hate it when you shut down like this. What's going on? Is he or isn't he?"

I said, deadpan, "Yes, he is."

She lay back down, banging her head against her cushion. She said, "Bastard." She sat up again. "You talked to him then? What did he say?"

A woman with a navel ring on the next lounger who had been reading *Marie Claire* had looked up during this. I glared at her until she looked back down. I said, "If I tell you something, do you promise you won't hate me?"

"Of course not."

I put my hands over my eyes. "I'm seeing someone too."

Mel swung her legs over her lounger and bent over me. "What?"

I took my hands away. "I'm seeing someone. I'm having an affair too. Now do you hate me?"

"Of course I don't." She was frowning.

"So only I hate me then."

She said, "Who? Who? How? When?" and I told her about Pete coming on to me and how eventually, after finding out about Claire, I'd given in and she said, "What, my Pete?" and I said yes, even though she'd never actually met him. I told her how at first it had bucked me up and given me something else to think about and made me feel better about myself, more on a par with Jake, physically better as much as anything, but that now I felt awful and angry all the time. And she said gently, shaking her head, "What were you thinking?"

And I said, "I didn't think. I just did."

And she said, "Maybe it wasn't an affair you needed, but an exercise class." And I saw the girl with the navel ring smile.

I was called for my stack of treatments then—much to the disappointment of Navel Ring. I had ordered an eyelash tint, and an underarm, a half-leg, a bikini and an eyebrow shape—the full nicknack Paddle wax. As I lay there, the beautician said, "Any particular occasion?" and I wanted to say "Yes, I'm sleeping with someone I'm not married to; actually I'm sleeping with two people I'm not married to, but that's another story." Instead, I simpered and said, "Oh just August."

She said, plucking, "One does tend to have more flesh on display then, doesn't one?"

When she'd finished tidying me up, the beautician studied my face, rather like Mel had done earlier. "There," she said, rubbing an excess streak of blue-black dye off my cheekbone. "You'll feel more human now."

Mel was already dressed when I came out. She had to pick Milly up from her next-door neighbor and then she had to rush home to cook Piers a good-bye dinner. She hugged me and said she'd ring and not to worry, but that we needed to talk some more soon. "There was some statistic in the paper the other day," she said. "In forty percent of all marriages . . ."

"Someone is sleeping with someone else," I finished off. "Yes, I saw that too. But we're both sleeping with someone else. And we're not married, so where does that leave us?"

"It'll all come out in the wash," she said, and there was something comforting in the triteness of that, as if none of it was any more important than a good spin cycle.

I left Paddle on my own and wandered around Covent Garden for a while looking for salvation of a more transient nature, putting off going home. In one of the shops in the plaza I found a dress that reminded me of the frock Claire was wearing the day I'd bumped into her on Morton High Street, the dress she wore to dinner that night. This one had tiny straps and ribbon along the hem, and was, according to the assistant, cut on the bias, which she concluded was flattering "to the curvier figure." It did look nice, even with my sneakers, even with my post-wax rash, but the assistant said it would look even better with some kitten heels. "Maybe in pink or taupe," she said. "Have you tried our shop next door? And what about a little cardigan," she added. "Cerise would look nice. Or this one in bilberry? For evening."

I was laden down with bags when I finally got home. I'd

bought everything guiltily on the joint account, so it was a relief to find an empty house. I stashed the bags into the back of the closet, poured myself a drink, and went into the garden to read the papers. There was a small ribbon of sun left at the bottom of the lawn and I sat my deck chair on it, with the shade creeping up my legs. I hadn't got much further than the travel section and was imagining myself digging for turtle eggs in hot bleached white sand—when Jake arrived back with the children.

"Hello," he said, as Fergus hurled himself on top of me. "Nice day?"

"Lovely. Thanks," I said politely. The deck chair lurched to one side under the force of Fergus's hug. I put my spare arm onto the grass to steady us. "You?"

"We've had a great time, haven't we boys?" said Jake, straining to keep hold of Dan, who was reaching his arms out to me. "Such nice weather."

"Isn't it just?" I said, taking Dan from him. How nice we were. How civilized. What surfaces we could maintain. I said, "Thank you for looking after the kids," thinking "why do mothers always thank fathers? Good thing they don't thank us or there would be no room for any other conversation." I was about to repeat this thought, make a joke about it, a joke with an edge, but it seemed too intimate, too engaged with the daily ebb and flow of our relationship. So I didn't say anything.

Jake peered around the children. "Let's see," he said. "You look different."

"I know," I said. I stood up and put Fergus and Dan down on the grass. The spot of sun had gone altogether now. I started folding up the deck chair. "Fergus, mind your fingers. I am different. It's a whole new me."

•   •   •

Rachel was on to me too. On the following Monday, in the changing rooms at the swimming pool, she wanted to know what the new undies were for. "Classy," she said, as I slipped off my new "second skin" underwear from Lycra'N'Lace, a lingerie shop in the Southgate Mall that thinks it's in Beverly Hills, and stuffed them in a Safeway's bag. "Matching bra, hmm. Very nice. Very underrated, purple."

I was a bit too busy trying to prevent Fergus from scattering his clothes all over the damp floor while squirming into my Speedo to answer immediately. I grunted as I finally got the straps over my shoulders. "Crushed grape," I said non-committally, adjusting the Lycra under my arms, and whirling Dan round to sit on one hip, "Yup. Just got myself remeasured—after all that breastfeeding, you know. It's amazing how your shape changes."

"Isn't it?" she agreed, still eying me up.

The swimming pool, Splashdown!, as they'd recently renamed it, had changed since my day. Less of "a rec" (or wreck), more of a whole wraparound swimming experience. We used to come on Wednesday afternoons with school. In those days, the most exciting thing on offer was the illustrated notice banning "heavy petting." Wasted on me: I didn't know what heavy petting was then, but suspected it was something to do with gerbils. Now it was all elephant slides and wave machines and huge inflatable monsters. You used to get snacks and a can of drink from the machines in the foyer—you'd need the right change, then you'd tense as you waited for the clunk or the rustle that meant your money had worked—and you'd devour your booty on the steps with your ears still humming and an itchy wetness under your clothes. Now there was a whole café space, specializing in whale-shaped fish morsels and crocodile-mouthed chicken pieces.

I jammed the plastic bag into a locker, which was as crappy as they always had been, and slipped the rubber band around my wrist. Fergus and Harry, miniature Michelin men in their orange Floaties, with Fergus's skinny arms sticking out like matchsticks, ran ahead of us to splash in the ankle-deep beach-style shallow end. Rachel's pregnant friend Martha was waiting for us there already, sitting on her bum in the water, legs splayed like a Beanie Baby plonked on a nursery shelf. Her two-year-old daughter Phoebe frolicked with a piece of yellow foam at her ankles. Martha smiled weakly when she saw us. We shivered down next to her. It was not the water that was the problem, heated as it was to Caribbean germ-breeding balmitude, it was the air above it.

"How are you?" asked Rachel.

Martha sighed. "Exhausted," she said. "I'm just . . ."

I missed what she said next because the attendant blew his whistle loudly and started gesticulating crossly just to the right of us. I turned to see what the nasty big boys were doing, which small child they were dive-bombing, but all I could see was Fergus and Harry climbing on one of the crocodiles, and then hurling themselves off with enviable fearlessness.

"Toooooooooooooot," the whistle went again, shrill above the echoing cries of swimmers. The attendant was coming over, waving his tracksuited arms. He was heading for Fergus and Harry.

"No jumping off the animals," he said to them. "Or you're out."

I busied myself with Dan—"Whoosh," I said, twirling him

around, "Whoooosh"—to show they weren't mine, but Rachel stood up and, water flapping at her ankles, strode over.

"Can't you two behave for one minute?" she said. For once she didn't seem to be blaming Fergus. "Fergus," she added, "off!"

After that, Martha said she'd watch Dan, while Rachel and I waded the boys over to the deeper end. It was still only about three feet deep, but we slouched across, alternating between our bottoms and knees, keeping as much of our upper torsos as we could in the warmth.

When we reached the ropes separating kiddy chaos from the lengths lane, Rachel said, "God, Martha doesn't know how lucky she is. For one thing, Phoebe is very well behaved, and for another she has so much help it's untrue. She's got an au pair and Phoebe goes to nursery one morning a week, and her mother comes up from Guildford and helps out all the time, and her inlaws come down from Chester every other weekend and practically fight to have the children . . . "

"Gosh," I said, trying to stop Fergus from putting both his feet on the rope. "That is a lot." Nonworking mothers are all obsessed with other people's help, as if our children's preoccupation with fairness had rubbed off on us. Fergus was swinging on the rope now, his hands in mine, his feet pushing it back and forth. Rachel was saying, "And her husband's an angel. He gives her a lie-in every Saturday and is home two nights a week for bathtime. And," she lowered her voice, "she's getting a maternity nurse when the baby's born. So really, I don't know how she can say she's exhausted."

"Not like we're exhausted," I said.

"Exactly."

"ERRRR. Excuse me!" There was a cross, spluttering voice suddenly in my ear. I'd let my attention lapse and

Fergus had swung a little too forcefully and pushed the rope, complete with his feet, right into the smooth path of an oncoming swimmer. A wet face was staring at me, her hair dark and wet, two-ringed fingers flicking droplets of water from under her eyes. She was wearing a black halter-neck bikini, her slim, tanned body flickering brown and white under the water.

"Oh," I said, speechless. Oh. God. Her. Here. Together in the same water as me. Almost naked in the same element. How unspeakably awful. "Claire," I said.

"OH. Oh. Maggie!" Her annoyance dropped immediately, plunged into embarrassment instead. She started rabbiting inanely. *"Fancy* meeting you here. Actually, do you know, I was just thinking about you. I had this funny feeling I might see you. There were all these small children in the changing room and I thought, 'oh I wonder if Maggie brings her boys here'!"

Her duplicitousness was quite dizzying. How could she even think about mentioning my children? "Sorry Fergus kicked you," I said, wishing he'd done it a bit harder.

"Oh, don't worry. High spirits, etc. It just gave me a shock that's all. Small foot in the ribs. Doesn't matter at all. But Maggie, I haven't seen you for *ages."* She was burbling, launched into hyperspace with the awkwardness of seeing me. It was quite gratifying to watch. She was skewered on a pin. Most of us, under such circumstances, might nod wanly and swim away. Not Claire. Claire gushed. "You must think I'm *terrible*. I've just been so—well, it's been eventful, let me tell you. Just—oh God," she was shaking her head. "But we must get together again soon."

Rachel was smiling hopefully, with her head on one side, looking from one to the other of us, waiting for an introduction. I was silent. Claire gave a wide smile and said, "I'm

Claire. Maggie and I are old, old friends. We were at school together, weren't we?"

"Er, yes," I said, pulling myself together. I'd have to do introductions, but I didn't want to. "This is Rachel." She'd probably steal her too.

Fergus and Harry were whooping and splashing. Claire gave a gay laugh and said, "Oops, there goes my waterproof mascara!" as quite a lot of water ricocheted off their bodies into her face. "Where's your other little one?" she added.

I waited, hoping she'd lose interest. I didn't want her even to look at my baby. Finally, I said, *"Dan's* over there," pointing vaguely in the direction of Martha. Claire gave a dainty wave, one hand flapping invisible castanets open and shut parallel to her eyes, in his direction. Dan had pulled himself up on to the elephant's trunk. He didn't wave back.

Rachel was looking at Claire with fascination, clearly intrigued as to how someone as dull as me could have such a glamorous friend. "It is brilliant," she said. "It hasn't run at all. Is it Dior?"

"No, Clinique," said Claire bending conspiratorially. "It's worth its weight in gold."

"I must get some," said Rachel. "Now. I want some now. This minute."

They both laughed.

"And how do you two know each other?" said Claire.

Rachel told her about the post-natal support group run by the hospital, what a *lifeline* it had been when all those hormones were just *swimming* and you just felt so *isolated* . . . I could see Claire's interest wander, but I wasn't going to interrupt. I wanted to slouch away, low down, so she wouldn't see my body out of the water, but I also couldn't stop looking at her. I wanted to see what Jake saw. Suddenly, I was imagining them and . . . I said, "Oh Rachel, Claire's not interested in all that."

Rachel said, "Oh sorry. You forget how boring children are to people who haven't got them."

Claire smiled. She darted me a look. She said, "No, it's not true at all. I'd love to have children, only the man I'm seeing . . ."

I interrupted. I said, "Claire's boyfriend's married."

I tugged on Fergus's fingers until finally they came loose. I grabbed his toes under the water and made him squeal. I pulled him onto one hip and Harry onto the other and, with a child in each arm, splashed up and down in the water until they screamed with delight.

I still couldn't drown out the answer, couldn't hide from the nervous look Claire threw in my direction.

"They always are," she said.

•   •   •

I started asking Pete what he did when he wasn't seeing me. He said, "Hang out." But I wanted to know where. "Just about," he said. "Bars, you know."

"Which bars?"

"I dunno. Fiction. Oblivion. Anonymous. Meltdown. The usual."

"The usual," I said. "Sounds like my life."

He shook his head.

"It doesn't matter," I said. "Who with?"

"Mates."

"But who are your mates?"

"Lloyd. Some blokes I used to live with when I lived in Catford. People from about."

"Women?"

"There are girls there, Maggie, yes."

We were lying in the back of his van by the river at Putney, down the end, under the trees. It was midweek and quiet, though you could still hear muffled squeals and shouts from the playground across the road. Fergus was having lunch at Lucinda's. I'd left Dan with Fran on the pretext of a "Safeway's shop." I could tell she was feeling neglected. As I left, she said, "I wanted to ask you about toxoplasmosis . . ."

"FRAN!"

"Only joking." But she gave me a reproachful look nonetheless.

The week before we'd been in Richmond Park, but I'd felt exposed there, naked in the back of a white van in the middle of an empty parking lot. It was less conspicuous on the embankment. It was lurkers' paradise. There were several people apart from us in locked cars, mainly old couples sharing a Thermos and the view. Unlike us, they tended to sit in the front.

Pete was pulling on his clothes. He had looked at his watch and said he'd better be getting on. I lay there, with my arms crossed behind my head.

I said, watching him burrow into his T-shirt, "I know, let's do something different for once."

"Different from what?" His head emerged.

"From *this.*" I sat up, pulled my knees into my chest. "We could go on a date. Go somewhere normal. Maybe not Oblivion. But we could find somewhere. Do something."

He winced, turned away from me toward the door. "Bit tricky . . ."

"I could manage it. I could work it. It would be good. It's important."

"Whatever," said Pete sunnily. He chucked my clothes at me. "Get your kit on. I haven't got all day."

I wriggled into my clothes, and Pete crouched down to undo the back doors. He clambered out and then bent to fiddle with the number plate on the back of the van. It was held on with string and was hanging on by one side. I followed him out and went to stand against the railings, looking down into the sludge below. It was low tide. There was a Dulux paint can among the driftwood, sticking out of the mud. A dog went by, nose down, tail up, followed by an owner, trudging in shorts and boots. Jake and I had talked about getting a dog, though we'd decided it wouldn't be fair. Not in London.

I said, "I should bring Fergus here. He'd love it down there."

Pete, still with his head under the bumper, said, in a half-grunt, "Huh?"

"He could dig around with sticks," I said. "In the mud."

I turned, but Pete wasn't listening.

The relationship, once the initial charge had left, wasn't following the kind of pattern I was used to. I was not, in these hot August days, at my most clearheaded, but I thought I knew two things. One, that I didn't want it to carry on the way it was, and two, that I didn't want it to end. Or did I? Did I want to try to make something more of it? Did I want to think about a future with this man?

I stood and stared at the strip of river, sparkling in the sun like the Mediterranean. "What now?" I said, turning again. "Where do we go from here?"

"Well." Pete was jangling his car keys. "I've got to pick up some bedding plants at the nursery. And I've got an appointment at Lucinda's at 3:00 p.m."

I think we both knew that wasn't what I meant.

Then he said he wasn't going my way, so could he drop me at the station? "Be a sport," he said, kissing the top of my head. "It's only one transfer."

Chapter 18

"I can't believe we're doing this," I said. "We must be mad. Out of our heads. Criminally insane. How did I let this happen?"

"It's too late," he said. "We've gone too far."

"I can't bear it," I said. "I'm leaving behind my house, my garden, my life."

"Tough," he said. "There's no turning back now."

We were in the car, Jake and I, on our way to Suffolk, the guests of Ed and Pea, who had invited us, along with Mark, another of Ed and Jake's colleagues at TMT&T, and his wife Louisa, to a cottage booked through Barn D'Or. Barn D'Or was the Rolls-Royce of holiday cottage companies: exposed beams and properly lagged hot water tanks, yours for two nights, for the cost of a small Learjet. "The house is 'price code B,'" Ed had said on the phone, before I passed him to Jake. "I've told Pea we'd bloody well better get a thatched roof for that."

The weekend had been in the *Cosmo* date-book for ages, but I'd filed it away in the region of my mind labeled "Get

Out of That Nearer the Time." What with one thing and another—small children, unfaithful husbands, rampant sex with near strangers in bushes—I hadn't got around to it and suddenly there we were, on our way, hardly speaking, Mr. and Mrs. Dysfunctional, having to put on a brave face for a Bank Holiday weekend with other people.

I was in a terrible mood. I hadn't managed to see Pete all week, but I'd managed to pin him down for our date, which was to take place the following Tuesday. In the meantime, if I'd had my choice, I would have spent the weekend on my own with my kids, thinking about things if I was feeling brave, burying them if I wasn't, but at any rate not forced into artificial merriment.

"I don't even understand why they've invited us," I said to Jake crossly. We had endured the Friday night traffic on Tower Bridge and were now heading haltingly up the White-chapel Road. "She hates me as much as I hate her."

"No, she doesn't," he said back, calmly, infuriatingly. "She's probably just a bit confused by your attitude. She's probably just waiting to like you, if you'd let her."

"What about Ed?" I said.

He was staring ahead at the bumpers in front of him. "You may not like him, but he is my friend and my colleague. And I don't see why we shouldn't socialize with them once in a while." He darted me a look and then glanced away again. "It's embarrassing not to. Particularly as Clarice and Fergus aren't so far apart in age."

"Fergus hates Clarice."

"No, he doesn't. And she's perfectly sweet really. She might even be a bit of a calming influence."

"She's a monster," I said.

"Don't be ridiculous," he said, quite harshly for him. "She's only a child."

We lapsed into silence. Fergus and Dan had been asleep since we crossed the river. Two months ago—was it only that recently?—a traffic jam with comatose children could have been classified as "quality time," a chance to catch up, listen to music together, chat idly. As it was, it felt like purgatory. Over the last month, things had, if it were possible, become even more strained. Jake had become withdrawn to the point where even the routine politeness between us, the going-through-the-motions, had seized up.

I said, after a while, "Well at least I like Mark and Louisa."

Jake grunted. It's true, I did. They lived in north London, and in the way in which friendship as you get older is increasingly dictated by geography, we never saw as much of them as we'd have liked. They were a bit unconventional, or as unconventional as anyone we ever knew was, which wasn't saying much. Mark, a copywriter at Jake's agency, was one of those energetic people who is always said to be "brilliant" with children. He was the one who'd run the barbecue and organize the kites and untangle the lines for tickling the crabs. He was the one his children, or anyone's children for that matter, ran to when they scraped their knees. Louisa, on the other hand, would emerge death-white at 10:00 a.m., grope for a cigarette and a mug of black coffee, and wail what a terrible mother she was, while wishing she was somewhere else. We always had a nice time with them. Or we used to.

I looked across at Jake and noticed how gray around the gills he was looking. There were bags under his eyes and a nick on his chin, with a scab on it, where he must have cut himself shaving. Probably using the razor I borrowed to deal with the regrowth from my Paddle wax. I said, suddenly disarmed by his vulnerability, "Are you exhausted? Would you like me to drive?"

"I'm fine," he said coolly.

We had reached the fast bit of the highway. When the traffic had cleared after a roundabout, Jake had put his foot down sharply on the accelerator and we had swerved to the left so aggressively I had gripped both sides of my seat. I continued to grip, chin jutting into my chest, right foot stretched out on an imaginary brake, just a little bit longer than was necessary—to make a point.

After a while, when the point wasn't picked up, I said, "So what's happening with Kyushi?"

There was a pause. Then he said, as if it didn't matter, "They liked our pitch best. So, er, yup, they're sticking with us."

"Really?"

"Yes,"

"Really? Jake? When? When did you find out?"

"Yesterday. It's what I was celebrating last night. I thought you realized."

"But I didn't . . . When you said you were having a few beers, I thought . . . You might have said."

"I didn't think you were interested," he said. "As long as I bring in the money . . ."

"I cannot believe you said that," I said. "It's unfair."

"Is it?" he said, turning to look at me. "Is it?"

"Yes, of course. Anyway, I wish I'd known."

"Too late now," he said briskly. "And Maggie, do me a favor. At least pretend to enjoy yourself, okay?"

• • •

Five things I swore I'd never do when I had children.

1. Add the baby's name to the list of people unable to get to the phone right now, on the answering machine.

2. Send Christmas cards of specially mounted family scenes.
3. Carry any sort of padded bag, with nursery animals on it, even for "changing" purposes.
4. Wear pastels.
5. Go away with other people.

So far I had managed to abide by the first four of these promises. But nobody's perfect.

• • •

It was dark when we arrived at the Old School House, Cotley. Ed and Pea's Kyushi Adventurer (4-wheel drive; profile: would-be urban warrior or adman keen to make impression with client) had already rammed a path up to the front door. A Renault Espace was squeezed in behind it.

"Last here, then," I said, as we parked on the lane outside.

I got out and breathed in the sharp fresh country air, a cocktail of leaves and salt, mown grass and manure. Jake heaved our bags out of the trunk in silence and together we eased our way up the drive, past the kangaroo bars to the front door.

"Hello, everyone!" hailed Ed, coming to greet us at the door with a dishcloth in his hand. "Find it okay? Great. Come in. Welcome. Welcome. Lovely to see you, Maggie. How are you?" He put on his teensy-weensy little girl's voice for this last question, as if addressing a flower fairy.

"I'm fine," I said heartily, but he had already turned to Jake and was gripping his forearm.

"Kyushi, Kyushi, Kyushi," he said in his ear. "Fucking brilliant," he said loudly.

Jake said, "Yup. Isn't it?"

"What an evening," Ed continued. "I hear you were in the

office today. I didn't make it in. I was going to come in for lunch, but . . ." He flicked his finger across his brow.

Jake suddenly felt the pocket of his jacket. "Shit. I left it at home. I forgot to cancel something next week." He looked at his watch. "Is there a phone here? I might just catch Judy in the office."

Ed was steering us into the house. "There isn't," he said. "But you can use mine. It's in my jacket. In there—" He moved his head to indicate a door behind him, then turned to me. "Maggie. I'll show you round."

The house was charming. There was a series of interconnecting rooms on the ground floor, all so tastefully decorated you fully expected to find a film crew at work on some elegant English drama. The woodwork was painted powder blue, the floorboards were sanded, and the sofas loosely covered in various neutral shades of linen. It was warm, despite the chill in the air outside. A fire was lit in the main sitting room. And above it there was a collection of beautifully chosen objects. What else could you want? Central heating and a candle sconce in the shape of an antelope. A tumble dryer and the stars at night.

"Where are the others?" I said.

"Oh, right." Ed's voice lowered. "Pea, I'm afraid, has gone to bed. Migraine, poor love. She's had a terribly stressful week at work. She had a very important film to finish. It was about battered women, phw." He shook his head in admiration. "It really took it out of her. And the others—Mark and Louisa—have gone for a quick drink at the pub. I'm holding the fort. I didn't want to leave Pea on her own in case any of the children woke up. Clarice is out like a light, but the other two . . ." He gave a small shudder. "Bit *wild* I think."

It occurred to me that Mark and Louisa's children, who seemed no wilder on the few times I had met them than any other six- and eight-year-olds, attended a state school. It may perhaps have disconcerted Ed, whose daughter was at Bolton Prep, to meet children who didn't speak more poshly than their parents.

"We'd better get ours in," I said.

"Yes, come up, come up," said Ed. He bounded ahead of me up the stairs. "I'll show you where you are first . . . We're in here—" He lowered his voice to a whisper and waved to the room at the top of the stairs. "Clarice is in—here. Mark and Louisa have got this room so they can be next to the room with the bunk beds, and you're in . . . um . . . in here." He opened the door to a perfectly adequate room at the end of the corridor, its only immediate drawbacks being the extra mattress on the floor and the crib in the corner. "Thought you'd want to have the children close to you," he said.

"Can Fergus not share with Clarice?" I said at the door-way, not even going in.

"Do you mind terribly if he doesn't? She's such a light sleeper . . ."

I stomped out to the car, muttering under my breath. Jake came up behind me and, when I told him about the sleeping arrangements, pulled me by the arm.

"Grow up," he said. "It doesn't matter."

"Oh right, you don't care if you don't get any sleep, then?"

"Of course, I care, but come on . . . it's only a weekend. Anyway," he added half under his breath, "it's not as if the children are going to interrupt us having sex."

It was the first time either of us had referred to the situa-tion between us, as if being with other people made it less dangerous. His words, which sounded almost amused, hung in the air as we took the children out of the car. Then we heard giggles coming up the lane behind us and Mark and

Louisa appeared round the corner. I was always taken aback at how handsome they both were. He looked like a male model with a chiseled jaw and rangily muscular body. She was tall and willowy with a large nose and hanks of gingery hair, which she pulled up in a collection of hair clips. On this occasion, some glittery turquoise butterflies, possibly borrowed from her daughter, fluttered above her ears. She was holding Mark's hand inside one of his pockets. That was the other thing about them: thirteen years of marriage and two children and you could tell they were still at it like rabbits, a suspicion that tended to make the rest of us rather grumpy. "Oh great, you made it!" called Louisa, crunching onto the drive. "Reinforcements!"

"I expect you need them," I said, bending to kiss her over Dan's sleeping head. "After a few hours of Pea."

She looked inquiring.

"I hear she's had a 'terrible week' saving the world." I mocked Ed's tone of uxorious concern.

Louisa laughed dubiously. Jake said, "For Christ's sake, Maggie. Behave."

He clapped his hand around Mark's back. He looked visibly relieved to see them. Perhaps because they had rescued him from me.

. . .

After I'd settled the children (Fergus rose briefly to the surface of consciousness: "Why am I on the floor?" he asked sleepily. "Ask Pea," I said, but he'd already gone back off), I combed my hair and went downstairs to join the others for "a nightcap."

Mark was leaning back on one of the sofas. Louisa was reclining on a pillow on the floor, resting against his legs. Jake was at a table at the window reading out extracts from the visitor's book: "'Disappointing weather for June. Recommend the scampi in the basket at the Pig and Gristle in Appleton'; 'Wonderfully hot water. And exceptionally soft towels'; 'Most delightful. Information folder the best we have seen in any rental.'" I thought he'd look up when I came in, raise an eyebrow at me, particularly when he got to the bit about information folders, but he kept his eyes on the page.

"Maggie," said Ed, coming in from the kitchen behind me. "A glass of wine? It's a rather nice Chateauneuf du Pape. I think you'll be amused by its immaturity . . . And what about some Boeuf Bourguignon?"

"Goodness, where did that come from?" I said.

"I made it at home and brought it with us in a Tupperware," Ed said. "I thought people might be hungry."

Louisa stretched her legs out. "God, you are brilliant, Ed," she said. "I wish Mark could cook." She gave him a backward jab with her head. "What a lucky woman Pea is."

Ed went pink. "I don't know about that," he said.

"I should be so lucky," I sang, going over to an armchair by the fire and throwing myself into it. "I should be so lucky in love." The others, with the exception of Jake, looked at me oddly. "Sorry," I said. "Country air."

There was a lot of talk about the Kyushi pitch then. Ed said, "I knew, I just knew, when they started talking about Claudia Schiffer that we'd got them," and Mark said, "not to mention when they said we'd hit the nail on the head strategically," and I realized then, for the first time, what this weekend was all about. It had been planned as a celebration or a commiseration. One I'd let go over my head. I stood up then and said I was going to get a glass of water. Nobody seemed to notice me leave. I went into the kitchen, a small room for a house of this size, and filled a glass from the tap. I drank it with my back against the sink. I felt a pang for Pete. I longed for the feel of his rough hands. It had been a week, and a week in the life of passion is a long time. Just to hear him would be to take me away from all this. He was my escape from the rat race, my escape from the middle classes. I wished I'd managed to ring him before we left. I wished I could hear his voice *now*. Then I saw Ed's jacket, flung on the back of a chair, with the pocket hanging down as if it had excess weight inside it. Without moving, I put my foot out and felt it. It was his phone. I could hear the others laughing in the sitting room. "Bang on brief!" I heard Ed yell. I reached across and drew the phone out quickly. It looked pretty easy. I pressed a little red button at the bottom left. The screen flickered and emitted a series of beeps that seemed to echo round the kitchen. A voice from the other room suddenly got louder. I started and thrust the phone back into the jacket just as Ed came into the kitchen.

"Are you feeling all right?" he said, in his little girl voice. "Bit tired?"

"I'm fine," I said. I turned and clicked on the kettle. "Just making a cup of tea."

"Oooohh," he said, a church visitor on an old people's home visit. "That's nice." He picked up another bottle of wine and, with a grimace, opened it between his legs. "I'll take this through to the non–tea drinkers next door then," he said. "Are you sure you don't want anything to eat?"

I smiled jovially. "I'm fine. I'll join you all in a minute."

After he'd gone, I grabbed the phone again, quickly unlatched the back door, and slipped into the garden. The screen had dimmed. Maybe it needed reactivating. I pressed another button, green this time, which said "OK" and a number flashed up, followed by "Call?" It was a moment before it registered. It was the last number the phone had rung. The phone Jake had used only minutes before. Jake had said he was ringing the office. His office was an 0207 number. This number began with 0208. The phone was giving me the option to call it. I quickly looked over my shoulder and then pressed OK again and heard the number dial. It rang three times and then a machine picked it up. I knew who it would be even before I heard her voice. No matter how hardened I thought I'd become, I still felt winded. "Hi," she began, "you've reached Claire Masterson . . ."

I heard a noise behind me. Louisa had come into the kitchen. "Maggie? Where are you?" she cried, poking her head into the garden. "What are you doing out here?"

Panicked, I dropped the phone under some rosemary. "Just getting some air," I said. "Clearing my head."

I had to go down later when everyone was asleep to retrieve it. Pete's cell phone was switched off. Ed's smelled of lamb chops.

Chapter 19

Saturday. The Old School House. Cotley. Raining.

The day did not start well. It started early. Very early. Dan and Fergus were up with the lark. Didn't hear the lark. Just heard the rain pounding against the window and the wind rattling the hinges. And Fergus saying, "Is it morning? Is it MORNING?"—and waking Dan up.

I took them down the stairs of the otherwise silent house and into the kitchen where I tried to entertain them with a plastic colander, some metal measuring spoons, and a pack of playing cards I found in a drawer. The cards had naked women on the back, but no one seemed to mind. I tried to make card houses, but every time I had more than two floors balanced, Dan gave them a swipe like a kitten irritated by a fly and they'd fall down and scatter over the flagstones. Fergus would put as many screeched syllables as he could manage without giving himself a sore throat into his disappointment, and then swipe Dan back, a puppy irritated by a kitten.

Ed's phone was in Ed's jacket on the kitchen chair where I'd left it. Several times I thought about using it, but I couldn't see how without Fergus wanting to talk and making a scene when I didn't let him. It was also painfully early to ring a childless man, not least a childless man who may have been out half the night at Oblivion. I wondered who he'd been with and the thought made me feel jagged with a kind of jealousy that was new to me. It was as if, by sleeping with Pete, I'd opened Pandora's box and all the dark-sided emotions normally kept at bay by civilized behavior had started buzzing around my ears. I may have looked like a slightly underslept mother playing nicely with her children. But actually I was a witch.

It seemed like five days later when the others began to emerge. First Mark with Penny and Joe, all in their pajamas. And later Pea with Clarice. Pea and Clarice were already dressed. Pea was wearing a pair of neatly pressed linen trousers and a mushroom-colored shirt with tiny pearl buttons. Clarice looked like a summer bridesmaid, in a fitted linen frock the same color as puy lentils.

"Hello Pea," I said, getting up off the floor. "Lovely linen thing."

"Agnes B," she said.

"I meant Clarice's."

"That's what I said. Agnes B." There was a pause. "Did you sleep well?"

"Yes, thank you," I lied. "You?"

She sighed. "Bearably."

I wanted to say, "Well I didn't either then," but Mark nudged me out of the way to get at the cereal bowls.

"Come on, everyone," he said. "Breakfast."

He looked up when he'd gotten the kids settled. "It's raining then," he said. "Must be August Bank Holiday."

"Nothing wrong with a bit of rain," clipped Pea.

"Except we'll need a plan," I said. "Mine need to get out of the house."

"We could still go to the sea," said Mark. "Wrap everyone up."

"Or there's the zoo," I said. I'd had plenty of time that morning to study the leather folder in the kitchen labeled "Information" (the best information folder in any rental, as we now knew).

"The world's our oyster," said Mark.

"The sea, the sea, the sea," shouted the children. Fergus had already gotten down from the table.

Clarice, who was picking the raisins out of her muesli one by one, said, "I don't like the sea. It makes me wet."

"As if you weren't wet enough already," I muttered over by the kettle.

The kids were still chanting, so I didn't think anyone had heard me, but Mark came over to pour himself some coffee and said, "Oooh, back in the drawer, Ms. Sharp." I giggled, but then I noticed Pea studying me and I felt a bit bad so I hauled the children upstairs and got us all dressed. I didn't bother to keep them quiet anymore, and when Jake finally rose he looked stormy.

I said, "No need to look at me like that. It's nine o'clock."

Louisa was coming out of the bathroom. "Everybody happy?' she said. And then Ed appeared wearing paisley that hung loosely over his thin body. His blond hair was mussed up at the back like a piece of candy floss.

"Morning," I said. "Almost ready to go out?"

"No, he's not," said Jake. "None of us are."

"Well, I am," I said. But Ed had already scurried into the bathroom like a guinea pig darting for cover.

Louisa looked at me. "You're very smart," she said. "For the country. New clothes?"

"This old thing?" I said, damping down the dress I'd bought after my day at Paddle (my "Claire dress").

"You're going to be cold," she said.

. . .

Jake was stony-faced by the time we got to the small seaside town nearby. We'd taken two cars but Louisa came with us, which gave us an opportunity to bitch about Pea (well I bitched with all the twisted humor of my bad blood and she laughed) until Jake, who was driving with a set mouth, said, "Lay off, Maggie," and I had to make stupid faces at her instead. Then we couldn't park and had to drive around and around until, finally, we found a lot in a housing estate on the fringes. It was still raining. There was a Texaco on the corner, but otherwise we were miles from anywhere. Miles from the shops. Miles from the beach.

"Oh," I said, pointedly not undoing my seat belt. "We're in the middle of nowhere. And we've lost the others. It's just stupid. I'm sure there's a better place to park."

"We can't drive around anymore," said Jake. "Maybe you should have worn something more sensible. It's only spitting. What are you? A man or a mouse?"

"A woman," I said dully, still not moving.

Louisa had disembarked and was putting her raincoat on. Dan was grizzling in the back. Fergus had twigged my mood and was moaning too. "It's raining. It's wet. I don't want to walk. I want to be carried. Carry, carry, carry."

"Now look what you've started," said Jake.

Louisa yanked open the passenger door. She handed me my jacket from the trunk. "Come on, you lot," she said. "What are you waiting for? Stop being horrid. It's the Bank Holiday weekend. Everybody has to be nice."

"That's put us in our place," I said. Jake didn't say anything.

He got out of the car and walked off ahead. I got out and joined Louisa. We followed with Fergus and the stroller.

Louisa was chatting away about this and that, pointing out interesting cottages, telling me about the holiday they'd just had in California and this interesting career move of Mark's and that swimming badge of Penny's, and suddenly the monster that was screaming in my head started hammering to get out.

I said, without realizing I was going to, "I've met someone else. I'm seeing someone else. A man. Pete." It was a thrill to say his name out loud.

"You what?" said Louisa.

"A man. I've met a man."

Louisa had stopped walking. Her head was hanging at an odd angle, like one of those dogs that waggles in the back of cars. Her mouth was open.

"A man," I said.

"What kind of man? What do you mean, you met a man? What are you talking about?"

A car drove past and splattered us. I walked on. She followed. She was still trying to look into my face.

"Watch where you're going," I said. "I've met a man. I'm having an affair. Or trying to." I giggled, but she was looking horrified.

"I can't believe it," she said. "This is awful."

"No, it's not," I said. "It's extraordinary. You should try it sometime."

I paused to pull Fergus away from some dog shit.

"Are you coming?" yelled Jake, from the top of the road.

I called, "Yes, we are," and to Louisa I said, "it's nothing. I'm not really. Forget it. I shouldn't have told you."

It's true: I really shouldn't have told her. It was just, shameful as it was, I wanted to smash something up for a moment. I wanted to see shock on her face. Even though it belonged to a person I liked. And, after I'd said it, even though I knew I'd opened myself up to danger, that there was a risk to tread around now, I felt relieved. As if I'd taken it one step further. As if I was beginning to make it real.

Jake had seen the others on the other side of the street. They were crossing over to meet us. Clarice and Pea were looking sulky. When they got to us, Pea said, "I'm just going to look round the antique shops. We haven't got anything waterproof for Clarice, and anyway she doesn't want to get sand in her shoes. And I've seen some rather nice Scandinavian painted furniture in the town square. So we'll meet you later."

Ed's feet were shifting to and fro in his tight Italian leather shoes. "Darling," he began, but she had already started walking in the opposite direction. "Meet you back at the car in an hour then?" he said in a high, nervous voice. Clarice, who was holding Pea's hand, turned her head and stuck out her tongue.

When we got to the beach, the children galumphed down to the water and were soon hooting with laughter, playing Russian roulette with the North Sea. Mark and Jake joined them, picking them up one by one, turning them horizontal and pretending to throw them in, like life buoys being hurled overboard. Louisa wandered down too. She said, "Coming?" to me, with a frown, but I shook my head and carried the stroller over the pebbles to join Ed who had sat down on an upturned boat. He looked glum. It had stopped raining, and there were patches of blue in the sky. There were quite a few people around. Couples trudging up and down, hands in their pockets, and families pretending it was sunny, eating their sandwiches behind wind shelters, children calf-deep in frothing sea.

"Budge up," I said, putting Dan down so he could watch the waves and pulling my jacket down to protect my bottom from the damp wood. "Good news about Kyushi then."

"Yes," he said.

"Tight competition too."

"Yup."

We were staring ahead. Louisa had reached Mark and put her arms round him from behind. We both watched them for a bit. I said, "They're the perfect couple, Mark and Louisa, aren't they?"

Ed shrugged. The dance seemed to have gone out of him. His face looked pouchy and pale. An actor waiting outside make-up.

I said, "Put the rest of us to shame."

He made an indeterminate noise in his throat.

Louisa had taken off her shoes and was trying to splash Mark with her feet. There were shrieks as Penny and Joe joined in. Jake was showing Fergus how to skim stones.

Ed and I seemed to have nothing to say to each other, which was disconcerting. He was not usually one to let a silence grow beneath his feet. He was playing with some pebbles, shifting them between his fingers and throwing the odd one as if it were a cricket ball onto the sand farther along the slope.

I bent down to rearrange Dan's blanket. "Your Daddy and I don't behave like that do we?" I said chirpily.

Suddenly, from behind me, Ed spoke very quickly. "Look, I'm probably speaking out of line here, but I know that you and Jake are going through a bad patch. I know it's none of my business, but . . ." He swallowed hard. "But I just wanted to tell you that I think he's a great bloke and that he really cares for you and . . . that's all really."

"Ed!" I said, straightening up.

His voice sounded strangled. "Relationships can be very difficult."

I said, "What do you mean?"

"None of us is perfect."

"I know, but what do you mean?"

Ed began to take in a deep breath, as if he was about to say something, but then stopped it and didn't. He dropped the stones he was holding, dusted his hands on his trousers, and shook his head as if he'd changed his mind. He stood up abruptly, pulling himself physically together. "No," he said. "No, no, no. Forget it."

"Go on," I said. "What do you mean? Who's not perfect?"

"I was just making conversation," he said. "I didn't mean anything." He'd started moving away and down the beach. He began to run, careening downhill into his usual self. He put his arms out like an airplane. "Ngwooooow," he said, charging into Penny and Joe. "Okay, campers!" he hollered. "How about a bite of lunch?" Even from where I was sitting I could see him pretending to take a chunk out of Louisa's shoulder.

• • •

We should, in retrospect, have gone back to the cottage for warmed-up stew. As it was, we went to one of those cozy-looking seafood cafés, which pretends it's cheap and cheerful but is full of people eating seriously, and expensively, off gingham tablecloths, heads ducked so as not to bang against the plastic lobsters hanging from the ceiling.

Ed darted off when we got to the main square and returned with Pea and Clarice. Clarice had been bought a jigsaw puzzle from a souvenir shop and she started unwrapping it while we were still waiting for a table, dropping pieces left, right, and center, and squealing whenever somebody trod on a piece of the Little Mermaid. We were all squashed against the door, with our arms full of coats, because it was steamy in there out of the wind, and Fergus had his hands in the air, wanting to be picked up, and Dan was writhing in my arms, trying to poke his fingers through the fishing net that was slung across the window, and everyone else was milling and tripping over chair legs. People at the tables kept looking round to see what the commotion was, which, on the one hand, made me want to bow my head in apology and embarrassment, and on the other, I wanted to curl up under the table and cry.

I said to Jake, "Do you think you could take something? I've got my arms full here."

He said, "What do you want me to take exactly?"

"I don't know. Anything," I snapped. "Take Dan."

I was about to suggest we beat a retreat when Pea said from the floor where she was picking up pieces of puzzle, "I don't know why we're doing this. There's lots of delicious bourguignonne left back at the house." Suddenly, I was eating out's biggest fan. "Yes but no hot crab ramekin. I can't wait for my hot crab ramekin."

When we finally squeezed into a table, negotiating the high chair round the legs, settling each child in proximity to at least one parent, confiscating the menus before they were waved too wildly, and the napkin-wrapped cutlery before it was scattered, matters disintegrated even further. Fergus was overexcited. He was bouncing up and down in his chair. He was banging the table, chanting, "Er, er, er" in a moment of regression. The older children joined in too, turning it into a game. Joe got hold of the salt and pepper shakers and started banging those too, and he made Clarice cry by spilling her Coke. "Grow up all of you," shrieked Pea. "Enough, I say. Enough." We all turn into our parents in the end.

I was at the opposite end of the table from Jake with a small mountain range of children's heads between us. Ed was next to me on my right. Ignoring the chaos, he had his face in the wine menu. "White all right for everyone?" he said, as if he was offering us a choice, then, without pausing, to the waiter, "Pouilly Fumé, please." He sniffed it when it came, swirled it in his glass, and brought it to his nose. He nodded at the waiter without looking up.

"Aren't you supposed to taste it?" I said.

"Actually, no. A sniff's all that's needed. All you're looking for is whether it's corked or not and you can tell that from the slightest of signs."

"Like many things in life," I said, taking a large glug from mine. "The smallest of clues . . ."

He looked at me and then looked away very quickly.

I waited until the food arrived to ask him what he had meant on the beach. I was sure he had been about to say something about Jake's affair. Could he be an unexpected ally? But, before I did, I had trouble getting his attention away from Clarice, who wanted him to hear her count her scallops in French.

"Un. Deux. Trois . . ."

"So what's the name of your French teacher?" I interrupted.

"Madame Charbonnel," she said, still busy with her Coquilles St. Jacques.

Unfortunately, this caught Pea's attention across the table. She looked up from her pan-fried squid. "Not for long. Madame Charbonnel has announced she's leaving next half term, to have a baby. So *she's* in no one's good books at the moment."

Ed had caught Jake's eye. "Madame Charbonnel," he said, with his hand on his heart, pretending to swoon.

Pea said, "Except clearly in Ed's. Madame Charbonnel can't do a thing wrong as far as you're concerned, can she? Including," this to the rest of us, "leaving in the middle of a school year. It couldn't be more disruptive for the children."

A flinch of irritation contracted Ed's forehead. "I'm only messing about," he said.

"Yes, well, not in front of . . ." Pea inclined her head toward Clarice.

Ed's jaw stiffened almost imperceptibly. I waited until it got noisy again, until there was a rising tumult around us, blurred voices and children's cries, like the sea heard through a shell. I concentrated firmly on my glass. I could hear Fergus demanding ketchup for his goujons. Jake admonished, "Fergus!"

"Ketchup PLEASE," returned Fergus. I saw the contents of Dan's spoon, catapulted by an errant elbow in a 180-degree radius. I reached across for the Pouilly Fumé and poured myself another drink.

Ed was picking at his Easter bonnet garnish of twirled carrot and parsley next to me. When no one was listening, I said softly, "What did you mean, 'no one's perfect'? What were you referring to? I wish you'd tell me."

He looked frightened. You could almost see the cogs in his brain trying to think of a joke to get him out of it; urgently needed: an ejector seat of wit.

"I don't know," he said. "Look, this is a mad house. Let's eat up and go. Waiter? Check please."

He did some frantic invisible writing, which caught the eye only of his wife.

"What are you doing?" she said. "Aren't we going to have coffee?"

"I thought . . ."

She looked irritated with him and turned to the others as

if she had decided no longer to register his presence. "Who wants coffee?" she said.

I had been busying myself with Dan. I said, "Ed and I thought we'd take the children for a runaround. You lot have coffee. Jake, will you take Dan? We'll take the others."

Jake said, "Er, sure." He looked a bit nonplussed, though not as nonplussed as Ed who looked as if he wanted to curl up like the carrot on his plate. But I felt defiant. I wanted Ed on my own. I wanted to know what he knew.

We bundled up the children and went outside into the gusty grayness. We walked back to the beach without talking. I hadn't brought my jacket. I wanted to feel the cold wind again after the hotness of the café. I felt headachey around the eyes as well as pink in the cheeks.

The children had run off back down to the sand. I stopped to take off my shoes and perched on the edge of a break-water, pulling my dress around my knees. "Listen, you started to say something earlier and then you bottled out."

"What?"

"Come on, you know you did."

He looked flustered. "Did I?"

"Yup. I know we don't really get on, but I liked you for it. I appreciated the fact you wanted to talk to me about it."

"Really?"

"Yes. It made me realize you are my friend as well as Jake's."

"Did it?" He flushed. He started picking at some dried-up seaweed, which had stuck to the breakwater. "I don't know what to say, really."

"Well, you don't have to say anything else, because I know about her. About Claire, I mean."

"Do you?" He sat down on the stump next to me. It was

wet, but he didn't seem to notice. The red had drained away, leaving his face white. "Did Jake tell you?"

"I worked it out. I'm not stupid."

"Oh." He picked at a bobbly string of seaweed attached to the breakwater next to him.

The children were huddled together farther across the beach. Penny was kneeling on the sand and was poking at something with a piece of driftwood. The others had their heads together watching her.

"So?" I tried to make my voice sound light. "How serious do you think it is?"

Ed rubbed his eyes with his seaweedy hands, pushed them back through his hair. "I think it's very serious. I wish it wasn't. I wish it wasn't . . ."

I didn't know what I was expecting, but I don't think, until this moment, that it was this. Part of me had assumed that Jake's relationship with Claire was just about sex. The fabric of my dress suddenly seemed very thin. I said, shivering, "Oh fuck."

Ed was looking paler than usual. "It's a terrible mess," he said in a tight voice.

"You can say that again."

He had turned his head to stare at the olive sea. There were some sail boats out there now, white envelopes cutting through the waves. I pulled on his shoulder. "So what are you saying, Ed? Time to leave?"

There was a pause before he turned his head back to me. "Maybe. I know Pea wouldn't stand for things if she knew. I don't know. What do you think, Maggie? It's a hard thing to ask, but maybe you could talk to Claire. See what's going through her mind. That's one thing I don't know."

"The last thing I want to do is talk to Claire," I said. Then I said, "Fuck." I didn't have the energy to pretend anymore.

The children had moved apart from each other now. Penny was taking something on the end of her wood down to the water. The smaller ones were following her, but Clarice had started back up the beach toward her father, her face screwed up. I said quickly, before she got to us, "So is it just about sex, Ed? Or is it love?"

He paused before answering. "Are they different?"

Clarice, sobbing, was a few steps from us. "Fergus . . ." she began.

"I wish I knew," I said.

Chapter 20

That evening, after I'd put the children to bed, I told everyone I needed some air and walked down to the pub in the
village. It was your typical country affair: video games built
into low tables, wide-screen TV, and local guys discussing
crack cocaine in a gaggle in the corner. I ordered a gin and
tonic and sat on a stool listening to the landlord talking with a
rather dapper middle-aged man in a velvet jacket about the
director's cut of *Apocalypse Now*: "The original version was
much more intense, but the new one's much longer." There
was a chunky plastic pay phone on the bar. I pushed coins
into it and called Pete. But the line was engaged.

I sat on the stool nursing my drink. I didn't know how
long I could be away from the house without drawing attention, but I had to speak to Pete. Ever since my conversation
on the beach with Ed, I'd been feeling desperate. It would do
me good to hear Pete's voice, to hear him be nice to me, to
check that he was still all right for Tuesday. All this would
quell my confusion. Jake didn't want me anymore, but Pete
did. Didn't he? And, naturally, I wanted to be with him. Why

wouldn't I? Why would I feel anything for Jake anymore? Not after how he'd behaved. Not if things were serious with Claire. There was no point thinking about that. Obviously Pete and I didn't know each other very well, but that was soon to change. We were proceeding in the right direction. Or were we? Oh, hell.

If the landlord had known what was going through my head, he would no doubt have told me to pull myself together. Worse things, worse things by far (especially in the uncut version) had happened in Vietnam. But he didn't.

I tried the phone again. This time Pete picked up straight away and said, "What happened there?" as if he was in the middle of a call with someone else.

I said, "What do you mean? Nothing. It's Maggie. You were engaged."

He said, "Oh, Maggie. Hi. Right. Sorry. I was talking to someone else and . . . er, they were cut off."

I said, "Do you want me to ring back?"

And he said, "No, it's all right," but after that I felt wrong-footed, as if I had to talk fast and get off.

"I just needed to hear your voice," I said. "It's awful here. I'm longing to see you. It feels like ages."

"I'm sorry, Mags. I've been busy as shit."

"It's all right, I understand. But you're still on for Tuesday?"

"You bet. Can't wait. A whole evening of . . ."

"Yes, but we're going to go out, aren't we? Do something? You're still happy to do that?"

"Oh yeah. Of course. How are you?"

"Oh God. You wouldn't believe . . ." I began to tell him about the weekend, but he cut me off. "Look, my little pumpkin"—he said this ironically—"I'm sorry. But I'd better go. There're some people waiting for me upstairs . . ."

"Oh, okay," I said. "Do you miss me?"

"Of course. Mmmmmm." He paused. "See ya, all right?"

"See you."

I didn't feel much better after this conversation, but I could at least take comfort in having spoken to him.

There was an uneasy atmosphere when I got back to the house. Pea was clattering about in the kitchen, making a meal out of cooking a chicken. Louisa and I had wanted to get take-out from the Thai restaurant in the village, but Pea had insisted. When I asked if there was anything I could do to help, she told me it was all under control *now*, thanks. She had been cool with me ever since Ed and I had taken the children for a walk. "Can I get you a drink?" I asked, pouring myself a glass from the bottle of wine by the sink.

She flinched. "Oh. I'd set that aside for the gravy. Never mind." A clipped, martyrish smile. Then, eyebrows raised, "Maybe I'll wait until Mark and Louisa have got their children to bed. If they ever do."

It was 9:30 p.m. before they did and 10:00 p.m. before we sat down for supper.

Pea was visibly steaming with irritation—Clarice had been in bed since 7:00 p.m., and the chicken had been in the oven for hours.

"It'll be fine," said Ed.

"It won't," she said under her breath. "It'll have completely dried out. Anyway, I don't know what I'm doing with this oven. I don't know where I am with gas."

"Do you have electricity at home?" asked Louisa with calming interest.

"No. I have an Aga."

"Natch," said Ed, looking at Jake.

Pea had been halfway out to the kitchen. She stopped in the doorway. "Sorry?"

"Nothing," he said. She was still looking at him, a glare that turned the rest of us to stone. I expected Ed to whimper apologies. That's what the old Ed would have done. Instead, he said, "It's just having an Aga over in Morton. It's a bit ridiculous, isn't it? It's the sort of stove you expect to find in a country farmhouse. But we never wear wellies, we never go out in the rain—Clarice doesn't even own a proper mack— we don't have a cat. We never cook cakes or bread or . . . I don't know whatever else an Aga is supposed to be good for. We're out at work all day, and yet sitting at home, cold and empty, except for the au pair doing her fingernails, is this complete replica of a country kitchen. In the suburbs of London. It just seems a bit . . ."

"A bit what?" Pea's teeth were gritted.

"A bit pretentious."

Everyone else started talking very quickly then.

"Raeburn . . ." said Louisa.

"Wet socks . . ." said Mark.

Jake told a story about his college room and a hot plate. I began to recount the time I'd left a burner on all night. But Ed went very quiet, and Pea left the room.

The meal passed awkwardly. Mark and Louisa tried as hard as they could to rally spirits—*heaping* compliments onto Pea, *insisting* she not lift another finger, *tearing* into each other's table-clearing techniques ("Don't scrape, Mark—that's so common. That's the worst thing you can do apparently. Straight to the bottom of the social order." "You're one to talk; you're spilling!"), knocking each other around the head in mock fury, as if it was totally normal for one half of a couple to be at the other half's throat. Unfortunately, this display only served to point up the solidarity between them. Jake and I were polite, while Ed and Pea were like opposite ends of a magnet. Ed turned to me a few times and asked the odd gentle question about my daily life, out of sympathy for my plight, I supposed. Pea glared from the other end of the table.

We were having coffee when the subject of the country came up again. Mark had gone outside for a cigarette, and when he came back in he said something about how wonderful the stars were when there weren't street lights in the way and that he'd thought he'd heard an owl. "I don't know," he said, "but maybe I could get used to this."

Pea, who hadn't said much up until then, said suddenly, "Well exactly. It's no wonder that some of us want to live in the country. It's not 'pretension.' The quality of life is much better here."

"You mean we could afford a bigger house," Ed said. "That's why the quality of life would be better."

"Maybe. But there are other things. Fresher, cleaner air. The great outdoors."

"Remind me to buy you your very own waxed Barbour country jacket."

Mark jumped in quickly. "You're right, Pea. No traffic. No trucks. No airplanes taking off and landing at all hours. No Tube strikes. No speed bumps. No multiplexes and play zones. Fresh air and country walks, and pissing about in the garden. That's what I did when I was growing up."

Louisa's nose was wrinkled up on one side. "Mark," she said. "Don't tell me you're serious. I'd hate it. Stuck with the children in the middle of nowhere. Roads full of mud."

"I might be," he said.

"And Clarice would love a pony," Pea said, still directing her comments to Ed.

"Pea. She doesn't even like dogs."

"Well, I just think it's madness. When you think what we could have . . ."

"Vegetables." This was Jake's first contribution. "You can never find fresh vegetables in the country. They pack them off to town as soon as they've dug them up."

"You have to grow your own," said Mark, warming to his theme.

"Or get a gardener to grow them for you," I said. They all looked at me, puzzled for a moment.

Then Pea said, "Of course, there is a problem with the people. You wouldn't have many friends. There'd be nobody to discuss Truffaut with . . . But you'd just have to ship your friends down at weekends."

There was a lull as everyone registered what she had said.

Jake, who had been tearing his napkin into little strips, suddenly bunched it together again and chucked it into the middle of the table. "It's just a dream," he said. "Mark, Pea, you're just imagining ideal lives in the country. Like other people's photographs, when the light's just right and everyone's smiling. Real life isn't like that. Real life in the country is just like life in the town only slightly different, more complicated in some ways, easier in others. It's still school runs and trips to Woolworth's and finding ways to keep the children quiet at weekends. I bet you'd find a multiplex and a play zone in the nearest town pretty damn quick. You make friends where you can. You try and make the most of anything wherever you are, don't you? It's all about muddling through."

"Muddling through?" I said. "Is that what life is?"

"Yes," he said, looking at me. "Isn't it?"

"Shouldn't one expect more than that?"

"I didn't say muddling through didn't make one happy."

I felt confused for a moment. But Mark was still enjoying himself, winding Louisa up, or pandering to Pea, or whatever he was doing. "All I'm saying is," he drawled, getting up and going over to one of the sofas, "I wouldn't mind going to bed every night with those stars over my head."

"Exactly," said Pea. "That is so beautifully put."

"I'll give you stars over your head," said Louisa, bashing him with a cushion.

· · ·

It wasn't long after this exchange that Louisa, clearly keen to emulate a weekend in the country with jollier companions, suggested we play a game. I said I was tired and that goodness knew what time Fergus would get up in the morning, but she told me to pull myself together. Pea, sitting stiff-backed on the edge of a hard chair with the bottle of wine on the sidetable next to her, wanted to know what kind of game.

"Mr. and Mrs," Louisa said. "We played it in Cornwall at New Year. It was hilarious. One half of a couple leaves the room and you ask questions about them to the other. Then they come back in and answer the questions themselves. Their partner gets a point for each correct answer. I got everything wrong about Mark. I even got his high school grades wrong."

"You know nothing about me," her husband said, pretending to sob.

"Yeah well, I know more now than I did. It was quite an eye-opener. Stag weekend indeed . . ."

"All right," said Pea. There were two bright spots on her cheeks. The bottle by her side seemed to be going down suspiciously fast.

The rest of us agreed too, largely, I suspect, through fear of being considered dull.

Louisa left the room first and Mark answered questions on 1) her favorite film ("Easy. *The Silence of the Lambs*"), 2) her favorite food ("Toad in the Hole. My mother taught me how to make it and she *loves* it"), and 3) her favorite flowers ("Tough one . . . er . . . carnations I think"), all of which he got wrong. Her answers, when she came back in, were 1) *An American in Paris* ("How can you say *Silence of the Lambs?*" "We saw it on our first date." "Yes, well just because I remember it fondly doesn't mean I *liked* it"), 2) Scallops with bacon ("But you love my Toad in the Hole!" "Oh sorry, of course, scrap scallops, put greasy sausage in artery-thickening batter. My mistake"), and 3) Night-scented stocks. When informed that Mark had guessed carnations, she sighed and shook her head pityingly. "All men think women like carnations. It's one of the great tragedies of life."

Their score, so far in the game, then was nil. "Which just goes to show," Louisa said, snuggling up to her husband on the sofa, "that knowing things about each other, just like 'having things in common,' is a greatly overrated quality in a marriage."

Pea was the next woman out, which meant that this time Mark and Louisa had a hand in the questions. Ed floundered as to whether Pea "scrunched or folded" her toilet paper. "Shit," he said. "She's quite anal so I'd say folded, but then if you are literally anal I suppose you scrunch. I'll have to guess on this one. I'll say scrunch." Her desert island luxury caused him equal trouble. "If it hadn't been for earlier I'd have said an Aga, ha ha, but apart from that . . ."

"Vibrator?" suggested Louisa.

"Phh." He made a sound like a horse snorting through its mouth. "No. Perfume? No . . . There's some face cream she's always going on about, but . . . Um, I know: her contacts book. That'll be it." And, as for whether she had any recurring nightmares, he tapped his fingers on the side of his head, and went "nnnnnn" in thought, like an airplane coming in to land. Finally, he said, "I don't think she likes heights much."

Pea smiled brittlely when she came back in. She'd taken her drink with her, and I noticed she was swaying a little bit. "So," she said. "What revelations?"

She looked a mite offended at the scrunch/fold question but admitted to scrunching, awarding her marriage one point. For her desert island luxury, she said quickly, "My photo album; I'd like to have my loved ones with me," which made Ed pretend to slink under the table in shame. And for her recurring nightmare, she said, staring at me, "Discovering my husband has been unfaithful." I felt myself go red. Did she think I'd been flirting with Ed? Or did she know about Jake and Claire and was being cruel? Or was I being paranoid? I opened my mouth to say something, but Louisa had gotten up and was bustling me out of the room so that Jake could be questioned. I stood in the corridor, taking deep breaths.

When I came back in, they were all staring at me. Jake was looking embarrassed. Louisa said, in the honeyed singsong tone of a travel show host, "from the table, to the bathroom, to the bedroom . . ." Then in her own voice, "Tough luck, Maggie. We're braving sex now. The first question: with whom did you lose your virginity?"

"Easy," I said, smiling but not looking at Jake. "Patrick Unwin. Lower Sixth. His bedroom. 'Is She Really Going Out With Him?' on the stereo."

Jake looked relieved. "Well done," said Louisa. "One point to the Priton/Owens. Next question: have you ever had a one-night stand?"

"No," I said. "Unless two nights count?"

"They don't. Sorry." Louisa marked a cross on her piece of paper.

"So who do you think I had a one-night stand with?" I asked Jake.

"I don't know," he said. "I just thought you must have done."

"Well, I haven't."

Louisa cleared her throat and then said in a rush, "And finally, not my question this, Mags, blame Pea . . . Have you ever been unfaithful?"

"Sorry?" I said. My heart was thudding in my rib cage. My mouth was dry, my face hot.

Pea said, "Have you ever been unfaithful?"

"What?" I tried to laugh.

Louisa and Mark had started horsing around on the sofa, busy with a private joke on their own. Ed was looking anxious. Jake was studying his fingernails as if he wasn't even listening. But Pea was glaring at me. "Come on," she said. "Answer the question."

"No," I said. I tried to breathe normally. "No. Never."

Jake looked up. "Liar," he said.

I stared at him. I felt the color drain from my face. My eyes felt like bones.

"What about with me?" he said.

"What about with you?" My voice sounded choked.

Everyone was looking at us now.

"*And David.*"

It was a moment before I understood what he was getting at, and then I felt relief flood through me. I took an enormous breath. "Oh, yes," I said. "I'd forgotten. Of course. There was, shall we say, a slight matter of overlap between David the lawyer and Jake . . ." I put my hands up in an act of surrender.

"Thank you," said Jake.

"Which," said Louisa, back in official mode, "puts the Priton/Owens in the lead with two points."

The next round passed without incident—until it was Jake's turn to leave the room. I failed completely to come up with a figure for his golf handicap. I didn't even know what kind of a figure to be playing with. Finally, wracking my memories of P. G. Wodehouse, I said, "Fourteen under five," which made Mark fall off his chair laughing. I also didn't know what the first account in his first job was. "Oh dear," I said. "I should know, shouldn't I? Can I have a clue?"

Mark said, "Who's a pretty bird then?"

I said, "Something to do with animal feed, um . . ."

"Pretty Polly," he hissed.

"Oh yes," I said, "I knew that . . ."

But it was the next question, asked by Pea, that really got me. "Does Jake have any secrets from you?" she said. Did he have any secrets from me? Oddly, my first instinct was to laugh. I thought of saying yes—I mean everyone has some secrets, don't they?—but her eyes were boring into me, and I suppose it was dignity or pride that made me say "no."

When Jake came back in he didn't seem particularly amused by my ignorance on questions one and two, but he smiled when he came to this one, or it might have been a grimace. Ed said, "Unfair question. Don't make him answer it," but Jake replied with remarkable cool. "Yes," he said. "I do. Doesn't everybody have some secret or other?"

Pea was looking triumphant. I couldn't let her. I said, suddenly feeling sober, "No, you haven't. You think you have. But you don't."

I got up and went to the door. "Anyway, we're disqualified," I said. "We're not married."

• • •

The following day, Jake and I had arranged to take the children to visit his parents, who lived just across the border into Norfolk, a short drive away.

"I'm not coming," I told Jake when we woke up, after a short night (it had been past two by the time we finally made it to bed). My head throbbed with exhaustion and hangover and misery. It felt like a child's toy, my brain clonking against my skull like the sound box in a mooing cow. "You can take Fergus and Dan on your own. They're your parents after all."

"But you're the one they'll want to see," he said. "Please come." He bent across Fergus, who had gotten into bed with us in the night, and said quietly, "Let's be friends. It's awful being like this."

"I know," I said. We looked at each other, but I was the first to look away. "I just don't feel like coming, that's all."

"About last night, Maggie. The secret . . ."

"Look," I said. My head pounded. "I don't want to talk about it. I don't want to know."

I got up and went down the corridor to the bathroom where I could hear splashing and squeals of "get off" and then a sort of lapping sound. Mark and Louisa were clearly having sex in the bath. Depressed, I went back to the bedroom where Jake was mucking about on the bed with Fergus and Dan.

"Fine," he said without rancor. "We'll go without you then."

The expression on his face made me want to kiss him. But I couldn't. It had been too long.

They set off quite soon after that. Pea and Ed took Clarice off to a museum in a local market town so she could do some work on her Ancient Roman project. Penny and Joe made a camp in the garden. Louisa wanted to know if I was all right.

I told her everything was hunky-dory.

"So who's this bloke?" she said, chucking the *Sunday Times*' Style section on the floor. "Are you going to tell me about him?"

I told her he was nobody really and that it hadn't been going on for long. That he was a gardener. That he had hands like sandpaper. That he had earth under his nails. That he was younger than me. That maybe it would be better if I didn't talk about it.

"Whatever," she said.

We went for a walk down the lane to a little bridge over a stream.

"Do you ever worry about missing out?" I asked her. "Do you ever for a minute doubt that Mark isn't right for you?" She didn't say anything, just looked sympathetic.

"Stupid question," I said.

"You're bound to have up and down patches," she said. "We all do. You met him young. It's so difficult with small children. Ninety percent of all divorces take place in the first year of the second child's life. Or something."

"Another two months to get through then," I said.

We stood, looking down into the water, a trickle at this time of year, with a few snack wrappers entangled in the weeds.

Louisa bent to fiddle with her flip-flops. "I quite like Pea, actually," she said.

"You like everybody," I said. "It doesn't count."

When we got back to the house, Ed, Pea, and Clarice had been back, packed, and left. Mark was standing up, eating a sandwich in the kitchen.

"They said they wanted to beat the Sunday evening traffic," he said. He took another bite, dropping lettuce onto the floor. "And Clarice had her Sanskrit homework to do. Or something."

Penny and Joe trailed in, covered in mud. "We're starving," said Penny.

"Shoes!" yelled Louisa.

Mark started cutting more bread into big, big chunks with cheese spilling out of the edges. My stomach turned. I went upstairs and lay down on the bed. The noises of the house drifted up. Mark was playing some energetic game in the garden. "Da–ad. Da–ad. Over here." Their voices got fainter and fainter. I felt a deep sense of unease. Something was nagging at the back of my mind. Something not right. Images came into my head. I could see box hedges, clipped into the shape of birds and animals, circles and spirals. I walked along a row of them toward a man in the distance. He had pruning shears in his hand and was bending over. His back was broad and he was wearing combats. When I got closer, he straightened up and turned toward me, and I saw then that it was Jake.

I must have slept for a long time because when I woke up the room was getting dark and the pillow beneath my cheek was wet.

September: Spiders

Chapter 21

It had been stormy in London that weekend too. When we got back there were leaves all over the common—green leaves, but harbingers of autumn nonetheless.

A change seemed to come over Jake and me, something less zingy and more subdued. When he said he was really sorry but he did have to go into the office on the Bank Holiday Monday to "tie up a few loose ends," I didn't tell him to "tie away" in reference to what I knew he was really off to do. I smiled and said, "Whatever."

"As long as you don't mind," he said, looking sad.

Fran had left a couple of messages over the weekend. She was planning a trip to Babyworld for all her nursery essentials. "So I could really do with the 'definitive Maggie list.' I mean what do you think of the three-in-one carseat/carry-seat/stroller option? Worth £500?" I could tell when I rang her back that she wanted me to go with her. Any item I mentioned, she made a sort of strangulated wheedling sound, as if it was all too much for her to cope with. "N'eghgh. What on earth are muslins anyway?" she said. "Don't you use them for making jam?" I told her she should probably just ask an assistant.

"When are you going?" I asked.

"Wednesday?" she said in a small voice.

"Good luck then," I said heartily. When I put the phone down, I felt lost for a moment, but I couldn't have gone with her, played the jolly sister-in-law. Not under the circumstances.

I had a strange sensation in the pit of my stomach all day Tuesday, the day of my date with Pete. I didn't know if it was excitement or anxiety or dread, but I felt breathless and jumpy. I had to go to the bathroom every five minutes too. I spent a long time getting ready. I'd waxed my legs and repolished my toenails when Fergus was napping. Scarlet Lady, the polish was called. And I used body lotion before getting dressed. I wore my Claire dress and my new taupe kitten heels. Jake was baby-sitting. I'd told him in the morning that I was having a girly night out with the "playground mums" and that I'd get Merika, but he'd frowned and said that he could do it, which felt a bit odd. I was surprised he could get away from work. "You look nice," he said, standing in the hallway as I left.

I got the Tube. Pete and I had arranged to meet down the line, in a district composed of street upon street of identical thirties housing. Safe houses. A long way from anyone we knew. Pete's van was waiting outside the station. He was sitting in the driver's seat, with his elbow out the window, reading the *Evening Standard*. He closed it when he saw me and leaned across to open the door. I hadn't seen him for more than a week. I'd expected him to look different. He was still in his work clothes. His hair was dull and unruly. He had more dirt than usual in his fingernails. He kissed me. "Look at you, all done up," he said.

"Yes, and look at you!" I said. "You haven't exactly made an effort!" I laughed, but I felt foolish suddenly in my new frock, my new heels at the bottom of my newly waxed legs, my cerise cardigan slung over my newly Clarins'ed shoulders.

Pete had taken his arm from my shoulder and had turned the ignition. "Where are we going then, Mags?" he said.

"I haven't booked anywhere. Shall we just drive until we find somewhere?"

"You're the boss," he said, pulling out.

We roved around, getting lost in an industrial estate, negotiating the same one-way system several times, rejecting this theme bar and that steak restaurant, until we came to a pub, The Three Bells, on a nondescript roundabout. "What about here?" he said. "It looks okay, doesn't it?"

It had filthy net curtains on the windows and a garish banner advertising some television event "Live." It wasn't quite what I'd imagined, some little local bistro with a menu on a blackboard and carafes of rough red wine. "Absolutely," I said. "A drink's a drink."

We got out and went in. Pete opened the door for me, with a semi-bow and then, shrugging his arm over my shoulder, steered me to a table. We had our choice. It was almost empty. There were a couple of teenagers playing pool and an old man in a sheepskin coat at the bar. A big screen television was showing MTV on one wall. It was still sunny outside, but it was dark in here as if it was underground. I sat down in the corner, next to a line of fruit machines flashing like Las Vegas.

Pete went to the bar and came back holding a gin and tonic in one hand and a beer mug full of Coke in the other. "Driving," he said, chucking two packets of cheese and onion chips from his pocket onto the table.

"That's a shame," I said. "You should have taken the Tube too."

"Maybe," he said, screwing up his eyes, then added, "Naaa," as if it would have been too complicated.

He opened one of the packets and started munching. He offered the packet to me. I shook my head and he delved his fingers back in again. Like a Big Mac, cheese and onion chips are delicious in your own mouth, revolting in someone else's. I tried to ignore them. He said, sympathetically, "So, your weekend? Bloody nightmare was it?" I started telling him all about it, describing Ed and Pea and the others. He was smiling as if interested, but he was also tapping the table in time to the music. Britney Spears was miming to the song on the screen above the bar, her tiny headset mike buzzing in front of her mouth like a large insect. And the only comment he made was "She sounds a corker; bit of a goer is she?" when I told him about Louisa.

"So how was your weekend?" I said. "How was your *week*?"

He said, "Fine, fine."

There was a pause. Pete continued to tap his hands on the table. I said, "There's a chill in the air isn't there? We had a picnic today, Fergus and Dan and me, I mean, on the common, and . . . um, there was really quite a breeze." Pete shook his head, back and forth, rhythmically. There was a smile on his face but I don't think he was listening. "And what else? We bumped into Lucinda, running in her new au pair. She told me, while the girl was poop-scooping after one of the dogs, that she'd looked 'high and low' and this girl was 'the best she could find.'"

I expected him to laugh, but he said soberly, "She does seem to have her hands quite full with all those children." And then he stopped drumming and opened his mouth wide to get a particularly large chip in.

We didn't stay there very much longer. I finished my drink and would have had another, but Pete said if he had any more Coke, he'd be "pissing all night." Then I said we should go for dinner but he gestured to the empty chip packets and said he wasn't that hungry so we idled back out to the parking lot and stood by the van wondering what to do. What did you do on proper dates? It had been such a long time. What did Jake and I used to do? I think we just used to talk. In fact, I think we'd sat in some pretty dingy pubs, but somehow . . . Well, that was then. This was Pete. Pete was different. This was a different kind of relationship. I'd had talk. This was something new.

Pete looked at his watch. He said some mates were meeting in Fiction at 10:00 p.m. and if I . . . I said, feeling scared and shy and old, I didn't think so really, did he? And he said, "Yeah, you're right. So er, what else then?" He didn't want to drink. He didn't want to eat.

I said, "There's always late night shopping at Safeway's." But he didn't laugh.

He said, "No, I've done my groceries this week. Look . . . I think I might head off back to the flat. I'm pretty knacked and . . . but if you want to come, I'd be . . ."

It wasn't the most fulsome of invitations so I was going to say no, but Pete nipped away for a moment, to the other corner of the parking lot, to help a couple push-start their car, and when he came back, cheerful, shouting "all right, mate" over his shoulder, and slightly breathless, I heard myself say, yes, I would. It was the first time I'd been to his flat. When we got there, Pete took the steps down to the basement two at a time and went straight in ahead of me, leaving the door open behind him. The hallway smelled damp and dark, musty like a cupboard that's been closed too long. There were pizza flyers on the floor, cab cards, some ruffled up plastic bag, and, on the wall, one of those buttons that switches on a timer light. The timer light went out.

"I'm in the kitchen," he called from a small galley off the sitting room. He was scooping instant coffee into "My Mate Went to the Tower of London and All He Brought Back . . ." mugs. He chucked the spoon into the pile of dishes in the sink.

"You're supposed to go, 'brrrrnnggngng,'" I said. Blank look.

"Like in the ad?" Incomprehension.

"It doesn't matter."

He said, as if something had just occurred to him. "Are you hungry?" He opened the fridge and, with a "ha-ha," brought out a boxed pizza. "What do you say?" he said, already ripping off the cardboard wrapper and trying to squash it into the microwave.

I said, "I say, I thought you didn't want anything to eat?"

He said, "Didn't I? Well, I guess I've got an appetite now." I took the pizza from him and cut it into quarters so that it would fit and stood back while he switched it on. He told me to go and sit down, to make myself at home, so I went into the sitting room. It looked like an unmade bed. There were papers on the chairs and cushions on the floor, mugs and dirty plates on the table, and towels draped over an exercise bike in the corner. I cleared a copy of *Loot* off the sofa and sat down. There was something hard and knobbly under my bottom. I put my hand down and came up with some dumb-bells, which I laid carefully on my knee, and stared at.

There was a ping and Pete came in, nudged the dumbbells onto the floor with his knee, and handed me a plate. "Tucker," he said. "Wrap your nostrils around that."

I took one chewy mouthful and said, "Actually. It's a funny thing. But do you know, I find I'm really not that hungry."

Pete, one eye on the *TV Guide*, said he'd have mine. Then he said, "Oh great: it's *Who Wants To Be A Millionaire?*" and put the television on with his spare hand. It was a very big television. I wasn't used to seeing Chris Tarrant so big. He was coaxing a flight attendant from Bicester up to £4,000. "In the famous quotation from Shakespeare's *Twelfth Night,* music is the food of what? Time, appetite, love, or ears?"

"Time," said Pete.

"Love," I said

"Nah," he said, wrinkling his nose. "Are you sure?"

"Yes," I said. "Everyone knows that." Then I caught his expression and added, "Well anyway. You know what they say: they're only easy if you know them."

"Yeah, all right, clever clogs," he said.

A little bit later, I said, "So Pete, what *are* your plans?"

Pete still had a mouthful of pizza. I waited, listening to the sound of his chews, until he swallowed. "What plans?" he said, finally.

"Don't you want to travel? Isn't that what all Australians do?"

"Yeah," he shrugged. He started another mouthful.

"And where would you go if you did?"

This time he didn't bother swallowing. "Thailand?" he said through his pepperoni.

"Anywhere else?"

"Phuket? I don't know. Can I phone a friend? Ha. Ha."

"No, I'm being serious," I said. "I'm just trying to find out more about you. I don't even know if you plan to settle in England or whether you're about to go back to Australia. Are you?"

He put his plate down, wiped his mouth with the back of his hand, and licked the remains of tomato off his fingers. He seemed to be giving it a lot of thought. "Dunno," he said finally.

I said, "But do you think you'll go back some time?"

"Maybe," he said.

"Soon?"

"Crickey," he said. "You and your questions. I dunno. Come on. Go 50/50." He wasn't talking to me now, he was talking to a sports instructor from Weymouth. I grabbed the remote control from under his plate. Chris Tarrant and the sports instructor disappeared with a hiss.

"We never talked," I said.

He didn't notice the change of tense. "Okay. Okay. Sorry. Sorry." He shifted slightly and put his arm around me. "So," he began, "let's talk . . ." Then I realized one of his shoulders was easing me down onto the sofa, that a hand was climbing up my newly waxed leg.

"That's not . . ." I said, beginning to protest. His hands were inside my new taupe heels, slipping them off. "What I meant," I said.

Chapter 22

Of course, I did sleep with him in the end. It would have seemed churlish not to. Not after all the fuss I'd made about having a date in the first place. But it was over. I knew that now. I'd probably, in the back of my mind, known it for some time, but it was the dumbbells that finally did it for me. The cheese and onion chips and the dumbbells. Our relationship had been all about sex, not because there wasn't time for it to be about anything else, but because that was all it was. There was nothing else to it, nowhere else for it to go. And even the sexual attraction was based on a false premise. I'd thought he was so natural, so physically in tune with the elements, with the plants he tended, but it turned out even his muscles were artificially boosted.

I cried a little bit in the taxi on the way home, but the tears stopped as quickly as they came. The realization in lots of ways made everything simpler. It was me and the kids now. Jake and Claire. Me and the kids. I'd make a life for us after the separation, on our own. We could start again. There was no point mourning the past, I thought, opening the door of my sleeping house. I just had to get on with things.

Mel had flown home from France on Tuesday night, while I was with Pete. She had one last day off before going back to work and was due to have lunch with Piers at Pizza Express. She'd missed him, she said. So we met in the park in the early morning. There was a chill in the air, and the sun made striped shadows through the trees.

Milly and Fergus had run off to investigate some boggy ground near a tree trunk. They were poking about with sticks, squawking with laughter every time they managed to fish a knot of brown foliage out of a puddle, whispering, daring each other to dip a sandaled toe.

"At least it's still warm enough not to mind," I said, as we watched them venture in, bent double with pleasure and naughtiness. "In a few weeks' time, we'll be shouting, 'No. Not in those shoes . . . You'll get cold feet.'"

Mel said, "So, come on. What's going on?"

We had talked all the way over, covering all the small inconsequential business that binds good friends; that tells you more about each other's state of mind than any amount of soul-searching. She had told me about her holiday. Nice house. Good pool. Irritating sister-in-law. I had burbled about some Ultima eyecream recommended in the Saturday papers. "Apparently it 'does as much for your bags as 100 years of sleep.'"

"In your dreams," said Mel. I knew we'd get to me in the end.

I said, "Do you think I can let Dan crawl around? He'll get very messy, but it seems unfair to keep him harnessed in."

She didn't say anything. She sat down on a bench and waited. I undid the straps on the stroller and put Dan down on a drier piece of ground. He set off immediately, scrabbling across the grass on his hands and knees to join the other two in their homemade bog. "Oh well," I said, "Doesn't matter. He'll dry off too."

I sat down next to her on the bench. Someone had written "Sue loves Pog" in small felt-tip letters on the wood between us (Sue I suppose), only they'd written "loves" in the form of a heart. I tried to rub the heart out with my finger as I filled her in. I told her I wasn't quite as mad as I had been, that I had the gardener in perspective, but that I did think things had gotten serious between Jake and Claire, and that he was probably on the verge of leaving me. It's like seeing a wall coming toward you, I told her. You know it's going to happen, you know it's going to hurt, but there's nothing you can do but brace yourself. I also told her that I had to take a lot of the blame, that I'd let it happen. I'd been awful. Brittle. Unapproachable. Worst of all, when I could have been fighting for him, I'd frittered away the time with some hunk from Down Under.

"Down Under being the operative words?"

"Well maybe."

"At least there's that," she said.

We both laughed. Or I tried to.

Milly and Fergus had run out of the trees and were heading away from us, elbows and knees and splashes of color across the yellowing grass. Mel said, "Do you think they'd make it to the border before we stopped them?"

"They'll come back," I said. "They always do."

We watched them reach the pond, where they leaned against the railings, looking over their shoulders occasionally at us, taunting us with their daring. Dark clouds with white edges billowed across the sky, skudding like missiles toward the sun. The pond darkened, and Milly and Fergus turned and started back, slowly, solidly, hand in hand, like an old couple. Mel put her arm around me. "I'm so sorry." I could tell she wasn't sure what sort of thing I wanted her to say.

I said, "You've got to tell me what to do. I'm in the middle of it. I can't see round it. I don't know what's what anymore. Do I want Jake back even if he wanted to come? Do I want the gardener? No. Or should I be on my own? I've never been on my own. It would be good for me, wouldn't it? What do you think I should want? What do you think I should do?"

She took a deep breath. She said, "Well. Maybe you should fight for Jake. If he can give her up, if you can forgive him . . . you won't be able to go back to how things were, but you can go on. You could make a life together, couldn't you? It might not be perfect, but you've got small children and they deserve some consideration in this. I mean, you always used to be so good together, so relaxed—no one else did cozy as well as you do—and I don't know. I don't think it's always a choice between being happy or being unhappy—I suppose I'm talking about Jake here—sticking in an 'unhappy relationship.' I think if you make a decision to stay and it seems hard, it doesn't mean you have to be unhappy for the rest of your life; you just have to try a bit harder to find happiness, root it out in the circumstances in which you find yourself. I don't think happiness is something that comes or doesn't; I think it's something you have control over."

"But if he really loves her . . ."

"Well maybe he does now. Maybe he doesn't. Who's to say how long it would last anyway? In a way, that's why I'm still with Piers. It's comfortable and comfortable only gets more comfortable as time goes by. Passion doesn't. Anyway, I have to say, I always assumed Jake really loved you, Maggie. I know he didn't say much, but he was just one of those men. Carried it deeply, not on his sleeve, but in his heart, which is where it counts. And actually I can't believe that's changed. Not really underneath."

"I don't know."

"This could just be an infatuation with Claire. Maybe you should see her for starters. Tell her to fuck off. Go round there. Cause havoc."

"Maybe Jake and I need some time apart anyway."

"Absolutely not!" Her eyes were bright. "That's the worst thing anyone ever does. Never ever have space. Don't give yourself space and don't, whatever you do, let Jake. It's space that kills relationships, not mistakes. Once you have space, then, all sorts of things start happening and none of them good."

I smiled. "Okay. Okay," I said. "Point taken." I got up to collect Dan who had crawled over to the trash can and was beginning to pull himself up to investigate its interestingly smelling contents. When I came back and had wrapped him up in the stroller, I gathered the V-neck of my cardigan into a bunch to protect my chest. It had gotten cold suddenly. "And what about my Australian?"

"Dump him," she said, standing up and brushing the bottom of her jeans. "Now."

. . .

I was cleaning out the bath a couple of hours later when the doorbell went.

"Coming!" I shouted, peeling off the rubber gloves and jumping down the stairs.

Pete was standing on the porch looking doleful. He was shaking drops of rain from his hair, moving his weight from foot to foot to keep his bare legs warm.

He said, "You rushed off so quickly yesterday. I just wondered . . . I mean, are you cross with me for not having been around . . . ?"

"No," I said. "Not at all."

He looked surprised. "And I was a bit short with you yesterday. To be quite honest I wasn't really in the mood but . . ."

"No honestly," I said. "It didn't matter."

"Oh." A look of relief came into his eyes, then he half-closed them. "I suppose I can't kiss you then, can I?"

I said, "No." I had Dan on one hip. Fergus was descending the stairs on his stomach. Head first.

"Look, I'm a snake," he told Pete.

Pete ignored him. He said, head on one shoulder, "When then?"

I didn't know what to say. Mrs. Allardyce was creaking by with her walker on wheels. She was wearing her raincoat. Not my nemesis anymore, my salvation. I waved. She peered round her plastic rain hat to say, "Hello, dear. Better get home before it pours."

I said quickly, "Any news?"

She smiled. "Well, it's not cancer. Old age probably. I've got a puffer."

"I'm so glad," I said. "Cup of tea later?"

Pete didn't turn around during this exchange. He said, "Aw, go on, let me in."

I didn't have the heart to turn him away now. We went into the kitchen. Fergus had stopped being a snake and was hiding behind my knees, trying to pry them apart and peer through the middle. Pete, recovering himself, pretended to lunge at him, and Fergus giggled and clutched one of my thighs, twirled round my leg as if it were a maypole. "Steady on," I said, almost losing my balance. "Come on, Fergus, let's see if the Tweenies are on!!" I raised my voice to a high, infectious pitch of excitement. "Yes!"

Fergus, infected, echoed, "Yes!" and ran through with me into the sitting room where he snuggled down happily into the sofa cushions, like a mouse nestling into hay. I left Dan on the floor chanting "balubalubalub," next to a bucket of Duplo.

Pete's hands were waiting for me in the kitchen. "Come here," he said, kneading me and kissing my neck. "I've missed this."

I pulled away. I was all angles. It wasn't me he'd missed; it was the danger. "Pete, I can't do this," I said.

"I can," he said, his voice husky, his eyes glazed. "Come here," and he pulled me toward him again and started kissing me. He had one hand on the back of my head. My knees weakened. I could hear the clatter, crash, clatter of Duplo being emptied onto the boards. Pete's hands were everywhere. There were alarm bells ringing in my head. This was wrong. It wasn't what I wanted. The alarm bells grew louder. More insistent. More ringing.

"Mummmeeee. Phone!"

"It's the phone," I said, pushing him away. "I've got to answer it."

Pete rolled his eyes and stood crossly, looking out the back door.

I grabbed the phone from under a tea cloth.

"Hello?" I said, breathlessly.

"Can I speak to Maggie Owen, please?'

"Speaking."

"It's Dr. Pulbrooke here, from Chelsea and Westminster Hospital." Even as she was talking, I could feel panic starting at my toes and working its way up. I moved on maternal autopilot to check the children in the front room. "I'm ringing on behalf of Fran Priton."

"What is it?" I said. "What is it? Is she all right? Is it the baby?"

"I'm afraid there has been an accident," said the voice. "Ms. Priton is in the operating room at the moment. She's going to be all right. Please don't panic. But she's been asking for you. Would it be possible for you to come in?"

"Yes, yes, I'll come now. Yes." I was gabbling. I'd forgotten all about Pete. "But the baby? What about the baby?"

"We're doing everything we can. We'll be able to tell you more when you get here."

She gave me the details of where to go, and I put down the phone and started throwing things into a bag—cups, bottles, diapers, wipes. Pete said, his laid-back delivery 100 miles behind me, "Is everything okay?"

"No," I said, "it isn't." I grabbed my car keys, switched off the television, drowned Fergus's cries of complaint with kisses, picked up both children for the sake of speed and started for the door. Pete trailed behind. Suddenly, I thought of something. "Your mobile!" I said. I'd felt it in his jeans pocket earlier. "I can ring Jake as I'm driving. Can I take it?"

"Er . . . Actually . . ."

"Thanks," I said, before he could say anything more. I reached for it out of his pocket. "I'll ring you later."

The children were muted in the car as if they sensed something was up. It had stopped raining, but the traffic was still heavy for mid-morning. Held up on the bridge, I fumbled with the phone until I got through to Jake's office. He was in a meeting, but I told Judy, his secretary, it was urgent. When I said it was Fran, I registered a nanosecond of relief in his voice as he realized it was nothing about the children, and then he sounded sick. "I'll come now," he said, his voice heavy and tight. "I'll meet you there."

The traffic was fine until the Fulham Road and then we

inched along, stuck in single file behind a parked truck. "Come on," I urged gutturally, like a businessman in a hurry or a Morton Park mother on a school run. "Come arnnnnn." I put my foot down when I turned into the side road leading to the parking lot, a quick spurt of relief—and then I braked hard. There was a line of cars in front. A Peugeot 205 with a fat man in the driver's seat was trying to turn around, but a bus had come up on the other side of the road and was jamming his path. Everybody else was just sitting, patiently, some with their engines off, as the line of cars idled its way, or rather didn't idle its way, down the lane to the parking area below. "Shit," I said, when I realized what was happening. "Shit, shit. Bugger, bugger." There were four cars ahead of us to the first bend. I looked at the clock on the dashboard. It was 12:40 p.m.—forty minutes since the doctor had called. A sign on the wall next to us said "NO stopping: offenders will be clamped." Why wasn't the road littered with clamped vehicles? This was a hospital after all: a place for screeching brakes and crashing doors, for relatives and doctors hitting the decks running. The man in front was eating a sandwich. But of course, outside of ER, hospitals are not places of rush and urgency and panic. They are about boredom and repetition and interminable waiting . . . But not now, not for me NOW.

"Oh no," I said through my teeth, as we entered the tunnel and I counted six cars in the flickering yellow light in front. I remembered the phone then, on the passenger seat beside me, and I picked it up to try to ring the ward, but the screen dimmed. No signal. "Oh no," I said again, chucking it into my bag.

It was 1:00 p.m. by the time the barrier had coughed us in, and ten past by the time we reached the elevator. A heavily pregnant woman and her husband got in with us. She had her bag with her; he was carrying a bottle of Perrier. There were no obvious contractions between floors. I wanted to say, in that irritating manner that women who've been there do, "Go home. You'll only have to sit around and wait," but the doors opened and I was out of there, rushing to the desk and identifying the floor and the "Lift Bank," scooting past the stall selling pastel knitted rabbits, and the visitors with their plastic-wrapped bunches of flowers, the sculptures hanging like shop window decorations in the atrium, past the cappuccino machine, and the "café-style" cafeteria, up in the Pompidou-style elevator to the ward.

Fergus said, "Are we going swimming?"

"No, darling," I said, pushing open the double doors. "We're going to see Fran."

The sister, a petite brunette who looked about twelve, frowned at us when she saw us. "Mother's own?" she said.

"Sorry?"

"We don't allow any other children!" she said sternly, but she melted when I told her who I'd come to see. She said, "Well, in that case, *one minute.*"

I said, moving Fergus out of the path of a woman in a nightgown who was inching her way along the hall, "I'm sorry. I was just in a hurry. I didn't really have time to make arrangements." A small, hiccuping kitten cry started up at one end of the corridor. "How is she? How's the baby?"

"She's in here," she said, leading us through a series of swinging doors to a room at the side. "In recovery." She paused before letting me in. "She's fine. She's a bit upset and shaken up obviously. It's been a big mental and physical shock. She's very sore. We're giving her morphine and voltral for the pain. And she's had to have quite a lot of blood."

"What about the baby?" I almost shouted. "Where's the baby?"

"Sssh," she said, too kindly. "The baby is in the Special Care Baby Unit. She's very little. Thirty-two weeks is quite early . . ."

"So she's had the baby?" I said, one part of my brain saying "It's a girl!" and the other dampening the hope down. "Is she going to be all right? They say thirty weeks is okay, isn't it? I mean, it's fine isn't it?"

She frowned. "The doctors gave her a Caesarean," she said, speaking slowly, as if this was something I was already aware of. "The placenta as you know was damaged in the accident and so delivery had to take place as quickly as possible. As I said, the doctors are doing everything they can." I must have looked stricken. She said more gently, "They're very good, the doctors. She's in very good hands. Now . . ." And then she opened the door, and there was Fran lying on a high hospital bed with tubes coming out of her and drips hanging next to her and a strange oblong-shaped ridge under the sheet where her pregnant swelling had been. She looked very pale and very small. There was a nurse, fiddling with a clipboard in the corner of the room. And next to her, look-ing very solid and calm and comforting, was Jake. He was cradling her head in his arm and stroking her hair and talking to her in a low voice, and before he looked up and saw us, he had just put his finger on her cheek and said something that made her smile.

"Daddeeeee!" Fergus had leaped into the room. Jake looked up and nodded his head at me, telling me with his eyes how things stood, reassuring me and cautioning me, as he cushioned the blow of his careering son away from Fran.

"Sweetie," I said. I abandoned the stroller in the doorway and went over to the bed. I bent down to put my arms round her. She flinched. There was a bruise on her forehead, a small cut above her mouth. Her eyes looked slightly odd, the pupils small. "Maggie," she said. "Oh, Maggie." And she started to cry and I was crying too and kissing her hair and saying I was sorry, so sorry, meaning sorry for all this and sorry for not having been there, for not having rung, for not having gone to Babyworld with her, to have driven her there, for not having stopped this from happening. And over and over I was saying, "It's going to be okay. It's going to be okay."

Fran was saying, "It's so early. Is she going to be all right? Please tell me she's going to be all right. I really wasn't driving that fast. The van just sort of came . . ."

"Sssh." Jake had put Fergus down and was stroking her hair again. He gave me another look, a serious look.

"I want to see her," Fran said. "Please." She turned to me. "Please, Maggie, ask them if I can see her now."

Jake put his hand on her forehead. "You'll see her very soon," he said. "As soon as you can be moved, you'll see her, I promise. And she's got Rain with her. She's not on her own."

The nurse came over then and flicked at the tube of blood. "They're taking very good care of her," she said. "They're doing everything they can."

Fergus was being very quiet. He was sitting on Jake's knee, staring at Fran and the tubes coming out of her. He seemed very interested in the nurse's flicking. But Dan was beginning to protest, unimpressed by the lack of attention coming his way, arching his back against the stroller straps, kicking his legs and crying in a cross way.

Fran said, "Hello, Dan," without moving her head and then closed her eyes. "Hello, Fergus," she said, opening them again. Fergus was pressing himself back against Jake's knees.

I said, "I'd better . . ."

But Jake said, "Don't worry. You stay here. I'll take them downstairs to look at the fish."

After he'd gone, Fran started telling me what had happened, going over and over it, as if she couldn't stop herself. "It just came from nowhere, the van. It was a red van. I remember that." She closed her eyes. "One minute it wasn't there, the next . . . I was so excited to be getting all the nursery stuff, muslins, you know. I was so excited about getting there and I was taking that shortcut, Maggie, you know, behind the Fulham Road, and we'd been stuck in traffic so I was sort of whizzing and then suddenly it was there, in the middle of the road. And I tried to brake . . . but I went right into him. There was this horrible crunch. And I knew something was wrong, you know? I knew. At first I just thought, oh, and then I realized . . . it was really hurting in my back and here, this terrible pain, and Rain had put his arm out . . . and there was blood everywhere and I thought it was me . . . And then the ambulance came and . . ."

She was crying again. I was wiping the tears away with my fingers, kissing her wet face. Two accidents in one summer, two red vans. "Sssh," I was saying. "It's okay. It's okay."

"I'm so cold," she said. "I'm so cold."

I asked the nurse if she could have a blanket, and she went off to see what she could do.

"The doctor said we were lucky we were so close," Fran said, tugging at the skin on her hand. "But they don't know. Please, God, I wish . . . Oh God, if only I hadn't . . ."

The nurse came back in with a sheet and a towel, which we draped over Fran as well as we could. "I'm sorry I can't find a blanket," she said. "There's a shortage of blankets." I said something about selling some of the art downstairs to buy some and she raised her eyes to the ceiling. "But apparently it cheers people up," she said doubtfully.

The door opened and Rain came in, his face calico-white against his rook-black hair. He looked lost and drawn. "Hello,

Maggie," he said. I asked him if he was all right. His arm was in a bandage. There was blood in his fingernails. He shook his head and said he was fine as if he hadn't even noticed. I stood up so he could have my chair. He sat down and put his head on the pillow next to Fran and started telling her things about the baby. "The doctor says her lungs aren't as mature as they could be at thirty weeks, so she can't quite yet breathe on her own, but she's a good weight. She looks tiny but she could have been much smaller . . ."

"What do you mean she can't breathe?" said Fran.

"She's on a machine to help her breathe," he said. "So there's a tube going into her mouth, and there's something for her temperature, and something going into her stomach, and there's a drip in her scalp, um and that's for . . ." He looked anxiously at the nurse, who was doing something with the line in Fran's hand.

She said, "That's to keep a vein open so they can keep testing her blood and oxygen levels. It looks awful, but it's all very necessary."

"And she's sedated so she doesn't pull the line out," Rain said. "And she's under a light because she's a bit jaundiced . . ." His voice began to break up.

The nurse said, "That's very common."

But Rain's head was bowed. Fran was clutching onto him, and they were sort of rocking a little bit together. I felt in the way then and suddenly, with a pang, I wanted to see Jake again, and my children, so I said, "I'll be back in a minute"— for the nurse's sake, because I knew they weren't going to hear me—and I left the room. First I went downstairs to the aquarium tank, but there was no sign of them. Then I went to the café place, but they weren't there either. So I went through the big revolving doors at the front, which move so slowly you want to punch through the glass, and looked up and down the road outside. I thought perhaps he'd taken them to Starbucks, but they weren't there. And they weren't under the "town square"-style trees. I felt a little murmur of anxiety as I went back inside. I was on my way back to "lift bank D," when I saw a familiar caravan coming toward me— not with Jake, but with my mother.

"Mum!"

"Oh, hello darling," she said, as if I'd just bumped into her in Woolworth's. "Jake rang and asked me to pick up the children. We just went to say good-bye to you, but as you weren't there, we left a message with that lovely nurse. Now we're going to go back to Granny's house, aren't we Fergus, and we'll have a lovely lunch and maybe a lovely walk and then mummy will pick you up later."

I was momentarily stunned by her tone of efficiency. "What about . . ." I began to say.

"Aqua aerobics can wait!" she said. "All that matters now is Fran."

Then she turned the children around before they could complain and marched them briskly off in the direction of the front doors.

"Where are you parked?" I yelled after her.

"On a yellow line," she called, without turning around. "This is, after all, an emergency."

I went back up to the ward when my mouth had fully closed but turned around just before I got there. I asked the nurse for directions and took another elevator up to the next floor. I couldn't work out where to go at first. The first room I peered into had a Beatrix Potter frieze along the walls and mobiles hanging from the ceiling—it looked cozy and jolly, even the couple of small babies who were crying seemed to be doing so in a healthily demanding sort of way. But there was a nurse coming out, and she said I was in the wrong place;

she directed me farther along the corridor, and there were no babies crying down here. There was a man at the door, when I got to the right room, with his back to me, his face against the glass. He was wearing a suit, a familiar dark gray linen suit from Paul Smith, which was all baggy at the knees and crumpled across the bottom of the jacket. It needed a dry cleaning. Someone who cared about him should have taken it to be dry cleaned. He moved so that his elbows were up against the door, his hands cupping his head.

"Hello," I said.

He turned around, and on his face was a gentleness I hadn't seen for a while. There was tenderness in his eyes and hope and desperation too.

"Hello," he said. There was a catch in his voice. He moved aside. "Look," he said.

I stood next to him with my head next to his and looked into the room through the glass. There were a lot of people inside, banks of high-tech equipment, and seven or eight tiny incubators. The lights were on full. There was no crying here, just bleeping.

"She's over there," he said. He pointed to the farthest incubator, over by the window. You couldn't see much, what with the wires and the plastic. You could just make out a shape really, an unimaginably small, bony shape in its artificial womb, a tiny smidgen of life.

We stood there, with our heads resting together, for a long time.

Chapter 23

When we got back down to the room where Fran was, she was sleeping, her head to one side against the pillow, her mouth open. Rain was standing by the window looking out across the roofs to the hotel towers around the Chelsea football ground. He said he'd been waiting for us to come back so that he could go home and get some things, but Jake told him that we'd go, that he should stay in case Fran woke up.

On the way down to the parking garage, Jake said, facing away from me, "Do you remember when Fergus was born?"

"Yes, of course." I'd been thinking about it too. It wasn't to this hospital, with its light and its art, that we'd come, but to another nearer us, a sprawling Victorian building with endless additions and corridors in which people seemed to wander about in constant confusion, amid a smell of fried food and antiseptic. We'd spent hours there, waiting for dilation, and then when things had sped up, I vaguely remembered a room and a bed and a midwife, but most of all I remembered Jake gripping my hand, allowing me to dig into it with my nails, proffering water through a bendy straw, and then his face when the baby came and his face again, when I was too whacked to do anything but watch, when he rocked him, held this little bundle in his lap and sang.

"God, we were lucky," I said.

"Yes we were," he said.

He took my hand for a moment and squeezed it. And then the elevator doors opened, and he walked out ahead of me into the garage.

⁘

When we got to Fran and Rain's building, we parked on a meter and let ourselves in with their key. There was something very poignant about the state of their flat, about the fact that they'd let themselves out only that morning not knowing they wouldn't be walking back in in a few hours time. There was a half-empty cereal bowl on the kitchen table, with dried muesli round the rim. A carton of milk had been left out by the kettle. And the button on the coffee machine was still shining orange: half a jug of viscous mahogany liquid waiting for a later that never came. The overhead light was on too—a weak beacon in a room full of slanting sun—as if they'd left when it was still dark. "Oh God," I said. "Of course, it was raining."

Jake said, "The road was wet. She'd have braked in time otherwise."

Together, we cleared up the kitchen and made the futon in the bedroom—"God, how do they sleep in this?" gasped Jake, rubbing his back with the effort of bending—and tidied the sitting room, plumping up the cushions, emptying the ashtrays, straightening the copies of *My Pregnancy* into a neat pile on the floor by the sofa. There was a book of babies' names on the television. A sheet of paper fell out as I picked it up to put it on the shelf. It was Fran's birth plan—the one Jake had effaced earlier that summer: "Pethidine, Epidural, Emergency Caesarean," it said. "Christ, Jake," I said, showing it to him.

Jake looked grim. He shook his head and closed his eyes. "I didn't know . . ." he said, sitting down on the plumped cushions.

I sat down next to him and put my arm round him. "I know," I said. "Of course, you didn't. Anyway, it was my fault. If only I'd gone with her. If only I'd picked her up in our car . . ."

"It's just one of those things that happens," he said.

We sat there for a bit and then I said, "Okay, suitcase, where do you think they keep it?"

And Jake said, patting his thighs, "Stuffed under the bed . . . if I know my sister" and we got on with the business of packing her a bag.

"Right," Jake said, as he piled things in, "Pajamas—will this do?—bathrobe, underwear." It touched my heart, his lack of self-consciousness, the big brother sorting out his sister's briefs.

Before we left, I popped back into the kitchen where earlier I'd noticed a packet of KitKats on the side. I hadn't eaten since breakfast and was suddenly starving. When I got there, the packet was empty. "Jake!" I called.

"What?" he said from the bathroom where he was getting Fran's toothbrush.

I said, "The KitKats?"

"Ooh, it's funny you should mention them," he said, poking his head around the kitchen door. "I was in the kitchen about five minutes ago and suddenly I felt weird and when I came to, there were crumbs all over . . ."

"Yeah, yeah," I said. "All right." But I laughed anyway.

When we finished, Jake went off to the police station to sort out Fran's car and I went to Marks & Spencer to buy her fruit and cookies, and we arranged to meet later at the hospital. Fran had been moved to a bed on a ward when I got there. She was propped up in her cubicle, with the curtains drawn on one side. There was a bit of color in her cheeks, and her pupils looked more normal. She still had a couple of drips with her—glucose and morphine—and she still had her catheter tucked discreetly by the mattress, but they'd finished with the blood. She said, "They said I can go and see my baby soon. When Rain gets back they're going to wheel me up in a wheelchair. I won't be able to hold her, but I'll be able to stroke her. Rain says there isn't much of her you can touch, what with the nappy and the bonnet, which she has to have to keep the thing on her and . . . and the lines. Do you think you could find someone, Maggie, and ask them? See whether I can go now? And I'm going to start expressing milk and freezing it for when she's bigger and can take it . . . Oh, Mags, thanks. Did you bring a blanket? Oh brilliant. And my pajamas."

I made her some tea and sat next to her for a while until Jake came. She was much calmer when he was there. She smiled at his jokes. And when he kept telling her that everything was going to be fine, she seemed to believe him. He'd brought her some magazines, which I hadn't thought to do. And as we were leaving, he said, "Oops, almost forgot this," and took something out of his jacket pocket. It was the book of babies' names. "Here you go, Fran," he said, putting it on the bed beside her. "You'll need this."

· · ·

It was early evening by the time we picked up the children. My mother was still chirpy when we got there. She had the Travel Scrabble out on the floor and was introducing Dan to the pleasures of the game. "Look," she was crying as we came in, "Granny's spelt INGRATE. No. No, Dan. No grabbing. No." Dan was trying to mash the rest of the letters into his mouth.

"That's my boy," I said. "You show her."

There was a flash of lacy stocking top as she got up off the floor. "You used to love Scrabble. Remember those lovely holidays in Cornwall?"

"Yes," I said, extracting a wet P and a tooth-marked Q, fending off an image of a hotel lounge, with crimplene chairs, a silent dining room. "I do."

I had picked Dan up and was holding his firm little body to me. He was jerking up and down, salmon-like, with excitement. "Umumamum," he said. His hair was sticking up and I kissed it down. His head felt warm and smelled of kittens. He turned his mouth and held it open against my cheek. I wanted to absorb him. I wanted to hold him forever.

Jake had wandered farther into the sitting room. "Christ," he said. "I mean, gracious. What's been going on here?"

The back half of the room looked like a bomb had been dismantled in it by disposal experts in a hurry. There was a big dented cardboard box in the middle of the floor, trailing tape, and white polystyrene prawns all over the carpet.

"Ah!" said my mother, coyly flirtatious for Jake's sake. "The new television. It arrived earlier. It's flat screen. DVD."

I left her showing him the finer points of Optimum Picture Control and went out through the kitchen into the garage where Fergus was helping Frank have a go at mending the old television. Fergus had a big Phillips screwdriver in his fist and an expression of such knitted concentration on his face it was like suddenly seeing him grown up. He looked so separate. My heart contracted. My stomach muscles tightened. I said, "Hello, chap."

Fergus looked up, and bounced down off the wooden counter, narrowly missing the inner workings of a manual lawnmower. "It's my mummy!" he said to Frank, throwing his arms round me. "It's my mummy." Then to me, climbing up my body, using my arms as crampons, he said, "We had lasagna. And do you know? I liked it!"

"Did you?" I said, kissing his nose, his eyes, his ears. I smiled at Frank. Frank in his overalls. Frank in his garage. Frank, surrounded by his tools and his gear and his long-term projects. Frank who had been here, I realized, for really quite a few years now and who looked as if he was here to stay. "Now, let's get you home."

· · ·

Both children, exhausted by an afternoon of board games and appliances, went to bed without a murmur between them. Jake and I made cheese on toast and sat and ate it outside in the garden. The wooden chairs were slightly damp, but it was all right if you sat on your jacket.

It was dark and still out there. Occasionally I felt myself shiver as if someone had opened the door and let a draft in, but it wasn't cold. There were stars in the sky and a great big tangerine moon, an Edam without the skin.

"Harvest moon," said Jake. "Time to get the crops in."

"Gather ye what ye sow," I said. And then wished I hadn't.

The moon was casting limbed shadows in the garden, which moved when the wind blew. The lights in the houses on the next street blinked at the same time. There was a rustle in some far bushes. It was loud enough to be a person. But then the next-door neighbor's tabby streaked across the lawn, a patchwork Tom on a patchwork night, rattled over the fence, and was gone. Not a cat burglar, just a cat.

Jake broke the silence. He said, "Maggie, thank you for everything today. I know Fran appreciates it. And . . . um . . . I was glad you were there. You know, it . . . um . . . made it easier for me having you with me."

"Of course, I was there," I said. I touched his arm across the table. "I had to be there."

He'd changed out of his suit when we got back. He was wearing jeans and a soft blue sweatshirt that he'd had since school, washed so many times it was as thin as felt. He didn't look that much older than when we'd first met.

I said, "It just makes you think, doesn't it? Your life is just chugging along and you're in your own little bubble and something like this happens and it's just bang, you realize how vulnerable we all are, how thin the difference between safe and not safe. At least, they're both, they're *all,* alive." I squeezed the wooden table.

"Thank God," he said.

There was a pause. He said, "I'd better go and ring Mum and Dad."

"Yup."

He got up to go, and then he leaned across the table and kissed me. "Sorry," he said, pulling back.

"It's all right," I said, looking up at him.

There was a flicker across his mouth. "For a moment there I forgot that we didn't kiss each other these days."

"So we don't," I said.

"Look—" He rubbed his eyes and raked his hands through his hair. "I'm sorry things have been so strained between us.

I've had my head full of work, and I know I've been irritable and distant. I shouldn't have let it come between us."

"Maybe it hasn't come between us as much as Claire," I said.

"Claire?" He looked taken aback. He sat back down.

"There were clues," I said calmly.

"Oh. Clues." He sounded more surprised than mortified. "But, is it really? . . ."

I felt a wave of exhaustion. "Well, let's not talk about it now. I'm too tired. We're both tired. But I just want you to know that I know. We can talk about it another time, okay? And there are things I have to tell you. I wish I didn't have to but . . ."

Jake rubbed his eyes again, this time with his palms, and then looked at me. "I hated having secrets from you."

I said, "Me, too." I was churning inside.

Jake bit the corner of his thumb. "And there's something I've been meaning to ask you . . ."

He sat back, crossed his arms behind his head. "Here goes . . ." He began. But he must have moved a fraction because a tendril from the climbing rose on the wall next to him caught in his hair. He moved to detach it. "Ow," he said, getting it tangled in his sleeve. Then, he said, looking at me closely, "Whatever happened to that gardener bloke you found?" There was a quizzical expression on his face. "Did he disappear?"

He turned away and was trying to extricate his sweatshirt without further damage. "Everything goes a bit mad in August," I said.

He freed his shirt, bent his head to inspect the little hole the thorns had made. "Anyway, where was I? Oh yes." He gave an awkward laugh. "What I wanted to ask you . . . What's that?"

"What?"

"That noise?"

I leaned forward, with my ears straining. It was music, or a noise, like one of Fergus's broken tapes playing backward.

We both got up and went to the kitchen door where the sound got louder, still muffled but more regular. It sounded like a synthesized musical box. It sounded electronic. I was still nervous about Jake's imminent inquiry, or I suppose my reactions would have been quicker. Jake had bounded down the hall and gotten to the stroller, folded up amid its usual wrapping and juice box detritus by the front door. Under it was the Safeway bag I'd packed earlier that day. Jake rummaged and I remembered what I should have remembered earlier: Pete's mobile. It was playing Vivaldi's *Four Seasons.* *The Four Seasons* by Motorola.

I leaped down the hall and grabbed it from him. "What . . . ?" Jake began.

I pressed green. "Hello?" I said, turning my back on Jake so he couldn't see my face.

A voice answered. It was a female voice, posh, anxious, asking for Pete. Jake was looking at me quizzically. "He's not here," I said. "Try again tomorrow." I pressed red. I was getting good at other people's phones now. And then I switched it off.

"What's that doing there?" Jake said. He was standing right behind me. "Whose phone is it?"

"Oh." I thought quickly. I said the first thing that came into my head. "It's Rachel's. I borrowed it."

"Oh. But you said 'he.' You said, 'He's not here.' "

"Guy. Rachel's husband."

"Oh." He must have been convinced because he seemed to forget all about it. He said, "Oh God, I'd better ring Mum and Dad before it gets too late," and went into the sitting room. I went to bed before he got off, but I lay awake for a while, feeling hopeful for the first time in ages, running things over in my mind, thinking how to sort things out. Something else nagged at me too: the voice, the voice on Pete's phone. I recognized it, but I couldn't quite place it.

Chapter 24

It was a week before Fran and Rain's baby came off the ventilator. For three days one or the other of us sat at the end of her incubator, stroking the square inch of flesh that wasn't covered in bruises or a diaper. Early on the fourth day, Fran rang with the news that our niece was no longer "critical," but "stable." She'd been moved to the room next door, where they switched off the lights at night—a gradual movement toward normality. Fran had given her some milk through a tube from her nose into her stomach and she had digested it. She had actually held her—albeit amid a tangle of wires. She also told Jake, who had answered the phone, that they'd finally chosen a name. I was standing next to him when she told him. "Arabella!" he cried, rolling his eyes for my benefit. I let my jaw slacken in horror, but Jake started nodding his head, looking mollified. He put his hand over the receiver and mouthed, "It's the name of the nurse."

"Oh," I said, and felt sheepish.

I'd gone in to see them every day. Fran was expressing milk for England and in need of much chocolate. Temporarily, she also seemed to have forgotten her principled belief in the right of all living creatures to freedom and dignity, not to mention her fear of mad cow disease, and had developed a passion for Marks & Spencer's beef and horseradish sandwiches. So there was a catering job to be done and also a chauffeuring one: the Pritons had come down to be near their daughter and were staying in Fran's flat. Stricken by my negligence during the Suffolk weekend, I was bending over backward to make them happy, ferrying them from the flat to the hospital to our house, for supper—nothing too spicy for Derek's digestion—and back to the flat.

Crisis, as ever, seemed to bring out the best, and the worst, in people. Rachel had been a brick. She brought around several ready-made meals: large casserole dishes, or *tagines* as she called them, awash with chicken and almonds (Claudia Roden), or saffron and cod (Jane Grigson), none strictly necessary in practical terms, but invaluable in terms of moral support. "You're a good friend," I said, giving her a hug at the door, and really meaning it.

"Oh it's nothing; I enjoy cooking," she said, over her shoulder, nipping back to her car, which she'd left with its engine running in the middle of the road. "And you can fuck off," she said to the man beeping her from behind. I liked her even more after that.

Lucinda had also revealed hidden depths—or hidden shallows. She rang the day after the accident in a complete state, caused, it turned out, by a missing member of staff. "Maggie. Thank God I've found you in. Do you by any chance have another number for Russ?"

"Who?" I said.

"Russ. Russ the gardener. I'm desperately in need of him—the lawn is a total shambles and I cannot but cannot get through to him on his mobile."

"Oh Pete," I said. "Er . . . yeah . . . Hang on . . . Sorry, we're having a bit of a time of it here . . ." And I told her what had happened.

When I finished, she said, still flustered, as if she hadn't even listened, "Oh right. Oh dear. The number then?"

"Thanks for the concern," I said, after I'd put the phone down. Jake raised his eyebrows.

"Never liked her much," he said.

Jake had taken the week off work. Things had eased off since the Kyushi deal and though there was trouble brewing at Pot Noodle—new flavor, new campaign—he'd decided after Fran's accident to put all hot snacks on the back burner. "Family comes first," he'd said. He'd said it in a funny voice, as if self-conscious with the sentimentality, but I knew he meant it.

Fran wasn't the only person happy to have him around. His mother, Angela, who was delighted with her new grand-daughter, seemed even more pleased to have unrestricted access to her son. His birthday was only three weeks away and she spent every spare minute pinning sections of knitting to his chest. "Just make sure it's not too tight around the neck," I heard Jake say once in a moany voice, "or too itchy," as if he was thirty-five going on eight.

I liked having him at home too. A lot of things were still unsaid between us. I didn't know whether he'd finished with Claire or not, but for the moment, it didn't seem to matter. He was at home, or in the hospital, at my side or at Fran's, all week. He seemed wrapped up in us, in his children. He seemed happier than he'd been for months. There was no obviously suspicious behavior. There was no sneaking out to buy lightbulbs.

Of course it was possible that, while Fran was in hospital, he had simply put the relationship on hold, and would pick it up with renewed vigor when she was out. I couldn't put this thought entirely out of my mind. Particularly in view of the phone calls. Someone was definitely trying to get hold of him—or me—or both. Pete rang once without leaving a message. I knew it was him because I heard the sound of a buzz saw before he managed to hang up. But there were other calls too, which I didn't think were him because the phone went dead when I picked it up. I dialed *69 but the caller had withheld their number. "God, kids," Jake said the third time it happened. He was catching up on some paperwork at the kitchen table. "Haven't they got anything better to do?"

"Or burglars," I said thoughtfully.

"Nothing to burgle here," he said absent-mindedly, head back down.

I still hadn't dealt with Pete. I was dreading meeting him. I would have to confront my own foolishness as well as his possible anguish. I kept putting it off, and it became more and more difficult as the days went by. Not least because the last time I'd seen him, when he'd come around to the house, he'd seemed so keen. Letting him down was going to be hard. But it had to be done. Also, I still had his phone.

So on a Saturday morning, almost two weeks after the accident, I told Jake I had some things to do. He didn't seem that bothered. His parents were coming around for coffee at 11:00 a.m. It wasn't raining.

I drove to the other side of the common, along the row of beautiful Georgian houses. When I got to the flat, I sat outside for a minute or two. There were battalions of small boys playing soccer on the common. It was quite warm, but the sky hung low in a mottled panoply as if the world had a false ceiling, the boys' cries bouncing off the clouds. The suburban idyll: grass and bare knees and fathers running up and down the touchline shouting, "Hoi, hoi. That's it, that's it. In. Go on. Through ball. Through ball. Hoi—aaaaaaa."

I took Pete's phone from the glove compartment, where I had put it for safekeeping, got out, and crossed the road, sticking my head between Pete's van and a Mitsubishi Shogun, before I did so. The Mitsubishi looked familiar and there was a yapping and a mad scratching from its back windows, as a couple of Highland Terriers tried to scrabble through the glass at the sight of me. They looked familiar, as well, but I was too preoccupied to think anything of that then. The road was busy today—because of the soccer I supposed. There was a bus, a Hopper, revving noisily as it waited for the oncoming traffic to let it through, forced into single lane by the cars on the edge. The bus stop was right outside the house, and there were a couple of old men taking the weight off their feet and sitting on the step when I got there. The one who eased himself up to let me pass was wearing a stained tweed jacket and a spotted bow tie. They were remarking on each car as it went by. "Toyota: they make a good car," the older man on the step was saying as I clambered through.

"Absolute bloody sods, the Japanese," said the man in the bow tie. "Bloody awful what they did in the war. I couldn't buy Japanese because of that. Sorry, dear."

Once past, I paused for a moment and then I went up the steps. I'd go down later. I'd do this first. I had to see Claire. I had to talk to her. I rang the bell and waited, convinced she was out, clenching and unclenching my fists, my toes curled in my sneakers. And I heard footsteps, the jangle of the chain, and then there Claire was. In her pigeon robe with the lace thing underneath. Ten o'clock in the morning and still in bed.

"Oh," she said.

Now she'd opened the door, my knees were trembling.

"Can I have a word?" I said, my voice unnaturally high.

"Er, yeh, hello, Maggie. Yes, come in."

She went ahead into her flat, and I followed. The curtains were drawn in the sitting room and it smelled musty. There was an overflowing ashtray and red wine rings on the coffee table. A candle had been left lighted on the mantelpiece and had dripped down onto the slate hearth below, splattering wax like molten honey. There was a cloying sweetness in the air. Perfume and cigarettes and, to my nostrils, something danker, like other people's husbands.

Claire had gone into another room. She came out again almost immediately. "How are you?" she said, closing the door behind her. "I haven't seen you for ages. Not since the . . . er . . . swimming pool. It's been a bit . . . hectic around here. Coffee?"

"Um, all right." I felt my resolution weaken. She was on her way to the kitchen now, on the move as if to keep what I had to say at arm's length. "It'll have to be instant," she called. "I've run out of real."

She came back in after a bit and rooted around in the sofa next to me until she found a packet of cigarettes. She pulled one out, sat on the arm of a chair, and tucked her robe—pashmina, I decided then; it had to be a pashmina—around her knees. But not before I'd caught sight of a web of broken veins on the inside of her thigh, like river tributaries on an ordnance survey map. She wasn't wearing make-up either, and close up she looked tired; there were shadows on each side of her mouth, dark smudges under her eyes. "So, what's up?" she said.

I sat on my hands to stop them from trembling. "Look," I began. I stopped.

She said, with a half smile, "I'm looking."

I cleared my throat. "Look," I said again. "This is awkward I'm sure for both of us. I expect your heart sank when you saw me at the door."

"Not really," she said. She was so cool I wanted to scream.

"It must have," I continued. "You must know what I've come for. You must have some idea what I've come to tell you."

Claire was smoking. "I have no idea," she said. "Though when we met at the swimming pool I could tell you felt some anger toward me."

"Of course, I feel anger," I said. I was clenching a velvet cushion. "What do you expect?"

She was still smiling at me, her head politely cocked to one side. She was still smoking, but she seemed to be gripping the cigarette more tightly between her fingers. There was a click from the kitchen. She looked at the door and then back to me. "I'm just going to go and make the coffee," she said, enunciating each word clearly.

When she got up, I got up too and followed her in. She had her back to me. "Fuck it," I said. "I don't want coffee." The kitchen showed signs of a meal, only idly cleared away. There were dirty plates—two—still on the table, saucepans soaking greasily by the sink. I said, "I just want you to tell me something. I want you to tell me that you're not going to try and see Jake again."

"What?" she didn't turn around. But she stopped what she was doing, which was pouring hot water into two old-fashioned Portmerion mugs, the kind with botanical prints on them. Her grandmother's Portmerion. Even Claire's china belonged to someone else.

"Yes, I know about it. I know about Jake and you. And I know something else too. It's over. Okay? It's over between you. You may think he loves you, but he doesn't. I know he loves me. And I know he loves his children. And if you think for one minute that he's going to leave us you're very, very wrong. I will fight you all the way." Even as I was talking, it struck me as odd how it's in moments of crisis that one falls back most readily on clichés, as if to force unwieldy emotions into something manageable. Claire turned, making a noise in her throat, but I carried on. "I am not going to give him up. We belong together now. We've made something together and if you think otherwise, you're . . ." I flailed for a moment, my arsenal of clichés temporarily exhausted, before I plucked another from the ether, "absolute bloody sods."

Claire was clearly fighting to control herself. I had gotten her. For the first time ever I had gotten to her. I had proved I wasn't mousy Maggie—forever boxing in her shadow. I was a force to be reckoned with. She was biting the corner of her lip. "Maggie," she began.

But I was unstoppable now, I had thirty years' worth of things to say. "Of course men like Jake are going to fall for you," I said, shaking my head. "You're gorgeous and you always look fantastic—mind you, you should, you get enough sleep—and you're out doing interesting things, you've got time to do them, and so you've got interesting things to talk about. But it's not fair. It's not an equal playing field. I'm boring and downtrodden because I look after children, Jake's children. And I've got no conversation because I've given up my life to do that. Not to mention my nights and half my brain. But this is what most people's lives are about. They're not about meetings with agents and weekends in New York. They're about getting through things and muddling on and finding shared pleasures in small things, like your child's first word or a random unbroken night and graduating, maybe, to the odd weekend away. They're about not getting on all of the time, and sometimes not getting on a lot of the time, but about growing old together, learning to fit together."

Claire said, "Maggie. Stop. STOP. You've got it all wrong. I am not seeing Jake. I have never been seeing Jake. I've never had anything to do with Jake. Or not really. This is nothing to do with him. You've got it all wrong. You've got the wrong man."

"What do you mean the wrong man?" I was gripping the back of a chair.

She was looking horrified and yet slightly amused at the same time. "Maggie. I don't know where you've got this from. I am having an affair, yes. But not with Jake."

"Who then?" I screeched, still disbelieving.

"With Ed."

"ED?"

She had started giggling. "Sorry, sorry." She straightened her face. "I know it's not funny. It's just your expression. Maggie, I'm so sorry. I don't know how this has happened."

I was staring at her. I could feel rushing in my ears. I was still holding onto the back of the chair, but to keep my balance now. I felt disbelief and confusion, something else glorious which must have been relief. "Ed?" I said again. "Ed Brady? I don't believe you. You're lying."

She was grinning. "I'm not. He was here only a minute ago, and you could have seen him with your own eyes." She looked at her watch. "He'll be back in a couple of hours if you want to wait. Look, sit down." She put her hand on my shoulder and guided me into the chair.

I said, "I don't believe it." Though I did now. There were just 100 things I didn't believe, like how I'd gotten it all wrong. "How . . ." I began.

"I promise you, I'm telling the truth," Claire said. "Why would I lie?"

I just stared at her. "I think you need that coffee," she said. Claire tipped the mugs into the sink and began to reboil the kettle. She made a little "tum-ti-tum" sound as she did so. Normal service had resumed for Claire; a minor misunderstanding had been mopped up. But what was minor to her was monumental to me. I sat, still unable to move, at the table. I was running through everything in my mind—trying to adjust how I felt to this new information. There were fish leaping in my toes, but they hadn't reached my head. How could I have been so wrong? How could I have misread the situation so badly? Or had I wanted to read things my way? Did this make things better? Or did it make them much, much worse? I realized I was crying. It must have been relief or shock or pity or guilt or all of those things. A couple of fat drops rolled down my face and fell on some documents next to the dirty plates in front of me. I put my palms up to my eyes and then used my sleeve to dab at the paper. I saw then that it was estate agent particulars. I picked the top one up: it was for a two-bedroom flat in Notting Hill.

"Are you moving?" I said.

"Well, Ed and I . . ."

"Ed and you?"

"Yes." She brought the Portmerion over and sat down next to me. She passed mine over. Violets. Violets for . . .

I said, "But I don't understand. I saw you together . . . I . . ."

A door slammed, and I didn't finish. There was the sound of hurried footsteps and a voice, getting louder, calling, "Forgot my bloody squash kit! I'd forget my balls if . . ." and the door to the kitchen opened, and there was Ed.

". . . if they weren't in a bag," he said dumbly, seeing me.

"Ed," I said, getting up.

"Hello, Maggie." He grimaced, then shrugged. "Caught in the act now, eh?"

"Ed," I said again. Both my hands were clutching the top of my head, as if in a gesture of surrender.

He came around the table and kissed me on both cheeks as if we were at a cocktail party. "Lovely to see you," he said. "I was so sorry to hear about Fran . . ."

I couldn't concentrate on the small talk. I glanced at Claire and then back to him again, "Ed, I don't understand." I emitted a small high laugh. "You told me Claire was having an affair with Jake."

"I told you what?" He pulled away.

"We talked. We had that conversation in Suffolk. About Claire and Jake."

He looked over at Claire, who looked baffled. "There is no Claire and Jake. There's only Claire and me."

I rubbed my head. Could this be possible? "But you did. You were so sympathetic."

"I was sympathetic? You were sympathetic. You encouraged me to pack my bags."

"I did?"

"Yeah." He was frowning at me as if I'd gone mad.

I turned to Claire. I realized I was supposed to be feeling embarrassed now, but I was still too bewildered. "I don't understand. You knew all about Jake's business trip—you knew about Kyushi. He knew all about what you were up to. I heard you on the phone to him arranging lunch. I followed you. I saw you together. I saw you embrace him."

"You embraced him?" Ed said.

"I was trying to get back with you. I was desperate. He was being kind."

"And what about all the other things?" I said. "All the coming round to our house, inviting us here, there, and everywhere. I won't flatter myself that it was for my company."

Claire had the grace then to look ashamed. "Yes, I know, I

used you and I used Jake. I used him to get to Ed when Ed wouldn't return my calls and when Ed's secretary, who had been my ally, suddenly developed a conscience . . ."

"And Jake didn't?"

"I don't think he liked doing it."

"Yes, well, I'm very grateful to him now," Ed interrupted. "It was the right thing and I think he had my best interests at heart."

"But not mine," I said. "He didn't tell me. If he'd told me, none of this would have happened."

"I made him promise not to," Ed said. "I was just so petrified that Pea would find out and . . . well then anyway, you told me you'd guessed. But Jake said you didn't want to talk about it."

"When? When did I say that?"

"In Suffolk. The night after the parlor game."

"I didn't want to talk about *him* and Claire," I said.

"Not *Jake,*" Claire said again.

"Fuck," I said. I put my forehead in the palms of my hands and kneaded it. I stared at the table through the crack between my arms, overwhelmed by my own foolishness. I could see the corner of the estate agents particulars. I picked them up again and held them out.

"Does Pea know?"

Ed said, "Yes. She does. She's staying with a friend in Bath this weekend to think. She suspected something was up even before I told her. Actually—" He started laughing at the ludicrousness of what he was about to say, "she thought I was having an affair with you! In Suffolk, anyway. She said we kept sneaking off!"

I smiled. I said, "Yeah, well, stranger things have happened."

There was a pause. "So you're leaving her?" I added.

Claire got up and was facing the sink. "Yes." Ed's face straightened. "Yes, this time I am."

"Poor Pea."

"Yes and no," he said. "She's angry with me now. But she's always been angry with me. I was never quite what she wanted me to be, never successful enough or driven or whatever she would call it. I frustrated her. She thought she deserved more than me."

"And what about . . ."

"Clarice. It's awful. But I'll see her all the time. I won't let anything come between us. I . . . Actually," he looked at his watch, "I said I'd ring at lunchtime. If you'll excuse me, I'll just go into the bedroom and do that."

Claire turned back from the sink after he'd gone. "It's not true that I only go after married men. There were only ever two. Marcus—who told me he was single when we met and was a disaster anyway, I don't know what I was doing, talk about rebound—and Ed. I would be lying if I said I hadn't known Ed was married. I knew right from the beginning. But we tried to stop it. And we split up for all that time . . . We did fight it."

"But it was too strong for you?"

"Don't be mean, Maggie."

"Sorry. I'm still stinging from my own mistake, still wondering what I would think if it was me."

Claire sighed. She twisted her hair and tucked it into the back of her robe. She did look thirty-six. A beautiful thirty-six, but thirty-six nonetheless. She was what she was. "He wasn't happy, Maggie. I know some people think you should stay 'for the children,' but is that fair? Would you want to be Pea in those circumstances? Or Clarice? Knowing, or sensing at any rate, that your father had given everything up for you?"

I said, "My friend Mel thinks you make your own happiness."

She shrugged. "Who knows," she said. "Maybe you do, maybe you don't. Maybe Ed and Pea could have been happy. But he met me and they weren't. These things happen. Some relationships last. Some don't. Who knows why that is. Maybe it's just luck or circumstance. You can kill yourself analyzing, but . . . nothing is clear-cut."

She got up and started looking for something in the cupboard above the sink. One half of my brain was still flicking back. Something struck me.

"Why," I said, "when I bumped into you in Morton High Street, did you say that thing about Jake being boring?"

She turned around. "What thing?"

"You made some reference to Jake being dull. Dullsville, you said. If you'd been seeing Ed, you'd have known that Jake was with me, that he was the father of my children. Why did you say that? It stuck with me. It made a difference. It was a horrible thing to say. Why did you say it?"

Claire smiled, as if amused by some private joke. "Oh, yes," she said.

"Why?" I insisted.

"Look." She bit the corner of a nail. "It was cruel, I know. It was a moment of spitefulness. It's just there you were, with your two lovely children and your fresh-faced outdoors complaisance and your shopping bags full of meals for two. You were the woman who had it all, who had everything I wanted: children, a family to shop for, a house to go back to, a busy little bee making her own happiness as your friend Mel would say, and I just wanted to dent it a bit. See that smug smile slip."

"Smug?" I said, shaking my head. "I was feeling desperate. I was at the end of my tether. I felt downtrodden and unloved.

You were the one who shone. You were the one who looked smug."

"Yes, well, things always look different from the outside."

She was grinning at me now, and I found I was grinning back. Ed came back into the room and Claire stretched up to bring down a rusty Quality Street tin from the top of the cupboard. "Chocolate brownie either of you?" she said, "I made them myself."

. . .

When I left the flat, the old men had gone and the small, muddy boys were being shepherded into cars. Pete's van, along with the Mitsubishi Shogun and its yapping inhabitants, were still there.

I crossed the road and walked a little way across the common to a bench over by the railroad tracks. I sat down. Pete's phone was in the back pocket of my jeans, so I stood up again to take it out. I placed it in my lap and stared at my feet. I could hear people going by along the path next to me: the rattle and squeals of children on bikes pedaling frantically ahead of their dawdling parents; a dog sniffing my shoes and then off; the parents, plastic bags swinging from reddening hands. But I didn't look up. I kept my eyes on the tufty, turdy grass under the bench, the candy wrappers, the dead matches, the cigarette butts.

There are very few moments in life when you see yourself for what you are. Not how you'd like to be, or how you think other people see you. These moments are very sobering.

I was the only one in our relationship who had been unfaithful, the only transgressor. Everything that had gone wrong in our relationship was my fault. I'd been selfish, self-obsessed, absorbed in my own world. Spoiled. How could I have done what I had done? Jake had done nothing. Or if he had, falling for Claire's charm to the extent that he'd agreed to act as Pandarus, it was a trifle to what I'd done. To him. To my children, because they weren't insulated; it *was* to do with them. How could I have done that? How could I have lost touch with what really mattered? With what was true and good?

I felt a surge of panic rise and stick like vomit in the back of my throat. Had I thrown it all away now? Was I going to lose everything? Would Jake forgive me? What would happen when I told him? Because I would tell him, I *had* to tell him, how do you live with yourself otherwise? But the thought of the hurt on his face was almost unbearable.

I got up then, brushing away the tears on my face impatiently, and walked back across the common and down the stairs to Pete's flat.

A strange man answered the door in his boxer shorts. "You must be Lloyd," I said clearly and firmly, "Is Pete in?"

He paused, then said unconvincingly, "Nnnnno. I don't think so."

"Are you sure?" I said. "It's just his van is there."

"No honestly, he isn't." His eyes widened in indignation.

"Do you mind if I check?" I said, maneuvering past him into the darkness of the flat. "Unlike him not still to be snoozing." I was sure he'd be in, his van was here, the curtains to his room were still drawn, and it was Saturday morning—where else would a single man be—if not in bed? I had to make sure, because I wanted to get it over with now. While my courage was up. I wanted to be free of it all. I could begin to have my life back. I made for Pete's bedroom. Lloyd was behind me, making ineffectual noises. I pushed open the door.

"Hey," he said. "I wouldn't . . ."

A navy blue velvet shoe with a buckle was dangling from the post at the foot of the bed. An olive green Coach shoulder bag was lying, splayed open, on the floor; its contents, a Harvey Nichols date book, a mobile phone, a pair of tiny pink ballet shoes, a packet of Pampers wipes, were spilling out onto what I could tell from the door was a pair of Boden tartan checked pull-on trousers and what I believed the catalog described as a "lamby half-zip." Pete was in bed. On top of him, her thick, curly locks not forced back in a hairband, but tumbling down her back in an attitude of sweaty abandon, her broad shoulders not tensed but arched in ecstasy, was someone to whom I had recommended his services and who was, at that very moment, making the most of them. Someone, I was glad to see, who did occasionally let her hair down.

"Oh, hello," I said. "Walking the dogs?"

Lucinda, hearing a voice, gasped and dove under the covers. Pete sat up quickly, tucking the bedclothes over her head and across his waist as if I was room service bringing breakfast in bed.

Pete said, "It's not what it looks like," which made the air escape explosively from the sides of my mouth. He must have thought it was a sob because he leaped out of bed, grabbed a grubby cotton bath robe, and hustled me out of the door and into the hall. "She was feeling unloved," he wheedled. "She needed affection. I've been trying and trying to get hold of you and you're never in or he is—and then when you answered I kept bottling out and . . ."

"What do you mean, 'bottling out'?"

"I'd hang up."

"So it was you. Why?"

He gave a pathetic shrug. "I dunno. Partly, I wanted to see you, but I thought you might have found out about—" He gestured toward the bedroom. "Also, I needed my . . ."

"Your phone." I reached into my pocket. "Sorry, I've taken so long to bring it back." I held it out. I was whispering now.

I didn't think Lucinda had seen me, and I realized suddenly how much better it would be if she didn't hear my voice either.

Pete put out his hand to take the phone. But he was already holding something. We both looked at it: a padded tartan hairband.

"Ah," he said.

"Ah," I said.

I turned to the door, smiling to myself, but by the time I reached it, Pete had recovered himself and had lunged forward, clinging to my arm like bindweed around a rose. "Maggie," he spluttered. "Please. I'll ring you. It's not what it seems."

I took in his handsome tanned face and his muscular arms, and the golden legs poking out of his too-short bathrobe. I looked at his mouth, his handsome mouth, the dimples high up on his cheekbones. At the tartan hairband nestling in his golden locks. I said, "Honestly, it doesn't matter." I gave him a peck. "I should say thank you, really." And I turned my back, climbed the steps, and crossed the road to the car.

· · ·

When I got home, Fergus was dive-bombing Dan in the sitting room. There were Lego bricks all over the floor and plastic cars all over the sofa, and the animals from Dan's Alphabet Caterpillar had been scattered everywhere. Fergus appeared to have brought his duvet down too, and the television was on—but no one was watching; you could hardly hear it above their squeals. Angela, Jake's mother, was in the kitchen, talking to my mother, who had popped around so as not to be left out. "We saw a super play at the National last night," my mother was saying when I walked in. "It was part of the Irish season. Do you get to the theater much? Oh, you don't?"

Derek was in the garden, studying a drainpipe with Frank, who was standing in the doorway to get a better angle. "Think I might just pop home to get my tools," he said, backing into the kitchen and stepping on a dump truck. "Oops. Better get something to mend that too."

And there was Jake in the middle of it all. His dark hair, tousled and pushed back from his face, his feet bare, pale after their summer in the office. He was standing at the oven in an old blue sweater with a saucepan of boiling water in one hand and an open tin of tomatoes in the other, and he was smiling. He had the phone under one ear. "Yes," he was saying, tipping the shiny tomatoes into a pan of sizzling onions, "Come round. The more the merrier. Maggie's just walked in. Do you want a word . . . No, no. Come straight round now. Mel," he said to me, putting the phone down, "she's bringing Milly to lunch." He had picked up another pan to drain the pasta but he kissed me over it, a hot, steamy kiss followed by a blast of cold air as he turned to empty the pan into the colander. "Then when we've had lunch, I said we'd drive Mum and Dad to the hospital—the nurse said we could take Fran for a walk today, and Mum wants to go to Marble Arch M&S if there's time before catching the train. They want to take the five-ten if they can. So I'll take her, shall I, or would you like to? And can you ring Rachel? She wants to know if you put ground almonds in your shortbread."

Was I going to tell him? Was it the right thing to do? Would it destroy everything we had? "Oh and—" Jake looked over his shoulder at our mothers, now happily discussing the Goya at the Hayward, and said in an undertone, "Christmas. They want to know what's happening at Christmas."

"But it's September!"

"Never too early," he sang under his breath.

There was crying from the next room. "I'll go," I said because Jake was already at the door. And I went through into the sitting room where Dan was sitting, sobbing with a bump on his head, with Fergus, who may well have been the perpetrator but it was too late to tell now, the evidence (probably the remote control), having already bounced off, sitting next to him trying to give him a kiss. "Don't cry," he was saying, "Don't cry." But Dan didn't want Fergus's kisses and was trying to push him off, which made Fergus cry, too, so soon I was having to cuddle them both, trying to fit both on my lap, stroking their soft baby hair, caressing their tears away. "I only wanted to cuddle him. Sorry," Fergus wailed, and I had to tell him that sometimes sorry was what people wanted and sometimes it wasn't. And I knew that I wasn't going to tell Jake about Pete, that *not* telling him would be my punishment. Maybe it was cowardly, or maybe it was brave. But to tell him would be to seek absolution, to beg forgiveness, and maybe that was the most selfish thing of all. And absolution didn't come that easy. Maybe absolution could only come by bearing the weight of my mistake myself. It wasn't a case of kiss and make up. It was a case of carrying it along with me, proving to myself, day after day, that, in the general, unruly, messy, disheveled state of things, it really wouldn't matter that much.

"Come on," I said, wiping away the last tears. "Lunch."

Chapter 25

It wasn't until several days later that I got around to asking Jake what it was he wanted to ask me that evening after we'd returned from the hospital. We'd put the children to bed and had eaten our supper. In the kitchen with the doors closed: it was getting chilly out there at night now. We were in the sitting room now. Jake was reading the papers, and I was sorting through some photographs. It was something I did from time to time, organize them into piles in preparation for putting them into a book. But I never actually got round to putting them into a book, and in the meantime they'd get all muddled up again—newborn mixed up with second birthday—and I'd have to start all over. It didn't matter. It was an excuse to flick through our life as much as anything.

I'd just come across a picture of Jake and me on holiday BC (Before Children). We had balanced the camera on a wall, set the timer, and we were crouched down, unnecessarily squashed together, with the Lake District stretching out, in a lopsided way, on either side of us. We weren't wearing quite enough clothes—we never had serious waterproofs like proper walkers—and our faces were pinched white with cold. But we looked happy, lineless. "Look," I said. "How young we were."

Jake looked up from his papers, said "Hmp," and went back to them.

I carried on staring at the picture. After it was taken, I remembered, we'd decided we'd had enough of scenery and we'd walked down to the car and gone back to the rental house—"A delightful cottage for two," it had said in the brochure, and we'd referred to it like that all holiday. "Shall we go back to our delightful cottage for two?" And that day, when we'd gotten back we realized we'd run out of firewood and we couldn't be bothered to go out again, so we'd gone to bed instead. At 4:00 in the afternoon. And we'd stayed there until the next morning, and I remember thinking I had never been happier than that night and would never be happier again.

Jake looked up. I was still staring at the picture and I could feel my eyes pricking. "Are you all right?" he said.

"I'm fine," I said, slipping it back into a pile of Fergus's first Christmas. "But what was it you wanted to ask me? The night Fran went into hospital you said there was something."

Jake froze. He looked down. "Er . . . oh it doesn't matter. It can wait," he said.

"No, no. Tell me now. Now will do."

I curled my legs up on the sofa, leaving the photographs on the floor. I'd had a bath with the children and was wearing Jake's pajamas and a pair of socks.

"What, now?" he said.

"Yes, now. Why not? Let's talk about whatever it is now."

He put the paper down. He ran his hands over his face and then through his hair. They were shaking slightly, his hands, and the corners of his mouth were down. Suddenly, he looked terribly serious. For one thudding, piercing moment, I thought, "he knows."

I said, "Actually . . ."

He said, "I've just been thinking and I know this summer . . . well, things weren't right . . . and I suspect . . ."

"What?" I said. I was gripping my toes through the socks.

"Well, maybe things would have been different if I . . . if I pulled myself together and . . ."

"What?"

"Well, whether you might like to get married."

He was grinning at me now. I put my hand to my mouth to stop myself from bursting into tears. I could see it all. A white wedding—a white frock for the bride (skittishly ironic, of course), a black coat for the groom, and all our friends in rows, and glasses raised, crystal catching fragments of light, and dancing, and small children twirled aloft by tipsy uncles, and the maid of honor getting off with the best man and someone's cousin being sick in the bathroom, and bad speeches, and good ones, and a white pagoda cake, with tiers to shed tears of joy over, and drinking and merriment and, as Mel was always reminding me, lots of presents with my name on them.

And I looked at Jake, sitting there next to me with a crooked smile on his face, the face I knew so well I could trace it in my sleep, and I thought of the children asleep upstairs, and I felt a great thud of joy in my heart. Because this wasn't an ending or a beginning. It was a continuation. I realized I didn't need to wait for something to happen. Something was happening all the time. I kissed his face, the rough bits around his chin and then his soft mouth. "Let's not," I said, switching off the television and wrapping my holey old tartan robe around him. "Let's stick with sin."

DURRANT   Durrant, Sabine.

Having it and eating
it.

DATE			